Prior Futures

Dan Kopcow

Black Rose Writing | Texas

ISBN: 978-1-68433-836-8
PUBLISHED BY BLACK ROSE WRITING
www.blackrosewriting.com

Printed in the United States of America
Suggested Retail Price (SRP) $20.95

Prior Futures is printed in Jansen

Author photo by Rachel Philipson

*As a planet-friendly publisher, Black Rose Writing does its best to eliminate
unnecessary waste to reduce paper usage and energy costs, while never
compromising the reading experience. As a result, the final word count vs. page count
may not meet common expectations.

Praise for
Prior Futures

"*Prior Futures* is a clever, biting work of satire. Rich with humor and horror, it transitions with ease from the silly and absurd to the powerfully allegorical."
—Fredrick Soukup, author of *Bliss*

"Dan Kopcow builds an aesthetically pleasing world and weaves a hauntingly inclusive tale of technology and wealth gone sour, as Jeremiah Prior searches high and low for redemption and, hopefully, a way to turn his life and many others around. In a decadent future, and in the era of the Mod, Prior is an unsung hero. World shaping honed, Kopcow is clearly a science fiction writer to look out for."
—Lawrence Dagstine, author of *Espionage First*

"An imaginative and stirring blend of hardboiled detective noir and science fiction, *Prior Futures* shows a dystopia where nanotechnology has taken wealth inequality to horrifying extremes. Crackling with wit, creative and richly detailed views of a frightening future, brilliant social commentary about wealth and technology, and a call for humanity, *Prior Futures* is an enjoyable book with a satisfying and moving conclusion."
—Matthew Arnold Stern, author of *Amiga* and *The Remainders*

"Dan Kopcow's *Prior Futures* is a smart, satirical thriller with a hardboiled, political edge, hilarious dialogue, and a loopy optimism all its own. With knowing nods to *Flatland* and *The Maltese Falcon*, the tale spins out in a swarm of nanos, cops, detectives, and mad scientists. As the bodies pile up, sparks fly off the page. A great ride."
—Jon Frankel, author of *GAHA: Babes of the Abyss* and *Isle of Dogs*

"*Prior Futures* challenged my concepts of the limits and potential dangers of future technologies gone amuck without control. It ultimately gave me hope for the humans who survived an experiment in population control gone horrifyingly wrong. It encouraged and thrilled me as the humans proved they had a strong will to survive the worst circumstances as old proven technologies prevail over corrupted new ones."
—Sharon K. Middleton, author of *The McCarron's Corner* series

"The sci-fi paranoia of Philip K. Dick meets the hardboiled sleuthing of Raymond Chandler. *Prior Futures* is a fast-paced and enigmatic trip through a nightmare world lost to its own decadent affair with nanotechnology and two-dimensional beings. Atmospheric and thought-provoking, this book will have you looking over your shoulder for nanos. It won't help, though. You can't see them."
–David E. Sharp, author of *Lost on a Page*

"Sam Spade meets *Blade Runner* in this mind-bending story of a dystopian world where two-dimensional beings rule. Dan Kopcow has created a cynical detective, worthy of Raymond Chandler, who shuffles, floats, and warps among a cast of eccentric characters in search of his own Maltese Falcon—a blood-borne art treasure that may hold the clue to survival for both the powerless and the powerful. Fast-paced and provocative, *Prior Futures* does not disappoint."
–Steven Mayfield, award winning author of *Treasure of the Blue Whale* and the forthcoming *Delphic Oracle U.S.A.*

"An ambitious take on a classic, set in a quirky, upsetting reality, *Prior Futures* is a delightfully imaginative take on the classic noir detective. Exploring what we are willing to risk for family, for integrity, for identity, it ponders the age old question –what makes us human? Creative, full of twists and turns, it takes the best of the detective genre and puts a fantastical cyberpunk spin on it. Hold on to your hat. This is one wild ride!"
–Alice Kaltman, author of *Dawg Towne*

"What does it mean to be human in a world where nanotechnology separates the rich and poor, the Mod and the Fringe, into two or three dimensions? Set in the near terrifying future, where extreme weather patterns have become the norm and nanotechnology has reached terrifying heights, *Prior Futures* places crime noir into a chilling dystopian landscape where class has become dimensional, and the human 'Fringe 'subject to the whims of the 'Mod.' *Prior Futures* asks what would you sacrifice for immortality? For redemption? For family?"
–Alicia Gilmore, author of *Path to the Night Sea*

*To Roz, for the decades of
encouragement, laughs, and listening.*

Prior Futures

Dreaming of turning Mod and leaving your measly Fringe three-dimensional life behind? Of course you are! You've accumulated wealth in stocks, bonds, and currency futures...but have you considered investing in yourself?

For the ultimate liquid assets, lock in your own nano-chemistry price in a blood futures contract! Blood futures are traded on the exclusive and discerning Futures Exchange. And since they are backed by NanoGov, they are perfectly safe! Welcome to the type of investment any Mod would be proud to have in their two-dimensional portfolio!

Please make your respectful enquiries to the Authentician Firm of Prior and Feynman, LLC, located in the downtown Fringe section of Manhattan, NY. Providing discreet antiquary and biological discoveries and confirmations since 2072.

–Old-Timey Mod Advertisement

Chapter 1

The turquoise morning ocean makes a prism of the sunlight and hurls Jeremiah Prior's distorted reflection back at him. Despite the floating trash and debris from last night's devastating storm, Prior's reflection skims the water's surface, occasionally bobbing with a gentle wave or pierced by a bamboo roof shingle seeking its way back to the Antiguan shore. Prior stands still, knee-deep in the Caribbean, gazing at his ocean reflection as if it is detached from him. Peter Pan's shadow. Behind him, pieces of his hut, formerly on stilts, float or sink, splintered and shredded; his home no longer where it once stood.

Prior is bare-chested, as he is most days when he's not working at his shop in town. His pink skin has turned a golden bronze since he moved to Antigua. His brown hair has grown a bit gray. What used to be short and business-like is now wild, tangled, and ropy. The cool ocean floor sand and smoothed pebbles feel like family on his bare feet. His rolled-up pants slowly get saturated as the tranquil waves lap forward and splash up to his waist.

Prior's gaze catches two rectangles floating amidst the detritus that used to be his belongings. The ocean is pulling the rectangles to sea, to his former home across the Atlantic, to New York City. He reaches down and rescues the rectangles, gambling they are real, three-dimensional objects and not Mod.

Framed photos. One of Felice, the other Molly. Each a posed head-and-shoulder shot from a lifetime ago. The photos, flimsy and worn from a lack of protective glass, have taken on water and warped. He loves these photos. The only ones he has of them. He contemplates his ex-wife and daughter's water-logged faces. It's only been four years since he left New York, back in 2086. Of course they remember him. They just don't want anything to do with him.

Last night's storm was worse than usual. Since NanoGov took over the planet, extreme weather patterns and geo-storms have become the norm. No one ever predicted that. But then, no one predicted any of this.

He places the framed photos in his net and takes a cautious step, scanning the ocean's surface for anything else of value. Depending on his mood and perspective, it's all valuable. And on other days, none of it is. The irony doesn't escape Prior. One day, you're one of the world's preeminent Authenticians; the next, you're dumpster-diving in the ocean.

Something smooth and fast glides past Prior's feet. It shimmers through the water until it disappears. Prior grabs what he can and trudges back to shore, hoping whatever that was already had its breakfast. He's heard rumors from his shop customers of a giant parrotfish on the other side of the island. More science gone mad. More global nano-evolution landing at his doorstep.

When Prior feels dry sand under his feet, he drops his cargo. He sits on the hot sand and stretches. Antoine has invited him to a pig roast tonight. The thought makes Prior smile. He hasn't smiled in at least three weeks. When Molly was little and learning her first words, she intended to tell Prior that he was a fine human being. It came out "ham being." Prior realizes his daughter was right. He's like the Three Little Pigs, continually trying to build a more durable house that the Big Bad Wolf can't blow down. He won't attend the pig roast.

Today, he'll finish collecting his things to dry. Tomorrow, he'll start to rebuild again. Same spot on the shore. Same rotting stilts. He knows it's the mark of madness to expect a different result with the next inevitable superstorm. But what other choice does he have? Mod have seen to that.

The next day, Prior wakes up from his bed of leaves on the sand. The cool island breeze is his blanket. He's alone on this part of the island. Just the birds, frogs, and fish. He's shaded by the indigenous palmettos and seaside mangroves. He suspects that soon the locals and refugees will inhabit his little slice of Antigua and he'll lose what privacy he has.

The tide has washed ashore the remainder of his former hut. At least the parts that didn't sink or move on to other islands. He drags the bamboo, branches, and woven leaves back to their address. When he's done, he picks a banana from his tree for breakfast. The banana is still hard but his teeth are strong. As he chews, he scans the sky. A piping plover flies by, optimistically searching for its breakfast.

He's not on the lookout for birds. He doesn't care about their plumage. The birdsong doesn't permeate his heart or lift his spirits. He's searching for Mod. The new dominant species. Transparent wisps of former real people. Two dimensional. Practically invisible. He searches in vain as always. He hopes he never sees any again.

A few days later, Prior's hut is practically built. He's leveling his floor when he hears rustling in the tree line behind him. He steps outside his hut.

"You should be wit us," says Antoine. He's in his forties, a native Rastafarian with a powerful build and stare. Antoine is Prior's only friend on the island. He's a refugee three-dimensional Fringe, having escaped Jamaica several years ago. He carries a cardboard box.

"Mr. Prior," says Philippe, standing behind Antoine. "The storm was terrible but in the village we sheltered together." Philippe, another Fringe islander, younger than Antoine, also carries a box. Philippe is always smiling. When Prior first met him, he thought Philippe had sipped too freely from the ganja. But Prior has discovered that Philippe is just a happy young man. In Prior's eyes, Philippe is more of an antique than anything Prior ever catalogued back in the day.

Antoine and Philippe have arrived to go fishing with Prior. They visit him every few days. Prior suspects it's really so they can check on him. Prior doesn't mind. It helps him fight the boredom of hiding from the world.

"Can we...?" says Philippe.

Prior nods and points his head towards the newly constructed hut. Philippe enters respectfully into Prior's hut, signaling his approval at the craftsmanship so that Prior notices. Prior doesn't mind that they store their boxes in his rafters. He has the room. They understand the risks of their boxes being washed out to sea. No one else on the island lives as close to the shore. But Prior needs to keep an eye out.

"How are you, my friend?" says Antoine in his deep voice.

Prior shrugs and Antoine proceeds into the hut to deposit his box in the rafters. In exchange for free storage and no questions about its contents, Antoine and Philippe show Prior the best fishing spots within walking distance from Prior's home. It's a good trade and has helped Prior survive.

"Tank you again, Jere," says Antoine, exiting Prior's house with Philippe.

"If you ever want to open..." says Philippe.

"Just some Wadadli voodoo shit," says Antoine, shooting Philippe a stare that would spear a frog. Wadadli is what the locals call Antigua. Antoine turns to

Prior. "Perhaps one day you can authenticate what we store. Tell us what is what, as dey say."

Prior shrugs and puts away his tools.

Antoine marches down to the beach and Prior and Philippe follow. Antoine rolls a spliff, lights it, and offers it to Prior, who waves it away. Antoine shrugs and takes a deep drag. He exhales and a halo momentarily forms around him before dissipating into the island breeze.

"Like I told you, Jere, change your mindset, change your life."

"Come on," says Philippe, running along the shore. "Before the fish all swim away."

The shore is a sparkling infinity of white sand and turquoise water. Half a mile down the beach, Philippe pulls out a small wooden boat that the storm hasn't destroyed. He digs out dead leaves and some branches from the hull. Prior and Antoine help drag the boat into the water, their nets hoisted over their shoulders. They pull out the secured wooden paddles from inside the boat's hull and make their way into the blue-jeweled water of the Caribbean.

Antoine and Philippe do most of the paddling. Prior steers but still hasn't gotten the hang of seamanship. When they get to their target spot off the Antiguan coast, they cast their nets. Each quietly fishes from a different side of the boat. Prior is grateful for the silence. The boat bobs with the slight waves and allows his mind to wander.

There was good money in being an Authentician in the old days, back in New York. He and his partner, Richard Feynman, had a respectable business going. At first, it was easier than being a detective or a cop; both of which Prior had been. Better money too. Fringe would bring their objects into Prior and Feynman's office and Prior would do the research. Try to discern if it was a forgery or the Great Golden Fortune. Their secretary, Penny, would help with research. The neighborhood kid, Lachende, would be sent on errands to dig up the object's history. People were going crazy for antiques. Every month, a different fad. Then, Fringe started coming to Prior with treasure maps instead of objects. They paid Prior good money to go and find their treasure and authenticate it. There was good money in that too. He and Feynman didn't see the trouble coming. Prior realized too late what Fringe were doing. They were stockpiling objects, hoarding them. Not like collectors. Like junkies. But junkies with a focused purpose. Fringe were buying up antiques in anticipation of converting to Mod. And by the time

Prior pieced it all together, there was no percentage in authenticating an object's worth. Not when your customers were turning into your oppressors.

"No goddamn fish," says Philippe, lifting an empty net. "Should be fish here."

"Really?" says Antoine.

Small bugs buzz around Prior's head. He takes his tight-mesh fishing net and tries to catch the bugs, hoping to drown them. The assault is unsuccessful and the bugs continue to fly around him. Resigned, he places his net back into the water.

"I remember when I was a boy," says Philippe.

"Here we go," says Antoine with a laugh.

Prior has heard this complaint before and not just from Philippe.

"So many fish then," says Philippe. "You could practically reach into the water with your hand and choke one."

When NanoGov had broadcast their Mod revolution to the world, one of their promises was resources becoming more plentiful for the planet. It sounded good at the time and folks were desperate for any quick solution that didn't involve self-sacrifice or more work. But the opposite happened. After Mod took over, resources became scarcer despite a major drop in the existence of three-dimensional people. No one counted on Mod being so ravenous. Of course, in hindsight, it was obvious.

Prior's net flinches. He's caught a big one. He pulls up his net as Antoine and Philippe beam with pride. The fish lands with a thud on the boat floor. The flat three-pounder, iridescent purple with blue striping, two eyes on one side of its head, gasps for air. Prior hits the fish with a crude, wooden mallet until it stops gasping. He reaches in and takes it out of the net. He hasn't seen this fish before. He holds it up, the weight of it incredibly satisfying.

"It's the most beautiful fish I've ever seen," says Prior, already thinking of several ways to cook it. It's flat so fillets will be easy. "I mean, have you ever seen anything more delicious?"

Antoine and Philippe burst into laughter. Prior gently puts down the fish, not sure if they're happy for him or think he's an idiot.

"You're an idiot," says Antoine.

"When will you learn?" says Philippe. "Look beyond the surface." He pokes at the fish with a crude stick. "This fish, its flesh is too oily."

"And, by da way, poisonous," says Antoine.

"Yes, let's not forget poisonous. How you survive this long?" says Philippe.

Prior dumps the dead fish into the water, feeling stupid for many reasons, including killing this fish that could have swam away if Prior had waited thirty seconds.

"Mr. Prior," says Philippe. "As always, think fat fish, not flat fish."

"Ugliness has no bearing on taste," says Antoine.

They fish in silence for another half-hour. The sea is largely empty, like the islanders' stomachs. It isn't supposed to be this way.

Prior jiggles his fishing line with his index finger, hoping to entice a passing customer when something bumps the bottom of the boat. Antoine and Philippe instantly grab their wooden bats. Prior reaches for the netted bag of fish by his feet.

A second bump. Something big. They're all quiet, listening for clues, trying to determine if this is a friendly encounter.

The surrounding ocean suddenly erupts into a fountain, spraying them violently. A monster breaches the surface. A large parrotfish, green with blue stripes. It's at least six feet long. Its teeth have been fused by evolution into a makeshift beak. The beak allows it to scrape algae off coral and rocks. That's when the parrotfish is at its normal size of six inches. It's grown exponentially, trying to scrape humans off the boat instead.

It surveys the humans in the boat as it arcs in the air, covered in the ocean spray it created. Its tail lands on the small boat, knocking Philippe into the water.

Antoine lets out a yell and bolts to the side of the boat, gripping it tightly while extending his bat to help Philippe. The giant parrotfish dives back into the water and the waves it creates nearly capsizes the boat. Prior sits still, trying not to get tossed into the water. Philippe grabs hold of Antoine's bat and starts to lift himself back into the boat.

Despite the air bubbles, Prior can see into the clear water. The parrotfish is swimming quickly towards them.

"Jere, grab Philippe's arm and help me pull him in," says Antoine.

"What the hell is that thing?" says Prior, not moving.

"You know exactly what..." says Antoine. He shakes his head at Prior's stillness and drops the bat. Antoine wedges his feet against the sides of the boat, and grabs Philippe's arms with both his hands. Philippe gets most of his weight over the side and throws himself into the boat, glaring at Prior.

"Hell is wrong with you?" says Philippe, wiping his face.

"I...I can't..." says Prior.

Philippe sits down, exhausted, drenched.

"Goddamn Nanos. Mod. Nature gone crazy," says Antoine.

"All three." says Philippe, rubbing his shoulder. He picks up the bat.

"You okay?" says Antoine to Philippe. Before Philippe can answer, Antoine yells, "Watch out!"

The parrotfish shoots out of the water alongside the boat, its mouth open, its sharp razor beak like a thrusted sword. Another foot to the left and it would have swallowed Philippe. The parrotfish lands in the water with a splash and soaks them all. Prior stands up, scrambling for something to hit it with but there is no bat for him. The parrotfish leaps out of the water again and Antoine and Philippe get in a few swings before it dives back into the water. It hits the boat with its tail, rocking it, throwing Prior overboard.

Prior tumbles into the water, his arms and legs pumping, trying to get back to the surface. In the mayhem of the ocean, he has no sense of direction. The bubbles dissipate and he sees the water surface, punctuated by the strong Antiguan sun. He reaches the surface, still in a panic, the boat behind him. He eyes the shore and swims frantically towards it, clutching his netted bag of fish. He doesn't want to lose what little catch he has. He figures that Antoine and Philippe can take care of themselves. He swims a few yards, the adrenaline doing most of the work. Behind him, there is the sound of splashing.

Prior realizes he has no defense for a parrotfish in the water. He's not in his natural environment. He clings to his netted fish as he desperately swims to shore. He feels something heavy on his shoulder.

"Mr. Prior, grab the bat," says Philippe.

Prior turns around and the boat is right behind him. The parrotfish lies dead on the boat, taking up most of the space.

"Come on, Jere," says Antoine.

Prior takes hold of the bat. Antoine and Philippe drag his netted fish onto the boat. Prior stays in the water, holding onto the side of the boat. They paddle towards shore with their giant catch while Prior kicks his feet to help move the boat towards his hut.

"Goddamn fish," says Antoine.

Prior remains quiet as he paddles.

"Don't even taste that good," says Philippe. "For a fat fish."

Chapter 2

Prior slides the wooden bolt open from the locking mechanism on the front door of his antique shop. There is no more metal on the island. Metal would attract Mod. The wooden lock won't keep out anyone who seriously wants to break in and loot the place but there's not much in the shop worth stealing.

The antique shop, located on the northern beach near Hodges Bay in the town of Turtle Cove, is an hour-and-a-half hike from Prior's home. He owns the shop, as much as anyone can own anything these days. He tries to get there several days a week but there are weeks that go by when he stays home in his hut. The locals don't seem to mind. The shop is there more for entertainment and conversation than for any real trading. Even calling it a shop is grandiose. It's a one-room wooden hut with a banana leaf roof and several shelves and a counter to fool someone into thinking it's a store. But the antique shop is how Prior applies his education. It is where the river of his experience runs.

He brews his coffee in a clay pot and sits behind the counter, gazing at the swaying palm trees. Antigua is a hundred-square-mile overgrown jungle ripe with wildlife and displaced Fringe. Some are local. Most Fringe have gotten away from their native countries to escape Mod and live off the nano-grid. The island's dense canopy of trees and thick understory of bushes and gnarled tree stumps make it ideal to avoid Mod detection. The strong island breezes also make it an inhospitable climate for Mod's nano-search parties.

When Prior first arrived at Antigua, the locals were wary of him. They were wary of all outsiders. They didn't believe this notion that regular people had become second-class citizens called Fringe and that two-dimensional Mod were the advantaged ruling class. It sounded too far-fetched. When boat after boat of Fringe refugees arrived at their shores from around the world, each bearing the same terrible story, the locals began to believe.

At first, Prior filled his shop with the mainland anomalies he managed to bring with him on the boat. The antiques were from his past cases. He traded these for his island life necessities. Now, he mostly sells rare Antiguan bric-a-brac that he obtains from the locals.

The shop is located away from any foot traffic, just outside the tree line by the beach. When he first opened his shop, he rarely raised his voice above a whisper or considered the local Fringe straight in the eye for fear that it would draw attention. He wanted to remain detached, anonymous. But he was the shiny, new curiosity. Fringe, Antiguan and foreign, would stop by and request his story. Rumors circulated the island quicker than a sandpiper.

One day, a crowd had gathered in his shop, ostensibly to evaluate his merchandise and make a trade. But they were really there to inspect the new refugee to their shores. One of the locals, a beautiful woman in her forties, wearing a green scarf on her head, picked up a faded, cracked leather wallet, its edges curled from years of use and abandon.

"What is dis," said the woman with the green scarf.

"A wallet," said Prior, not sure if she had ever seen one.

"Not a regular wallet, I tink," insisted the woman, opening it and revealing a large empty space that was meant to hold something heavy and large.

The shop quieted as everyone gave a serious inspection of the wallet. Suspicious eyes turned to Prior.

"Dis for badge," said another woman, holding her child closer.

"Dis yours?" said the woman with the green scarf.

"Leave da mon alone," said a large black man, walking through the crowd. "He means you no harm." He possessed a deep voice and commanding presence. He wore a Jamaican tam and faded red shirt made from an old quadrille dress; his Rastafarian dreads held at bay by a Jamaican flag bandana.

The locals immediately hushed when Antoine approached the counter. Antoine must have taken a shine to Prior. He rarely smiled but everyone witnessed his grin aimed towards Prior that day. Prior later learned that Antoine was considered a shaman among the islanders.

The locals continued staring at Prior like he was on trial, as if his next statement to the jury might result in harsh sentencing.

"Yeah, I used to be a cop," said Prior, his voice cutting through the air in the silenced shop like a razor.

The dozen local Fringe turned back to examining the old objects to see what they could trade for their homemade spears and nets.

"Will you be bringing peace and order to our island, Mr. Prior?" said Antoine. "Is dat why da Gods sent you?"

Prior smiled as the customers became still again, craning their necks so they could see Prior's response.

"Used to be a cop," said Prior, quietly. "Many, many years ago. A lifetime."

Not willing to share more that day, Prior turned his back on the villagers. They got the message.

Later that day, the woman with the green scarf returned to the shop with more than antiques on her mind. She told Prior her name was Tindonna and that she was a widow. She smiled broadly and took the scarf off her head to show him she had nothing to hide.

But Prior was still heartbroken over his ex-wife, Felice, and wallowing in his misery about his daughter. Molly had told him she never wanted to speak to him again for what he had done. His heart wasn't open for business. He was cordial but remained strictly on a shop keeper-customer basis with Tindonna.

Over time, the villagers discovered more about Prior's past through rumor or direct disclosure during Prior's few unguarded moments. They learned that he left the New York City Police Department to start a detective agency with his partner, Richard Feynman. After a few years, it became apparent that being an Authentician was a more lucrative business. Feynman even bragged about the gold bars he occasionally skimmed off the top. Prior didn't mind. You did what you could to survive. Prior and Feynman were Authenticians for five years before Prior escaped to Antigua. No one seemed to be able to pry any more details from this American.

Prior hasn't disclosed much about himself to the locals since. Merely the broad outline of his resume. It's hard to know who to trust. He trusts Antoine but even Antoine isn't privy to Prior's darkest secrets.

Prior came to understand early on that the island residents needed to co-exist in order to survive. After thanking Antoine for his help in resolving the Great Wallet Dispute, Prior started growing out his hair in hopes of having dreads.

Later that week, Antoine dropped off his first gift to Prior: a natural fiber red-gold-green tam like he wore.

During his fours years on Antigua, Prior continued to interact with the locals but generally avoided the foreign Fringe. Sometimes, he overheard their distant conversations in the jungle as he took his afternoon walks. Mostly, the discussions were about the ever-increasing changes in the world's civilizations. Every new Fringe that found their way to Prior's Antiguan shores seemed to bring news of Mod dominance and Fringe enslavement.

This morning, sitting in his shop, Prior stares at the framed, warped photo of his daughter, Molly, that he saved. He says his little daily prayer that she is doing better than just surviving.

Antoine enters the store, holding his satchel. Prior hopes that Antoine isn't too mad at him for not helping them kill the parrotfish yesterday. Prior can't afford to have Antoine upset with him. He's his only link with this world.

"Mr. Jere," says Antoine, placing his satchel on the counter. "How's business?"

Antoine reaches into his satchel. Usually, this is the part when a local takes out a fishing lure or wooden statue to trade for one of Prior's Victorian glass ornaments or cigarette holders. Instead, Antoine takes out two Red Stripes. These are sacred among the islanders. They're not making beer any longer. They're not making anything for Fringe any longer. And Mod don't need beer.

"Come on," says Antoine. "Let's take a walk."

Prior follows him to the rocky shore of a nearby cove where they've spent many evenings sitting, smoking, discussing the state of the world, and avoiding the sand fleas on the beach. After they've sat awhile, Antoine cracks open a Red Stripe and hands it to Prior. It's still cold and sweaty from being submerged in an underground stream somewhere near Antoine's home.

"I'm sorry," says Prior. "I don't know why I froze."

"Your apology is not to me, my friend. It is to Philippe."

Prior nods and makes a note to go find Philippe tomorrow. He takes a deep pull from the Red Stripe and it's like a time machine, bringing him back to an era when three-dimensional humans were enough for the world.

"My God, that's excellent," says Prior. He hands the bottle back to Antoine. They will share this one sacrament. Opening a second bottle is merely formality. They are too precious to waste in one evening.

"How's America?" says Antoine.

Prior has observed that Antoine is so hungry for any news from America, he will listen endlessly to Prior go on about his life.

"How would I know? I'm not really looking for any news."

"You're in dis world, you know," says Antoine, taking a small sip.

"It's hard to think that way," says Prior. "I'd rather…"

"You can't disappear. Your daughter." Antoine stands up, hands the beer to Prior, and lights a spliff. He gazes at the breaking ocean waves.

Prior stares up at him. From this low angle, Antoine is a Sky-God, his head haloed by deep clouds and ganja smoke.

"Look at dem sand fleas, scratchin' their way around," says Antoine in a deep whisper. "Da ting you got in da world now is fleas on top of dogs. You got yourself da nanos. Dey is run by Mod. Dey, in turn, is run by NanoGov. You watch yourself if you eva' go back, Jere. You remember you a flea fightin' a dog."

Prior laughs at the thought. He laughs because he knows he's never going back. And he knows in his gut that Antoine is dead right. There's a linear connection between everything in this new world. A new hierarchy. Humans aren't in charge anymore. Well, not traditional humans. But it's pointless to worry about it.

They finish the one beer and spliff in silence, Antoine beaming the whole time. Then they shake hands and go their separate ways home. Prior is guessing that Antoine is satisfied he's dropped some knowledge on Prior. Prior isn't sure if he's willing to trade on that knowledge yet.

The next day, no one's shadow crosses the shop's threshold so Prior leaves early. He'll finish sitting around and staring at the ocean from his home. He hikes the well-worn path several miles across the island, brushing the broad leaves away from his face, back to the isolated shores of his hut.

Prior clears the trees and arrives home to where his hut should be. Immediately, he realizes that another violent storm has blown through his side of the island. His hut, fortified this time with coconut leaves and reeds, has been blown away again into the ocean, his life strewn everywhere.

Chapter 3

After pulling his belongings from the ocean and dragging them to dry safety for the second time in a week, Prior sets up his makeshift bed far away enough from the shore so the tide and sand fleas can't get to him. He lays on his side and faces the ocean waves, listening to them crash against his shore. The constant, rhythmic sounds should lull him to sleep. He has purposefully set up his home and bed to face America.

He misses his life there. He misses his status. But mostly, he misses his wife and daughter. The irony isn't lost on him that the ones he yearns for don't want anything to do with him and the ones who want to see him, he has little interest in spending time with. Except Dr. Brewster and Professor Belden back in the old days. He was always happy to work with them.

The next morning, he begins to organize his belongings again. He's not sure what else he can do to fortify his hut aside from moving it closer to the other side of the island with the rest of the populace. But he's not ready for that. The self-imposed exile suits him perfectly right now.

Prior picks up one of the boxes that Antoine had been storing in Prior's hut's rafters. It's heavier than he expects. He's tempted to open this box. He observes the dozen or so other boxes leaning against the palm tree and he suddenly gets the urge to open them all up. Antoine has intentionally not told Prior what sort of contraband he is hiding. Prior imagines that, as the village shaman and de facto leader, Antoine sells ganja to the locals and refugee Fringe and this is simply his surplus supply to trade for other things.

Prior puts down the box. He needs to draw the line somewhere. If he opens Antoine's boxes, he'll lose the only human connection that remains viable to him on the planet. If he loses Antoine's friendship, he literally has nothing left. He starts in earnest on his hut reconstruction.

In a few days, Prior completes his home makeover for what is at least the fourteenth time since he arrived on the island. His hut is a bit shabby but sturdy enough to survive a mild storm. He decides to hike to his shop in case someone needs something to trade. He's also hungry for human contact but doesn't readily admit that to himself until he's climbed the first mountain towards the village.

As he passes Paradise View, he hears rustling nearby and spots Tindonna and her daughter. Tindonna wears the same green scarf on her head that she wore when he first met her. Since then, she has found a new husband who had a daughter from a previous marriage. The daughter is around ten. Tindonna smiles across the forest at Prior and offers a friendly wave. The daughter looks shyly at him, then turns her head. The mother and daughter remind him too much of Felice and Molly. He stops. He's having trouble breathing. He squats, trying to hide from onlookers who might be foraging. He tries to compose himself but it takes an hour before he can stand back up.

His shop sits on a lonely path by itself. The other nearby shops are clustered together for support and warmth. Prior wanted to keep his distance when he got to the island and this tradition has been upheld with great dedication. It does, however, make him feel he doesn't understand the rules here. Back in America, he knew all the rules and became successful at figuring out how to slip past the ones that were in his way.

No one is waiting for him at his shop as he unlatches the door. Anyone could walk in and take what they want but there is an honor system in Antigua that still astonishes him. He supposes all the Caribbean islands are like that. Filled with refugees whose lives have been upended when the world turned inside-out, the only way to survive in Fringe society is to work together. The thought occasionally gives him hope even as the lack of hope binds the Fringe together.

Prior boils some water in his clay pot for tea. As the tea seeps, he gets his first customer of the day. It's an old man wearing tattered white and gray zigzag camouflage. He has a spotty beard and his face is weathered from wind burn and strife. A refugee. Probably from Russian or one of the Baltics. Things are bad everywhere. He plods slowly, favoring his right leg, and places his hands on the counter. Prior notices the small satchel over his left shoulder.

"Sveiki. Turiu užsiimti prekyba," says the old refugee.

Prior shakes his head, indicating he doesn't understand him. How has this guy survived this long? Prior doesn't recognize him. Maybe he just arrived on the island.

"English?" says Prior.

"Ką duosi man už tai?" says the old man. He places a small black-and-white photograph of a family on the counter and slides it over to Prior. "Mano šeima. Mano šeima."

"Look, there's no market for…" says Prior but the old man's eyes are insistent. Prior picks up the photo. A family posing. Father, mother, two daughters, a baby. The photo is printed on thin paper that is glued to heavy card stock. It has a classic antique sepia tone. The father in the photo looks like the old man. Prior points to the baby. "This is you?"

The old man smiles and nods enthusiastically. "Taip. Taip. Tai aš."

The old man appears so hopeful. Prior knows that no one is interested in someone else's past or memories. Memories are the only valuable commodity left but they hold no currency except to the bearer.

Prior holds up his finger, indicating to the old man to hang on. Prior walks to the corner of his store and comes back with five small sticks of boar jerky. The old man's face lights up, his wrinkles temporarily dismissed from duty.

"One for each of your family," says Prior, pointing at the photo again.

"Ačiū," says the old man, taking the jerky. He grabs Prior's forearms and squeezes, looking him in the eye. "Ačiū."

The old man turns and leaves, never glancing back at the photo. Was it even his family? Prior is doubtful. The old man was definitely not the baby. The photo is a carte de visite, the first type of photography to use a glass negative to make copies, circa 1859-1889. That was over two hundred years ago. All this accumulated knowledge and years of study just to know that everyone lies.

The old man turns out to be the only customer of the day. As the sun sets, Prior closes up shop and decides to take the long way home. The island is big enough that he still finds new trails back to his hut. And the dense foliage makes him feel protected as he maneuvers the twisting branches, tall grasses, and ground vines.

He's climbing a large rock to get a better view and discern if he should remain on this path back home. At the top of the rock, he spots a distant fire. The smoke curls up over the tree line. It must be near Potters Village towards the center of the island. He stops breathing and listens carefully, trying to block out the sounds of mosquitoes, frogs, and the wind. He hears a small crowd of people talking over one another. Or maybe it's just the echoes of a few people that land in his ear. Then, a voice carries over the rest. A commanding voice. Their leader. The voices sound familiar and non-threatening. Mod and NanoGov aren't that subtle. These are locals tending to their business which has nothing to do with Prior. He climbs down the rock and finds his way back home.

The next day, Prior decides to go to work two days in a row. Antoine and Philippe are waiting for him outside his shop. They don't have their fishing equipment so this is an official visit. Philippe must have been appointed deputy at some point. They smile as Prior approaches.

"My boxes still secure or did da sea make me a widow?" says Antoine.

"I was able to retrieve all of them," says Prior. "Why didn't you warn me about the storm the other day?" He unlatches the shop door and holds it open. Antoine and Philippe enter.

"Dese are tings you must start to figure out by yourself, Jere, if you are to trive here."

"Thrive and Mr. Prior are not words that go together," says Philippe, holding in a chuckle. Prior apologized to him yesterday about the parrotfish and Philippe waved it away as an unnecessary gesture.

"Careful, Philippe," says Prior.

Antoine laughs and Prior knows this isn't a serious visit. It's a curiosity call.

Philippe is staring out the shop window, transfixed by a reproduction canvas David Hockney print hanging between two trees. The intrigued expression on his face. It reminds Prior so much of Molly.

"First tings first," says Antoine, tapping Philippe's shoulder.

Philippe opens up his satchel and takes out a bundle of boar jerky, tied together with a thread of banana leaf. Prior accepts it and stores it in the corner.

"Payment before services rendered?" says Prior. "Now I can't refuse to help."

"Helping is how you survive," says Antoine.

"Surviving," says Prior. "I'll work on thriving next year."

Antoine reaches into Philippe's satchel and takes out a banana leaf parcel. It is rolled tightly, almost like one of Antoine's spliffs.

"Isn't it a bit early for..." says Prior.

"Wait," says Antoine.

Antoine unwraps the banana leaf and Philippe takes a cautious step back.

Prior leans in to contemplate. Resting in the middle of the large, unfurled banana leaf is another leaf. This one is dull green, lance-shaped, about six-inches long and half-an-inch wide.

"What's this supposed to be?" says Prior.

"We were hoping you could tell us," says Philippe. He keeps his distance, distrustful of the leaf exposed to the air, like it's a bomb waiting to be detonated.

"Well, my considered professional opinion is that it's a leaf," says Prior. "I don't know if you've noticed, Philippe, but the island is filled with them. Most of them sticking out of those things. What do you call them? Oh yeah, trees."

"Dis is not like any leaf we have eva' seen," says Antoine. He picks it up and hands it to Prior. Prior takes a step back, tucking his arms behind him. "A villager found it on da beach. Dere were no other leaves or twigs anywhere near it."

"Probably washed up from the storm a few days ago," says Prior.

Antoine places the leaf back in the nest of the banana leaf. "The storm did not visit our side of de island," says Antoine. "Only yours."

"We were wondering if you could tell us anything of its origin," says Philippe. "We are very suspect of foreign leaves."

"Leaves and people," says Prior, his hands still behind his back, peering at the leaf.

"Please, Jere," says Antoine.

"Is that what you were discussing last night at your meeting?" says Prior.

"We all decided you could be trusted," says Philippe.

"We do trust you," says Antoine.

Prior points to the leaf and Philippe turns it over. It's the same dull green color on the other side. "Tell me what you know," says Prior.

"No more," says Antoine. "Like I said, it was on de shore by itself, almost like it wanted to be left alone and had willed de rest of de leaves to go away."

"Hey," says Philippe, chuckling, pointing at Prior. "Dis leaf and you are de same."

"Can you authenticate it?" says Antoine, ignoring Philippe.

Prior examines the leaf carefully without touching it. "Well, to start, this leaf shouldn't be here. I mean, there's no way this should exist. But then again, we're not dealing with traditional physics and universal laws any longer."

"Why shouldn't it be here?" says Philippe.

"Have you welcomed any refugees from Australia recently?" says Prior.

"Australia?" says Philippe.

"No," says Antoine, gazing at the leaf.

"Because this leaf is from the eucalyptus michaeliana plant. Commonly known as Hillgrove gum," says Prior.

"And is not indigenous to this island?"

"You said no one here has ever seen it," says Prior. "No, it only grows in Australia. Specifically, in the woodlands on sandy soils. You talk about thriving? This little guy only grows between St. Albans and Wollomombi in New South Wales."

"I told you he would know," says Antoine to Philippe.

"Is there anything you don't know?" says Philippe.

"Yeah," says Prior. "Why it's here. Knowing where it's from is cheap and easy. And, in this case, useless. Sorry I can't help you further."

"Can we leave it here for now?" says Antoine.

"Our village is a little freaked out by it," says Philippe.

"One day. Two, tops," says Prior. "I don't need a new voodoo totem that attracts crowds."

In the distance, there's a thundering explosion. It sends a rippling shock wave that bends back the bamboo poles that support the shop. Prior, Antoine, and Philippe are pushed back by the force and fall to the floor. Antoine and Philippe crawl behind the counter. There's a second explosion and this one causes the banana leaf that was on Prior's counter to blow across the room. Prior pokes his head up and sees the eucalyptus leaf on the counter, unmoved, defiant.

"De fuck is dis?" says Antoine.

No one responds. They wait a few minutes and stand up. Antoine gapes outside. "Come on," he says and runs out. Philippe follows him out of the shop but Prior stays behind his counter. He stares down and sees he has unconsciously covered the eucalyptus leaf with an inverted wooden bowl.

He hears Antoine and Philippe running towards the explosions, their feet and hands cracking twigs and dried leaves as their steps take them closer to the invading sounds.

Prior puts a heavy coconut on the bowl, not wanting to lose the eucalyptus leaf. He picks up everything that fell off the floor and re-arranges all the objects so they are back in their place. When an hour has gone by, he pokes his head out of the shop, listening for any excuse to stay or go home. He doesn't hear anything unusual so he wends his way slowly on the same path that Antoine and Philippe took.

He climbs to a high vantage point on one of the smaller, forested mountains on the island. He peers through the leaves towards the cove near the village.

Anchored a few hundred feet from shore are three enormous, majestic pirate warships. Each is brand new, like they've never been kissed by the sun or the stormy sea. They're identical with three tall masts, sails billowing in the wind, two tiers of decks, and heavy cannons pointed at the shore. Small row boats hang off the sides of each ship like vulgar jewelry. No flag is hoisted. No men are on board. Three shiny new ghost ships.

One of the pirate warships has a missing rowboat. Prior spies the rowboat on the beach. There are some footprints on the sand leading from the rowboat towards inland.

Mod are too arrogant to soil their feet on this island so they have sent their Fringe representatives.

Prior's breathing becomes labored. He thought it would be several more years before Mod invaded this island. Even though the warships are right there, in plain sight, Prior knows it's all an illusion. Nanos have created this. And Prior gets that horrible, sour feeling in his stomach he had when he saw his first Mod. It made him want to leave America.

Years ago, when the earth's population was exploding into unsustainable numbers, the planet's resources were being depleted at an exponential rate. Everything that was needed to survive quickly grew scarce. The planet was stretched thin.

Just when the world headed for the brink of what seemed like the breaking point, a small, exclusive party saw an opportunity and took over. The world's governments, in partnership with multi-national corporations, formed the global entity NanoGov. The leading scientists and profiteers had been brought in to solve the crisis. Anton Ferri, NanoGov's chief scientist, made his immortal name. Things were taken to their logical extremes.

In less than a decade, they had created, and the world embraced, the nanotechnology revolution. The nanos had reduced the demand for resources. Through the nanos, NanoGov had created longer lives, flying cars, solar cells, better medicine, food substitutes, cleaner water, and stronger crops.

And Mod were born.

At first, Prior supposed the idea of the nano-revolution and turning Mod was appealing. The world's economy got flipped with the advent of Mod. Businesses weren't needed as the middle men anymore. Mod just thought of what they wanted and their nanos provided it to them. Mod literally took up no space. They didn't need to eat. They just needed a little bit of water. That meant no more manufacturing, no more global warming, no more overpopulation. But there was a hefty, unexpected price to pay.

And now Mod had landed on Prior's shores. The nanos may have created the surface of the pirate warships but the threat is real to the island Fringe. Maybe Mod aren't even on the ships. Prior knows of Mod so powerful, with a vast, accumulated storehouse of nanos, that they can commission Mod ambassadors to do the actual physical work of accumulating more mass for more nanos. It is a never-ending cycle of consumption.

Whatever they are, be it Mod, Fringe representatives, or Mod ambassadors, they are not here on friendly terms. Maybe they've already pillaged other Caribbean islands and are just spreading like a virus to this one.

Prior runs back to his shop, grabs a towel, and uses it to pick up the eucalyptus leaf. He stuffs it in his pocket and bolts home. This isn't his fight. Antoine, Philippe and the rest of the islanders have survived this whole time. Like Antoine said, they have even thrived. They can handle this. And Prior could be wrong. It could just be local pirates from a neighboring island hunting for food. That's probably what it is.

He gets home, breathing heavily but relieved no one is there waiting for him. His hut seems unmolested. The weather on this side of the island seems the same, just cloudier. But better cloudy than filled with Mod pirate warships.

Prior looks up at the sky, shielding his eyes from the glare. These aren't clouds. Millions of butterflies are migrating towards the other side of the island. They are each different colors but they move as part of a unit. They sail by silently, their wings flapping but leaving no reverberations in their path.

Prior ducks inside his hut, glad to be protected from the sky. He sits down at his table, unwraps the towel and lays it at the center of the table; the eucalyptus leaf stubbornly still there.

Prior takes a deep breath. He touches the eucalyptus leaf, picking it up tenderly with his right thumb and forefinger. The leaf vibrates, shaking as if there is a stiff tropical wind blowing through Prior's hut. The leaf's vibrations pick up momentum until Prior can't hold on to it. It flies away, forcing Prior to stand up and paw at the air, trying to grab it.

The leaf lands in the chair opposite Prior and is still again. The leaf is bent in the middle at a ninety-degree angle, like a person sitting up.

"Have a seat, Jeremiah Prior."

There's a crunching sound followed by a deep droning bass line. The crunching sound is rhythmic, almost like a march performed by thousands of little feet. Prior isn't sure where the sound is coming from. He looks over at the leaf. It vibrates again but this time, it is also being pulled and stretched like taffy. It grows with each pull, changing shape. It remains seated the entire time.

"Please sit down, Prior."

Prior sits and peers down at the floor. Hundreds of island insects are marching in an organized fashion across his floor, crawling up the table leg, converging on the leaf like it's a homing beacon. The bugs are enveloped within the leaf as it grows. Prior stares in amazement, completely still. The leaf is as big as Prior now, having absorbed the mass of bugs. Prior anticipates further action, perhaps his execution. But the room is silent again. No attacking nanos or Mod.

There is a silky noise as the giant leaf pops into its final shape.

"Hello Prior." The leaf-voice is soothing. Familiar. "How's tricks?"

It's Penny, Prior's secretary from his Authentician agency. He must be hallucinating. Maybe Antoine gave him some doctored ganja and he is just now feeling the effects. Penny's long, brown hair covers her beautiful, angular face which rests atop her curvy body. Her determined eyes don't miss a beat. This can't be happening. The last person he wants to face is Penny.

"Well, say something," says Penny, sitting across from him as if she was invited for afternoon tea.

"You aren't real."

"You need to come home," says Penny. "You've been away far too long."

Prior gets up and crosses the room. Her eyes follow him.

"Can you hear me?" says Prior. "Is this a telegram or a phone call?"

"Come home," she says. "I want to work with you again. Your Authentician license is still active. I've paid the annual fees these past four years."

Prior sits down across from her again. She doesn't blink. She's just a message. He thinks about just running out. Again.

"I also kept the lease going on our small office. Please," she says.

That doesn't hook him. He has feelings for Penny but not the kind that would make him want to go back home. Then she drops the big news.

"They've solved my husband's murder. You're free to come home. The Feynman case is officially closed. Your name is cleared. Please, Jere."

Prior grabs a table and throws it across the room, knocking over the chair that Penny-leaf is sitting on. Hundreds of insects are released from the nanos and scatter across the room, looking for the quickest exit. They're confused about what just happened to them. Prior knows the feeling.

The eucalyptus leaf is back to its original size. Prior picks it up off the floor, using a towel, careful not to touch it. The leaf-nanos must be triggered by his molecules, his touch. He folds up the towel and tucks it into his pocket.

He walks outside and looks up at the fluttering objects in the sky. They aren't butterflies. They're not paper kites, hummingbirds, or leaves, despite his fantasies that they are.

The objects are Mod. Regular people who have chosen to undergo a ridiculously expensive procedure to give up their mass and become two-dimensional. They sail across the Antiguan sky like wind-blown silk handkerchiefs, leaving Prior feeling deeply alone.

Chapter 4

Prior slowly creeps though the dense jungle so sound doesn't give away his position. The birds in the trees and ground mice are noisier as they hunt for food. He's making his way across the island. He needs to be with people. Needs to talk to Antoine. Every hundred feet or so, he looks around to make sure he's not being followed.

How did Penny find him? How did she manage to pull the resources to get the letter-leaf to him? Despite what she's telling him, Prior doesn't want to go back home. He's safe in Antigua. His antique shop is surviving. He has a good friend in Antoine. There are no traces of the real world here. Maybe those are real pirate ships. That would be excellent news.

Prior recalls there used to be donkeys on the island years ago but no more. Prior's heard rumors that they were eaten. Maybe he'll go the way of the Wadadli donkey.

He is relieved that they closed the case on Feynman's death. Prior's partner was never a careful man and his death didn't surprise too many people. Damn good Authentician, though. Feynman sure knew his stuff. Too bad he couldn't distinguish what was real and what was fake in his own life.

Prior wonders who they nailed with the conviction. He's pretty sure that committing murder is still a crime in America. Maybe they just randomly pick a Fringe to send to jail or slavery or whatever the Mod and NanoGov are doing these days. Maybe they pinned the murder on Lachende, the kid in his office who helped out.

After Feynman died, Prior left and swore he'd never go back home. He doesn't think that Penny's message changes the conviction of his decision. It would take a lot to outweigh the guilt Prior feels in his gut over Feynman's death. After all, how else could he feel when he was having an affair with his partner's wife. He and Penny were consenting adults yet Prior can't get past believing that he is to blame for the whole damn thing. If only he had been a better detective.

Between the recent storms washing his hut out to sea and the appearance of the leaf-letter, Prior has taken the precaution of carrying Molly's photograph in his pocket. He doesn't want to lose it. He left Felice's framed photo back at the hut.

The thick brush and rocky terrain make him advance slowly. He's in no rush. He can't outrun his past anyway. He stares at his daughter's photo. It's never the good stuff he recalls. It's the garbage. The disturbing vision of his ex-wife, Felice, deciding to become Mod. Days later, Felice leaving him. Molly running away. But not before Molly saying she hated him for ruining their lives for having an affair with his secretary. Prior was the author of all this chaos. The one-two punch of seeing his family dissolve and being responsible for Feynman's death. That's when he chose to escape to Antigua.

Prior reaches the village and walks down the main street. There are some villagers standing around but no one talks to him. They have clearly heard the rumor that he received a nano-letter and are immediately, and rightly, suspicious of him. There are no more explosions this morning. Prior makes inquiries and finds out that Antoine is on the other side of the island.

Prior suddenly feels abandoned. There is no one else he can share his Penny-leaf news with. There is no one he can share his rage with. Even in this island of outcasts, he's an outcast.

He leaves a note on the front door of Antoine's hut and heads back to his shop. The walk is just as slow and flooded with memories of his life back home. His past is a swarm of gnats buzzing around his head, following him regardless of his location or hand-swatting.

Prior finds someone standing inside his shop. It is a white man in his thirties, cleanly shaven, dirty-blond hair neatly pomaded like an ice cream cone, expensive three-piece suit, crisply tailored, leather shoes shining. An arrogant smile filled with more white, perfect teeth than someone should have. Obviously not a local.

"Can I help you, friend?" says Prior, closing the shop door behind him. Prior searches the shop. This guy appears to be alone. This Fringe in a suit is working for Mod. He's a Mod ambassador. The suit's a sure sign. And the attitude.

The man leans on the counter, casual and confident, as if he not only owns the shop but the whole damned island. He continues to smile, sizing up Prior.

"Your shop, it amuses me," says the man in a high, effeminate voice. He's slightly ridiculous now that there is a sound attached to his appearance, like an old silent film actor with a squeaky voice who couldn't make it in the talkies.

"Glad you're enjoying it. Anything in particular..."

"You already bore me," says the man, heading towards Prior, who steps out of the way.

"Yeah, sorry for the lack of excitement here but..."

"I'm speaking now," says the man, his hand on the shop's front door. He opens it and faces out towards the beach, even though he is addressing Prior. "There is new management here. New owners." He lets out a strained, little laugh. "A contingent of Mod will be taking over this island, this Antigua, as you call it, very soon."

The pirate warships.

"Who the hell do you think..."

"Including your shop and all its contents. I've taken inventory. Most amusing."

And just like that, before Prior can say anything, the dandy steps outside. Prior runs after him but the guy has disappeared. There's a swishing sound from above. Prior looks up at the sky and sees a giant banana leaf blowing away. The guy in the suit, the dandy, was Mod. They're impersonating Fringe now. Jesus.

Prior scans the horizon. No sign of the warships. Mod are toying with the islanders. It's all about their amusement.

Prior goes to the beach where he does his best thinking. The cool ocean laps its waves on his feet. How could Mod have changed things so much? How could so many people have blindly accepted the change?

Prior wonders why Mod would be interested in Antigua. Probably for the pirate gold. Hence, the ludicrous warships. Little children playing with their toys. It's odd since Mod prefer to live in cooler climates. Gold nanos melt at room temperature. But Prior figures Mod are too greedy to pass up on endless pirate gold. It might take all their focused energy not to have their gold nanos melt in warm climates but it would be worth it for the bragging rights to other Mod. It's all about bragging to the other exclusive club members.

Prior and Feynman had started their agency because there seemed to be a genuine interest in rich people collecting gold, artifacts, and valuables. Prior hadn't realized he was actually helping Mod by operating a successful Authentician agency. The rich wanted to ensure their possessions and investments were the real deal. Bragging rights were so important to them. For five years, he and Feynman researched, travelled, catalogued, interviewed, and negotiated on behalf of their well-paying clients. Prior didn't realize it was for the same cause. Mod conversion.

In order for a rich Fringe to convert to Mod, they needed to amass a huge inventory of possessions as well as grow themselves into massive physical proportions. The larger the mass, the more nanos one had to control when one became two dimensional.

And the thing that put Prior over the edge was that his wife had been secretly working on the Mod project on behalf of Anton Ferri and NanoGov. Prior knew she was working on some government project but never dreamed that it was something so insidious. Ferri and NanoGov were working on the ultimate game of rock-paper-scissor and finally figured out a way for paper to forever beat rock. Weeks later, Felice converted to Mod, moved out, and Molly ran off. Feynman was murdered and Prior hightailed it to Antigua.

And in the end, is the world really better with Mod? Not to Fringe. Not to Antoine and everyone on this island. And not to Molly back in New York. Prior hopes she's safe. He'll never know. The kid wouldn't want to see him again. Maybe he can just hide and this will all blow over like a passing hurricane.

The next morning, Prior wakes up in his hut and it is still there. That's always a good sign. He didn't get a good night's sleep, though. There was a humming and rhythmic clanging above his hut all night. He assumes it was the warships or a bad dream. Same thing.

He's wondering whether to get out of bed or just pull his thin blanket over his head when a muffled voice interrupts his plans. The sound is coming from outside his hut. Getting up and stretching his back, he tentatively opens his front door to investigate the muffled voice.

It's coming from the sky. More specifically, it's emanating from the enormous Sky-Screen that NanoGov has installed over the entire island. It's oval, several miles wide, and floats in the sky like a contact lens, adjusting its angle based on its viewers and position of the sun. It's the main communication device for NanoGov to deliver news to Fringe.

Currently, the news anchor, a smarmy Mod Ambassador with styled graying hair, is reporting on a missing Georges Seurat sketch. The sketch was stolen from an underground vault thought to be the hidden treasure cave of a Fringe on the verge of turning Mod. The Fringe is presumed dead; the laws don't prevent Mod from killing Fringe for their convenience or amusement. These scavengers will eat their own if it gets them more treasure and mass.

Prior knows this Seurat sketch. At least, he's seen pictures of it. The fact that he's got a giant screen staring right back at him from heaven doesn't disturb Prior as much as it should. Maybe it's the part of his brain that momentarily feels like he's back in business, pondering stolen artworks.

The Sky-Screen newscaster turns his attention to a commercial and it brings Prior right back to reality. The world he escaped has followed him here. And if Mod are here, there's nowhere else to go.

Then Prior realizes how Mod found him and why they chose to pillage the island now. They followed Penny's letter right to Prior. That's when it registers that none of the locals are safe. He has to warn Antoine.

He jogs the worn path that emanates from his hut through the thick vegetation. He hasn't tired of these trails. He decides to forge a new trail about three miles from home, occasionally hacking his way through the underbrush with his machete. It's a slog but he finds himself enjoying blazing a new trail. The small animals in his way are puzzled by his intrusion but most continue on with their busy, scurrying lives as soon as he passes. He knows he's heading towards a mountain top and that should provide enough of a vantage point to orient him towards Antoine.

Antoine will know what to do. He's wise beyond his years and never seems troubled by current events. He takes it all in stride, as if everything is unfolding as it should. Then again, he's lived through a Jamaican revolution that brought him to this island which had its own terrors. But that crisis was human scale. Antoine has never experienced the heart of the nano-revolution or the horror of human civilization being engineered out of existence.

Prior reaches the top of the mountain at nightfall and is momentarily disoriented. The village bonfires are not where they should be. He smells smoke arriving with the northern breeze. He stands perfectly still, leaning on a nearby tree. He hears the distant hum of people talking. The sound circles back in echoes and continues to tease his ears.

He advances down the mountain slowly, cautiously, talking care not to rustle the underbrush or snap any twigs with his approaching steps. The mosquitoes bite him but he doesn't make his usual swatting movements or yell at them. He remains silent and covert, approaching the sound of voices like he's on a hunt. As he gets closer, he also hears the crackle of a large fire.

Prior peers through the broad leaves and spots the bonfire, feeling its warmth. The bonfire is surrounded by many of the islanders he knows as his customers and fishing companions. They sit in front of the roaring fire, drinking and eating. But there is no merriment to the proceedings. No joy in their eyes. They are focused in the same direction, listening attentively to a large man standing on a tree stump, orating with great fervor. Next to the man, silhouetted by the fire behind him, there are crude drawings mapped out on the skin of a long-ago slaughtered animal.

Prior adjusts his eyes and takes a step closer, still trying to be stealthy and conceal his position. The large man speaking to the crowd is Antoine.

Over the roar of the fire and call-and-response between Antoine and the villagers, Prior can barely make out what Antoine is talking about. Something about a rebellion. Violence. Maybe a secret factory.

Maybe they're all high. It wouldn't be the first time that Prior has seen the locals congregate, get stoned, and talk about fixing the world's problems. People are the same everywhere.

Prior retreats back to the mountain. This isn't his fight. As he treks back, he realizes that although he has known Antoine for four years and shared many bottles of old rum and stories with him, it turns out Prior doesn't know him at all.

He feels ashamed for spying on this secret society but he's also angry for not being invited. Would he have shown up if they had asked him to attend? There are no secrets among the islanders. They rely on each other to survive. They'll figure out a way to defend their village or co-exist with Mod. Like a seashell that keeps out the ocean. Prior decides to never mention his stumbling upon their meeting to anyone.

Chapter 5

The air feels thick, the night sky devoid of stars. The Sky-Screen blocks any ambient light and with no one watching the news or commercials at this late hour, the Sky-Screen reverts from a two-way mirror back to its actual intention: a giant camera spying on the populace.

By the time Prior gets home, it's almost dawn. He's exhausted and doesn't know what to do. If he has to flee, he doesn't know where to go. And there are some possessions that he doesn't want to lose.

He's taking stock of what he absolutely couldn't live without when he hears the roaring boom. The explosion is followed by a rush of wind and the splash of water.

Outside, there is only smoke and the choking wind, filled with sand and broken leaves swirling past Prior at dangerous velocities. As he makes his way out of his hut, shielding his eyes with his arms, he hears birds migrating to a safer spot on the island.

He runs through the swirling sand that dances and twists in the wind, trying to get a better vantage point. He needs to understand what the source of all this chaos is. He's hoping it's a natural storm, one in a long string of storms that have plagued the island over centuries. He sees a coconut tree and shimmies twenty feet up its long, bent skin. His feet and left hand grip the rough bark while his right hand continues to shield his eyes from the sand, leaves, and shells that form most of the immediate atmosphere.

He tries to block out the white noise of the wind rushing through him. Focusing intently, he hears an unmistakable boom of cannons and his heart sinks. He knows this is not a natural phenomenon. It's a pirate warship.

The Mod invasion has officially begun. The explosions the day before were only foreplay. They're taking over Antigua. He only hears one cannon firing but it's impossible to see anything through the smoke and sand. Prior figures Mod are having fun playing war and have taken the other two ships to other side of the island.

A strong wind blows across Prior's beach and he is offered a blessedly small vision of the chaos underway. The pirate warship floats a few hundred feet from shore, its cannons pointed over his hut, firing relentlessly. The cannon isn't shooting cannonballs. Mod aren't interested in wholesale destruction of property. They want to accumulate mass that they will convert to nanos so they can own more. They want to clear away detritus to make room for their crazy two-dimensional fantasy resorts. These resorts and all their contents will appear to be real but they'll just be a facade, a two-dimensional picture created by the nanos. Just who they are trying to impress is anyone's guess.

The cannons shoot a pulsating ring of energy, flat and slightly blue in color, that spins and expands, like a smoke ring from a grossly sized mouth. The ring grows as it spins until it lands on a large portion of the Antiguan forest. The ring descends like a fog but instead of dissipating, it turns every useful resource within its circumference to nanos which travel instantaneously to its Mod master. Anything not deemed valuable, like animals, wood, and dirt, is thrown into the ocean. The final effect as the ring touches down is an enormous, perfect circle that has been cleared of everything, ready to receive its new structure. The pirate warship fires dozens of these rings through its cannon like frisbees. The island is quickly and efficiently being reduced to the spotty appearance of a mangy dog.

Prior hears something sailing towards him, its humming getting louder. He prays the cannon-ring isn't coming for him.

It's a giant wahoo. Confused but still hungry, the twenty-foot sleek fish, expanded to freakish proportions from its normal two-foot length by the mad science of nanotechnology, shoots through the air like an arrow, opening its pointed, silver mouth as it spots easy pickings hanging off the coconut tree.

Prior jumps off the tree, then lands and rolls as best he can into the sand. The wahoo flies overhead, landing on the beach several yards away from him, its mouth stuck in the sand like a spear, its tail flopping in the air.

Prior feels bad for the fish. He tries to pull the wahoo out of the sand by its tail but it's too big. He takes a running start and throws himself into the side of the fish. The fish is dislodged and flops on the sand, spinning around like a bottle at a teenage party. Gasping for air, the wahoo isn't interested in eating Prior any longer. It just needs to get back to the sea. Prior manages to grab its tail and tugs at the fish. Sliding along the sand, it's not as heavy as Prior expects. Maybe because it's so thin.

Prior reaches the tide and rolls the wahoo the rest of the way in. He's not sure if it's even alive at this point. Overhead, the pirate warship continues to decimate this part of the island with its nano-attack, continuing to convert the landscape to its liking. A wave takes the wahoo back to the ocean and it's gone as quickly as it arrived on land.

Prior turns and spots an antique "Don't Mess with Texas" flag waving on the pirate warship's mast. He begins to get an idea.

Antigua is a small island and there's nowhere to hide. Prior figures his only chance for survival is to find Antoine. Probably half the island is having the same thought. Standing still is suicide. His hut is still untouched but that's not going to last long. He leaves everything, including the chaos, and runs into the forest towards Antoine's.

He gets a few hundred yards into the forest when he hears his name being called. It's faint at first and he thinks it's just his mind or heartbeat pulsing in his ears playing tricks with him. He stops, catches his breath, and hears his name again. Clearing the brush away, he sees Philippe standing in the distance, waving his arms at Prior. Philippe is yelling something else now but its hard to hear over the booming of the cannons and trees being torn from their roots and flung into the ocean.

Prior motions Philippe to stay where he is. As Prior heads towards him, a blue nano-ring, fired by the Texas warship, is coming right at Philippe. Prior breaks into a full run as Philippe covers his head in fear. The nano-ring is about to touch down to the tree line, ready to envelop, destroy, and reset everything within its circumference.

Prior tackles Philippe, putting his arms around him, as the two fly through the air to safety. The nano-ring lands, making a crashing sound, as Prior and Philippe roll away, out of its reach. They smack into a pile of black pineapples, looking back to see if they are still in immediate danger. Philippe has a cut on his forehead but otherwise looks fine. Prior is out of breath.

The blue nano-ring, about two-hundred feet wide, forms a dome and begins to vibrate, like a demented snow-globe. Trees shoot out from the dome; unwanted building materials. There is a swirling cloud within the dome followed by a buzzing sound. The dome lifts and in the place of the forest and part of a mountain, is a giant, gleaming Alamo-themed pinball machine. It stands on perfectly level ground that resembles Italian marble.

"The Mod's goddamn playground," says Prior. "Some spoiled brat got an arcade fetish when he was twelve and this whole ecosystem has to die so he can have his toy."

"Thank you for saving my life, Mr. Prior," says Philippe.

"Shit, Philippe, call me Jere."

"Are you OK," says Philippe, getting up. He swabs at the cut on his head.

"What the hell are you doing here?"

"Antoine sent me to find you."

"Is it the same on the rest of the island?" says Prior, already knowing the answer.

"Worse. Come on."

Philippe helps Prior up and they head east towards the center of the island. Prior trails a few steps behind Philippe, keeping a careful watch. In the distance, the thunderous boom and crunching continues.

"Antoine is this way," says Prior, indicating a northern trail.

"Please, Jere, follow me," says Philippe.

They continue east without stopping. After two hours, they hear another ring-dome touch down nearby. Prior notes it didn't come from overhead so it must be from another warship. He tells Philippe to stay put while he investigates. Philippe readily agrees and sits under a tree, nursing his cut head.

Prior approaches the ring-dome cautiously. After the noise has dissipated and the dust has settled, Prior arrives at a clearing that wasn't there two minutes ago. Every tree within the dome's reach has been ripped from the earth. A large pond and the creek that fed it have been diverted or simply removed. In their place stand two perfect trees, one-hundred feet tall. The trunks are white and pencil thin. The tops of the trees are a solid mass of green like a lollipop. The trees are without blemish; the kind of trees that a four-year old would draw. Strung together between the two trees are hundreds of hammocks in varying colors. They are stacked on top of each other along the height of the trees and the overall effect is of a giant corset ready to be sewn up. Each hammock has an "I Love NY" logo on it.

Bingo. Prior calculates the general direction and distance where this nano-ring was shot from.

"What is to become of us?" says Philippe when Prior returns. "My whole family is here."

"That's what I'm hoping Antoine can tell us."

"I fear I may have gotten us lost," says Philippe. "In all this confusion."

"Why did Antoine send for me?"

"Of course," says Philippe. He reaches into his front pocket and takes out a fresh spliff.

"Philippe, we need all the lucidity we can get."

"Antoine gave this to me. For emergencies. For when I have to find him."

"I'm sure he meant..."

Philippe holds the spliff by the end, like a divining rod. The rolling paper unfurls in the wind, revealing the ganja within. The ganja doesn't blow away. Instead, it shimmers.

"Now watch this," says Philippe.

Philippe lets go of the spliff and it floats in the air. It completes unrolling and becomes its original rectangular, flat shape, suspended just below eye level. The ganja continues vibrating and begins to reorganize itself on the paper's surface. Soon, the ganja has formed itself into the shape of an arrow, pointing towards the forest in front of them.

"It will get us to Antoine," says Philippe.

"This is impossible," says Prior.

"Come," says Philippe, running in the direction of the arrow in front of him. With each step he takes, the floating paper stays a step in front of him, the arrow adjusting slightly like a compass needle.

"This technology doesn't exist," says Prior, running after Philippe, who just shakes his head.

They continue their guided stealth run into the island's heart. An hour later, the paper and arrow stop moving. Prior looks around, not seeing anything new. He and Philippe are standing in the forest on the other side of the mountain. The booming from the nano-attack seems more distant from this location. Philippe puts his hands to the sides of his mouth.

"Antoine, we are here," says Philippe.

Then, as if a curtain has been lifted, the surrounding forest disappears. But instead of being destroyed by the Mod, these trees and mountain are an illusion, a painted landscape that folds into itself. Revealed behind the curtain is an enormous factory. Prior recognizes it as the old sugar mill where the old slaves from several centuries ago were forced to work for their rich plantation masters.

Antigua used to be owned by the British, the ruling class exploiting the pineapple plantations, but there are no longer any world governments or countries, in the traditional sense. NanoGov took care of that. The rich got what they finally craved: everything whenever they wanted it. They became Mod. And no one was there to stop them. The world became bifurcated so easily into the Haves and Have-Nots. Mod created a world-wide Fringe population dedicated exclusively to worshipping them. And Fringe that didn't want to worship became the help or slaves. Or died. And all because of Ferri and his invention of the nanos.

Where the old sugar mill machinery and still-pots used to be, there is now a sleek, efficient, modern factory. Thousands of thin pipes shoot off in all directions as if a kid has dropped a container of old-time plastic straws on the ground. The pipes lead to small reactor vessels, each quietly humming and gleaming in the factory overhead light. There doesn't appear to be any input or output to this machine process; just an infinite loop of whatever is being produced running quietly through the thin pipes.

Antoine appears from behind one of the tall vessels. He's dressed in full Rastafarian garb, including a dashiki and flowing pants, all in the colors of his beloved Jamaican flag. His dreadlock hair is pulled back into a lumpy ponytail. He waves at Prior like a kid welcoming his playmate into his toy-filled room.

Philippe gives a little salute to Antoine, pats Prior on the shoulder and heads out.

"I forgot how much I missed metal," says Prior. It's the first thing that jumps to mind.

"Jere, I am so happy you are safe and dat you are here. Come."

Prior walks over to a table and sits with Antoine. Antoine pours some water into two clay jars.

"Antoine, I don't understand. What is all this?"

"First, tell me about dat letter you got. Da leaf-letter. What did it say?"

Prior takes a sip. It's the best-tasting water that's crossed his lips in several years. "What is this?"

"Was it from your daughter?" says Antoine.

"The letter? No, Molly doesn't want anything to do with me," says Prior with no remorse or self-pity. He hasn't spoken much about his family with Antoine.

"No matta'," says Antoine. "You must go back."

"Back?"

"Before you even tell me, I know dat letter is callin' you back to New York. You gotta' answer it."

"I can't," says Prior.

"Why?"

Prior finishes the water and puts down his jar. He decides to trust Antoine with this dark part of his life. "Because I might have murdered my partner."

"Ah," says Antoine, not flustered one bit. "Penny. Your old secretary. She sent da letter. Tell me, how did she get it here?"

Prior stands up. "Can we talk about what the hell this all is?"

"Answer my question first," says Antoine. "Because my guess is da answer to my question and da answer to yours are da same answer."

Prior inspects one of the vessels. The machine hums along on its own without any assistance from a human. It's just Antoine in here with his vast network of pipes and vessels. Prior faces Antoine who is still sits languidly, sipping slowly from his jar.

"I feel terrible about that letter," says Prior.

"Because of your history with Mr. Feynman and Penny," says Antoine.

"Because I think Mod followed Penny's letter to me. I think that's why the warships are here and the island is being taken over. Aren't you worried? I'm responsible for all this."

Antoine gets up and approaches Prior. He places a gentle hand on Prior's shoulder. "Dat's why you got to make tings right and go back."

Prior takes a step back and puts his hand under one of the delicate factory pipes. It's smooth. Prior can hardly detect any motion inside.

"It's picas, isn't it?" says Prior. "You're making pica threads."

"What else?" says Antoine.

"What do you mean, what else? I was just kidding. This technology doesn't exist. NanoGov hasn't figured out how to do it. And if men like Ferri aren't smart enough…"

"Easy, mon. Easy. The question is, why would dey make picas when dey got it so good? You don't see sharks inventing guns. But we poor islanders, we need all da protection we can get."

"And what exactly does this machine do?"

Antoine reaches into his pocket and tosses a fabric circle to Prior. It spins with perfect balance in the air, flashing the same Jamaican colors as Antoine's clothes.

Prior has to hand it to Antoine. With complete secrecy, Antoine has built a pica factory on this little island and is manufacturing pica-fiber tams. It's the only technology Prior figures can ward off Mod. Mod are ruled by nanos which are about one-hundred-thousandth the width of a human hair. A billionth of a meter.

But a picameter is a thousand times smaller than a nanometer. And Antoine's pica-tam is woven with the pica-fibers produced in this factory. Which means that Mod and their nanos will get caught in the pica-tam like a school of tuna in a giant pantyhose.

The ground shakes, causing Prior to catch himself on a railing. The pica factory machines keep humming along, not bothered by the chaos and destruction outside. Prior figures the factory exterior has been covered with pica threads and is largely immune to the nano attacks.

Antoine is checking some gauges, nodding at the readouts. Prior still can't believe that Antoine has managed to gather the materials and build this place right under the nose of NanoGov. These pica threads could change human history and bring it back to some semblance of balance.

"Why don't you ship these out to the world and overthrow NanoGov?" says Prior.

Antoine sighs. "Dere's no appetite for dat kind of meal," he says. He checks on another screen readout. "People not ready. Dis is all defense. I do dis for protection. For Wadadli to survive until something betta' happens. Dere's no way to beat the system, Jere. All we can do is take care of our own."

Prior understands and realizes that Antoine is right. What good could this little factory on this tiny island do except help its own?

Prior notices one of the factory monitors shows the Sky-Screen above the island. The Sky-Screen is broadcasting "World News Live" and portrays a calm Antigua in real time, the gentle waves lapping upon the pristine shores. It shows Mod arriving in peace and the beholden Fringe getting down on their knees in gratitude that their saviors have arrived to pull them out from their horrible, drab existence. According to the live report, the island Fringe are practically delighted to become slaves again.

"It's time to go," says Antoine.

"Go where?" says Prior. "I thought we were safe here."

"Nowhere is safe. You watch and do like me," says Antoine.

Antoine grabs his pica-tam, sitting on the mop of his dreads, with both hands and pulls it down past his ears. The tam seems to expand. He continues to pull the tam down and it envelops his entire body, the vivid colors stretching and wrapping him like a condom. A moment later, Prior watches as the giant body-flag that was Antoine quickly vibrates, then disappears. Prior is left standing alone in the factory.

He thinks about staying in the cold isolation and security of the factory, knowing that it will probably remain undetected by nanos. However, there was just the slightest look of fear in Antoine's eyes, as if he wasn't entirely sure his invention would be as effective as he thought against the onslaught of Mod.

Prior places the tam on his head and pulls down. It gives easily, like unfolding a bed comforter over him. Soon, he's enveloped in the Jamaican flag colors. It's warm inside the cocoon. He can hear the ocean. And Antoine laughing. How is that possible?

Prior pulls up the tam and it snaps back to its original shape on top of his head. He's standing in his own hut on the other side of the island. Antoine sits on the floor next to him.

"Not bad, huh?" says Antoine, chuckling.

"What happened? Was I out?"

"Out? You were not unconscious, my friend. We have strung pica fibers all over da island. Dey act as our own interstate system."

"You mean…"

"Once you put it on, the pica-tam got on the express lane of da fiber that leads right to your hut. Da trip took as long as it did for you to blink. Good for short distances. Lucky we on a small island."

Antoine stands up and dusts himself off. He reaches into the rafters of Prior's hut.

"Let me guess," says Prior. "You've been storing your pica-tams here the whole time."

"I hope that is all right."

Prior takes a deep breath. "Antoine, after I'm gone, you can store whatever you want here."

Antoine smiles and nods his head. His face shows that he is pleased by Prior's decision.

"Jere, I have to tell you something very important."

"I need to make sure my name is cleared back home. Repair my Authentician reputation. But I have to go," says Prior, "before I change my mind."

Antoine studies Prior as if the past four years haven't been enough time to evaluate the trustworthiness of the man. "OK, yes, I will tell you."

"You don't have to."

"No," said Antoine, "I must. I am with da Fringe Underground Movement."

"The...Underground?"

"Da FU, we call it. Because, of course we do."

"That's not a real thing," says Prior. Prior had heard rumors but they were mostly daydreams and mist.

"It is true."

Prior thinks about that gathering in the jungle, the villagers surrounding the bonfire, Antoine preaching to them. He decides not to reveal witnessing their meeting. He doesn't want Antoine to think that he was spying on him.

"All dis time, all dis time. You see what you look for," says Antoine.

"But how..."

"Da hope. It is my life's dream to reclaim da planet from da Mod. Our planet. Da Fringe. So we start da FU here. A chapter anyway. It is everywhere. We know we cannot do anyting. But da hope. Da hope has to be kept aflame."

"I don't know what...Why are you telling me this?"

"Are you not my friend?" says Antoine.

"But why spend so much time with me when there are so many other refugees here?"

"I would tink it's obvious. You a white mon from America," says Antoine. "Why would a white mon from America come to our little island?"

"I can't even save myself."

"Before you leave on your journey, join our movement." Antoine stares at Prior for what seems like a month.

"I...I can't," says Prior.

"Yes. Tink of the good you can do."

"Not interested. Not why I'm going back."

Antoine sighs and nods, a gesture Prior has witnessed many times before. Antoine turns and takes inventory of the stored boxes in the rafters.

"Here," says Prior, taking off the pica-tam and handing it to Antoine.

"Keep it," says Antoine. "For your salvation in a savage world. For your protection. Use it wisely. It contains powerful juju."

This is something Prior isn't going to miss about Antigua. He never got used to the reliance on protective, invisible forces or belief in evil spirits out to ruin your fortune.

Antoine continues to rummage through Prior's rafters for boxes. He's doing more than checking his inventory. He's searching for something. Outside, the booming is getting louder. In a few hours, the island will be completely run by Mod.

Prior tried to keep his distance from everyone, only allowing himself to get close enough to people to survive. Then he met Antoine and made his first legitimate friend in a long time. And by extension, he befriended the rest of the islanders. He can't leave them all like this.

Antoine steps off the chair and faces Prior, a burlap bag in his hand.

"You da only one I could trust. You da only one on dis island not a FU member. Da other refugees come here, dey join right away. Not you," said Antoine.

"You suspect a mole," says Prior. His entire concept of this island and what's been going on has been turned upside-down. He supposes that's what he gets for living by himself on one of the deserted coves on the island.

"If da members of da FU are caught and interrogated, dey would reveal my box contents. Da Mod would know about my tams. And we can't have dat."

"I'm sorry," says Prior. "The Mod showed up anyway. Penny's letter."

Antoine offers Prior the burlap sack but Prior waves it away. He's not ready to accept parting gifts from his friend. He suddenly has a thousand questions but knows that a thousand answers await him back in New York.

"Come with me," says Prior. "They're here now. There's nothing protecting you. Why don't you escape too?"

"My people need me to protect dem," says Antoine, as if it's the most obvious thing in the world. "My old home in Montego Bay was destroyed. Dis is my new home and dese are my people."

Antoine throws the burlap sack at Prior who is forced to catch it.

"To help you escape," says Antoine. "Dis isn't your home. Dese aren't your people. Do you know how to get back?"

Prior rubs his pica-tam with his thumb and forefinger. It doesn't feel like his tam yet. The woven material is smooth, almost plastic.

"Thank you, Antoine. I can get to one of the warships with your tam. And from there, hitch a ride back home."

Prior opens the sack. It's filled with a few tams and bottles of jerk sauce.

"My friend," says Prior. Antoine smiles and Prior realizes he's going to miss him more than he thought.

"Get da hell out while you can," says Antoine, giving Prior a hug.

Prior places the pica-tam on his head and pulls it down. It elongates and covers him completely. He takes a small step and pulls up the tam. He's standing on the shore of Guard Point. The Mod warship with the New York flag is docked slightly offshore, still shooting its nano-rings onto the land, almost complete with its renovations. The center of the island has no trees or creeks. It's a giant toy chest filled with every pastime imaginable.

Prior knows that this sudden glut of new mass is something that Mod can't help but brag about. Their mindset isn't just consumption. It's bragging about it; showing it all off. He speculates this particular New York Mod is arrogant enough to show off his new-found wealth to Mod back home right away. Prior pulls the tam over his eyes which blocks the sunlight but allows him to see the Mod's nanos at work.

The New York Mod has built a temporary nano-bridge from his warship all the way back to Manhattan. Prior knows its temporary because after the Mod gets bored with showing off his newly amassed mass, it will retract the bridge and use the nanos for something else to amuse him.

Which means that Prior has limited time to get to New York on this bridge. He's counting on the Mod's limited attention span to get him back home. It's a terrible plan. But it's the only plan that will work for now.

Prior slips the tam over himself again and jumps onto the bridge. Nanos can't detect him now. He becomes invisible, pica-level. He takes out Penny's leaf-letter and touches it. It unfurls and guides him back home over the nano-bridge. He feels the rush of crossing the Atlantic in a matter of seconds.

He's still over the water but can see the Manhattan shore. He can swim the rest of the way from here rather than being caught as soon as he arrives. Prior takes off the pica-tam and immediately heads towards the exit off the pica-highway. He pockets the leaf-letter as he jumps into the cold water, temporarily disoriented. There used to be debris in this river but the mass has been consumed by the new landlords. He swims towards the tunnel.

Chapter 6

The Holland Tunnel is longer and darker than Prior recalls. The flat stripes of slanted natural light in the middle distance tells him he's still several hundred feet from the end. He starts to make out old city sounds. The clip-clop-clop of the horse-drawn carriages, the atonal buzz as Fringe messenger boys run by blowing into their kazoos, the fluttery omnipresent whirr of the remaining Fringe going about their daily routines. The city wind rushing and echoing in between the buildings.

He hears faint music. The kind of music that was popular fifty years ago when digital was considered high tech. These sounds are so familiar, as if his four-year absence meant nothing.

He shakes the notion free from his head. He can't have been expected. Up until this morning, he didn't even know he was returning. And he still isn't sure if he's staying longer than a night.

Back in Antigua, he'd heard things had gotten extraordinarily worse in New York since he left. He heard that Mod had appropriated all forms of plastics for themselves, leaving Fringe with mostly ancient wood-based technology. Mod aren't interested in making the lives of Fringe convenient. Fringe are left with scraps. They are left with what Mod find devoid of value.

The tunnel isn't easy to slog through. It's filled with ankle-deep thick muck. But at least Prior's island living has prepared him for the muck.

The two-lane tunnel hasn't seen a car for ages. It smells awful. It was built around a hundred and forty-seven years ago, back in 1943. Maybe no one leaves the city anymore. Prior feels like he's the only person stupid enough to slog back in.

Small animals, having long taken residence as squatters, dart back and forth into their makeshift caves made up of old leaves, rags, bones, and whatever else they dragged in. Tunnels inside of tunnels. Graves within graves.

Something drips on the back of Prior's neck. He instinctively jumps back, landing on all fours, his hands pressed against the forgotten, wet filth. It's cooler than he expects. Even the trash in this city feels like a stone-cold corpse. He looks up at the cracked-tile ceiling. An overhead pipe covered in wet mold leaks its gray fluid.

He crawls ahead on all fours, thinking he's safer down low. He whispers to the rats and cockroaches, figuring they are the only living things left that haven't been corrupted.

"So how do you like being closer to the top of the food chain?" says Prior. There's a skitter of furry movement accompanied by an echoed squeak. "I mean, things have got to look a lot less crowded for you guys now. More food. Less chance to get squashed."

He seeks their company, their camaraderie. He wants the bugs and rats to know he's on their side. He sympathizes with them. They go about their business, tolerating the momentary infestation of this rare Fringe crawling through their home.

Prior stops his locomotion and arches his neck up. In the narrow view of the tunnel exit, he makes out confetti flittering through the air. There seems to be some kind of parade going on today although it doesn't sound like a celebration. Or maybe they're leaves scattered by the early evening breeze or butterflies looking for their next nectar fix or stringless kites flying against the orange sunset of the sky.

He's been out of touch with this world, living nano-free like any Fringe lucky or clever enough to escape to a hidden corner of the world. Still, there is no point in deceiving himself. He knows what those fluttering objects are. Just like the ones on the island yesterday. Even if he has only seen a few in his lifetime, even if the first one he saw was enough to make him leave this place.

It makes it harder to go on. As much as he tries to prepare himself, he's not ready for this world. But there comes a time, he supposes, when every baby is given its womb eviction notice.

Some larger mammals, scurrying around his boots, stop long enough for him to identify them. Mostly raccoons and squirrels. Some woodchucks. They investigate him, wondering who this stranger is with the antiquated clothes, long hair, and forty-year old frame. Their bodies, at least, are adapted to the unnatural change in the world's conditions.

He's a few feet from the tunnel exit. There's a sudden lack of noise, as if the air has been sucked out of the tunnel. All the animals bolt towards the dark warmth of the middle of the tunnel. That's how they've survived for so long. They know when to run.

Prior reaches the edge of the tunnel and takes a long, suffocating breath. There is no movement around him. The congregation of people is blocks away, the distant noise a bit louder and more raucous. He can still make out faraway music. He picks up a piece of broken glass and cuts his hair so it's less feral. He pushes off the muck with his hands and stands up, swinging his backpack into place.

He decides to leave the package of pica-tams and jerk sauce in the tunnel opening. The last thing he needs is the Mod Police giving him a nano-search and finding an illegal substance. He finds a small hatch and opens it. The rusted hinges on the lid groan with atrophy from years of neglect. He hides the bundle in the hatch and closes it tight. It'll be safe here for when he needs to get back to Antigua. He hopes Antoine and the rest of the islanders are safe.

No welcome wagon but then no alarms either. Mostly, he just can't believe he is back. A muffled noise approaches him from behind, in the tunnel, low to the ground. It gets louder. Hundreds of fingernails on hundreds of chalkboards. It's the rats sounding the alert. Letting everyone know of his presence. Totally selling him out. Even vermin are on the take in this world.

A bright, blue beam of light descends on Prior like a waterfall. He freezes. When the light reaches the edge of the tunnels, the rats, having earned their government cheese, skitter back into the darkness.

The light spirals around Prior in a way that is completely unnatural. Light isn't supposed to bend this way. It curves, re-thinks its direction, moves the other way, responding to the search of Prior's body. The light is searching for rogue nanos.

The light isn't really light, of course. It's the arm of the law. Because nanos are in charge. And they are in search of the only thing that can threaten them: their own kind.

The nano-inspection is painless in the physical sense. It takes about five seconds but feels longer. And the whole time, Prior gets the sense that he has never left. And that they are going to find out why he is here.

Prior resolves right then to not let anything get in the way of making sure his name is cleared in the murder of his partner, Feynman.

The bright, blue beam turns green to indicate he is cleared. No rogue nanos upon his person. No enemy combatants being smuggled in his blood or backpack. The colored light beam is a condescending system that implies that stupid Fringe can't figure out when they have passed the nano-test. Prior figures it's meant to keep Fringe in their place.

The nanos grant him access to the city. Prior is left once again to fend for himself in this wasteland of a world. The daylight is almost entirely faded as the night sky beckons him, growing larger in diameter as he leaves the tunnel. The dead city presents itself to him, hungry, smiling, large gaps in its skyline like a rotten set of teeth.

Chapter 7

Prior walks among thousands of Fringe, filled with the knowledge that he is re-entering the island where his wife left him flat. He promised himself this island would never again feel the weight of the bottom of his shoe.

The Fringe are in shambles. Frail, ill-clothed, frightened, devoid. They shuffle past Prior along the sidewalks, pursuing their daily lives along authorized routes. The sharp, raw sewage smell cuts through everything. The gray decay permeates the air. Occasionally, the Fringe gaze upward at a specific portion of the sky as if each owns a small tract of cloud. Prior looks up, knowing that palm trees and black pineapples aren't in his future. Above, a Sky-Screen shines high above the city, covering two-thirds of the heavens.

Prior's eyes trace the Sky-Screen to its edges like a wandering child. Prior catches a glimpse of the one thing he does not want to see right now. The fluttering objects on the periphery of the Sky-Screen glide effortlessly across the sky, their glow swelling in direct proportion with the approaching darkness.

Prior forces himself to focus on the Sky-Screen when he should be concentrating on the ground and getting out of here. Getting away from the gathering Fringe.

A blue light bathes Prior. The Sky-Screen projects placid colors and abstract images calculated to sooth and calm Fringe as they go about their business. No material objects are portrayed. Also, no sunsets, oceans, or flowers. No visions of natural beauty for Fringe.

There are no news stories being reported on Feynman's murder being solved. Nothing about Prior's name being cleared. It is, after all, an old news story and thousands of fresh horrors have certainly come to replace it. Prior searches the crowd for Molly. The growing throng is vast and his memory of Molly is anything but recent. He knows he won't find her here but he continues to look just the same.

He detects frantic 2020s retro-punkflapper music playing at a faint volume. A Sky-Screen DJ introduces each song, adding some smarmy, incorrect anecdote about each band. Prior's ears twitch when he hears the DJ. The voice sounds familiar. The Sky-Screen, this world-wide tranquilizer, appears to do its job effectively. Prior scans the crowd. The Fringe don't seem agitated or upset as they scrape their calloused feet along the street, each step heavier than the last.

With no warning, the Sky-Screen flickers like a centuries-old fluorescent-bulb, bringing foot traffic to a halt. The Fringe stop in unison, obedient, staring up. They rock in place, nervous from having their walking comas disrupted but unable to fight the urge to listen and obey.

Prior shakes his head, disgusted. These third-world, third-class, three-dimensional citizens. All flesh and blood and mass. Their shadows betray them. The sound of their steps seal their fate, as does their utter lack of hope.

Prior stands in the middle of the Fringe crowd that has gathered at an abandoned intersection. Everything dims to a silence. Prior's breathing gets heavier. He wanted to arrive under the radar, off the grid. He isn't here to listen and obey. He starts charting his run back to the tunnel.

The retro-punkflapper music volume diminishes. A newscaster, resembling a well-dressed Fringe, flickers on the Sky-Screen, looking down at everyone with a great toothy grin. The Sky-Screen is oriented so it appears to Prior that the newscaster is staring right at him. Prior is sure this is the intended effect. He's been back in this two-dimensionally-dominant world for less than an hour and already that familiar paranoid anxiety is over-filling his gut.

"My fellow Mod, my fellow Fringe," says the newscaster in a rehearsed velvet voice, "I am saddened to interrupt the 'Golden Oldies' hour but I am obligated to report world news as it happens."

The Fringe cease their rocking. They brace themselves. If possible, it gets even more quiet.

The fluttering objects in the sky effortlessly halt their gliding and hover in the air, swaying slightly with the weak breeze.

"Anton Ferri, our leading scientist in the nano-revolution and father to Mod, has gone missing," announces the newscaster. "I will report more as we learn of the search for his whereabouts. No foul play is suspected at this time. Mod Police are investigating all leads. Now, don't change that dial, it's back to the 'Golden Oldies' hour."

The Sky-Screen flickers again and the flint-blue night sky returns along with the distant background music. The fluttering objects in the sky vibrate with tension, banging into each other violently as if their traffic rules have disappeared. In a few seconds, order is restored. They resume their hovering and gliding, generally behaving like a swarm of organized bees.

In the time it takes Prior to reach the sidewalk, the once quiet and obedient Fringe crowd begins to riot. There is no garbage or broken bottles to throw in the desolate streets, no cars to overturn, and no streetlights to upend. Lacking alternatives, Fringe quickly digress into a weaponless mob, raising their fists into the air.

"Damned kidnappers!" a Fringe cries out.

"Mod wouldn't do this!" yells another.

Prior slowly backs himself against a cracked concrete wall. He clings to it, trying to remain invisible. At first, he figures the Fringe are upset at NanoGov about the nightly disruption. But then, he realizes that the Fringe are genuinely disturbed by Ferri's disappearance. Old Anton still means something to them. Ferri is still revered. And the Fringe are not taking his disappearance well.

Prior doesn't blame them. Ferri is one of the few people, if that's the word, on the planet that might have been able to help them. If something bad happened to Ferri, the streets are now more hopeless than ever.

A dozen Fringe collect around Prior and he decides to inch away from the wall. Suddenly, there's a cracking noise and part of the building wall gives way. Dense chunks of concrete are plummeting straight down towards the Fringe a few feet from Prior. The Fringe see their impending death but do nothing except to simply stare up at their destruction.

Prior draws a heavy breath and hurls himself at the Fringe group, their bodies light and weak, pushing them all away. They fall backwards on the street and barely escape the crash of the building debris. Prior scrambles back up, having scraped his hand. No one thanks him. No one even acknowledges that he rescued them. Or that anything happened. Prior walks away but turns back to make sure they are okay.

One of the Fringe, a pale, middle-aged woman in her twenties with a soot-colored streak in her otherwise blond hair, is hoisted up on the shoulders of two other Fringe. The middle-aged Fringe tries to calm the crowd but no one seems to hear her. She motions to her assistants and they let her down. In a well-rehearsed move, five Fringe get on their hands and knees in the muck. Prior cringes. It reminds him of his trek through the tunnel. Four Fringe climb on top of the five, then three climb on top of them and so on until there is a Fringe pyramid assembled next to Prior. Prior looks down, trying not to move, pretending not to notice this impromptu circus act. The Fringe leader with the soot streak in her hair stands atop the human pile, surveying the chaos. She begins a speech but her voice is drowned out by the Fringe mob's shouting.

Prior reaches into his pocket, caressing a bit of Antiguan sand. He tries to shift his stance, attempting to creep sideways to escape the growing attention that this Fringe pile and speech will create. He is still mapping out an emergency route back to the tunnel. What was he thinking coming back here? He doesn't fit into this world that was once his. What's the point of an Authentician when there's nothing left that's real?

The screaming Fringe cause Prior to continue making love to the concrete wall. The impromptu Fringe leader stands atop her lieutenants, still shouting at the crowd to behave. Prior can't move. The surrounding Fringe crowd gathers ever more tightly around him. The Fringe leader, waving her arms in the air in an increasingly frantic manner, violently jerks to the side. Her leg gives way and she tumbles off the Fringe pyramid to the ground. This captures Fringe attention. The crowd finally goes quiet. Against his better instincts, Prior moves to get a better look to see if the Fringe leader is hurt.

The soot-streaked Fringe, full-figured just a moment ago, violently shakes on the ground, parts of her bubbling and foaming. She is melting. The Fringe leader's right foot liquifies as if a strong acid is being poured on it. The liquid is quickly absorbed into the ground. Next, her right hand does the disappearing act accompanied by agonizing yelps. The melting of limbs continues, traveling up her right arm and leg, eventually spreading down to her left side.

Prior stares in horror as this Fringe disintegrates in front of him. What's left of the Fringe leader is splayed on the street, her body quickly dissolving.

The Fringe leader's diminishing, agonized screams burst out of her in horrible, liquid streams. Prior looks away, trying not to focus on the despair and plight of this melting Fringe.

The crowd looks at Prior. He recognizes that look. It's the look that is asking desperately for help. Prior thinks about Feynman. Prior came back to save his dissolved reputation. He needs to know if his name has been cleared.

The wind shifts and Prior gets a full whiff of the melting Fringe. It makes him gag. The streak of soot in the Fringe leader's hair trembles upon the head that momentarily remains, eyes rolled up in anguish, while the rest of her continues to vanish. The crowd stares aghast at the sight but the acrid odor does nothing to sicken them. Prior figures they must be used to it. Their empathy and fear seem focused on this ever-expanding vacuum. Some of the Fringe look up and observe Prior who is emotionless. They appear puzzled at Prior's impassivity.

The Fringe leader lets out a final gurgling scream before she implodes into a deep, red mist that hovers over the space where she had just lain. The bloody mist then completely vanishes into itself. The vaporization is over in ten seconds.

The Sky-Screen, apart from lighting the scene, has been filming every excruciating moment, registering the event for posterity. Perhaps for future study. Perhaps for future recrimination. The Sky-Screen briefly shines a spotlight on Prior before searching the crowd.

Prior doesn't like it one bit. He turns away in disgust, having never watched someone get devoured. Or melted. Or whatever the hell just happened.

Judging from the reaction of the crowd, no one has ever taken part in this particular type of movie. Although they witnessed in silence, now that the event is over, the nearby Fringe begin screaming in terror, mirroring Prior's thoughts. Muffled gasps provide a bass line to the unbearable symphony. Fringe brush aside the air from their faces as if this Devourer of Fringe is some type of airborne disease. Maybe it is. Who really understands nanotechnology?

The Sky-Screen flickers before whipping back to its blue ambient hum. It shows an old commercial with Modela Nova, the first Mod ever; her beautiful face hawking some product. The sudden lack of light plunges the Fringe into further distress. Fringe are panicking, picking up clumps of mud and throwing it at brick walls. Others yell at the sky before running off in Byzantine patterns to avoid detection. Prior notices that the Fringe don't turn against each other. They take care not to hurl mud or expletives towards their fellow Fringe. It's all hopelessly directed to some sinister abstract around them. The Fringe crowd scatters in all directions, leaving the streets vacant.

Prior impetuously wants to reach out and talk to these escaping Fringe. To comfort them and find out what's going on. His hesitation leaves him alone on a post-riot street, save for the fluttering objects still peacefully hovering above. His only immediate companion is the stinging feeling in his gut to return to the tunnel and try this another day. It wasn't supposed to work out like this.

After hiking a few blocks, making sure to cling to the shadows of the city's building rubble, Prior realizes his escape route will be closed off. The nano-inspectors will no doubt alert the authorities that he has returned. Not knowing where to go for the moment, Prior digs himself into some rubble to catch his breath in the night air.

But the baggage handler in his head is an incompetent one. His thoughts get forwarded to a destination near rock-bottom. Usually, he tries to re-direct his thoughts to a better place. He doesn't consciously attempt to think of the worst moments of his life. It just comes naturally.

Since Prior has been back, he's already been witness to bad news about Ferri's disappearance, some ferocious new Fringe-melting disease, and a subsequent riot. The melting Fringe, the nano-scan, this desolate husk of a city, the Fringe reduced to a quality of life that would be looked down upon by the Middle Ages, the glorious, decadent palaces of the Mod he's heard about. They're all the same thing.

He reaches into his shirt pocket and rubs Penny's leaf-letter. It vibrates a moment before it is still again. Knowing the tunnel is closed, he readjusts his backpack and starts the long, heavy walk to visit his old partner. He hopes the graveyard is still there.

Chapter 8

Prior gulps a deep breath, feeling the desperate cold air and gray ash take purchase in his lungs. When he thinks it's safe, he wends his way back to the Holland Tunnel. It takes two hours for the coast to clear near the tunnel. Prior retrieves Antoine's package, stuffing it into his backpack. No alarms sound.

He proceeds down the city street, not wanting to appear like a tourist. The thought amuses him. As if there are three-dimensional tourists anymore. He turns a corner and creeps along a broken-down street that looks familiar. He's aware of a tugging at his chest. It's homesickness groping around his body cavity, trying to massage his heart and coax a repressed corner of his memory. He unzips his backpack and pulls out his pica-tam.

The Sky-Screen is reporting an attack on one of the Mod Clinics by a Fringe terrorist group. The report states the terrorist group is ridiculous to try to make any kind of impact on such a world-dominating force. The smug announcer then moves his attention to the flourishing paradise created by Mod on various Caribbean islands.

Prior walks for miles and arrives at a new neighborhood. It is an incinerated hellscape. The hollowed-out storefronts breathe fire and belch smoke. Fringe inside burn what they can, coiling themselves around their fires. Despite the ash and smoke, there are pockets of air that smell cleaner. Prior figures with fewer people breathing the air and exhaling waste, things smell better every day. That's one way to obtain progress.

Prior proceeds cautiously down the street, fighting the feeling that he's being watched. He keeps to the sidewalks and the shadows, stepping over garbage and sleeping Fringe.

The familiar blue-steel light beams down on Prior from the sky. Prior squints his eyes but can't make out the source. The lights swirl around him, starting at his ankles and traveling up his body. Prior takes off at a full sprint, zig-zagging to avoid the light and garbage on the street. He leaps over the larger heaps of trash like an ancient Olympian. The light eventually loses interest; unless its intent was scaring the crap out of Prior and reminding him that he is always under observation.

He slows down and sidesteps a Fringe who's crouched in the middle of the sidewalk, draped completely in a large burlap sack. The Fringe's head is barely visible, shrouded in the night's shadow.

"Help a fella out?" says the burlapped Fringe. He looks older than Prior. Maybe it's these streets.

"Sorry," says Prior. Prior's voice is groggy. He looks straight ahead, trying to keep his focus on what's in front of him, not crouched beside him.

Prior gets a few yards ahead when the old Fringe says, "You won't find the graveyard anymore, if that's what you're looking for."

Prior practically trips on his own heels as he spins around. These nanos have taken a massive evolutionary leap forward and are now astonishingly real. Prior approaches the Fringe, really studying him for the first time.

"Come again?" says Prior.

"I was saying..."

But the old Fringe doesn't repeat himself once Prior kicks him hard in the side. Old technology always beats new technology.

The old Fringe rolls over, clutching his side, as a gasp escapes his sooty mouth. Prior rushes over.

"Oh, hey, listen, old-timer," says Prior, leaning down and righting the old Fringe so he's in a sitting position. "I'm sorry. I didn't think you were real there for a moment. Only way to tell, really. Sorry again."

The old Fringe tries to take a deep breath but all he can manage is some wet wheezing.

"Must be new around here if you can't tell Mod from Fringe."

"It's the burlap bag," says Prior in a shameful excuse.

"Oh, well, that explains it then," says the old Fringe, craning his neck. He remains seated. "That makes it all fine and dandy."

Prior gets the first clear glimpse of the old Fringe's eyes. They are a piercing green, at least in this darkness.

"How did you know I was going to the graveyard?"

"Had that look about you," says the old Fringe, rubbing his side. "Like you was haunted by something and needed to see where it lived. I get that all the time."

"Where's the graveyard now? How did they move it?"

"I'll tell you," says the old Fringe, licking his crusted lips. "But you gotta give me something. I don't know what island you've been living on but that kind of information doesn't come free around here. What you got in the backpack?"

Prior considers the old Fringe's request. Sooner or later, he's going to have to embed himself in this new world. He's disappointed that it had to happen so soon. He throws his backpack down and unzips one of the compartments. At the bottom are several tall, thin glass bottles. Antoine's going-away present. Prior always hated Antoine's jerk sauce. He pulls out one of the bottles. Gold flecks are suspended in the thick orange-red liquid. The gold flecks are some type of local herb. Antoine's secret ingredient.

"Do you know what this is?" says Prior.

"Can I drink it?"

"I wouldn't advise it but I suppose if you have the constitution…"

"I do," says the old Fringe before Prior changes his mind.

Prior waves the bottle just out of reach of the old Fringe. "Where's the graveyard?"

"The bottle," says the old Fringe. A thin reed of an arm pokes through a hole in the burlap to retrieve his bounty. Prior hands it to him. The bottle disappears inside the burlap sack.

"Well?" says Prior.

"Well," says the old Fringe. "There's graveyards and there's graveyards. If you're looking for headstones, forget it. Gone. Most were plastic so the Mod reclaimed them. Bodies, on the other hand, bodies are right where we left them. Just down the corner, five blocks to the left."

Prior looks in the direction the old Fringe has charted out for him. When he looks down, he's not surprised to see an empty, wet patch where the old man sat.

Prior approaches the end of the street. Waiting for him, basking in the glow of a streetlight that was not there moments ago, is his old office building. There is no electricity for Fringe. There are no streetlights. All the buildings are husks. And yet, there, right there in front of him, shining with prosperity, is his old office. There's the small bronze sign on the lavish red-lacquered door.

Prior and Feynman
Authenticians
Enquire Within

The building practically gleams with its extended invitation to Prior. But Prior knows not to go inside. Not because there are too many memories waiting for him in there. Not because he'd have to face the ghost of his deceased partner. And not because he isn't ready to deal with Penny.

Prior doesn't go in because it's obviously a trap. Because the building isn't real. And if the building and the streetlight and the glow aren't real, nothing inside can be trusted. This is the work of nanos. He doesn't have too much experience with the world of Mod and NanoGov but he knows enough not to be stupid on his first day back. There will be plenty of time for stupid later.

The nanobots are following him. He can't see them of course. Small doesn't really grasp the minuteness of the nanos. Humans were never meant to comprehend such scales. Prior heard it put this way: a nanometer is the length of facial hair a man grows in the time it takes to bring a razor to his face.

Prior stands frozen. If the nanos suspected anything, they would have made their move already. Maybe, they're waiting to vaporize him the way they did the Fringe leader earlier. Right now, they're just testing Prior. Stretching him like dough to see what he's made of. Evaluating his intentions. As vastly powerful as nanos are, they can't contemplate your soul while they're scanning you for rogues. But they can learn your name, tap into their files, and replicate the building where you used to work.

Prior forces his feet to shuffle past his building. He snaps his neck the other way so he won't be tempted by a nano-version of Penny waving at him through the window. He focuses on the graveyard a few blocks away. Prior wonders about Lachende, the kid he took in and mentored as an Authentician. Has he survived all this? Did Prior teach him enough?

As Prior clears the city perimeter, the trees rise to take up the dead space. The Sky-Screen flickers on for the evening news. The leaves don't weave a complete canopy overhead and Prior gathers snatches of the NanoGov report on the still-missing Anton Ferri. The Sky-Screen notes that, due to Ferri's disappearance, there is rampant and extensive Fringe rioting all over the planet.

Prior thinks this is a grand time for him to poke his head back into the goddamn world. He wonders again if the nanos can point him towards the Holland Tunnel so he can get the hell out of here.

Gathering his stability and momentum, he reaches the graveyard. Or at least what used to be the graveyard. Like the old guy in the burlap sack said, the headstones have been reclaimed. The trees have been cleared. In their place, standing magnificently and defiantly in front of Prior, is a fifteenth-century cathedral. Its spires soar towards the heavens while its flying stone buttresses practically dare Prior to deny their existence.

Ever since NanoGov came to power, more and more basic things have been constructed out of plastic. Headstones, which for centuries never needed improvement on their stone design, found themselves subject to the high-density polyethylene craze. Now Prior understands why. Mod, and by extension, their nanos, primarily live off plastic by reclaiming its mass, its molecules, as their own, synthesizing it into whatever their whims allow. Mod force Fringe to manufacture plastic so they can ravenously consume it.

Prior's partner may still be buried somewhere beneath this monstrosity but Feynman's headstone, along with everyone else's, has been commandeered to benefit some insecure Mod douchebag with a Middle Ages monk fetish.

Testing out a theory, Prior quickly jumps to the side to examine the cathedral from a slightly different angle. The cathedral momentarily looks transparent before readjusting its index of refraction and appearing three-dimensional again. Prior runs at full speed to the other side of the cathedral and watches it try to keep up with him like a damaged revolving door. Clearly, the Mod owner doesn't have enough nanos in its mass to construct a full cathedral so it rebuilds a façade for itself and any observers. The nanos are working full-time around the clock to keep up appearances for its owner. It sickens Prior that this charade is viewed as more valuable than the final resting place of his partner.

Prior promised himself he would clear his name. He can't dwell on his old partner. Prior assures himself that Feynman was a tragic casualty. That it wasn't really Prior's fault. As usual, Prior does a lousy job of lying.

He tries to take another step but can't bring himself to do it. His feet are stuck in the tar pit of time. Feynman's grave will have to get paid a visit some other day.

Prior rests at the front door of the cathedral, catching his breath, wondering if the owner is even home. Someone grabs his shoulder. Before Prior can turn around, his eyes instantly go to the door, suspecting some type of nano-security or perhaps the owner himself. But the grip on his shoulder is too substantial, too three-dimensional and warm for it to be Mod. He spins around and finds a beautiful face, quite unchanged, those liquid eyes staring back at him.

"Jeremiah Prior," says Penelope. "I knew I'd find you here." Her voice is as smoky as he remembers. It curls around him in an embrace. "Still sniffing around the past?"

"Penny," says Prior. "I got your note."

She walks past him but not before her silhouette rattles his insides.

"Hold up. What do you know about this building?" says Prior.

"What building?" she says.

Prior spins around and the nano-façade is gone. Penelope just nods, clearly not wanting to discuss the subject out in the open.

A few blocks away, Penelope glides open the office door latch with the same efficiency she guided Prior back to his old, real building. Prior smells something in the air. It isn't nanos. He doesn't think nanos have learned to smell like this yet. Mod wouldn't place a value on a smell to benefit Fringe. And this smell is aimed squarely at Authenticians by their desirable secretaries.

"Welcome home," says Penelope. "I was here earlier. Redecorating a little."

"Penny," says Prior, surprised he gets that much out.

"It's still Penelope, Mr. Prior," she says. Her voice takes up residency in his ear as if it's never been given an eviction notice.

"Mr. Prior, huh?"

She moves over to the window and pulls down the shade. She is as stunning as he remembers. That makes her dangerous. He tries to convince himself to be wary. The only way a beautiful and smart woman like Penny has remained Fringe these days is to strike an unsavory deal with some shady characters. He should stay away from her.

"You'll always be Prior to me," she says, satisfied with the shades. She walks slowly towards him, her shoes barely making noise on the wooden boards. She encloses her arms around him. "I've missed you."

Before she zeroes in for a wet one, Prior pulls back.

"Your new hubby miss me too?" he says, pointing at her wooden wedding ring.

She throws a frustrated look out the window. She lets go of him, snapping her arms back to standard-issue position. "Yes, my husband. Beauregard Sanders. He's a placeholder," she says matter-of-factly. "Word travels fast around here."

"Beauregard Sanders?"

Antoine warned Prior that people came cheap in this new world. Penny appears to be going for a gold medal in setting the bar lower.

"Just until you came back," she continues. "Plus, he's a rich placeholder. Who do you think paid for all this?"

"I'm sure he knows where his money's going."

"Marriages don't mean a whole lot anymore," she says, approaching another window. She appears to prefer the window's view to Prior's disapproving eyes.

He stands silently, watching her, trying to figure out her angle.

"I guess this isn't the sort of homecoming you expected," she says. "Got a smoke?"

"Sorry."

Marriages stopped having meaning ever since Fringe started saving enough money to turn Mod. And Mod remained unfettered and selfishly alone. Or if you were Fringe, what's the point of marriage when you could be separated from your spouse at any moment and relocated to act as cheap labor for Mod.

But Prior has a hunch that Penny is referring to her first husband. And the thought that Prior might have had something to do with getting his old partner killed pops up again like a persistently nasty garden mole.

"It's hard to forget old times," he says, breaking the silence.

She turns back and shoots him a hungry look. "Prior, I'm so happy you're back. You don't know what it's been like."

He wants to move towards her. It's been a long time since he's felt a woman's touch. His legs resist, remembering the trouble these types of urges have gotten him into before.

"Look, Penny."

"Penelope."

"First of all, thanks for arranging to get me back home. And for keeping the old office going. I owe you big. But let's just concentrate on work right now."

Her shoulders drop a bit as the air goes out of the room. She sits down on a cardboard box. She puts down the little red purse she's been holding. "You need my help in finding you a place to sleep?" she says.

"Thanks anyway. Where'd you get the purse?"

She looks down at her little red purse like it's a criminal. Objects like her purse are in short supply.

"My husband. Bought it at the company store. For good luck," she says.

"Great luck so far," says Prior. "Look, as soon as we get paid for a case or two, I'll find a place to flop. People still need stuff authenticated, don't they?"

"Didn't I tell you?" she says. "We have a case. That's why I came to find you tonight."

"That's why."

"Yes," she says. "I got a letter from a new client. Some lady." She reaches into her purse and pulls out a wrinkled piece of paper. "Miss Simmons. Sounds like she'll pay. You know, the usual desperation and all that."

"You were always a great secretary."

"I told this Miss Simmons you'd meet her. Hope you don't mind." She gets up and does that drifting slow-walk right up to Prior again. This time, there's additional emphasis from the hip-swinging contingent. "I figured you just wanted to hit the ground running."

"Thanks," he says. He swallows hard. This is going to be tougher than he thought.

"What else can I do for you?" she says.

"Nothing," he says with as much finality in his tone as he can muster. "I just want to hold on to what little personal integrity I packed with me. This is just professional."

"Right, Prior."

She backs off and heads towards the door.

"Penelope, wait."

"Yeah?" she says, with more excitement than she probably intends.

"You said your husband's case was closed," says Prior, hoping her face lines up with her response.

"Did I?" Penny's face looks angry, her tone coy.

"How did you get that note to me?"

"Worry less about your precious reputation," she says. "What you should be doing is getting ready for your new client."

Penny's right in one way. If he's going to survive here, he needs to maintain a front and a clean image. Especially if he still has to clear his name.

"Feynman's case wasn't solved, was it?" he says.

"You need to find Molly," says Penny.

"Felice turned her against me."

"And we need this new case," says Penny. She leaves, closing the door behind her.

She's up to something. She wants him. He's hanging on by a thread. Seems like old times.

Chapter 9

Prior's old office hasn't changed. Mod took anything of value. Now, it's just four fading walls wrapped around a rotting wooden floor. Two old chairs, a few cardboard boxes, and a bookcase are the only objects filling the musty room.

He spots an old cardboard box where Penny was sitting. He opens it up and a musty smell smacks his face. Mostly old files. He rummages around the box and his hand finds something hard. He pulls out a small box, covered in a silk handkerchief. The handkerchief is probably worth more than anything inside the box.

He unwraps the box. Inside is a thin wooden square, slightly smaller than Prior's hand, with a small, red button sticking out of the middle. It's a Framer.

These things are illegal. Good for getting out of jams with Mod. You don't want to use it unless you have to. Where the hell did Penny get her hands on one of these? Probably her new husband. He pockets the Framer.

One of the two filthy windows looks out onto the city. It isn't a bad view considering the office is on the ninth floor. There are hardly any lights on in any of the buildings. There is plenty of light out in the city, just not from the buildings. Fringe have to rely on candles. They are given a small amount of electricity to power small things like decades-old cell phones in case Mod want to reach out to them and can't be bothered with the three seconds it takes to send their nanos.

The light comes from Mod. Their dedicated nanos allow them to glow in the dark as they sail across the night sky like lightning bugs.

Prior lights a candle. Penny must have left it here for him. He notices she also left him a charging cell phone which he unplugs. It's one of the really old models, about the size of his thumb, the kind you have to actually hold in your hand. So old even Mod aren't interested. He throws it into the corner.

Though some of the Antiguan villagers claimed to protect Prior from evil forces on the island, he never felt at home there. Prior feels strangely secure in his office, despite his awareness of the omnipresent threat all around him.

It has something to do with his love for the world's past. He'd always felt more comfortable studying distant cultures through their antiques. When he was in the middle of an investigation of a stolen antique, he was at his happiest. He used to immerse himself so deeply into the mindset and world of the past, he was never quite sure what period he was in when he emerged back into the present. He still treasures history deeply, especially when little awaits him in the present.

As he contemplates being back, that safe feeling is nudged aside by paranoia. A prickliness in the office air descends upon him. He doesn't flinch. He waits for something to make itself known. Nanos? In this new world, he is never truly alone.

Prior decides to leave and see if this feeling will accompany him on a walk. He's in no condition to solve the Feynman case and clear his name now. He isn't sure when he will be. It's been too long and the trail must have gone cold. This ambivalence circles him down the stairwell. He is glad of it. Prior will embrace his own tornadoed-trailer emotions over nano-intrusion any day of the week.

Back on the desolate streets, Prior goes hunting and gathering for some basic provisions. Since he'll be sleeping in his office for a while, he needs some shaving supplies and soap. Also, a change of clothes. While he's here, he'll have to start earning a living again and find a real place to live. The neighborhood is rotten. He wishes that, years ago, he had picked another office location in a better part of town.

He figures he shouldn't complain. This neighborhood gave him his start. And his end. The last case he worked was right here. Just before he left Felice and hopped a boat for the islands.

His caseload had been mounting as his first-class Authentician reputation grew. It paralleled the increasing number of Mod. One of his last cases involved a Mod with a penchant for Etruscan friezes of small boys. Prior never understood these people. Mod got bored quickly and always followed the tide of changing tastes. The week before Prior's last case, Norwegian violin cases were the thing.

Mod were insatiable and their nanos knew no bounds to satisfy them. When Mod gave up being three-dimensional for two-dimensionality, they expected a lot in return. The nanos would turn into whatever their Mod masters desired. A Louis XIV drawing room, a Native American carved pipe, it didn't matter. The nanos were there to simulate any whim. Real objects, on the other hand, were available for the seizing. They were solid and represented real value. The more unique, the better. Any Mod could lay their hands, or flaps, on an object, get their nanos to absorb it into their amoeba-like existence, and then no one else could have the real thing. It would be converted into the unity of their little nano universe.

That's where Prior came in. He'd be hired by Mod agents to find and authenticate these increasingly rare objects. It was a business that didn't exist twenty years before and wouldn't exist ten years hence. There were only a finite number of objects of value left and Mod were ever-increasing and famished.

On the night of the handoff, when Prior brought the Etruscan boy frieze to the Mod's agent, it was on the corner where Prior is standing now. The agent, a shifty-eyed Fringe who wore his hair long in the back to compensate for being completely bald in the front, smoked a cigarette under the streetlight. Prior knew this guy was trash. Only a Fringe with a Mod master could afford to smoke these days. But this guy had Mod protection so nobody could touch him. How else could he walk around with a stupid trench coat and a balding mullet?

In the old days, when there was a shred of honor among his clientele, Prior would offer up the object along with a historical report and certificate of authenticity. Also, his bill. This night, the agent puffed on his cigarette and asked, "You got the thing?"

"Maybe."

"Really?"

"Listen, pal..."

But Prior never finished his sentence. He felt a tugging at his sleeve followed by a buzzing sound that enveloped his head. A few seconds later, the sound and the tugging ceased instantly. Prior stood alone on the street corner, confused, out one Etruscan frieze, and stiffed of his sizable bill. Where was the honor in these so-called higher classes? Good thing he didn't have a partner anymore to explain this to.

The news footage on the Sky-Screen is live. It shows a young woman being pursued by NanoGov and the Mod Police. The camera's point of view is at a high altitude so it's difficult for Prior to make out details. The young woman darts in and out of alleys but the efficient, gray police force continues to gain ground. The police turn a corner and almost catch her but the young woman jumps down a manhole.

The Sky-Screen abruptly turns off the news and goes back to its tranquil color, laying music.

Was that Molly? Was that footage specifically directed at Prior, as a warning that he should get off this island? How has Molly survived in this world? He knows he can't answer these questions tonight.

Before he proceeds down the street, Prior spots a guy with spiky red hair in a trench coat following him. He knows a tail when he sees one. Prior ducks down an alley and zigzags his way around the city until he loses the tail. It can't be NanoGov since they don't have to sneak around. And Prior hasn't been back long enough to make enemies. Which means it's someone from his past.

There's a dilapidated drug store on the corner. It looks worse than Prior remembers. He walks in anyway. Inside, rows and rows of empty shelves gaze blankly at Prior. A red spider clinging to a cobweb welcomes him. At the back of the store, a stack of cardboard boxes pretends to be a pharmacy counter.

"What it be?" asks a voice behind the counter.

Prior peeks over and spies an old Fringe woman sitting on the floor. Her hair is a blunt gray and there are deep creases on her canyon of a face. The kind that indicates she plays around with a lot of drugs when she's bored. Prior doesn't recognize her.

"What happened to Jacob? Does he still run this joint?" Prior says.

She can't be bothered with standing for every customer. "Jacob dead," she says simply. She wheezes. Her cough is a pulsing blender that comes alive in her throat.

"You should really take something for that," he says.

"I take everything. No trust any of it," she says. Some mental calculus tells her it's time to stand. She cranes herself to a respectable hunch and falls into a stoop over the counter. "Now, what it be?"

"Just some basics."

She lets out a grunt.

"You know, soap, shaving cream, razor, toothbrush," says Prior.

"We got lye cakes. I give you lye cakes."

She leans back to get some momentum, turns and shuffles off behind a curtain before Prior can respond. He looks down at the spot where she's been sitting. The dust that surrounded her creates a negative image of her silhouette on the floor. A red spider crawls through her warm spot, intersecting her circle with his tiny line.

Since Mod took over, Fringe life expectancy has dramatically reduced. A healthy Fringe can expect to live until their mid-forties at best. Mod appropriated all modern medicine, pharmaceutical research, hospitals, even cleaning products. Anything useful and new. The only thing left for Fringe are Mod leftovers.

The old Fringe returns. "Old medicine," she says, shuffling over with great effort. "I got me one lye cake," she says. "What you give for it? Need something good." The old lady's breath wheezes out of her, trying to escape her slight frame.

"I don't really have anything."

"Then no lye cake. You come back when you make good trade." She takes the lye soap bar off the counter and sits down on her dust-outline floor.

"Wait," says Prior. He reaches into his backpack for the second time this day and pulls out an Antiguan red fish jerk sauce bottle. These are doing him a better service than he expected when Antoine gave them to him. "Here. You've never seen this before. Jerk sauce. Special juju."

The old Fringe stands up again, but this time, a little quicker. She snatches the small bottle of red liquid. "This just red sauce. Where is juju?" she says.

"Juju. It's like magic. It will help you."

"Help me how? Get rid of nanos? Mod?"

How the hell does Prior know? If he had that figured out, he'd be king of the world. He looks around her empty store.

"It gets rid of red spiders," he says.

She looks at the bottle with renewed awe, then disdainfully at her filthy shelves.

"Goddamn spiders. Red ones. Okay, you got yourself lye cake," she says. "But you come back next time and I still got cobwebs? I smile pretty. Then I kill you." Then she adds, for the sake of clarity, "I kill you for permanent."

"You going to offer me a choice of paper or plastic?" says Prior, grabbing the lye cake.

"What?"

"Old joke. You have yourself a pleasant evening."

Chapter 10

"Penny, looks like we're back in business."

"It's Penelope, Mr. Prior," she says with a scowl. She's come in and actually made the place resemble their old office. She sits by the door behind some cardboard boxes. She's back to all smiles.

"Like old times," says Prior. "Only…"

"What?" She stands up and approaches him, her hips keeping time with his heart. He senses that danger in her. He doesn't bite.

"Stop tailing me," he says. "It's unnerving that everyone always knows where I am."

"Welcome to the real world, boss."

He walks across the common area, away from her, and steps into his office, leaving her frustrated and alone. He feels bad for her but the last thing he needs is to cannonball into the whole Penny thing again.

Right before Mod took over, there were good times. Feynman and Prior solving crimes. Penny wrapping up paperwork. Lachende, the neighborhood kid, helping out. Felice sometimes waiting for him at home.

Felice was a gifted nanotechnologist and colloidal chemist. Prior figures she still is. She used to tell him that it didn't bother her that she was married to a blue-collar mug like Prior. What did he know? They had Molly. Even with his busy work schedule, it always turned out that he was the one taking care of his daughter. Felice's schedule was hectic and she always seemed to be on the brink of some major discovery that required burning the midnight oil.

Her star was in ascendance and caught the attention of Anton Ferri, who brought her onto his team. This was the most sought-after scientific position in the world. Ferri was a God on earth, literally, as he created nanos and Mod. Soon, Felice was his right-hand person in the development of some super-secret nanotechnology breakthrough. Ferri took all the credit, of course. Genius though he was, Felice had her share of brilliant discoveries on his team.

She was increasingly working longer hours at Ferri's lab. Prior was too busy between his casework and raising Molly to notice. Felice was having an affair. It was a classic case of an Authentician's private life. He was the last one to figure out the mystery.

When Prior confronted her about it, she swore that she broke it off months earlier. Prior had trouble breathing that week, the wind swiftly knocked out of him.

Then things started getting strange. Strange enough that it made Prior regret getting into the whole Authentician game. Felice's jilted guy started stalking her and leaving threatening notes. Prior tried trailing him but the guy was elusive. Prior thought of himself as being good at his job but this guy was always one step ahead. Prior couldn't think of a worse scenario for someone in his field. It drove him crazy.

"Prior," says Penny, drawing him out of his daydream. "Our new client is here."

Prior straightens his hair and puts on his game face. It's been a while since he's met a new client. He steps into the main part of the office. All of a sudden, the room feels hotter, smaller.

"This is Miss Simmons," says Penny.

Miss Simmons is slender, tall, and beautiful. She has the kind of face that keeps photographers in business and the kind of body that does wonders for sculptors. She's wearing a wide-brimmed hat but Prior detects blond hair underneath. After the initial sunspot of her beauty flares away, Prior notices an overall sadness about her. Still, it's a hell of a face that nature decided to hang on her. He figures it's his job to put a smile on that face.

"Miss Simmons? Jeremiah Prior, Authentician and antiquarian detective, at your service."

He offers his hand, catching Penny rolling her eyes. Miss Simmons takes his hand in hers and shakes it. Her hand is soft. It feels real. Prior hasn't touched a real woman in years. He's betting that the softness of her hand is just a preview for the whole picture.

"Mr. Prior, can we speak privately?"

Her voice is softer than her hand. Miss Simmons has tenderness in spades.

"Just Prior. It's what everyone calls me," he says. "I haven't heard the details of your case yet but are you sure you don't want a…how shall I put it…a female point of view?" He nods toward Penny. Penny smiles and takes a step forward.

"If you'll excuse me, I'd rather speak with you in private."

Prior points her to his private office. The tent poles of Penny's smile are blown away. She shrugs her shoulders even as her eyes throw daggers at his chest.

Miss Simmons saunters into his office as if dancing to an invisible samba band, a perpetual red carpet being unspooled in front of her. Prior has to admit, her rhythm section has a great beat. It occurs to Prior that something about her is familiar.

He closes the door behind him and throws down the wooden latch. "There, that's as private as it gets around here," says Prior, pulling out a cardboard box. "Sit down please. Now, tell me what I can do for you."

She draws a deep breath. "If I only knew where to start," she says.

"I always found beginnings to be boring. Why don't you start in the middle with what's troubling you?"

She smiles, as if she's just discovered an ally. "It's my brother," she finally says. "I want you to find him."

"Your brother, huh? Got a name?"

"Addison. Addison Simmons."

"Same last name. So, you're not married?"

"No. Can you help me find him?" she says. There is desperation in her voice.

"How old is he?"

"Thirty."

"Reason I ask, Miss Simmons, is that he's a big boy now. What makes you think he's missing? And what makes you think he wants to be found?"

"I know he's in danger. Grave danger."

"And how do you know?" She looks away, holding back. "Does he have enemies? Was there a ransom note or threatening letter?"

"I…I can't tell you. He's just in tremendous trouble and I need you to find him."

"Miss Simmons, I don't work that way. You spill everything you know or I can't help you. Believe me, I'm like one of those old priests. Your secrets stay locked with me."

"I wish I could believe you," she says. Prior can practically feel the cold water thrown at him.

"Well," he says, trying another tact, "let's look at it this way. I'm an Authentician. I find old stuff. Your brother is neither old nor stuff. Why don't you go to the cops for this?"

She stands up, as if he's offended her in some way. "The cops?" She grows more agitated. "Mod Police could never help. And Fringe cops? They've all been bribed. Or they're otherwise beholden to Mod. I would never trust them."

"Well, it's hard to argue with that," he says, knowing sound logic when he hears it.

"I want you, Mr. Prior."

"Just Prior."

"I've looked into you, Prior. You have no record or history of corruption. You don't associate with Mod."

Prior is taken aback by that. "You know, Miss Simmons, ever since I laid eyes on you, I keep telling myself I've seen you somewhere."

She sits back down and looks away, suddenly very interested in the blank wall. Being modest or coy doesn't fit with the rest of her.

"And never mind what you heard about me," says Prior, sitting down.

She purses her lips, her mind made up. "My brother is an art forger," she says, her voice soft again. "Mostly nineteenth-century paintings. A few days ago, he disappeared. I'm worried that Addison's customers, all Mod, of course, might have found out he was selling them forgeries."

She looks at Prior dead in the eyes for the first time. It's a good thing gravity still works in this mixed-up world or her stare might blow him back to the other side of the room.

If what she is spilling is true, her brother's a sap. There is no way to fool Mod for long with forgeries. They have all the technology on their side. Their nanos will eventually detect a forgery in any of their acquisitions if an Authentician hasn't done it for them. Practically all existing physical things, especially luxury items and art, have been appropriated by Mod. All sanctioned by NanoGov.

Yet, desperation makes people do stupid things. Prior figures that kind of desperation is what will keep him in business. After all, Fringe can become Mod by paying a lot of money for the conversion. And if Fringe like Addison can figure out a way to fool some Mod a little at a time, he can gather enough cash and win his Modhood. Maybe that's what Addison has done: figured out a way to beat the system.

"I'll need a description of your brother," Prior says.

"Addison? He's tall. Spiky red hair in the front that's too long in the back. And he usually wears a gray overcoat. Even in the summer. Here," she says and hands him a small bottle filled with a swatch of cloth. "It's a swatch of shirt that Addison wore. For DNA."

Prior's brain sounds the alarm. Addison's description matches the guy who followed him last night.

"So what kind of art was he working on recently?" he says.

"Working on?"

"Forging."

"A Seurat," she says, matter-of-factly.

"A fan of pointillism, huh? Well, Miss Simmons…"

"Yes?" she says, leaning in, looking more fetching up close.

"I have to say no."

"What?"

"Look, it's nothing personal. Believe me, nothing would give me greater satisfaction than to spend all kinds of hours with you."

"Then what is it? Don't you see there's no one else I can turn to?"

"The thing is I only go after real art stolen by Fringe. Not forgeries. I heard a real Seurat sketch was stolen recently. But your brother wouldn't have anything to do with that, would he?"

"I don't see why you couldn't do this for me."

"Plus, your brother probably contracted with Mod and I don't have authority to interview or tail Mod. It's illegal. And if you truly investigated my background, you'll know I just got back into town after being away for a long time. But I know enough not to be on the wrong side of a case against some pissed-off Mod."

He stands and unlatches the door. Leading her out to the main part of the office, he sees that she is truly crestfallen. He can't get the angle on her. Is she telling him the whole truth? As he opens the front door for her, she turns to him and reaches into her purse.

"Is it money? I have lots of money. Enough for you to turn Mod with this one case. Imagine. Just after being away for so long."

She's smooth. He has to give her that.

"Sorry, Miss Simmons. Not interested in becoming Mod. I like my density. Good luck finding your brother. I'm sure he'll be okay."

She closes the purse, turns sharply, and walks down the hall. Her rhythm section takes five and, in their place, sad elevator music gets piped in.

"You turned down the case?" says Penny. "What's with you?"

"Miss Simmons is lying."

"I know. If she has so much money, why isn't she Mod? But still, I think you really should re-think this. A lot of dough."

Prior walks back into his office. He opens the window and stares out at the big city, thinking about what Penny just said.

There's a queasy feeling in the pit of his stomach. That queasiness is usually right. But this feeling isn't pointing at Miss Simmons.

It's pointing at Penny.

Chapter 11

Prior takes an afternoon stroll through the park to get away from the city's decay and debris. The trees remain unmolested by progress here. It makes him recall the Antiguan jungle being vaporized by Mod.

Prior hears calliope music blaring. He spies a horse-drawn caravan turning the corner into the park. The circus music brings Prior back to the present. The garish red and gold-painted caravan is a traveling stage. Strapped to the stage by their ankles are two Fringe, a male and a female, wearing grotesque costumes. They hit each other on the head with foam bats. The Mod, adorned as a Ring Master, sits atop the stage on a red velvet throne, bemused. On further inspection, he appears a bit bored that more pedestrians aren't more keenly interested in his Fringe Punch-and-Judy puppet show.

Prior stays hidden behind an oak tree until the horror show rolls by. Even though the caravan is beyond his view, the circus music can be heard from a distance.

Prior conceals himself in the park until evening. He occasionally looks up through the trees to watch the news on the Sky-Screen. One of the news items that makes him ache nostalgically is a story that someone has stolen the last known Vermeer painting. Prior always loved the Dutch master's paintings. It is exactly the kind of case Prior would have killed for where he was a full blown Authentician.

When he thinks it's safe to leave the park, Prior heads to his old neighborhood and ducks into Wild Finnegan's. The seedy bar is so beaten down it doesn't look like it should exist. The unwashed smell slaps Prior on the cheek. The dive bar is candlelit, everything blurred in shadowy grey, brown tones, and smoke. The place is swarming with Fringe. By habit, they congregate in these dives even though everyone knows there is no alcohol. Mod don't need it so it doesn't exist. But water is still free. At least for today. So is shooting wooden dice. Not that there is anything of real substance to gamble on.

Glancing around the joint, Prior thinks about what Molly would look like. Four years is a long time, especially when you go from fifteen to nineteen. Hell, he doesn't even know how tall she is.

He's not so sure he wants to find her so soon. Maybe after he's cleared of Feynman's murder charges. After he re-establishes his reputation as an Authentician. Maybe, after he takes down NanoGov, like Antoine wanted. Prior laughs to himself and searches for someone to sell him a drink or smokes. Maybe he should go back to Antigua and submit to Mod there. He shakes his head, unsure if it's his thoughts or the smell doing the talking.

He eyeballs the guy standing behind some cardboard boxes serving water from a broken-down barrel. The boxes serve as the bar. The barrel exhibit signs of rust but no metal. The barrel's aching wooden slats squeeze together for a family portrait, held tight by a frayed belt of rope around its waist.

"Water," says Prior.

The bartender doesn't notice Prior when he leans over the worn boxes. Prior figures he looks like every other Fringe. And when you serve rusted water to lost people in a dark bar, everything appears the same.

"Hilarious," says the bartender in a flat voice. He dunks a cone, made of a thin strip of rolled paper, into the barrel and hands it to Prior. "We need more funny guys in here. Lighten the place up."

"You know a guy goes by the name Feynman?" Prior says.

"Whoa, whoa, whoa. What, do I know you? I hand you water. You pay me – which you ain't done yet. That's the extent of our relationship."

"Alright, calm down, Gunga Din."

"What you call me?"

The water-monger's voice gets louder. He's attempting to attract the attention of anyone interested in holding down Prior while he beats the snot out of him if things get ugly.

Prior gives the dive a quick glance. Nobody is even looking up to help the water-monger. They're all staring at the fire burning from the pit in the middle of the room. It gives Prior more confidence. The last thing he wants is to scrap with some nobody and have the Mod Police zoom in.

"Prior, you asshole," thunders a voice from the other side of the fire.

Prior cranes his neck to get a better view, readying himself for trouble.

Four beefy Fringe make their way towards Prior. He recognizes three of them. Fringe cops. The fourth must be a rookie.

"Grainger, you son of a bitch. You still traveling around in a pack?" says Prior. He's taking a risk. Grainger is a tough prick who is just as happy to snap Prior in half or buy him a funnel of gruel. And he's not waving any gruel vouchers.

Grainger's men gather around Prior like its feeding time at the zoo. Grainger still sports the same buzz cut and palooka face but has put on a few pounds. That can only mean one thing. He's working towards becoming Mod. Grainger puts his arm around the rookie.

"There, you understand now what I'm saying, Strutsky?" says Grainger to the rookie. "You asked me before what a refugee Fringe looks like."

"I did?" says Strutsky.

Grainger gives Strutsky's shoulder a little tug as a reminder not to improvise and just stick to the script.

"Sure. Well, here he is. The scum of the scum. Just sitting here like King Shit."

"The hell is that smell?" says Strutsky, finding his stride. The other two torpedoes stand solid, blocking any exit for Prior.

"It's that island crap," says Grainger. "How they all smell when they come back. And believe me, they all come back."

"Alright, Grainger, you done impressing your sycophants?" says Prior. He turns to the torpedoes. "He always needed an audience, this prick." Better to find out now where he stands.

The torpedoes glance at Grainger, looking for a signal, their mouths open, clearly having never heard anyone talk back to their superior this way.

Grainger laughs. Everyone relaxes. Their shoulders slacken. Prior remains stoic; all his internal soldiers still manning their battle stations.

"What's the word?" says Prior. "You got nothing on me."

"Oh, yeah, your precious reputation. Prior, you still have royal balls, you know that?" says Grainger through guffaws and a phalanx of bravado. "Those balls are something that should never be turned two-dimensional. No sir, museum-quality balls."

"Museum-quality balls." It's one of Grainger's torpedoes. The bigger one. In the relaxed atmosphere, he's forgotten he's still on duty. The man is bigger than an old brick-and-mortar storefront. But they do come smarter. Grainer turns to him, ready to shut him down. Before Grainger gets a word out, Prior notices Strutsky staring at his wristwatch. The little red light is flashing. The one that tells Fringe cops that the Mod Police are in the vicinity.

"Shit, we're out of our jurisdiction," says Grainger. He and his men stand a little straighter and turn to the front door like children being caught by their parents for doing something naughty. There's a spark of light outside and everyone freezes.

"Mommy calling you?" says Prior.

"Quiet," says Grainger. He's all business.

Strutsky puts his hand on Prior's shoulder, keeps him sitting. "Boss," says Strutsky. "Mod bust in here, they're gonna make this guy. What do you think we should..."

"All right, all right," says Grainger. He's nervous. He looks like he's pre-occupied making his bones with Mod.

Prior figures Grainger wants to find out more about him, what he's hiding, why he came back, what his plans are. Prior could be the big score that Grainger has been waiting for. But if he turns Prior over now, he gets nothing. Just another vagrant Fringe to process.

"They really got you by the short ones, don't they?" says Prior, able to read Grainger's thoughts on his giant relief map of a face.

"Shut it," says Grainger. The spark of light outside is getting closer. "Okay, Strutsky, you take Bob Marley through the back alley. I'll make my nano-report in the front and we'll meet you later. Got it?"

"On it," says Strutsky, grabbing Prior under his arm, pulling him up. Prior struggles but Strutsky's grip on him is hard and mechanical. Prior gets dragged through the back door without getting a chance for a proper farewell to Grainger and his men. Somehow, he thinks Grainger will get over the breach in etiquette.

Besides, Prior has more immediate issues at hand. Namely, this rookie pulling him into the deserted back alley.

It's dark but Prior can easily make out the debris spewed everywhere. The filthy asphalt is wet with the dingy soup of past vagrant occupants. The moon bleeds faint light through the abandoned buildings. The air is punctuated by sparks from nanos on the neighboring streets. Prior thinks it's a lousy place to die. Especially when he was just wiggling his toes on an Antiguan beach. He wiggles his toes in his shoes now to see if he can feel a grain or two of stowaway sand. Something to remind him he stupidly chose to leave goddamn paradise to come here.

"Right here," says Strutsky, all business, as if Grainger is in the alley with him. He lets go of Prior's arm and backs him against a wall. Strutsky looks over his shoulder, judges the moonlight, and moves Prior further into the alley's shadows. Prior figures the rookie doesn't want to actually see Prior die in front of him. It's bad enough the rookie will hear the gunshot pulled from his own trigger.

"You used to be tougher than this," says Strutsky.

Prior squints his eyes, trying to drink in as much moonlight as he can to get his bearings. What Prior sees makes his knees buckle.

Strutsky takes off his overcoat and disappears, leaving nothing behind but a few sparks. From the reflected light off a swampy puddle, a blue line begins to shimmer where Strutsky stood. The blue line flattens out, broadening in dimension, until it is in the shape of a giant paper doll.

"A hell of a lot tougher," says the paper doll.

Prior takes a breath.

"Lachende," says Prior. "You little bastard."

"Jeremiah Prior," says Lachende the Mod. "Goddammit, I never thought I'd get the chance."

"What, scare the hell out of me?"

"Save your ass."

When Prior last saw Lachende, he was Fringe. Prior met him years ago, when Lachende was a kid. An orphan. He couldn't be more than twenty-five now. Feynman took Lachende in. The kid became their informant and helped them on a lot of cases. The kid wanted to be an Authentician when he grew up. He wanted to be just like Prior. He also used to make moves on Molly until Prior got wise and set Lachende straight about how he had no future as an Authentician or as his son-in-law.

"What the hell happened to you?" asks Prior.

"Thing is," says Lachende, "since I turned, I can't seem to remember. Isn't that the funniest?"

"Hilarious."

"What, Prior, you don't trust me?"

"Can't imagine why. Let's get the hell out of here."

"This way," says Lachende, turning himself into a giant half-dome that covers Prior like a snow globe, leading them down the alley.

Chapter 12

Prior drifts inside Lachende's snow globe until they arrive at a safer neighborhood. The sensation is like a comfortable cab ride. Lachende halts at a street corner and retracts his protective semi-dome from Prior.

"You want to explain how you're posing as a Fringe cop?"

"You want to explain what you're doing back here?" says Lachende. It's a fair question. Years back, the kid would never have spoken to Prior like this. In the years since, he's grown a pair of three-dimensional coconuts that he had pressed into 2-D.

"Grainger know about you?" says Prior.

Lachende leads Prior through the shadows of the dark street. Where light leaks in from above, Lachende creates his own shadows to cover Prior. Prior knows these streets, this neighborhood. Lachende is taking him to the outskirts. Maybe someone there hasn't heard about Prior's past.

"Of course not," says Lachende. "But it's awfully amusing to take orders from Fringe."

"I heard about Mod slumming."

"Remember your old friend, Dr. Brewster?" says Lachende. "He's the one who got me this disguise."

"How the hell is that old chemist doing?"

"Fine, I guess. Still working with plastics. He remembered me from one of your old cases."

"I still can't get over you," says Prior.

"Slumming," says Lachende, his film of a mouth broadening into a smile. "Yes, that's it exactly. No sleep, you know. Something about keeping the nanos active all the time. They tell you that up front, before you convert, but the truth doesn't really sink in until the third or fourth night. You don't get tired, though. Now, it's all about fighting the boredom. The damn nanos, they're supposed to be my servants but, honestly, I feel like I work for them."

He's serious, thinks Prior. Fringe dying in the diseased streets, slaving away. And Lachende, the kid Prior thought he helped raise, is talking about fighting boredom.

"Lachende, I have to ask you..."

"Feynman?"

Prior nods.

"That answers why you're back. Of course it does. Makes sense."

"They still think I did it?" says Prior.

Lachende and his shadows stand still. Prior glances at the street behind him. No one is there.

"Didn't you?" says Lachende.

"Kill my partner? You crazy?" But there's something in Prior's voice that betrays him. He can hear it as the words escape his mouth.

"You seen Molly?" says Lachende.

"Not yet."

"Prior, you say you didn't do it, you didn't do it. I believe you."

"Okay," says Prior, not sure if he can fully trust the kid yet. "What does NanoGov have to say about it?"

Lachende stares at Prior and it's like a poster echoing back at you. Prior can't believe he's standing this close to a Mod.

"I think I know how to help," says Lachende.

"You always had a thing for Molly, didn't you?" says Prior.

"Thanks. I'd forgotten. Tell me more." Even as a sliver, Lachende is a pain in a Fringe's ass.

"Well?"

"Come with me. And don't fight it."

Lachende's shadows gather around Prior's feet, then encircle him. Quickly, Lachende and his shadows merge into a sphere around Prior. Prior stays perfectly still even though his heart rate ramps up to dangerous levels. Antoine told him this is how some Mod transport Fringe illegally. The sphere containing them lifts off from the ground, floating straight up until it clears the building rooftops.

"I said don't fight it," says Lachende, his voice somehow concentrated in the sphere. "Think of it as a crispy Lachende shell with a warm Prior center." Lachende laughs and its echoes are the thing that drive Prior over the edge. He feels nauseous. "No throwing up, Prior. Last Fringe I took in and vomited didn't end up so well. I opened at the bottom and they dropped out. Still, it saved my beautiful vintage satin shirt from untold stains."

"Feynman," says Prior between gritted teeth, trying to keep his stomach below his chest. He doesn't even consider looking down. "What happened that night?"

They're flying over the city towards the outskirts, slowly, gently, taking in the sights, bobbing up and down with the breeze, making sure not to attract any attention. The last thing Prior wants is the Mod Police spotlight on them.

"You should ask your old secretary. How is Miss Penny?" says Lachende.

"I'm sure you already know."

"Damn shame what's happened to Fringe women," says Lachende. "Did you know in order to survive, some Fringe women were kept as pets by Mod for the exclusive purpose of breeding? Some Fringe, depending on their point of view, called it slavery. Mod would inject their DNA nanos into these Fringe women and use them as incubators. The children would be tagged as Mod. Kids couldn't actually turn Mod until they were twenty, of course."

"Why not?" asks Prior, avoiding the true question about Molly.

"NanoGov found out by horrible trial and error. Now, no Fringe woman wants to be tagged as a Mod breeder. You could imagine. The women that weren't making future Mod babies? They were bred with Fringe men to make more Fringe. All done under strict NanoGov control, of course."

They descend in a zigzag pattern, slowly but with purpose. Prior can make out the city outskirts through the milky skin of the Lachende globe.

"It was never supposed to be this way," says Prior.

"Only Fringe can reproduce. That's the central problem," says Lachende. "Becoming a Mod means you give up the ability to procreate. Mod are okay with this. They leave the burden to these Fringe women."

"Another gift from NanoGov in their endless pursuit to make Fringe third-class citizens," says Prior. "Molly. She's almost at the age where she's gonna start attracting attention."

"You got here just in time," says Lachende. "What a hero."

More of that sarcasm. Prior feels around his pockets for a pin to pop this damn balloon now that they're only ten feet off the ground. No luck. They land and Lachende reconfigures himself as off-duty Strutsky the moment they touch ground.

"Now what?" says Prior.

"That way," says Lachende, pointing Prior towards a disheveled tent city under a grove of trees.

When Prior turns, Lachende is gone. Prior wonders if Lachende is really working for the Fringe cops or Mod Police. Maybe Lachende was assigned to get rid of Prior. No, that doesn't make any sense. If NanoGov wants to get rid of Prior, they'd squash him like a gnat. Like a hair on a gnat's ass. Shrugging his shoulders to no one, Prior adjusts his backpack, tightens his coat collar, and heads into the tent city.

The outskirts resemble an enormous dirty pile of laundry. Smoke from fires and burning rags rises above the hap-hazardously arranged tattered tents and lean-tos, blocking off the sky. This place has probably been here a few years but looks like it was just built yesterday and will be burned down tomorrow.

A crooked line of Fringe stretches endlessly, each Fringe hunched over in a defeated pose that Mod really can't replicate. Mod pretend to be Fringe at their Fringe Festival parties but it always turns out a cruel mockery of the twisted and burdened spines of most Fringe. Everyone in this tent city seems to be waiting on this line, each focused on shuffling forward at an excruciatingly slow pace. Not knowing what else to do or where else to go, Prior gets on the back of the line. No one talks to him. No one even notices him.

The night tries to put out the rag-fire but it keeps burning, turning the smoky air blacker than the absence of sun. Hours roll by and Prior shuffles forward. Food line maybe? Doubtful. Food isn't organized this well. There would never be this much food to distribute to a crowd this size. Then, after turning another corner, Prior sees the head of the line. A tiny tent. A small cardboard box turned so it is at its maximum height. An elderly man sitting on the floor, behind the box, writing with a frazzled quill. Real bottle of black ink at his side on the floor. He dips the pen in the ink and finishes his note. The Fringe pays him and walks away. The next Fringe approaches and begins dictating. The old man writes on a fresh piece of paper. The Fringe gives him an address, pays him, and moves on.

A Letter-Writer. Jesus. Prior thought he saw the last of them. Guy was probably an Authentician on the run. Like Prior. One of the few Fringe left who can read and write. Of course Fringe would line up for this. How else are Fringe communicating with their friends and family? The Letter-Writer takes their money, prepares their notes, and delivers them using Fringe children as messengers.

Finally, it's Prior's turn. He moves up to the front of the cardboard box. The Letter-Writer looks smaller, like a child playing with ancient crayons. Prior checks his pockets. He doesn't have any money on him. He's got no letters to write.

"Name?" says the Letter-Writer without looking up, applying a fresh piece of paper to the box surface. His voice is thin, tired.

"Feynman. Richard Feynman."

The Letter-Writer looks up with a surprised look. "Funny, you don't look like a dead guy."

"I was his partner. Jeremiah Prior."

"You need someone in a different line of work," says the Letter-Writer. "One of those old-fashioned gypsy mediums. You know," he says, really throwing himself into this ridiculous request, "one of those nice seance ladies with beads on the walls. I send letters to people who are still alive, Mr. Prior." He puts down his pen and stands up. It's difficult for him to move and he wheezes as his back straightens. At his full height, he only comes up to Prior's chest. He gazes into Prior's eyes, taking his measure, and lets out a disappointed sigh. It makes a harmonic counterpoint to the painful wheezing. Turning around, the Letter-Writer disappears behind a curtain, his little body moving as if intensely heavy.

Prior looks behind him but no one in line seems to be complaining or annoyed at this disruption to their routine. They probably have no place else to be today. Prior stands in wonder at this little center of organization and process in the middle of the chaotic world. Is NanoGov aware of this operation? Do they let it slide since it is harmless? Has the Letter-Writer and all these Fringe really figured out a way to operate under the nano-radar? Seems unlikely.

The Letter-Writer re-appears from behind the curtain. He's hiding something under his shirt. He sits down again, still holding the object close to his heart. His eyes are furtive, cautious.

"Jeremiah Prior," says the Letter-Writer. "Delivery for you. Came yesterday."

"How did you know I'd be here?"

The Letter-Writer peeks into his shirt like he's checking on a malignant mole. He has no regard for the hundreds of Fringe still waiting to send letters to their desperate loved ones elsewhere.

"You're here, aren't you? People know," says the Letter-Writer. "They always know where the important people in their lives are. Trust me. It's what I do."

"Let's see it."

"Not yet," says the Letter-Writer. "We haven't discussed what's important to me."

"Namely?"

"What do you have to trade?"

Prior unzips his backpack and sees what he can give this old, thieving buzzard. The sender already paid him but the bastard wants it from both ends. The Letter-Writer smiles, revealing a broken-tile mosaic of teeth while Prior fishes around his backpack. Prior's fingers wrap around one of the bottles of Antoine's jerk sauce. Maybe that's why Antoine gave him the jerk sauce; to pay for these kind of things. Besides, who better to give jerk sauce to than this relic?

"Ah, thank you," says the Letter-Writer, accepting the small bottle with the greedy fingers of his left hand while the right hand produces a small burlap-wrapped package from within his tattered shirt. "Antiguan jerk sauce. Very rare." Without opening it, the Letter-Writer smells the bottle, as if the jerk sauce odor permeates the rare glass.

Prior turns to the side so neither the Letter-Writer nor the crowd behind him can see what's inside the package. The burlap peels off like an onion, wrapping after wrapping, dropping to the ground. Already, a child with hungry eyes is crawling towards the discarded burlap, knowing it will serve some useful purpose or fetch a good price for food. Prior gets to the meaty center of the gift.

Prior's mouth goes slack. It's an old newspaper clipping. Prior hasn't held newspaper for so long, he's forgotten how delicate it is. It's ripped and shows an ad that spans beyond the tear of the page. He turns it over. The headline reads, "Inquiry Closed on Authentician Death. Ruled an Accident."

There are three small columns of the story that begin but don't end since the page has been torn. Prior pieces together the gist of it. After Prior left for Antigua, they interviewed Penny. Felice couldn't be found. No surprise. Penny didn't pursue any criminal action and there didn't seem to be enough evidence to convict anyone.

At the bottom of the paper, someone has written in red crayon in neat block print, "TRUTH OR DARE?"

Prior shoots a glance at the Letter-Writer who is already preparing for the next customer. He cranes his neck and stares at the sky. "Damn you, Lachende."

Chapter 13

Prior awakens to the sound of someone trying to open his office front door. The door has a wooden latch but that's not stopping anyone from breaking in. Prior springs up, jolted by the assault on his privacy. He misses the days when he had a gun. Hell, he misses the days he had any metal object.

Prior sneaks up to the door, stands with his back pressed to the wall next to the doorway, and slides the latch out of place. His heart is racing. The door slips open slightly. Then a wisp of a hand tentatively pushes the door completely open.

"Hello?" says the polite intruder, taking a step into Prior's office. Prior jumps out from behind the door and tackles the intruder. It's like diving onto a sheet of plastic wrap. Prior finds himself rolling on the floor covered by the intruder.

"Prior, simmer. It's little old me."

The intruder's voice is muffled since he's covering Prior's ears. Prior is finding it hard to breathe. Suddenly, the boa-constrictor pressure is released and Prior lies on the floor, panting. He looks up.

"Good morning," says Lachende cheerfully. He's formed his two-dimensional body back into its human-scale fullness.

Prior garbles something unintelligible.

"No one locks their doors anymore," says Lachende. "Who has anything valuable to steal?"

"You just goddamn wait until I open the door next time," says Prior, standing up and getting his wind back.

"I knocked," he says, looking around the office. "Hey, maybe you do have something valuable. From Antigua. Is it true they're still growing ganja down there? I've always heard about it but..."

"You wouldn't know of an illegal underground coffee place around here?" says Prior, brushing himself off.

"I don't drink coffee anymore."

"Yeah, I get it," says Prior. "Real independent streak. I hadn't noticed you were a tarp."

"Independent streak. That's code for big pain-in-the-ass, right?"

They walk out into the street. The air is biting cold and the wind almost blows Lachende away. He pivots and walks sideways so the wind won't affect him.

"How the hell do you live like that?" says Prior.

"I have my reasons. I recently converted. It takes some getting used to. We're not really meant to walk around like this. We're born to glide."

"I'm honored," says Prior.

Prior peaks behind them to make sure they're not being followed. In the bright sun, it's harder for someone to hide.

"I got your message, by the way," says Prior. He was hoping Lachende would have brought it up first.

"Message?" says Lachende innocently.

"From the Letter-Writer yesterday. Look, kid, if you have any evidence..."

"Prior," says Lachende. "I dropped you off there yesterday so you could try and reach out to Molly. I didn't leave any evidence."

"Then someone is trying to mess with me," says Prior.

"They should take a number." Lachende grins and Prior decides to trust him for a little while longer.

They walk down a wide boulevard that was jammed with traffic decades ago. A homeless person is sleeping in the middle of the sidewalk. They step over him.

"So, Mod have their wishes come true and a few Fringe turn out like that guy back there. All okay with you, huh?" says Prior.

Lachende stops crab-walking. The front of him flaps in the wind and, when he speaks, his voice flutters rhythmically.

"Hasn't it always been that way? Look, I'm not crazy about the state of things either, okay? And I don't need you to rub it in. We couldn't all disappear into a tropical jungle like you. Some of us had to stay here and make choices," he says.

Prior nods, not knowing how to respond to that. They continue another block before either one of them says anything.

"I just don't understand how this could happen," says Prior. "Everything blurs."

"Easy," says Lachende. "You're into antiques. You should know."

"Meaning?"

"Look at technology as it advanced throughout history. Each time there was a major advancement, it came exponentially sooner than the last one. Fire. The wheel. The boat. The Industrial Revolution. The Digital Revolution. The Cellular Revolution. Then, with Modela Novela and Ferri came the Nano Revolution. Each one coming at us quicker. Telescopically quicker."

Prior lets out a long breath and peers up at the sky. There are no Mod flying above like last night. He glances back and spots the Fringe with spiky red hair wearing a long gray overcoat walking about a block behind them. Miss Simmons' brother. Addison must notice he's been made because he ducks into an alley. Prior is sure he'll turn up again soon. He continues his walk with Lachende on the empty street.

"Where do all you Mod go?" says Prior.

"They'd never be out now. But you're special so I'm here with you," Lachende says.

"I saw them last night."

"Searching for Ferri. He's gone missing. I'm sure you heard."

"Yeah. Anyway, go on," says Prior.

"I was saying that each time, there was this reverse telescopic effect of technology where each advancement came in shorter and shorter periods of time."

"And?"

"And that's how it happened. That's how I came to give up my mass in exchange for endless shopping. One day, I was impressed with instant molecular imaging games, the next, I'm gliding free as a bird."

"But NanoGov. How can you trust them?"

"Who needs to trust them?" says Lachende as they cross the street. "Twenty percent of the planet is made up of Mod. We don't need anything to live. And NanoGov keeps an eye on the other seventy-eight percent of the planet so they can control the Fringe population."

They stop in front of a glass building.

"Wait a minute," says Prior. "That's only ninety-eight percent."

"Really? I was never good with the…what do you call it? The mathematics."

Prior gets a chill up his spine completely unrelated to the weather.

"We're here," says Lachende.

"Where?"

"Home sweet home."

Lachende turns and slips through the crack between the closed front door and doorjamb. Prior waits outside, disoriented as usual.

Addison appears behind them, keeping his distance. Why is Addison stalking him? Shouldn't it be the other way around? Normally, Prior would be suspect but he doesn't understand all the rules in this new world. Sometimes you say no to a case but the case doesn't say no to you.

After a moment, the door opens.

"Sorry," says Lachende.

Prior walks into the lobby. It sparkles with a light that doesn't originate from outside. The air is fragrant. A golden fountain roars in the middle of the beautiful entry, sending tendrils of water skyward before accepting them back into its pool.

"So this is how Mod live," says Prior.

"You have no idea. Shall we take the stairs?" says Lachende, putting on the air of the host and gesturing upwards.

"What, no elevator?"

"The residents merely float up."

"So the stairs are for the help," says Prior. "Well, if it won't demean you."

They proceed up the marble stairs which, even for a service stairwell, is luxurious. The rails are polished brass and glisten like a new church organ. Soft music, piped in, flits across their ears.

Lachende opens the door in a grand manner and lets them in. His place is opulent in a garish way. The kind of a place a child dreams of when they fantasize about being rich. It is devoid of adult temperance.

"Nice joint," says Prior. "Modest."

"It's home."

Lachende lies down on the Persian rug and momentarily disappears. Only when Prior's eyesight catches the slight distinction between Lachende and the rug does he realize that Lachende is just resting.

"How about that coffee?" says Prior.

A thin hand rises from the ground, snaps its fingers, then melts away into the rug again.

Prior looks down and a hot mug of coffee appears in front of him.

"Nanos. Marvelous servants. Will do anything I want," says Lachende. "That's the payoff."

"Yeah, but suppose you want to turn back into a Fringe. What do you do?"

"You can't. Not usually. I'd already agreed to become Mod, signed all the NanoGov papers, was checked for rogue nanos, the whole thing. A few weeks before I go in for the procedure, Molly and I got serious."

Prior detects a hesitancy in Lachende's voice that is the first sign of humanity.

"I'm not going to lie to you, Prior. I'm in love with her."

"Molly."

"You can see my dilemma. I fell in love with a Fringe but already gave up all my rights. But don't worry. I found a way."

Prior sips the coffee and it's the best that he's ever had.

"With the help of your old friend, Brewster," says Lachende. "Anyway, the day I turned Mod, he helped me. He re-wired my DNA code so I could turn back. Mod don't know. That's our secret, Daddy-O."

"Don't ever."

Lachende stands up. He shimmers translucently in the sunlight as he floats toward the front door.

"What is it?" says Prior.

Lachende picks up a piece of paper that someone has slid under the door.

"Careful," says Prior. "It could be Mod."

"Mod don't intrude on each other's space."

Lachende opens the note. "It's from your secretary. Your client is waiting for you."

"How the hell do they keep finding me?"

Chapter 14

"What do you know about a guy named Addison Simmons?" Prior asks Grainger.

Grainger and his cronies are holed up in their usual dive, lounging around the table drinking something that makes swill look like champagne.

"Where the hell's my rookie?" says Grainger.

Prior has spent a restless night debating on whether to take the Simmons case or investigate Penny further. As usual, Prior takes the path of least resistance.

"Who?" says Prior, laying it on thick.

"Kid threw you out of here the other day. Strutsky. The hell is he?"

"Haven't seen him. Big kid, though," says Prior, hoping the topic has played itself out.

"Addison," says Grainger, rolling around the name in his mouth. "Why does that name sound familiar?"

While he's engaged in rumination, Prior nods at the other two cops.

"So," says Prior. "How's life? Mod treating you gentlemen well?"

"Fuck off," says Torpedo No. 1. He looks like he could bend crowbars into pretzels. If they still had crowbars. Or pretzels.

"Now, now," says Grainger. "Let's not be rude. Prior here can't help it if he's jealous of us. Besides, he saved us a trip checking up on him." He turns to Prior. "Addison don't ring any bells."

"Thanks anyway," says Prior.

"Now you can fuck off," says Torpedo No. 2. The table bursts into laughter.

"Yeah, too bad he ain't a cop no more," says Torpedo No. 1, not knowing when he's ahead on points. "He would have loved this case."

"Say again?" says Prior. It hurts him to hang around this bunch but he's been in a curious mood ever since Miss Simmons walked into his office.

"The last of the world's masterpieces. Gone," says Grainger.

"The Seurat sketch?" says Prior.

"That's old news. I'm taking about the Vermeer. Stolen last night. Right out from under the Tate's security guard's nose. You'd think if you've got one giant building to house one small painting, you'd figure out a way to keep an eye on it. Stupid bastards."

"Scotland Mod have any suspects?" says Prior.

Grainger and his boys grow silent, watching him carefully. Grainger gets in closer to Prior.

"Here's the thing, Prior," says Grainger. "Everyone knows you killed your partner."

Prior leans forward so he's nose to nose with Grainger. He can smell Grainger's rancid breath. This is not going to end well for one of them.

"Repeat that," says Prior.

"We think it's awfully suspicious the Vermeer disappeared the same time you showed up."

"Are you saying I'm a suspect for this too? What else? My fault that you're overweight and have flatulent issues?"

"You gotta admit," says Grainger. "It's a pretty big coincidence."

"The farting?" says Torpedo No. 1.

"The Vermeer!" says Grainger.

"Ain't it?" says Torpedo No. 2, trying to get on Grainger's good side.

"You've got nothing, Grainger," says Prior, pointing his index finger at Grainger's bulbous nose. "Just stay the hell out of my way. You've got no cause. And if you ever say anything about my old partner..."

The table erupts into laughter again.

"Jesus, Prior, can't you take a joke? We're just busting your balls," says Grainger.

The torpedoes laugh along like one big happy family, drinking their sub-swill.

"Hilarious," says Prior, not backing off.

"Scotland Mod," guffaws Torpedo No. 2. "Like they care about some stupid painting."

Grainger glares at his subordinates. The torpedoes, realizing they're a beat behind, clam it.

"You should explain to your lap dogs how valuable this Vermeer is," says Prior.

The torpedoes get up, trying to replace their embarrassment with a threatening stance.

"Sit down, boys," says Grainger. They do as ordered and await further instruction. Grainger turns to them like a disappointed father. "It's real art," says Grainger, trying not to take Prior's side in this discussion but agreeing with him all the same.

"And it's the last of its kind," says Prior. "Now, you may think it's meaningless but ask Mod. Any Mod."

"Mod wouldn't steal it," says Grainger.

"Don't play stupid, Grainger. They'd all kill for it," says Prior. "They wouldn't think twice. And since NanoGov runs everything unopposed, who's to stop them? You guys? You'll do as you're told."

One of the torpedoes makes a move toward Prior. Prior kicks the chair out from under him and the guy hits the floor, banging his chin on the table on his way down. His gray drink splashes all over him. There are worse ways to have fun.

Grainger and his other goon shoot up.

"Come on," says Prior. "Tell me I'm wrong, Detective Grainger."

Grainger helps the torpedo up and sits him back down. They all stare at each other, breathing hard, seething, strategizing, while the torpedo rubs his chin.

Grainger breaks the ice. "You're not worth it, Prior. And here's why. You can't investigate the missing Vermeer. You can't even investigate this Addison guy. Your antiquarian detective license has been revoked as of this morning. When your buddies at NanoGov found out you were back in town, they pulled it. Now you apologize to my young colleague here."

The color melts away from Prior's face. He gets up, turns quickly, and makes a tactical retreat. He doesn't want to give them a chance to drop any more bombs. He's led a life of shelter for the past few years and can't tolerate this type of change that he has no control over. He's had more disturbing news thrown his way in two days than in all four years in Antigua.

Prior hits the street, the rough laughter of Grainger and his men still ringing in his ear. The cold wind slaps him hard but it's what he needs. He's got to sift through all these facts and determine where to go and how to navigate.

Through his peripheral vision, Prior is sure he catches a glimpse of Addison tailing him. The more time he spends in this city, the more his instincts are coming back, like atrophied muscles finally getting a workout.

Prior ducks into an old warehouse. He closes the door behind him and walks in, noticing there are no windows. Day and nighttime seem indistinguishable. The rancid smell hits him like a gut punch. Hundreds of Fringe men lay on the floor, sleeping.

Things are tough for Fringe women but Fringe men don't have it so good either. They are the workers, living on discarded scrap objects thrown out by Mod. Eating paltry food grown in sidewalk cracks. Water is scarce for them.

An emaciated dog pads slowly toward Prior and gives him a sniff. Prior gives him a pet behind his ears before the dog shuffles off. Years ago, Mod tried making their pets into Mod. It was a disaster. Then, not having learned their lessons, Mod took Fringe pets and tried making them into Mod. More disaster. The problem was that being Mod involved free will. Dogs and cats didn't really have free will and their nanos ran amuck, making a mess of everything. Dog biscuits and fire hydrants the size of houses soon littered the landscape until Mod had to put their Mod pets to sleep permanently. It makes Prior think of the giant parrotfish and wahoo that attacked him.

"Hello?" says Prior, his voice echoing throughout the warehouse. No one responds. The sleeping bodies don't even stir. It's then that Prior realizes they aren't sleeping.

Prior runs to the door, steps through and slams it behind him, shaking. He turns around, expecting to be outdoors. But the city breeze doesn't find him. The door leads to another room in the warehouse with another kind of breeze. It is a fetid smell, pungent and sour, as it crosses Prior's nostrils. The smell is rhythmic, like breathing.

Prior looks up in the faint light. His gaze is met by two red eyes the size of car headlights. The breathing stops momentarily and is replaced with a deafening chattering sound. Claws are skittering on the floor as something sniffs the air, trying to get a sense of Prior.

Prior doesn't want to stick around to find out whether he'd make a tasty dessert. Before he can turn, a giant gray mouse emerges from the shadows. It must be twenty feet high, its thin tail longer than a fire hose. It slowly approaches Prior, never taking its eyes off him.

Prior doesn't stick around long enough to figure out whether this is Mod controlling a two-dimensional mouse or whether this big bastard is real. He bolts towards the door. The mouse takes off after him, squealing and making thunderous skitters on the wooden floor.

The door is locked. Prior whips around, looking for other escape options. How could he be so stupid?

Before he can answer that, a blue tarp flies off a wooden crate from the rafters and envelopes Prior. It pushes him to the left, practically lifting him off his feet. He's in complete darkness but can hear the giant mouse getting closer. The tarp is pushing Prior in a specific direction and Prior is powerless to stop it. The momentum takes Prior further from the mouse and that's good enough for now.

Suddenly, the tarp is yanked away from Prior and he spills on the floor like a child's unwrapped toy. The mouse has the tarp in its mouth and is swinging it wildly. The blue tarp is screaming. The scream sounds familiar.

Prior looks around and sees a window nearby. It is large enough for him to fit through. But he can't leave the tarp there to be torn to shreds. He picks up a broken section of a wooden pallet, the jagged edge making a decent weapon.

Prior stands and screams at the mouse, momentarily distracting it from the tarp. The mouse stands on its hind legs to look more intimidating. The mouse is about to pounce when Prior throws the wood towards the mouse's exposed belly. The wood pierces the belly and the mouse opens its mouth and lets out a scream. The tarp flies away, crashing through the window. The mouse charges but Prior dives through the window after the tarp. As Prior lands on the sidewalk, he hears a crash against the warehouse wall. No doubt, that mouse was real.

Prior catches his breath and looks around. The street is deserted. No sign of the blue tarp.

He stands up by the window and is greeted by the mouse's high-pitched screaming. The mouse bites and growls, it's tongue trying to get a hold of Prior through the window. Prior is jolted by the sound and it takes a second before he moves out of the way. At the same time, a cloud of dust particles silently descends from the sky and stream in through the window. The mouse lets out one last scream before Prior hears it getting completely devoured by the particles. He didn't think he could feel bad for the mouse.

Prior calms down, not knowing where to go. He has to get out of this part of the city. He heads into the park, figuring he might run into an informant or two there. He needs to clear his head. Too much change too quickly.

Prior's mind races and comes to rest on his theory. Evolution is never that far behind or ahead of them. Their caveman ancestors are still close enough to be looking over their shoulders. Mod don't want to be reminded of that. They think they're so far advanced. But the Fringe stubbornly remind them of where they all came from. And Mod need Fringe, goddammit.

The park is still lush with tall trees and uncontrolled grass and weeds. At first, there's just the wind brushing against the leaves, coaxing a sad song. Then, Prior hears the dying groan of some beast through the trees. He dives behind a bush and sees a band of Fringe hunters chasing some wild horses.

Since there are so many Mod, and they all live indoors and don't consume any food, the animal population has blossomed tremendously. The animals tend to congregate in the park. To earn extra money, Fringe are hired by Mod to be animal hunters to keep some type of ecological balance in the hell on earth they created. They are given spears and each Fringe man serves out an annual tour of duty, thinning the local herds of whatever happens to roam the lands at the time.

The Fringe men are all shackled in chains. The chains stretch out several hundreds of feet behind them, held by a Mod flapping in the wind.

Prior feels a leaf land on his shoulder.

"Prior," says the leaf.

Prior jumps back, giving away his position to the Mod marching by with his fleet of Fringe hunters. The Mod, still flapping in the wind like an untethered sail, makes eye contact with Prior, scoffing at him. The Mod whips the chains and giddy-yaps the Fringe men to continue their hunting.

"It's me," says a familiar voice into Prior's ear.

The leaf unfurls into full human shape.

"Lachende, what the hell are you doing here?"

"I could ask you the same thing."

"The...the warehouse. There were Fringe..."

"The body shop. Yeah, don't go in there. Nothing for you. Once a week, they set fire to the inside. Thanks for saving my life, by the way."

"Only Mod could come up with something so incredibly horrible," says Prior.

"You should have seen what they used to do. This is relatively humane."

"Just like this," says Prior, pointing to the Fringe slaves hunting animals.

"Oh, that," says Lachende with a wave of his hand. "Look, everyone gets what they want out of it. The ecological balance is maintained, Fringe get some money and food, and Mod get to fantasize that they're wild African hunters or Pharaohs or chariot-racers or whatever the hell is fashionable this week."

"You still haven't told me what you're doing here," says Prior.

They walk back towards the paved portion of the city, emerging from the jungle wilds of the park.

"I heard about your license being revoked. Sorry about that."

"Dammit," says Prior.

"What?"

"I'm just not used to everybody knowing my business instantly."

"Yeah, well, you're lucky that everyone doesn't know everything about your business."

"Meaning?"

"Your secretary, Penelope?"

"What about her?"

"You know she got remarried, right?" says Lachende.

"Yeah."

"Well, Sanders, her new husband? He's real high-level with NanoGov. You see where I'm going with this?"

"Pretend I don't," says Prior. He's got an inkling where this is heading but wants to see what Lachende's play is.

"Penelope's husband, he arranged for your license to be revoked. The schmuck is jealous."

"Jealous," says Prior.

"The guy knows that Penelope still has the major screaming thigh-sweats for you. The poor guy just wants his wife back."

"Touching. But pardon me if I don't feel sympathy for a guy who just cut me off at the knees."

"Still, the guy loves his wife."

"I'm not getting in the way," says Prior. "Someone's going to have to break it to him that I may have a new client and may decide to take the case. In which case, I'll need Penelope to help."

"Without a license? The Mod Police won't like that."

"What the Mod Police don't like could fill a warehouse," says Prior.

"Yeah, the kind they burn dead bodies in."

They get to a large intersection, empty as usual. Though NanoGov keeps a clandestine presence, this global emptiness is presented as a good thing for everyone on the planet. There aren't any more wars since Mod live as they desire. Fringe are kept in check. The party line is that, due to the sacrifice of Mod, there is no more pollution, no more depletion of natural resources, no disease. What they aren't talking about is that the average lifespan for Fringe is down to forty years.

"Can you really trust NanoGov to have your best interests at heart?" says Prior.

"That again?" says Lachende.

"Fringe? Their entire lives are defined by work. Their slavery to Mod. Hunters, Mod-Dreamers, Breeders, who knows what else."

"Prior, no one asks these questions anymore. We're playing way past that."

They continue walking down the deserted street. The Sky-Screen gives an update that there's no new breaks in the missing Seurat investigation.

"How can I find out about Feynman? You think Brewster can help?" says Prior.

Lachende nods at the Sky-Screen, his translucent face lost in thought. "Fringe have free will. They just don't have 'Free Will,'" says Lachende, devoid of irony.

Prior walks off, leaving Lachende behind. He'd had enough of Lachende's company. Someone needs to see what is happening in the world and agree with Prior.

"Prior," says Lachende, floating over.

"What?"

Lachende leans in and whispers. "You've heard of the Fringe Underground Movement, right?"

Prior stares at him blankly, not willing to commit to an opinion in public. He thinks about Antoine and how he tried to get Prior to join.

"Well, here. This is for saving my life. Take it," says Lachende. He produces a fat brass key out of thin air and hands it to Prior. Prior hasn't felt metal since he's been back.

"What is this?"

"It'll get you in to our next meeting," says Lachende. With a slight turn of his body, he catches the wind and drifts away skywards.

Chapter 15

Prior decides to spend his day trying to locate some old friends. Allies who might still be alive and can help him make sense of this world. He starts with Brewster, trying to remember where that crazy, hippie activist lived. He'll search for Professor Belden later. If not today, maybe tomorrow. Belden was always more malleable and slippery than Brewster.

Prior hits the streets and finally recalls the route. It takes the better part of the morning. He keeps a lookout for Addison, making sure he isn't being tailed. Brewster's street is narrow and quiet. Old stone houses, bunched together a century ago when the city was worried about being too crowded with fully fleshed people, line each side of the street.

Prior approaches the foot of Brewster's driveway, thinking of what he's going to say to his old friend. He's put aside the Fringe Underground Movement for the moment. The idea that Lachende and Antoine might be connected by common cause is too vast a notion to contemplate at the moment. He'll deal with all that later. Right now, Brewster's light is on and he needs the good doctor's help.

He hopes Brewster has survived by his wits. Brewster was already a legendary chemist who railed against NanoGov when it first formed. For a while, he was known as something of a revolutionary. An anti-nano terrorist who helped organize the Fringe in their struggle. He begged Prior to stay and help him but by then, Feynman was dead, Felice had left, and Prior was on the last boat to Antigua.

Brewster had always been an invaluable resource to Prior, helping him with DNA evidence and other forensics to identify ownership of rare antiques.

Brewster liked solving history's riddles. "Bring clarity to chaos and you'll never be out of a job," Brewster was often fond of saying.

Prior is about to give Brewster's door a knock when he hears shuffling footsteps inside.

"It cannot be," says a gargled voice from behind the door.

"It is, man," says another muffled voice.

"Brewster?" says Prior. "It's me, Jeremiah."

"Go away," says the gargled voice from behind the door.

"Come on in," says the muffled voice.

The door swings open. The foyer is dimly lit and the musty smell of mold and rotting wood is thick in the air. Prior steps inside before the door is closed.

"Alright, who the hell is..." says Prior. He takes a step forward to get a better look at the couple hiding from him.

He is confronted with two faces growing out of two long necks.

One of the faces is an older version of Brewster, slightly wrinkled, graying more around the temples. Ponytail still in place, maybe a bit longer. He wears granny glasses like one of his old idols. His spherical face bobs up and down on his inhumanly long neck like a tulip bulb in the wind.

The other face is flatter, more severe. It's a version of Brewster the way Prior remembers him. He is young, vibrant, still with the ponytail and slight gray around the temples to indicate some sort of wisdom. But the joy has been washed out, leaving behind a void; an almost sinister anger and hopelessness. The flat face bobs away slightly, its neck tapering delicately as it gets closer to the face, and Prior sees clearly that this second head is two-dimensional. It reminds him of an old developing photograph dangling on a wire.

Both neck-stalks convene like rivers to the three-dimensional body of Brewster.

Prior takes a step back but he's up against a dank wall.

"Don't be afraid, man," says 3D Brewster, the left-sided head. His spherical face draws closer to Prior, the neck elongating to allow a more thorough inspection.

"He is not wanted here," says 2D Brewster. His paper-plate face retracts. "He smells of Fringe. Disgusting. I will not stand for this infestation."

"Brewster, what did they do to you?"

"It's cool. Come on in, Jere. Let's hang in the lab where the light's better," says 3D Brewster.

He points the way and Prior proceeds down the hallway into a lit opening, keeping an eye on both faces.

Behind him, he hears 2D Brewster complaining, "He is not with us. He seeks to ruin! Mod will not stand for this."

"You're harshing the room, dude," says 3D Brewster.

Brewster's lab is exactly as Prior remembers it. Prior spent many nights trying to decipher clues with Brewster about the origins of Etruscan vases, Monet paintings, Indian arrowheads, vacuum cleaners, whatever was trendy with the collectors at that time. Three black lab tables are set up in parallel, each lined with glass tubes, beakers, crude scales, and wooden bowls. On the walls are blackboards, each filled with unreadable chalk scrawls of gibberish in every color available. Words are circled multiple times and arrows point in dramatic arcs from one point to another. The curtainless window is stained with a brown scum.

"You used to be tidier," says Prior. He's trying to figure out how to approach this.

Brewster positions himself in from of the window, his smeared reflection creating the illusion of two additional heads, like a nightmare Medusa.

"I've had difficulty focusing lately," says 3D Brewster. 2D Brewster faces away, looking out the window. "Mod. They're still after me. Everywhere. Listening."

2D Brewster's head whips around and conks 3D Brewster, knocking 3D Brewster's head away. It makes a sound like two coconuts.

"Ah, this is treason!" says 2D Brewster. "Call the Mod Police. NanoGov! Get this Fringe, this murderer, out of my sight. He does not serve us."

Brewster's body, which is normal below the neck, from what Prior can tell, moves forward slightly. Brewster's right hand reaches for a small vial on the lab bench. He flips off the cork stopper with his thumb. Brewster's left hand grabs the vial, fighting him for temporary control of his body. With a practiced grace, Brewster's right arm shakes loose his left arm and brings the vial to his 3D mouth. Brewster drinks the vial's purple liquid like a tequila shot. Emitting a low growl, 2D Brewster's head expands in its square footage and wraps itself around the 3D head, hoping to force the liquid to come sloshing out of his mouth; plastic wrap trying to suffocate a grapefruit.

But it's too late. 3D Brewster has swallowed whatever was in that vial.

"I will report this insolence!" says 2D Brewster. "You can never truly..."

But that's all that 2D Brewster gets out. His neck shrinks at the collar bone, like a decaying vine, until it snaps off from Brewster's body. The detached 2D head and neck string begin to freely float through the air like a lost circus balloon.

"Sorry you have to see this," says 3D Brewster whose own neck has begun to take the dimensions and location of a Fringe neck.

Brewster takes the floating neck string and flings it towards his mouth. In one practiced move, he swallows the detached 2D Brewster head like a fruit rollup.

"Apologies. Strictly necessary," says Brewster, as if he accidentally belched in proper company.

"Alright," says Prior, trying not to make eye contact.

"And disagreeably temporary. That crotchety dude will be back shortly."

"What the hell, Brewster?" Prior thought about Brewster often when he was in Antigua. He hoped, as had many, that Brewster was the key to fighting the system and turning it over back to the people. Now, it looks like he can't even control his own body. Like he's suffered the ultimate home invasion.

"Despite what you must think," says Brewster, sitting down in an old chair, "no one did this to me. Experiments and science, Jere. It's what got us into this mess. That damn Ferri. Good riddance, I say. Science will get us out of this, man."

"You did this to yourself?"

"Looking for a cure. Now, obviously, I'm more motivated than ever. You see, I'm in constant pain and in fear that my Mod self will eventually pause from thinking about himself long enough to realize it's simple to completely take over the rest of me."

"And here I was looking for your help. What can I do?" says Prior.

"Should have stayed in Antigua where it's safe."

"Yeah, about that…"

"Better make it quick," says Brewster. "Our moon-faced friend is an impatient tenant. I can already feel him starting to bubble up."

"Jesus, Brewster. I'm so sorry."

"Empathy is in short supply around here, Jere, and refreshing to hear."

"I need to clear my name," says Prior, more nakedly that he cares to. "People still think…":

"Ah, the sanctity of your reputation. I guess things haven't changed all that much, have they, man?"

"Lachende said you helped him with a disguise so he could look like a Fringe. I need to get into Mod Police headquarters. Was wondering if you could outfit me with something."

Brewster stands up, adjusts his lab coat, and shuffles over to his blackboard of mumbo-jumbo. He stares at it, his eyes tracing the arrows and circled words.

"That's a lot of information you've divulged. A Fringe could get into serious trouble and pain if Mod found out what he was up to," says Brewster, his back to Prior.

Prior spies the exit and thinks he can make the lab door before Brewster could reach him. Worst-case scenario, Prior could jump out the window, although he's not looking forward to crashing through thick glass.

"Sorry to have wasted your time," says Prior, slowly advancing towards the exit.

"Don't be ridiculous," says Brewster, turning around. He's still 3D Brewster and Prior finds it odd that this sight is comforting. "I'm just asking you to be careful. Also, this never gets traced back to me."

Brewster opens a drawer in one of his desks, reaches in, and throws Prior a small packet. Prior looks inside the open packet. A stick of gum.

"For trucking in," says Brewster.

"Thanks, pal. What can I do for you?" says Prior.

"Go back to Antigua, for starters," says Brewster. There is a pained look on his face. He holds his stomach, looking sicker by the second. "My roommate is pulling up to the driveway. He's gonna crash here soon."

"I can't leave you like this."

"Careful, Jere. You don't know. There's a gathering. A threat more horrible…"

Brewster doubles over and crashes onto his knees.

"Brewster…"

"Go!" says Brewster, his voice muffled, his neck already shifting over, elongating, making room for 2D Brewster.

Prior runs to the exit.

Behind him, he hears 2D Brewster growl, "Hey Prior, tell Felice and Molly I say hello!"

Chapter 16

Mod Police headquarters squats in the middle of what used to be 52nd Street in midtown Manhattan. It is a solid cube, about three stories tall, made of poured concrete. There are thin slits of windows that run vertically along each of the four sides. The only door is on the Broadway side, an old wooden door that is clearly meant for bringing in Fringe for torture or interrogation.

A block away, in a dark alley, Prior pops Brewster's stick of gum into his mouth. As he chews, he carefully studies his reflection in a puddle. The chewing gum goes into his system and the nanos are instantly activated, emanating from his skin pores. They create a coat around Prior, effectively acting as a specific prism, bending light around him, allowing him to pass for Mod if you aren't looking too closely. While he maintains his weight and heft, his outer appearance changes to the perception of two-dimensional. Prior isn't sure how long the effect lasts.

Prior is making an educated guess. He's hoping that certain Mod Police members go undercover as Fringe to infiltrate and gather information about the Fringe slave population. He is betting everything on this because if he's wrong, his capture is assured and the penalty seems incalculable. At best, he would be sent back to Antigua to be a Mod slave. He hopes Antoine and his people got out unscathed.

He approaches the Fringe entrance to Mod Police headquarters. No self-respecting Mod would ever go through a Fringe entrance when they can flit through the more dignified Mod slots on the building. But Mod Police, disguised undercover as a Fringe, would still go through these doors to keep up appearances. It's part of their weird cosplay fetish.

Prior dances lightly through the door and the nano-security clicks on. Nanos surround him, swirling as they look for anything suspicious. This is when Prior realizes how much faith he has placed in poor, mad Brewster.

The nanos dissipate, unalarmed. Prior figures the nanos are rarely suspicious. Fringe would never dare infiltrate a Mod building. Prior continues to saunter with all the confidence of Mod. He proceeds down a hallway, looking for a sign to the Records Room.

"What are you supposed to be?" says a gruff voice behind him.

Prior turns around calmly, trying to take on an arrogant air. The gruff voice belongs to a Mod who has taken on the facade of an old, burly sailor with a bushy mustache. In earlier days, he'd be fighting Popeye for Olive Oyl's hand.

The Mod Police are mostly men, mostly re-living their childhood of playing cops and robbers. They don't stay with the job too long since it's more of a hobby or vacation to fight boredom. Since the general populace has been coaxed into submission, there is hardly a need for a real police force. Not when you have nanos to do all the actual work.

"Just turned in a gang of Fringe. Couldn't wait to get the stupid Fringe costume off me," says Prior. "How the hell do they do it? All that weight. It's exhausting."

"I hear ya," says Bluto and floats away.

Prior takes a deep breath and increases his pace. The sooner he gets out of here, the better. He jogs up a flight of stairs and spots a map of the building. The Records Room is on this level and he makes his way down the mirrored hall. Mod can't get enough of their image and even in a dismal concrete office building, where Mod slum and pretend to be blue-collar workers, their vanity is precious to them.

He struggles with the Mod image of himself. His features have been flattened as if a steamroller has driven over him. His flaws have been pressed out and he looks better than he has in years. He's healthy, strong, and youthful. He begins to see the appeal.

Prior arrives at the Records Room and tries to slip in between the razor-thin slit of the door and door jamb. He bumps against the door. He reminds himself he's not actually Mod, just a lumpy Fringe. His mindset has changed too fast, his brain too accepting of his perceived new reality. He needs to make himself scarce quickly.

He opens the door and lets himself in. Prior tries to keep his cool. No one's around and there are no nanos scanning him here. He figures no Fringe would ever dare come into the Records Room unescorted. Cameras perceive a Mod has entered and that may be enough to get him the time he needs. He'll worry about his escape later.

The Records Room is a windowless space with two major compartments. There are rows of file cabinets and rows of computer terminals. Prior sits down at a terminal and enters some preliminary access information. He enters some passwords from his old police force days that still work. The arrogance of Mod are their greatest weakness.

He spots a loose nano paper clip and sticks it in his pocket. This technology is hard to come by. Mod just leave this tech lying around.

He quickly does a search. After a few minutes, he locates a small video file. It's old surveillance footage; grainy, black-and-white. Prior takes another look around to make sure no one has spotted him.

He clicks play. The video, a few seconds long, has been entered as evidence of Jeremiah Prior's innocence for the murder of his partner, Richard Feynman. The video shows Prior and Penny, leaving a cheap motel together. It's night and raining hard. The two of them look happy, holding hands, running down the street, protecting their heads from the onslaught of rain. Feynman, hidden at first in a nearby alley, walks into view and follows them. The video stops and Prior plays it again, searching for any additional clues or details.

Prior checks the video's date: about a week before Feynman was killed and Felice left him. NanoGov and the Mod Police must know that Prior is innocent. There's motive for Feynman to kill Prior, not the other way around. Prior wonders why they're suppressing this information.

The Records Room door opens. Prior bolts up and heads towards the door. He encounters a Mod disguised as a Fringe, wearing a 1940s-era police uniform. Prior doesn't look the Mod in the eyes, just keeps on walking past him. They nod to each other, as if they're both on secret missions.

He feels his disguise slipping away, the effect dissipating. Prior walks confidently and leaves Mod Police headquarters still looking like one of them. Inside, he's all sweat. He doesn't know how long this Mod disguise will last but he's starting to feel ill from the effects.

He runs hard, making his way to a small alley adjacent to a ruined building. There, he covers himself with some old cardboard and wooden pallets. In this little fort, he can't be seen and won't be questioned by the Mod or Fringe as to what he's doing in the slums.

Though he gets thirsty, he stays under his shelter the entire night. He sleeps fitfully, dreaming of palm trees and warm sand beaches. When he awakes the next morning, it's cold and dry. He shifts a pallet aside and looks at his hand in the gray morning light. It's three-dimensional and most of him is happy to be his old self again.

Chapter 17

Prior trudges back to his office. The nanos have left his sluggish body sapped of energy, like a used battery.

"You look swell," says Penny as he enters his office.

"Rough night," he says, plopping down at his cardboard desk. "I'd give anything for a cup of good coffee. Listen, you said you had information about your husband's case."

"I don't know why you hold onto your precious reputation."

"It's all I have," says Prior.

Penny's shoulders drop a bit. She's holding onto the little red purse Sanders gave her, rubbing it nervously as if a genie might emerge. "You never asked me about Molly."

"I know," says Prior. "Not sure if I'm ready to…"

"Molly ain't with her mom anymore," she says. "Moved out a while ago. I tracked her address." She hands him a frayed slip of paper.

"What would I do without you," says Prior, immediately regretting his words.

"Beats me," says Penny. "I'll go see about that coffee." She heads to the door. She's got her hand on the doorknob. Before she turns it, she throws him an anguished stare.

"What?" says Prior.

"What did you find out?"

"I'll tell you what I haven't figured out," says Prior, rubbing his temples. "Why you asked me to come back. The Feynman case should be closed but it's not."

He stands up and approaches her. She leans on the door.

"What's your game here?" he says.

Penny looks tormented, the truth trying to escape but getting caught in her throat.

"Come on, Penny."

"I just wanted to see you, okay? Is that so horrible? I just wanted you and I..."

She runs out, slamming the door behind her.

No matter how sophisticated the world gets, women like Penny will be his ruin.

There's an electric hum in the room. Prior swivels to discover a 1960s-era television console sitting majestically in the corner of Prior's office. Its exterior shines with its mahogany polished luster. The twelve-inch screen displays a black-and-white test pattern. As soon as Prior takes a step towards it, the screen switches to a black-and-white soap opera that is already in progress.

Prior looks around but there are no nanos or Mod Police swarming in. He plants himself in front of the TV like a child, legs crossed. He squints and gets a better view of the fuzzy image.

On the screen, two figures are making out on the couch in Prior's old apartment. Close-up of the door slowly opening, letting in enough light to identify the kissing figures on the couch: Felice and Feynman. Prior enters the room, followed by Penny as the dramatic music picks up pace. The four of them argue but the sound is muffled. Smash cut of a hand picking up a lamp. Penny strikes Prior on the back of the head with the lamp. Prior goes down, crashing on the floor hard. A gunshot rings out and Feynman hits the floor, dead. Dramatic music gets louder. Closeup of a smoking gun. Pull back to reveal Penny holding the gun. Felice runs out of the room screaming. Penny plants the gun on an unconscious Prior and runs out the door. The screen changes to the soap opera title card, "The Authentic Detective." An announcer says, "Exonerating evidence of Jeremiah Prior's innocence brought to you by Lachende and undoctored NanoGov's records. Good to the last drop." The screen fades to black and the TV disappears. In its place is a small video drive.

Prior pockets the drive. Lachende always did have a flair for the dramatic.

In the afternoon, Prior heads back out to the streets. The Sky-Screen is broadcasting another story about the Fringe terrorist who has been plaguing NanoGov. The newscaster tries to put a positive spin on the story, claiming that this is a NanoGov operation meant to test their inherently perfect system and make it more perfect. But Prior sees through the bullshit. This terrorist has them worried. And the havoc that the terrorist is causing must be so great as to be obvious. Otherwise, Sky-Screen wouldn't be reporting it.

Molly's neighborhood is one of the nicer ones in the city. Her street is lined with brownstones from two centuries ago. The Sky-Screen is re-running some old movie from last century. The back-and-white images flicker over the cobbled neighborhood in an arm-wrestling contest of nostalgia.

Some Fringe attempt weak smiles as they pass Prior on the morning sidewalk. The sunlit old neighborhood puts Prior in a comfortable mood immediately. Maybe, thinks Prior, Molly's acquired a similar taste for antiques. Then it occurs to Prior that the neighborhood, the old movie, the morning sun, the slight breeze in the air: it's all a form of sedation.

Prior arrives at Molly's building and takes a flight of stairs up. He quietly walks down a dimly lit hallway, smoothing down his hair. He knocks on Molly's door and a flush of nervousness washes over him. What if she still doesn't want to see him? He's not sure that he wants to know the answer. Without knocking a second time or giving her the chance to come to the door, he pivots towards the exit.

Molly's next-door neighbor cracks open the door and pokes her head out. She is on the early side of middle age. Around nineteen. Molly's age. She's pretty in an impoverished way with long, stringy hair that she twirls around her finger. Prior spies something that glistens through her forest of hair. It peeks out while she pulls up her hair in a twirl.

"Who are you?" she says, nodding her head toward Molly's door.

"No one."

"She ain't here," she says, trying to put on a brave front.

"Molly?"

"Yeah, Molly. She ain't here. Who are you?"

"I'm..." Prior thinks about a response. It's tricky. In Antigua, whenever someone asked about his daughter, he always had a ready answer. It's not so simple here. "I'm an old friend."

"Ain't we all."

"I mean to say, I represent a Mod of some influence who would very much like to dialogue with Molly."

"Yeah? What about?"

This is going nowhere. Then, like a lucky dice roll, he comes up with a plan and everything is sevens again. Prior pulls out his badge.

"I'll tell you what the concern here is. It's about those gold hoop earrings you're wearing. Don't bother covering them with your hair. They've been witnessed by present company. And you can be assured that if I chanced upon them..."

"I told you I don't know."

"Fine. Tell me," says Prior, "where did you manage to locate the technology that would hide gold earrings?"

"Jesus, don't tell no one about these. I shouldn't even be wearing them."

"You have my word. But how have you kept them hidden from Mod?"

"Veiling tech. From Molly, actually. I think she got the tech from her mom."

"You'll let me know when Molly is back?"

"Promise you won't tell nobody?"

"Of course."

"I don't even know who you are," she says as Prior heads down the hallway.

"Someone to be trusted," he says without turning around. "I'll send a kid around in a few days."

"Right, like I've heard that before. Shit." She closes her door with a disheartened thud. The interview is over as quickly as it started.

Prior walks down the stairwell. He understands her apprehension. He gets back on the streets. When he's a block away from his office, he spots a small bonfire burning in the middle of the street. Fringe are gathered around for warmth. Prior cranes his neck and squints.

Standing in front of the fire is Grainger and his two torpedoes. Lachende/Strutsky is nowhere in sight.

"Grainger," says Prior. "If I didn't know any better, I'd say you were following me. You got a little school-girl crush?"

The torpedoes laugh until Grainger shoots them a look.

"Coming back and showing your face in this city," says Grainger. "Like I said, museum-quality balls."

The torpedoes laugh again, this time rumbling in a way that strikes Prior as rehearsed. Grainger lets them go on. They move towards Prior in a manner that suggests menace. The torpedoes crowd him. Grainger keeps his distance.

"Prior, you want to tell me how you got away from my rookie?" says Grainger.

"Question you have to ask yourself," says Prior, "is where's Strutsky now? Undependable. Not like these guys."

"Detective, you want I should..." says Torpedo No. 1.

Prior turns to him. "You want to dance?" says Prior, giving the torpedo a hug. "Is that why you're getting so close?"

The torpedo takes an awkward step back. Grainger chuckles. "You're still a freaky little anomaly," says Grainger. The torpedoes gather behind Grainger, glad to be away from Prior. "So what are you doing here?"

"I heard they were having a butt-ugly contest," says Prior. "I concede victory."

"What'd I tell you boys?" says Grainger. "This guy precious or what?" He waves his boys to cross the street.

"Follow me," says Grainger. "Pretty please."

They walk across into a bar. It's crowded but quiet. There's a fire burning inside the bar as well. The torpedoes go to the counter, leaving their boss alone. The fire blows smoke between Prior and Grainger. Grainger tries not to cough as the smoke swirls around his face like a gray mane. Grainger moves his chair and sits down next to Prior. Prior keeps his hand in his pocket, where he's holding the Fringe cop badge he swiped from one of the torpedoes during his hug.

"Listen, asshole, I've been watching you. So have my men. Ever since you walked out of that tunnel. Shit, you're here a couple days, Ferri's gone missing, the world's in a panic. I already got the Mod Police chewing me up about some Fringe who got melted in the middle of the street. Guy just got devoured. What the hell is that? Coincidence?"

"What's on your mind, Detective Grainger?"

Years ago, when Prior was on the force and working with Grainger, they were on a stakeout. Around hour thirty, Grainger turned to Prior and told him he was in love with Prior's wife, Felice. Prior never forgave him for that.

"It's like this, Prior," says Grainger. "I don't trust the fact that you used to work for Mod."

"I think you have me confused with you."

"Yeah, you worked for Mod," says Grainger. "Mister antiquarian detective. Mister Authentician. They hired you to find stuff for them. Anything."

"I never..." says Prior.

"Yeah, you were hired by some Fringe middleman but follow the money. It was Mod all the way. And when you were hired by Fringe, it was to get their stuff sold so they could get the money and convert to Mod. It stinks all the way. And you, a former cop."

"I don't remember your chest being so big. You've got a lot to get off it tonight."

"Prior, you used to turn in Fringe. Our own kind. Fuck that."

"Bullshit."

It isn't.

"Yeah," says Grainger, "you're a regular angel. Well, I'm keeping an eye on you. We got orders. Guy kills his partner, next thing you know..."

"You've seen the video, the evidence. You know I didn't kill him."

"Maybe. You see Felice?" says Grainger, softly.

"Good night, Grainger."

Unbelievably, the air smells worse outside. Prior walks fast, not knowing where. Just trying to shake this guilty feeling away.

He doesn't like where Grainger's line of questioning was going.

Prior hears echoing footsteps behind him in the shadows. He's being followed. Grainger isn't kidding. He has a tail on him. As he turns the corner, Prior spins his head back and catches a glimpse of the tail. It's Addison Simpson.

Prior turns to confront the guy but he's gone. All that's there to meet his eye is a decimated city street.

The next morning, Prior takes a stroll to the outskirts of the city. He doesn't think anyone is following him. He cases the old stables to make sure they're not under surveillance. Unless you're on Fringe animal-hunting detail, most Fringe don't use the horse-and-carriage mode of transportation anymore since everything they need are contained within a three-block radius. And Fringe working for Mod Police eventually find it cumbersome to include horses among their ranks.

Prior always liked the horse-and-carriage life. He had his own horse, Gluestick, back in the day, which he took great pride and pleasure in training. Besides Feynman and Lachende, Gluestick was his unofficial partner. Feynman and Prior made modifications to the horse. Nothing illegal, just the kind of thing that nano-equine technology allowed at the time.

Prior reaches the stables. A lone Fringe stable boy is gently bringing hay to some of the horses in the corral. Prior doesn't see Gluestick among them. Behind the corral, there's an old red barn with its doors closed. Inside, waiting in storage, is Prior's old carriage.

"Skippy," whispers Prior from behind the fence.

The stable boy stops what he's doing and glances over at Prior's direction. He has a knot of red, patchy hair and matching freckles.

Prior waves his arms. "Skippy."

Skippy squints his eyes. "Mr. Prior?" His voice has changed since Prior saw him last but he hasn't grown an inch.

"Hey, Skippy, how've you been?"

Skippy drops the hay and runs over, suddenly filled with energy. "Geez, Mr. Prior. I never thought I'd see you again. Last I heard…"

"Yeah, kid, it's probably all true."

"You here for Gluestick?"

"And my carriage. How are they doing?"

"Doing fine. I told you I'd take care of them. Everything is just like you left it."

Prior chuckles out loud. "Yeah, Skippy, I guess everything is."

"How's Molly?" says Skippy in an octave lower than four years ago.

"Look, the arrangement was I leave you some money, you take care of my stuff. Just show me to Gluestick."

The stables are more weather-beaten but otherwise look the same. The faded red paint on the stable's exterior still reminds Prior of better days.

The horse is a magnificent animal. He recognizes Prior instantly. His brown-red mane blows in the wind like royalty as he dances over to get a whiff of Prior. Skippy brings over some brushes and Prior grooms Gluestick for a few minutes. These solid, real things feel good and make Prior wonder why anyone would give up such simple pleasures.

"Just like you left him," says Skippy, entering the stable. "It wasn't easy. I mean, with Mod and everything."

"Thanks, kid. It means the world to me."

"Are you back because of Molly?"

Skippy always had a thing for her. Prior found it cute at the time. That was back in the day when Skippy was just a kid. Now, he's old enough to make a play for his daughter. Just like Lachende.

"I'm here looking up an old case," says Prior.

"You mean Mr. Feynman and the whole…"

"You're still quick, Skippy," say Prior, grooming Gluestick. The horse appears thrilled to be getting this kind of attention.

"You know, Mr. Prior, the news reports about what happened with you and Mr. Feynman, they got redacted and twisted. That's my opinion, anyway. It's hard to believe anything that was reported. One day, they said you were guilty, the next they said you were innocent. I never believed you did anything."

"Thanks kid, but the problem is I should've stayed here and done something about it."

"Molly's doing fine," says Skippy, putting down his brushes.

Prior puts down his brushes and leans on the horse. "You know, Skippy, when I said look after my things, I just meant Gluestick."

"Oh, you'd never have to pay me to keep an eye on Molly."

"Great. Well, I'll be back for Gluestick shortly," says Prior.

He pats Skippy on the back and walks off.

"Oh, Mr. Prior, I almost forgot. Letter came for you yesterday. I thought it was the strangest thing but I guess that's why the Letter-Writer gets paid for what he does."

He hands Prior a slip of paper. Prior is suspicious. He shouldn't have come here. He doesn't want Skippy mixed up with any of this.

It's a message from Belden, Prior's old Professor. He's invited Prior to his house for a social visit. Prior has never felt more popular. He should have become a refugee years ago.

Chapter 18

"You again," says Wild Finnegan's water-monger, remembering Prior's face and attitude. It's late and the bar is crowded.

Prior's decides to pay his visit to Belden tomorrow. For now, he's got something he needs to clear up besides his reputation. Prior sent a Fringe messenger kid to Molly's place earlier and the neighbor girl with the earrings sent a note back saying that Molly might be at this bar.

"I'll ask you for the last time," says Prior, his voice a growl. He's tired of going around in circles in this goddamn world. "Molly Prior."

"Who wants to know?" says the water-monger. He's defensive, trying to save face. Or his bar. Or Molly.

"Calm down, I'm her father."

"Her father? Her father's dead. Who the hell are you, mac?"

"Well, pal," says Prior. "The nanos must have figured out a way to make zombies."

"More jokes. Like I should trust the guy hanging around with Fringe cops."

Prior pulls out the badge he took off Grainger's torpedo. "Authentician Detective Prior," says Prior. "You want to keep arguing? This badge says I can shut you down if I want. Now, where is she?"

"Okay, okay. Jeez," says the water-monger, suddenly all smiles and good will. "Can't a guy have a little fun with his clientele?"

"Take the rust out of the water. That'll make them happy. Where is she?"

The water-monger sighs, defeated, hating the system, hating that even in this illegal, underground water barrel, he gets harassed by bureaucracy. "Saw her go into the back alley little while ago. Through the back door."

Prior walks through the bar towards the back alley. Before he went into private practice, he was a member of the Fringe police and had seen plenty of bad situations like the one he's walking into now. Only then, it wasn't his daughter. Prior swallows hard but it's more the memories than the water that leaves a bitter taste in his mouth.

The back of the bar is completely dark. Whatever is back here, no one is interested in seeing it by candlelight. He fumbles like a nervous teenager at a make-out party and feels around for the backdoor. Then he traces his fingers for the wooden latch.

Illuminated by the moon, the back alley is a thin strip of space between the bar and the next building. It looks different from earlier when Lachende escorted him here. The alley can't be more than five feet wide. Out of instinct, Prior's training kicks in and he checks out his escape options. One end of the alleyway is blocked off by a pile of gray cinder blocks. If the Mod Police show up, he'll be trapped with no escape. These alleys are famous for two things: illicit object trades and couples making out. Either one doesn't thrill Prior.

The alley is relatively empty. A few Fringe couples are making out but none look like they could be Molly. Maybe she isn't here. The bar door slips out of Prior's grip and slams shut. It's locked. His escape options are diminishing by the minute.

Prior's head turns towards the alley's dead end when he hears a scraping sound. The gray dead-end wall of the alleyway is rotating, the gray chunks of cinderblock pushing against the ground courtesy of some unseen mechanics. The grinding noise makes Prior's teeth chatter. As the cinderblock wall rotates, light filters through, revealing someone behind it.

A stone curtain is lifted, revealing Molly.

She's taller than he remembers, less baby fat. But there is no mistaking her. Molly's bobbed hairstyle is the same as when she was a child. He catches glimpses of her pretty face, obscured by the charcoal wall and the light. Like her mother's face. It's a feeling bitter and warm at the same time. It usually takes a few drinks for Prior to feel this way. That's why he mostly drank in Antigua.

Molly has her arms around the gray wall, clutching it for balance, groping it, her fingers widespread, occasionally caressing the rough surfaces, like she's rock-climbing. She's oblivious to the outside world. Prior wants to interrupt her, to protect her. At the same time, he wants her to remain oblivious to the outside world. Maybe by the time she lets go of the wall, the world will have changed for the better.

Prior squints his eyes. The wall shimmers, losing its heft. Prior suddenly realizes she's not holding onto a wall. She's making out with a Mod. Prior still isn't acclimated to Mod translucence, human and solid from straight on, but absent in profile. Prior sprints through the alley towards Molly while plunging his hand into his backpack.

"Molly, get out of the way!" says Prior.

She jerks her head back from the Mod and her eyes bug.

The Mod, whose nanos have supplied him with a two-dimensional gray trench coat, spins around like a dreamcatcher to see which Fringe has the audacity to interrupt his make-out session.

Prior whips out the Framer. He clicks the red button and throws it like a disk. Instantly, the Framer pops open into a large square perimeter that resembles an old picture frame. It spins fast and straight towards the Mod who doesn't have time to react. The Mod's nanos have grown lazy, not aware they can act as security as well. In this world, they've never needed to. The Mod is not used to being accosted. They've given up everything for their luxurious life and sacred entitlements.

The Framer grows in dimension as it spins towards the Mod. Instead of hitting the Mod square in the face, where it was heading, the Framer takes a ninety-degree turn upwards, momentarily hovers over the Mod, then plunges down around his body, threading him like a needle. By the time the Framer hits the ground, the Mod is trapped inside the frame, the canvas of his body stretched tight and caught on all four sides.

Prior makes a mental note to thank Penny later.

The Framer is effective but temporary. The Mod just needs enough time to calm down and re-arrange his nanos in order to break loose. Nanos are quick studies, having an intense self-survival mode after being threatened. Of course they do; they were designed by Ferri, a human. Prior doesn't want to be around long enough to witness the Mod get out of the Framer.

"Dad, just what the hell do you think…"

"Dad?" says the Mod in a muffled voice. His features are out of proportion, like an earlier century's funhouse mirror. "Prior?"

Prior turns back to Molly. "This guy knows me?"

"It's Lachende, you asshole," she says, storming off, lighting a cigarette. She takes a deep drag, exhaling as she walks down the alley, the smoke accentuating the growing distance between them.

"Prior? Little help here?" says Lachende, a living painting in the frame.

Prior leans down and picks up the frame. It's light. Mod don't weigh anything. Prior proceeds to the other end of the alley, holding onto the framed Lachende. Molly waits for them, her foot tapping on the dirty ground.

"Put him down," says Molly to Prior.

Prior holds up the frame to his face. "Lachende," says Prior. "What the hell?"

"Sorry, Prior, needed some time with Molly." His voice is muffled.

"Goddamn Mod," says Prior.

"Goddamn jerk," says Lachende.

Molly laughs. Despite the situation, her laughter sounds great to Prior.

Prior pushes the button on the Framer. Lachende pours out of the frame like melted plastic. He hits the ground, spreads out, and begins twisting himself into the size of a small cord. He's wringing himself dry of whatever touched him. Then, he stretches himself back into human proportion.

"Oh Mod, that's better," says Lachende.

"Now, you want to tell me what you're doing with my daughter?"

"Whoa, whoa," says Molly. "I don't see you for four years and you think you have the right..."

"Molly, kiddo, I'm sorry, but..."

"Don't kiddo me," says Molly.

For all the years he's imagined reuniting with Molly, Prior doesn't know what to say. He turns to Lachende.

"I'll walk Molly home," says Lachende.

"I'll walk her home, thank you," says Prior.

Molly shakes her head. Prior thinks it's a good sign that she doesn't tell him to go to hell. Maybe, inside, she's curious about what happened to him. Maybe she misses her Dad. Maybe she's just hurt. Maybe she told him to go to hell and he didn't hear.

"I can walk home by myself," says Molly.

"You look rough, Prior," says Lachende. "Not even a thank you for helping you solve your case and clear your name?" says Lachende.

"It's not clear yet," says Prior.

"So, what, I'm not good enough for your daughter?" says Lachende.

"Don't talk about me that way," says Molly.

"Because I have a job," says Lachende.

"Yeah, undercover for Grainger?" says Prior.

"He's worse than you told me," says Molly to Lachende. She won't look Prior in the eyes.

Prior turns to Molly. "You knew I was here?"

Lachende steps between them. "Hey, Prior, lay off."

"Big man," says Prior, taking a step towards him.

"Lachende is a Mod-Dreamer," says Molly.

"What?" says Prior.

"Multi-tasker," says Lachende, shrugging his shoulders.

"Jesus, you couldn't figure out a way to make a better living than being a Mod-Dreamer? After all I taught you?"

After the Mod population became the majority on the planet, Mod quickly grew bored with the endless shopping and activities their limited minds could conceive. They were all dressed up with nowhere to go. Fringe that exhibited a creative streak were turned to Mod-Dreamers. Over time, there was a huge demand for Mod-Dreamers. Their job was to dream up new and exciting things for Mod to do to avoid boredom. Mod-Dreamers created aspirations, goods, settings, causes, adventures, vacations, and fantasies so Mod could spend their days in luxury. In exchange, these Fringe were eventually granted Modhood.

"It's the best I could do," says Lachende. "But the thing that makes it all worthwhile is Molly."

"I don't want to hear it," says Prior, looking at Molly.

She looks like she's trying to adjust to this major intrusion and development. Deciding how to play it. She flicks her cigarette against the wall, turns, and heads down the alley alone. Prior follows her, unsure of what to say when he catches up. This is not how he imagined it would be.

"Prior," says Lachende. "Let's get together soon."

Prior looks back at him. "You won't tell your Mod friends I'm here, will you?" Prior says.

"They already know about it."

"Just stay away from my daughter."

"That's what I always liked about you, Prior. You're so old-fashioned." Lachende floats away into the night.

Prior walks alongside Molly. She doesn't acknowledge him. They proceed in the awkward silence through the empty streets. The moonlight floods the city, giving their night shadows a particular intensity. Even in this light, Prior's drab clothes form a striking contrast to the yellow and blue jacket that Molly wears. She leans forward slightly as she walks, hands deep in her pockets.

Prior tries to steal a glance to see what Molly looks like up close. Every few steps, he catches her doing the same with him. Just as he's gathering up courage to begin a conversation with her, a Fringe messenger boy runs up to them, out of breath.

"Jeremiah Prior?" says the messenger boy. He can't be more than seven.

Prior gives the kid a nod. The kid waits around while Prior reads the note.

"Prior, message from F. (can't believe she still had this address). She wants you to call her back right away. It sounded important so I figured I'd find you. Penelope."

Prior takes out a pencil and writes his reply on the back of the note.

"Penny, tell Felice whatever it is, the answer is no. Prior."

He gives the note back to the kid. The kid runs off, doing his job.

"What the hell was that about?" says Molly.

"Like I never left."

"And the first thing you did was come and embarrass me. How sweet."

"So," says Prior. "You and Lachende."

"Yeah."

"You thinking about turning Mod? Because that's the only way…"

"Maybe."

Prior doesn't like where this is going. But he doesn't want to drag out his soapbox.

"Look, Molly…"

"You go to hell. Why did you come back?"

Prior wants to tell her. But he also wants to have her forget the past and accept him right here and now.

They're at the edge of what used to be a park. Molly walks to an old wooden bench that faces some distant fire. Prior sits alongside her and she doesn't wince.

She looks at him for the first time with genuine interest. "Seriously, Mom said you were living in the Caribbean."

"What about you, Molly? How have you been?"

119

"Let's stay on you," says Molly. "My life's a little complicated now and I'm not sure I'm ready to tell you about it yet."

"Okay."

Molly's eyes shift past him to the middle distance. Her pupils dilate. "Dad, we gotta go."

She bolts up and takes off to the park's edge. Prior runs after her. She dives into some bushes and Prior lands next to her.

"What is it?" whispers Prior.

But Prior doesn't need a response. He hears the thundering drum of horse hooves on the packed dirt, the yells of an invading army. As the dozens of armed, bare-chested warriors ride through the park, chasing helpless Fringe, Prior adjusts his eyes. He's witnessing a Hun army. The poor Fringe have been made to dress like Romans and Visigoths, circa 450 A.D., in the Western Roman province of Gaul. The riders, possibly made up of two or three actual Mod, wear fur hats and wield their horse's reins in one hand and a brandished sword in the other. They are having the time of their lives. To them, it's just a way to kill a few hours.

Molly jumps out of the bushes before Prior can grab a hold of her. She reaches into her jacket pocket and removes two marbles, each the color of polished steel. She rolls them on the ground in front of her. One marble rolls a few feet while the other gains momentum, rolling another thirty feet before stopping. The moment the second marble stops, a blue beam of light flashes from each marble, connecting them right in front of the passing army. The blue light beam expands upwards until it instantly creates a large rectangle, a screen of light.

Molly gives a guttural yell as the Fringe pass unharmed through the blue screen. The Mod rear up their nano-horses, as their danger sensors start to blare. One nano-horse is too slow and passes through the blue screen, unable to stop. There is a sizzling sound and on the other side of the screen, nothing but mist. The nanos have been destroyed.

The Mod scream. They call back their remaining nanos, take on their sail-like forms, and evaporate into the sky.

"Just you come back here again, motherfuckers!" yells Molly. The Fringe shake their heads, disoriented at the evening's happenings. They skulk off into the darkness.

Molly approaches the marbles and kicks them with her toe. They don't move. "Spent. Damn." She walks past Prior, who looks at her in disbelief. "Well, you're not the only one with cool toys," she says.

She stands in silence for a few minutes, looking up at the Sky-Screen. Prior is amazed that the Mod Police haven't arrived to report her. She walks back to the park bench, seeming to be mildly annoyed by the disruption.

"Not that any of my shenanigans have any effect," she says, more to herself.

"Of course they do."

"Now, Nano-Ethics, that's where the action is," she says. "But you wouldn't…"

Prior sits next to her and puts his arms around her shoulder. She brushes it off.

Too soon.

Chapter 19

Prior stands outside the grand mansion, stamping his feet in the cold. Its scale is completely out of proportion to its surrounding and time. Composed of variegated gray and red stone, the mansion radiates craftsmanship and foreign laborers imported exclusively for this construction. The cost of the turrets alone would feed African Fringe for a month. But, as large and impressive a structure as it is, the silence gives it away. A place like this requires dozens of servants if it's real.

Prior approaches the massive oak front door. A small water nozzle pokes out from the ivy plant hanging from the front porch. The nozzle swivels towards him in a jerky manner and releases an aerosol mist. The mist, light purple in shade, swirls momentarily at Prior's eye level before streaming up his nose in a quick swoosh.

The mansion security-nanos take a few seconds to complete their interrogation through his body. This must be exciting for the nanos. They probably don't get many Fringe visitors here. The nanos finish scanning him for rogues. Having detected nothing, they escape through his skin pores and fly away, descending as a fine mist onto a garden gnome.

The great entry door swings open by itself. Prior enters the elaborate foyer as the door quietly closes behind him. The long hallway that greets him is no substitute for a butler or doorman. There's a shiny, silken red rug that Prior follows down the longest hallway he's ever walked. At the end of the hallway is a faint light that gets brighter as he approaches. He figures he crosses over two zip codes in the process. The hallway spills into an opulent drawing room.

Inside, the mansion's owner, looking round and prosperous, luxuriates on a circa 1767 Chippendale wing chair.

"Detective Prior. Welcome." His jovial voice sounds familiar, as if Prior were still attending his 18th and 19th-century history class. "You're looking so...what's the word I want...well, there you are." The mansion's owner lets out a puff of smoke from his 1828 mahogany pipe.

"Professor Belden."

"Professor," says Belden in a manner that implies nostalgia. "Retired now for three years. Tell me, Detective Prior, would you say retirement agrees with me?"

Prior advances into the room, walking its perimeter, taking in the sights. "What's with all this 'Detective' stuff?"

"Aren't you here on official police business?" says Belden. "Oh, please say you are. Vintage film noir flatfoot stuff, circa 1940s. How delightful."

"I'm not official police."

"Still, my question remains unanswered," says Belden.

"Which is?"

"How. Do. I. Look?"

"Like you're five minutes away from losing one of your dimensions," says Prior.

"Oh, from your mouth to Mod's ear," says Belden, drawing a fat grin.

"Somehow, I don't think you're joking," says Prior, sitting down on a wing chair opposite Belden.

"You must tell me of your island voodoo gods."

"Haven't you heard?" says Prior, crossing his legs. "Nanos are the new religion."

"You of all people, Jere, have to admit that God is an antiquated concept." Belden takes a long, satisfied drag on his pipe. "Still, religious artifacts make a tremendous addition to one's collection."

There is a lot about Belden that has changed. When Prior attended his class years ago, Belden was open-minded and believed that everyone deserved a square shake.

"Now you're going to tell me I'm not making any sense," says Belden.

"What doesn't make sense is an Authentician who still believes," says Prior. "And a Fringe Professor who doesn't."

Belden's pudgy hand takes the pipe out of his mouth. He places it on the brass ashtray and reaches into the folds of his coat. He pulls out a golden pocket watch and opens it.

"Still, the life of Mod is nothing to sneeze at," says Belden.

"I wouldn't know. By the looks of this place, you'll find out soon enough."

"Now, Detective Prior, sorry, Jere, it just takes a force of will to let in the nanos and turn your crass three-dimensionality into the glorious life of Mod. So far, I've exhibited superior strength and will. Remarkably, I've resisted."

"It takes cash, Professor. Lots of sweaty cash in exchange for your soul."

"Don't forget the shopping. Oh, Jere, my dear, the shopping!" Belden's fingers do a little dance at the end of his chubby hands.

Prior gets up and pretends to observe the books on Belden's shelf. Prior doesn't appreciate this change in Belden. He was hoping Belden had remained pure and unpolluted. Prior's attention is caught by a small wood-framed glass case. Inside are dozens of thin glass vials. Prior has seen these before.

"Ah, you have an eye for glory," says Belden.

"Thermoplastics," says Prior.

"A little gift from our old colleague, Dr. Brewster," says Belden. "Now, don't look at me that way. Not all of us had the luxury of escaping life and heading to Aruba."

"Antigua."

"The point. You miss it."

"I don't think so," says Prior. "I'm curious why you called me."

Belden winds his watch and puts it away. "And Felice? Molly? How are all the Priors femme these days, Jere?" says Belden.

"Never mind all that."

"So, this is official business after all. Well," says Belden, sitting up. "How exciting. Are you going to rough me up?"

Belden stands up majestically and puts his thick arm around Prior in a grand manner. He leads Prior towards a side door that wasn't there a minute ago. It opens to the outdoors. A stretch limo and driver await them. The driver is probably real. The limo has to be nanos.

"What's with the ride?" says Prior.

"An engagement. You're my Plus One."

Prior considers the situation. He needs Belden's help, maybe more than he cares to admit.

"I have things to show you. You'll adore it," says Belden.

Belden piles into the backseat. After a moment of deliberation, Prior follows him into the limo. Belden beams, looking like there was never a moment's doubt in his mischievous little mind.

The limo drives past Belden's iron gates and onto the main road. It feels strange being in a motorized vehicle. It's been years.

"Now, without all your subterfuge and attitude, what can I do for you, hmm?" says Belden, still at play. "Chasing down another forger?"

"You heard about the stolen Vermeer?" says Prior, searching Belden's facial expressions for any clues. "Johannes Vermeer's 'Officer and a Laughing Girl?'"

"Awful," says Belden. "But stealing an actual painting these days? I mean, that's so last season. Now, stealing someone else's mass? Well, that's charmingly enticing. That I could understand. What's the world coming to?"

"You don't think Mod would kill to own the painting?"

"A Vermeer? Of course they would," says Belden. "But that doesn't detract from how gauche it would be."

They make a turn onto a minor road, heading out of the city and into the suburbs. Prior is used to being on foot or riding Gluestick. He's forgotten what a smooth ride feels like.

"Any leads?" says Belden.

"Maybe. Guy who I think stole it? He might be a friend of yours. Does the name Addison mean anything to you?"

"Detective Prior, surely you're not implying that I would know the whereabouts of the Vermeer? Or this Addison chap?"

"Implying nothing."

Belden shifts his body to face the window until his broad back is to Prior. He looks like a well-fed petulant child. As one aspires to more material things, there is always an intense developmental regression into solipsism. Classic pre-Mod behavior.

"You still dealing in black-market thermoplastics?" says Prior, tentatively.

"My collection? An old line of work. Your friend Brewster is the one to see about those things. How is the good doctor?"

"Divided on the subject of Mod."

Belden, dripping with good will, turns around to face Prior again. "So, tell me all about Antigua."

"You know why I left."

"Something to do with murder and adultery, one suspects," says Belden as if reciting the day's weather.

"Something like that."

"Your precious name," says Belden.

"Professor, you know you want to show it to me," says Prior, deciding to try another approach. "That's why you asked me here."

He waits for the silence to take over.

"Oh, very well. At your insistence," says Belden. "You always knew I could never keep a secret." He reaches into the folds of his jacket and pulls out a large leather wallet. "You of all people will simply relish this."

Delicately, Belden pulls out a small bit of cloth. He tugs on a small corner of the canvas. It pops open and unfurls, revealing Vermeer's "Officer and Laughing Girl." Prior scans it intensely. The pigment, the lines, the shadows. It's the real thing. It's magnificent.

"Oh, dear boy," says Belden, practically crowing. "Your facial expression says it all. I couldn't pay for a better independent authentication of this painting. My friend, I shall sleep deeply tonight knowing full well that this is the real McCoy."

"Where'd you get this? Addison?"

"Honestly," says Belden. He rolls up the painting and pinches a corner. The painting reduces to a small swatch again. He places it gingerly back into his wallet. "We all know Mod. So why not profit from such relationships?"

The limo pulls up to an old-fashioned brick-and-mortar elementary school. The three-story stately building is nestled within large trees and a mountain like it's snuggling a lover. Prior knows this isn't a regular school. Fringe kids growing up to be Fringe slaves aren't allowed formal education. They are too busy making a living as messenger kids. This is a school for future Mod.

"Another speaking engagement," says Belden. "History of nanos. Very informative."

"Quite a lifestyle you've carved out for yourself," says Prior.

"It's all a grand artifice. Inside beats the heart of a true patriot, my boy," says Belden in a tone that a deaf man would find false. "Never doubt my loyalty to le cause."

Once you get a taste for the good life, once every whim is satisfied, once you realize you no longer have to wallow in your squalor, it is impossible to have the integrity to go back. Hell, Prior isn't sure how he's stood it for so long. The trip to Mod Police headquarters disguised as a Mod was enough to give him a taste.

The driver opens the back door of the limo and they proceed into the school. A school flag, bold with orange and purple school colors and emblazoned with the school fight song lyrics, drifts in from an adjacent hallway and lands in the foyer. The flag ceases flapping and assumes human shape.

"Welcome, I am the Principal of this peerless institution," says the former flag, in a flat, cheerless voice. He leads them towards the auditorium stage.

The auditorium is empty. The kids must not have gotten out of class yet. Any minute now, hundreds of Fringe children, each born with a Nano-spoon in their soon-to-be flat mouth, will come prancing down the aisle to take their seats. Each enabled, privileged, and with the assurance that their future will be devoid of furrowed brows and empty stomachs

Belden proceeds to the stage podium while Prior grabs a seat at the end of the first row.

"Excuse me for a moment," says the Mod Principal, "I will re-join you in a moment." He unfurls himself again and drifts away.

Belden unpacks some notes and slaps them on the podium. For added effect, to match his antique garb, Belden gingerly places a pince-nez onto his bulbous face. Prior shakes his head knowing that, in Belden's mind, he must think he looks spectacularly erudite.

Prior feels a small drop on his shoulder. Then another. He looks up and witnesses a slight mist descending upon the auditorium. Prior is reminded of the rat-trap rooms where Fringe children used to gather. The asbestos-riddled ceilings would rain down cancerous particles into their inhaling little Fringe lungs. The auditorium roof is too newly built to be leaking. And with the affluence that acts as the muscle behind this school, a roof would never be allowed to leak.

The mist turns to confetti. Suddenly, Prior is being showered with small bits of paper being generated from thin air as if he is a returning war hero on parade. The confetti streams down with increasing intensity. Prior brushes it away but it is replaced just as quickly with more and more. Soon, the shear mass of the confetti begins to restrict his movement. He's covered in it; the confetti trapping him in his seat.

Along with the avalanche comes an accompanying spray of children's laughter. Far away, there is a dull, booming sound. Prior is having trouble breathing. He can't see beyond his nose. The confetti is getting into his eyes. The only thing that Prior clings to for safety is that distant thunderous sound. It somehow is trying to help him.

"Children, please!" it finally booms in a clear and direct voice.

Just as fast as the confetti parade has arrived, it disappears. Prior shakes his body loose, rubbing his eyes and nostrils. Finally, he takes a deep breath.

When he regains his composure, he opens his eyes to find the auditorium filled with children. Thousands of them. They all sit with their hands folded on their laps. Their school uniforms are immaculately pressed, their faces angelic.

They are all obscenely overweight. Their tailored clothes cover their ample frames and conceal some of their dimpled elbows and knees. Their round faces and chin folds give them away. They are prime candidates for Modhood. The more mass a Fringe child has when they convert, the more nanos are at their disposal.

The Mod Principal speaks to Prior from the stage. "Please excuse the student body. They just had science lab and were practicing with their nanos. It's such a rare treat for them to play with a Fringe. They're not allowed to take home their nanos, you see. The little peckers."

Prior smiles at the kids, helpless to the situation, unable to express his discomfort. "It's alright. Just surprised me is all," says Prior.

The last thing Prior needs is these kids going home and telling their Fringe surrogate mother and Mod parents that some ex-Fringe cop interrogated them at school.

The Mod Principal gestures grandly and resigns the podium to Belden.

Amidst thundering applause, Belden takes a grand bow and clears his throat while the lights dim. The children quiet down.

Prior wonders if Belden gives the same speech about nano-history wherever he goes. This audience is filled with children who have been bred by Mod with Fringe mothers. They are the future. They've been told from the day they were born that they will inherit thrones of unimaginable riches, privilege, and power. Politically, it would be suicide to tell these kids how morally bankrupt Mod are and how equally downtrodden Fringe are.

Belden begins his discussion. The nano history lesson, made up mostly of falsehoods, has a decidedly pro-Mod bent. The children listen attentively, knowing that this man is one of the few Fringe who act as gatekeeper to their ultimate wish fulfillment. And judging by Belden's size and behavior, it won't be long before Belden joins these kids as Mod. Belden looks like an older version of the fat kids.

Earlier, Belden had reacted differently than Prior expected when Prior mentioned Addison. Prior doesn't think that Belden has anything to do with Ferri's disappearance either. Belden is too self-involved to think about intricate plans for others. Maybe Belden can still help Prior get to the bottom of the truth about Feynman's death.

Right on cue, as if he can read Prior's thoughts, Belden launches into a discussion on the Messiah-like mythos of Ferri. It is filled with the usual legendary facts and figures about how he put God out of work or, more precisely, took over for him. Then, Belden's speech takes a sharp right turn as he discusses Modela Nova and her brave role as the first Mod.

"One person, in this case, Modela Nova, can be so influential as to completely change society's values and priorities," says Belden to the packed auditorium. "For another example in history, one only has to look back a hundred years or so. Imagine a world, just like you've all been taught, before Mod. When only Fringe ruled the world. Plump three-dimensional people taking up much too much space and resources."

The kids in the audience titter at the ridiculous notion.

"Imagine people who get sick, have to wait in line, and be told they can't have something because there isn't enough," says Belden. "Unlike you here, there was no moderation and no balance.

"Now, into this world, consider Coco Chanel. She was a wealthy Fringe queen. Before her, only the poor were thin and tanned. The rich were pale. They didn't have to work outside and could luxuriate indoors. They were plump since they owned the food.

"But, Coco Chanel went on a cruise. And when she came back, she was thin and tanned. No one had ever heard of such a thing. She started a new trend. And very quickly, only the rich were thin and tanned."

There is awed silence in the room as the students, placing themselves into the center of the story, realize that they too are as influential to society.

Belden's speech ends in tumultuous applause. The students stand, reduce themselves to paper-thin dimensions, and float out of the room, again taking full advantage of their nano-science lab.

In the bustle of the students' exit, Prior ducks into one of the laboratory classrooms for a moment, fills his front jacket pocket with school contraband, and makes his way back to the auditorium. No one notices he was gone. He stands in the auditorium aisle.

"Well, what did you think of my little speech?" says Belden, trudges off the stage towards Prior.

"Is there room for God in their world?" says Prior.

"Let's just say heaven is emptier since God has made room for more of us here," says Belden. "If it makes you sleep better."

"Chanel a queen? You're re-writing history," says Prior.

"We make our own history."

Belden and the Mod Principal exchange a handshake before Prior and Belden return to the waiting limo.

When they're a few miles down the road, Belden turns to Prior and whispers, "Jere, there are people concerned that this Addison fellow might give away Ferri's secret."

"You know Addison?" says Prior.

"No, but I have penetrating access to information. For instance, I happen to know that Ferri is still missing. And he's being pursued by the very same people who are after Addison. Pernicious times we live in."

"Almost makes you want to turn Mod and avoid the whole damn thing now, doesn't it," says Prior.

"Now if I didn't know you better, I'd say you were being sarcastic."

Belden reaches into the front seat of the limo and grabs a large satchel.

"Jere," he whispers, "I know what you must think of me, what with the weight and my wardrobe and all. But I tell you, things have changed since you've been gone. Things are complicated. Tres complicated. It's all about survival now."

"What's it always been?"

Prior grabs the satchel from Belden and opens it. Inside, tied down by thick, black straps, is a plasma gun. These things are illegal, especially when in the possession of Fringe.

"I know you're mixed up in things I don't even want to know about," says Belden.

"Funny, I was going to tell you the same thing."

"Please accept this gift. For protection."

"And you don't need protection?" says Prior, pocketing the plasma gun.

"I'm covered."

"Belden, where did you even get this thing?"

"Confiscated it from one of the school children today. The little peckers."

Chapter 20

Addison seems to be at the center of all this. Prior decides to take the Miss Simmons case. It feels good to have a job, to be needed, his mind occupied with something other than Feynman. Everyone seems to have made their mind up about Prior being guilty regarding Feynman. He can't figure out why NanoGov would want to distort the evidence that exonerates him.

He lets Penny know where he'll be and heads out, deciding to share information with her on a need-to-know basis. He reminds himself that he used to be a good detective and those instincts don't just get up and crawl away. The trick is to out-maneuver Fringe, Mod Police, and NanoGov. He sets out to find Addison. That means going old school.

It takes him about an hour to hoof it down to the old Wall Street section of the city. The streets are deserted and that keeps him alert. He keeps looking behind him, in case Addison is following him. No such luck today.

The old buildings are mostly crumbled, their rubble shining in the morning sun. No one has bothered to tell the buildings that their remains are anachronisms. The days when this part of the world was the financial capital is ancient history. The buildings are used now to house displaced Fringe. Prior hopes they're not housing more dead Fringe.

He stands at one of the main intersections and asks himself where he would hide if he were trying to avoid the Mod squad? He doesn't know a whole lot about how Addison's brain works. Prior figures the guy is smart. Like any Fringe, he'd squirrel away in the least likely place. He'd hide in plain sight.

Prior spends hours snooping downtown but doesn't get anywhere. But tenacity is a quality he hasn't lost yet. Prior hoofs it to the old New York Stock Exchange building. Hundreds of Fringe are sprawled out on the concrete steps, sleeping. Their possessions, mostly ragged blankets and cardboard boxes, are huddled around the sleeping Fringe like pets trying to keep warm.

All Miss Simmons had given Prior to go on, besides his last whereabouts, was a DNA sample. Prior takes out his pica-tam and wipes it against the concrete steps by the sleeping Fringe until he collects a representative sample. He quietly retreats back to the street and reaches into his backpack, pulling out the portable DNA scanner he stole from the nano-school during his visit with Belden. The scanner is no bigger than Prior's hand. He draws out Addison's DNA sample, a swatch of a sweaty old T-shirt, and wipes it on the scanner. Then, he wipes the pica-tam on the scanner as a control and waits for a match.

Prior holds the scanner in the air as it vibrates and sniffs the faint Fringe molecules wafting in with the upwind current. The scanner's readout tells him that Addison is the seventh Fringe from the right on the third set of steps. Prior looks up to locate Addison but he's gone. In his place is an obvious break in the pattern of sleeping bodies.

Shit. This is going to be tricky. Now Addison knows he's being followed. Prior switches to Plan B. He always has a Plan B.

He's back at the stables. Just as Prior instructed, Skippy has outfitted Gluestick for the day's travels. Gluestick is joyous to see Prior and keeps rubbing his face on him.

"Alright, pal," says Prior to the horse. "We'll have plenty of time for this later. Right now, I need you to help me find this guy."

He rubs behind Gluestick's ear while Skippy wheels out the carriage. Prior helps the kid connect the small wooden four-wheeled two-seater to Gluestick. Everything is smooth, well-tended. Prior nods at Skippy, who glows with pride. Life couldn't have been easy for Skippy the past few years. Prior's not sure if he wants to know what Skippy did to survive.

Prior sticks Addison's old T-shirt swatch under Gluestick's tremendous nostrils. They flare as Gluestick's head rises. The wind is right. Even Prior feels right. He climbs aboard the carriage and they head out.

At first, Gluestick circles around a few blocks until he picks up Addison's scent again. Prior has trained the horse for exactly this kind of investigation. Even if Addison is on the run, there isn't a Fringe that could outrun old Gluestick.

Suddenly, Gluestick bolts, almost throwing Prior off the carriage. They head straight back to the stables.

"No, boy, you'll get your feed after we find this guy. Where are you going?"

The carriage bumps up and down as its wooden wheels roll with fierce velocity along the cobblestone streets. The wooden poles that attach the carriage to Gluestick seem to be holding up fine.

They ride in fast past the stable entrance and barrel up to the barn. Gluestick lets out a ferocious whinny and abruptly stops.

Standing before them is Addison, shaking, his face a canvas of tension and sweat. Pressed up in front of him, held there by gleaming knife point, is Skippy. The kid looks terrified, having never felt a real metal blade at his throat. Skippy's legs are dangling, his feet kicking in protest while Addison keeps a tight grip on him. Addison is completely still and it appears as if Skippy is stuck to a giant magnetic statue.

Prior leaps off the carriage. How the hell did he outrun them? How did he know to come here?

"Mr. Prior...get this guy...off me," says Skippy in strangled gasps.

"Addison, he's just a kid. Let him go. No one's going to hurt you." Prior takes a step forward.

"Just...go...away," says Addison. His voice is thin, weak. It sounds like it's being projected through a long, narrow tube.

"Can't do that, Addison. Not until you let go of the kid." Prior takes a few more cautious steps forward. "Easy does it."

Addison releases his grip and Skippy drops to the ground, tearing off across the stables almost before he touches down. Prior watches to make sure Skippy is safe.

"Skippy! You okay?" Prior says.

"Yeah."

When Prior looks back, Addison is gone.

Gluestick neighs. Prior spins around as Addison hops onto the carriage and leads Gluestick away.

"What the hell!" Prior cries out.

"Here..." says Skippy, trying to catch his breath.

Prior jumps on the saddled horse that Skippy has brought out and takes off down the city canyons after Addison. He turns a corner and sees Addison and Gluestick three blocks ahead. They're headed uptown. Prior crosses over a small patch of grass and turns a hard left, racing down a small alleyway that his new horse barely fits through. He turns right and has closed the distance by a block.

That's all Prior needs.

Prior whistles and Gluestick slows down and starts circling around towards Prior, despite Addison's attempts to keep Gluestick on track. Addison finds the whip under the carriage driver's seat and draws his arm back. Prior whistles again and Gluestick takes off, running directly toward Prior. The sudden motion knocks Addison back but he's still seated.

Prior can't wait to get his hands on this guy and show him what happens when people try to run from him. Especially on his horse.

Prior is a half block from Gluestick who is still trotting towards him at full speed. Addison looks wild at the reins, screaming into the wind like something out of a child's nightmare.

Suddenly, the carriage disengages from Gluestick and shoots into the air past Prior. Addison looks down from his flying chariot and gives Prior a little salute before taking off. Gluestick stops next to Prior, looking into the sky, as bewildered as Prior.

"Who the hell is this guy?" says Prior.

Prior jumps off the borrowed horse and mounts Gluestick. They race along the streets, heading uptown again, keeping an eye skyward to chase their quarry. Prior's horseless carriage flies alongside the buildings, Addison fleetly maneuvering and banking the vehicle. Gluestick is no match for its speed.

Prior can't understand what's happening. It's just an old carriage. Skippy doesn't have the technology or smarts to soup it up like this.

With one hand on the reins, Prior reaches over and opens his backpack. He feels around inside for what he needs.

Addison enters the airspace over Central Park. Prior is in pursuit but still several blocks behind. The carriage banks sharply downwards to avoid a row of large trees. It turns just as quickly to the left, barely avoiding a stone bridge. It spins wildly, trying to maneuver under the bridge. Prior calculates that once the carriage gets through to the other side of the bridge, Addison will lose them in the trees.

Prior takes out his Framer, taps the button, and flings the device towards the carriage. The Framer takes off like a rocket, zeroing in on the carriage's nanos. It collides with the side of the carriage and expands, momentarily disabling the carriage's nanos. The carriage starts smoking before it curls up and explodes, instantly turning to ash. The Framer burns with it. This wasn't part of Prior's plan.

Prior shields his eyes from the sun and explosion. Through squinted eyes, he tries to get a read on what's happened to Addison.

Unconscious from the explosion, Addison floats down like a windless kite into the waiting reservoir below.

Addison is Mod. Shit.

That's when Prior realizes he's in serious trouble. Someone set him up. Under the best of circumstances, there is no way he is allowed to pursue or meddle with Mod without a warrant. These warrants are never given anyway. And he doesn't have a license. He's in way over his head again.

Prior is apprehensive about approaching Addison. He wades into the reservoir, approaching Addison's unconscious, floating body on the surface. Addison looks like a life-sized, two-dimensional tarp. A spent parachute. The reservoir's undulations continue rippling through his smooth body.

Prior pulls Addison out of the reservoir, twisting him to ring out the water. He folds Addison up and secures him with the nano paper clip he stole from Mod Police headquarters. He places Addison in his wallet and puts the wallet in his inside jacket pocket, hoping that Addison doesn't wake up soon. That could be awkward.

Chapter 21

Prior is at his fourth bar. He drinks his diluted swill alone, chewing his rat jerky, listening to the conversations that surround him. He keeps his eyes to the ground or on his drink, not wanting to attract attention or have anyone recognize him. Addison is still nestled safely in his wallet. Prior's tuning into people's conversations. So far, there's no mention of what he needs to hear. Just Fringe discussing their sad and desperate situations.

At the fifth bar, his ears perk up. Two Fringe guys sit at a table behind Prior. They look like they just came off a night of mandatory hunting.

"So, tonight. What's it about?" says the first guy, dressed in a woolen hunting outfit straight out of a 19th-century fox hunt painting.

"Dunno," says the second guy, outfitted in gray camouflage. "Same old shit."

"Jeez," says the first guy, gulping down his drink. "But one night, it's gotta be about something, right?"

"You mean besides how to build bonfires."

"Jeez."

"Hear they're really cracking down lately," says the second guy.

"You mean ever since…?"

The second guy lowers his voice to a whisper. "Yeah, since that Addison came down and fuckin' devoured that guy."

"Jeez."

"We're doing the right thing, ain't we?"

"FU?" says the first guy, looking around.

"Yeah."

"We're doing the right thing," says the first guy. "I mean, someone's gotta."

"Yeah, good luck with that," says the second guy.

Prior spins around on his stool and faces them.

"Excuse me," says Prior.

"Who the hell are you?" says the first guy.

They sit up straight, their eyes darting about the room to assess their situation.

"No need to get paranoid," says Prior. "It's just that I couldn't help but overhear your conversation and…"

"We ain't done nothin'."

"Right," says Prior. Now it's his turn to look around the bar for anyone overhearing him. "I'm Detective Prior. I'm looking for…"

"Prior?" says the first guy, sounding relieved. "You hear that, Stan? We got ourselves a living legend in front of us."

"Jeremiah Prior," says Stan. "Shit, Harry, I heard he was dead."

The two of them stand up and face Prior. Their faces turn grim and Prior knows the discussion has taken a turn away from the friendly tone he is trying to set.

"Stan. Harry," says Prior. "I'm looking for…"

"Looking for a bad end to your night," says Stan.

"We know all about you, Prior," says Harry. "You turn in your own."

They advance towards Prior. Prior takes a step back, his mind racing. He's calculating whether he can take them both on. The closer they get, the bigger they look.

"Things ain't bad enough with Mod keeping us down, we got Fringe like you haulin' our asses in jail for some made-up infractions?" says Stan.

"Jeez, breaks your heart," says Harry.

They flex their hands, warming them up for the pummeling they're about to administer. None of the other bar flies even look their way.

Prior braces himself, holding his ground. "Listen, guys, you got it all wrong," he says, reaching into his pocket.

"Oh, do we?" says Stan.

"How about that," says Harry.

"You want to be assholes about it?" says Prior and whips out the brass key Lachende gave him.

Stan and Harry stop cold in their pursuit as if the brass key is some kind of pause button.

"Harry," says Stan, "you believe this? He's one of us."

"Jeez, where the hell did you get that?" says Harry, suspicion in his voice.

"That's what I've been trying to tell you. I've been gone a couple of years. Joined in Antigua. You guys believe in repentance?"

"Repentance?"

"Where's the next meeting?" says Prior.

"This legit?"

"Does the Movement give out keys to Fringe who don't believe in the cause?" says Prior.

"Could be stolen."

"Would you guys allow an asshole like me to steal this?" says Prior, waving the key.

Harry and Stan consider this question, looking to each other for an answer. Finally, Stan grins and says, "Why didn't you say so?"

"Come on," says Harry. "Jeez."

Prior follows Harry and Stan through the grubby streets. They laugh off their implied physical threat and blame it on their frustrations at having a bad hunting day. Still, Fringe or not, Prior trails behind them. He doesn't trust meatheads with grudges and bad judgment.

Harry and Stan lead Prior to an abandoned movie theater. At the box office window, Stan slides a small wooden latch aside, revealing a key slot. Each of them takes turns sliding in their keys, giving it a half turn, then sliding it out. Each time a key slides out of the slot, the theater doors open and close rhythmically, allowing them in one at a time.

"How did Fringe pick this place?" says Prior, as they pass through the lobby.

"Good acoustics," says Stan.

"Other buildings have holes in the walls or crumbled ceilings. This place is relatively intact," says Harry.

Prior wonders how Mod haven't noticed this glazed, roasted duck on their global buffet table.

They enter the candle-lit theater. A low murmur wafts in the air. Hundreds of Fringe are in attendance, seated in rows of cardboard boxes. There is a crude wooden stage where once stood a glorious proscenium. Each Fringe sits alone; close enough to feel like they're participating in a committed organization but far enough away from each other to disassociate from the rest of the group if the Mod Police arrive. Even Harry and Stan split up and sit a few rows apart from each other.

The walls on the inside of the theater are covered with aluminum foil. It is stunning to see so much metal in the possession of Fringe. Fringe must have saved it for years. Somehow, they still believe it will keep out nanos. Prior guesses the foil is doing its job. Somehow, in the decades-old advertisements for aluminum foil, they never mentioned that the product would keep Fringe civilization fresh under wraps, preserving hope in the process.

Prior slides into the back of the room, standing, overhearing bits of conversation, learning what he can. It's a Nano-Ethics conference, already in progress. There is no main speaker, just Fringe factions arguing with each other.

"This is patently unsafe."

"Exactly."

"Mod could rip in here any moment. What a feast they would make of us."

"You're crazy. Follow the nanos."

"Mod tolerate this type of public address because…"

"Because at the end of each one of these conferences, nothing is accomplished."

"Except re-hashing our miseries and woes."

"And don't forget cursing our fate."

"The futility of it all."

Prior has never attended a conference like this before. Giant pity parties aren't his idea of a good time.

Prior cranes his neck and spots Molly, remembering that Nano-Ethics are one of her big causes. He makes his way to the front near the stage and spots Molly and Lachende sitting in the first row. From the way they hold hands and whisper into each other's ears, this is not a first date. Prior takes a closer look and sees something on Molly's hand. He stands in front of them.

"You want to explain that?" says Prior, pointing at a small scrap of foil wrapped around Molly's ring finger.

"Dad," says Molly, clearly annoyed.

"Oh, right," says Lachende, still holding her hand. He puts his arm around her. "I forgot to mention I gave your Dad an FU key. Seems we could use all the help we can get."

"Waste of time," says Molly.

"Molly, I just…" says Prior but he doesn't know how to finish what he started.

"We want to take this whole shit bag down," says Molly to Prior. "Are you telling me you're suddenly a committed rebel?"

"Give him a chance," says Lachende, trying to be loyal to both warring factions. "His heart's in the right place. He's an innocent man."

"His heart is probably somewhere on a hammock in Antigua," says Molly.

"Can we go somewhere and talk?" says Prior. He notices there are no empty seats around Molly and Lachende. The others listening in to this private conversation aren't budging.

"Later," says Lachende.

Prior looks up at the speaker who has taken the stage.

"Sit down," says a Fringe to Prior. "You're blocking my view."

Prior takes a seat on the floor of the aisle, craning his neck to get a look at the speaker.

It's Belden, looking more rotund than usual, intermittently puffing on a pipe.

"Ladies and gentlemen, if we may stop this bickering and continue," says Belden in a booming voice that reverberates throughout the building. "My fellow Fringe, I bring dire news."

The Fringe fall into a deadly silence. The acoustics of the movie house are muffled by the aluminum foil and everyone leans in to hear better.

"Dr. Anton Ferri," says Belden, "an esteemed scientist I'm sure we are all familiar with, helped create NanoGov. And starting with the advent of Modela Nova, Fringe rights were quickly deleted, one after another, while Mod were allowed to live on endlessly."

Belden pauses for effect. "I find it amusing that NanoGov later turned on Dr. Ferri himself. Many speculate that Ferri's recent disappearance was the direct result of NanoGov's actions against him."

Prior looks down the row. Molly and Lachende remain transfixed by Belden. They're still holding hands.

"Just like we all learned as toddlers," says Belden. "Nanotubes and bucky balls are composed solely of carbon and their strength comes from the special characteristics of the bonds between the carbon atoms. This strength is the basis of Mod immortality and the source of our frailty."

Now Belden is getting esoteric. Prior can tell he's losing his audience.

Belden's stagehands blow out some of the candles as he dramatically reaches the climax of his speech.

"History has shown that the price-performance and capacity of information technology always doubles in less than a year," says Belden, using increasingly exaggerated gestures. "Which means an expansion by a factor of a billion in the next twenty-five years. This exponential dilation applies to our knowledge of the brain, of biology, the environment, and all other aspects of technology that we can describe in informational terms.

"So what does this mean to you and I? Well, it is how the Fringe will come to their end in less than two generations."

Prior sees Molly roll her eyes. Everyone's heard this talk before. Not only is life expectancy for Fringe down to around forty years of age, but they'll all be extinct shortly.

Good old Belden. Taking speaking fees from all sides. He always excelled at endlessly circling the drain without actually plopping in.

"Previously, we thought we had made inroads to Mod weaknesses. We were preparing to strike. But, with the arrival of this latest evolution, the balance of power has shifted. This will entail more investigation on our part. We must be diligent. We must be thorough. And most of all, we must continue to be patient."

The murmur throughout the theater is one of disappointment. Prior observes that most of the audience seem to blindly believe what Belden is telling them. They shake their heads. Prior can't make out if Molly and Lachende react the same way. Any flicker of hope is all but extinguished.

"I am sorry to report this news for it weighs heavily on my heart as I'm sure it does yours," says Belden. "But, simply stated, at this time, we cannot overthrow NanoGov. There is too much risk. Too many uncertainties. For now, we must continue working on achieving a better life through negotiation."

There is a faint, but defeated, applause.

"But mark my words, my fellow Fringe, our day will come. When things settle, our day will come."

The applause grows louder. Belden surveys the crowd, a proud look on his face. He is clearly having fun with this speech.

Belden's eyes cross Prior's and the speaker nods in recognition. As the applause dies down, he waves his hand. Prior quietly gets up and makes his way backstage.

"And now, a report on the northern sector," says Belden. He steps off the stage as another Fringe takes the microphone and begins his report.

"Detective Prior, we meet again. How enchanting," says Belden as soon as he arrives backstage and away from his audience's ears. "I never pegged you as part of the Movement."

"Clam it, tubby. The hell do you think you're trying to pull with these people?" says Prior.

Belden flinches at the crude remark. He composes himself, then leans in. "These people? Why, Detective, to hear you phrase it, one would think you're not a Fringe yourself. Considering conversion, are you?"

"Sorry to disappoint. One traitorous sack of shit around here is enough," says Prior, drawing himself in closer to Belden until they are nose to nose.

Belden looks into Prior's eyes for a moment, then smiles again. He pulls back and lights a cigarette.

"You've got a lot of rage, Prior. You should have that checked out. You're at the wrong end of your lifespan."

"Tell me about it. Now, what did you mean by 'the latest evolution?' Just what are you doing here?"

"I would think it's obvious. In fact…"

Before Prior can react, Belden pulls him onto the stage. The Fringe speaker wraps up his northern sector update. Belden takes the microphone.

"Friends, we are in luck tonight. As a surprise speaker, we have someone who has intimate knowledge on the comings and goings of Mod society. I give you Authentician Detective Jeremiah Prior."

There is a noticeable shift in the mood of the audience. Where they looked to Belden with loving devotion, they glare at Prior, daring him to prove himself worthy in their judgmental eyes. Leading the glare is Molly. Lachende looks as disaffected as usual. The crowd sits in stony silence, waiting for Prior to explain why he is standing there, infecting their gathering. Belden stands next to him, clutching his arm, ever the showman.

"What the hell is this traitor doing here?" someone yells out.

"Now, ladies and gentlemen…" says Belden.

"Yeah, we know all about Detective Prior," yells a Fringe.

"Friends," says Belden, quelling the crowd, "we've all done things we're deeply ashamed of. Detective Prior here is no different. What's important now is what he can do to help us. Isn't that right, Jere?"

The crowd grows silent and waits. In these desperate times, they are even willing to listen to Prior, hoping that he will unveil a magic answer.

"Belden…" says Prior.

"Come now, don't be shy. You've been gone for several years. Since you've been back, you've witnessed much about Mod. What have you to report to the good cause?"

"Well," says Prior after a moment, "the main thing, I guess, is that no one, and I mean Mod nor Fringe, seem to know or care how nanos work."

"That's fascinating," says Belden. "But not entirely true. As I recall, your wife, sorry, ex-wife, Felice, seemed to be a genius at understanding nanos. How is the old girl?"

"Fuck you," says Prior.

The crowd gasps at the disrespect. Molly stands up and turns to leave. Lachende looks up, ready to go after her as she races up the aisle. Some members of the audience follow Molly's lead. Clearly, their loyalties are still with Belden.

There is a loud voice booming outside. It's slightly muffled from the room's acoustics. The outside sound tries to enter at full volume but gets split apart and put back together in everyone's ears. The room quiets down to listen.

It's the NanoGov newscaster making a breaking news announcement on the Sky-Screen. NanoGov has increased the volume. They must know that the FU is meeting indoors somewhere in the city.

"Again, we have breaking news," says the newscaster in his oily-smooth delivery. "NanoGov, through perfect detection, has identified the terrorist suspected of planning attacks on various NanoGov centers."

One of the technicians at the FU meeting switches on a live Sky-Screen feed to a crude screen on the stage so everyone can see what is being broadcast.

"These attacks were always futile but society must be protected from such disruptive practices," says the Sky-Screen newscaster. "The terrorist at large has been identified as Molly Prior. If you see her, contact the authorities at once. She is presumed armed and dangerous."

A picture of Molly wearing a mirrored bodysuit and black hat is shown. She's holding some type of flamethrower. Prior scans the crowd but Molly and Lachende are gone. Prior hopes the Sky-Screen photo is doctored.

"She's the daughter of known murderer Jeremiah Prior who has illegally entered the country after years of having evaded the Mod Police. A warrant for both their arrests has been issued."

Sky-Screen switches from Molly's photo to a shaky video that suddenly begins to play on a loop. It's Prior's old apartment. Prior and Felice are there as well as Feynman and Penny. The video is grainy but they can all be clearly identified. They're arguing but the sound is muffled. Prior draws a gun on Feynman and shoots. Feynman sails back across the room and is suddenly out of frame. Penny and Felice scream. The Sky-Screen switches back to sedate music.

Prior reaches into his pocket but the video file that Lachende gave him is gone.

The crowd gets up and advance toward the stage.

"What is it with you people?" says Prior. "We're all on the same side here and you trust the news? Think about it. Just think about it."

Four large men stalk menacingly onto the stage. Prior grabs Belden by the scruff of the neck.

"Belden, tell them to back the hell off or I'll snap your Moddamn arm off."

"Yes!" screams Belden, never a man of action. "Do as he says."

Prior backs up to the stage door with Belden in his firm grasp. The men stand their ground but don't advance.

Suddenly, one of the large men blares out a convulsive scream. The other three men back away, unsure of what is happening.

"Oh dear," says Belden.

The large screaming man brings his trembling hands to his head as if trying to keep his skull from exploding. In an instant, his head has disappeared and his headless body stumbles around on the stage, his arms waving maniacally, trying to gain some sense of equilibrium. As his body falls to the stage, there is a sucking noise. He is completely gone as his shredded clothes hit the stage floor.

Everyone in the room goes into a panic and takes cover. Prior looks up just in time to see a flurry of particles descend from the theater ceiling like snow. It's not like the confetti-kids at the Mod school. These particles are barely perceptible. Everyone screams as the mass of the other three large Fringe men get devoured.

"No hard feelings," says Prior and hurls Belden at the snow fall. Belden collapses off the stage with a thud. Prior takes that as his cue to fling open the stage door and duck out the back alley.

So much for Prior's initiation into the Fringe Underground.

Chapter 22

Prior races down the alley to the main street but it's clotted with Fringe, each in a panic from the advancing Mod Police. Chaotic screams can be heard from every direction. Prior doesn't know which is worse: The Mod Police raiding their FU meeting or everyone witnessing the Fringe that were vaporized or devoured or whatever the hell happened to them.

Prior turns and runs the opposite way, hoping that the other end of the alley isn't a dead end. It's hard to tell from this vantage point since much of the alley is covered in debris and smoke.

The alleyway opens to a narrow street. Prior climbs some wooden crates that act as a makeshift wall against the street. He moves aside some tarps and cautiously raises his head over the debris pile. As soon as he gets a bead on what's in front of him, four Mod Police cut off his retreat. They're pointing some type of weapon at him that Prior doesn't recognize. He doesn't want to get a closer look.

One of the tarps he's standing on pushes back. It grabs Prior by the ankle and turns it, causing him to fall back on the debris pile. Momentarily, he's out of view of the Mod Police. Prior throws off the tarp, seeing who's under it. There's no one there. The tarp puffs up like a balloon, floating next to him.

"Come on," says the tarp.

Prior takes a closer look. "Lachende, where's Molly?"

"In here, of course," says Molly from inside Lachende's tarp-bubble.

"Room in there for me?" says Prior.

"In a minute," says Lachende.

The Mod Police are running towards Prior from both ends of the alley now. "What the hell are you waiting for?" says Prior.

"This," says Lachende.

A small beam of light emanates from Lachende towards the Sky-Screen. The news playing on the Sky-Screen is interrupted. A different newscaster now speaks to the denizens below.

"Citizens, the fugitive Jeremiah Prior, has been caught. He had previously released several look-alikes into the city to confuse the Mod Police but we are too smart for those type of Caribbean voodoo tricks."

The Mod Police stop in their tracks and stare up at the Sky-Screen like calves waiting for an available teat.

"Repeat, the fugitive Jeremiah Prior has been caught. We now return you to our regularly scheduled program."

The Mod Police turn off their weapons and retreat back into the smoke.

"A little counter-programming," says Lachende. "Molly's idea, actually." Lachende extends his two-dimensional body so the tarp extends over Prior. Prior looks around for Molly but there is a tarp barrier between them. Even in the small space, she has compartmentalized him from her life.

"Where to?" says Lachende, as if he's a taxi picking up pedestrians.

"Penny's place," says Prior.

"Oh, great," says Molly from behind the opaque curtain.

Lachende floats up, appearing to be like any other Mod on their way to wherever they feel like going. Prior sits still in the back of the bubble and watches the city below. He sees pockets of Fringe crowds running from the Mod Police. None of them fight back. They are immediately submissive.

"Molly?" says Prior

"What?"

"Is any of it true?"

"What about?"

Her voice sounds annoyed. Prior isn't sure if it's intentional that Molly is seated up front in first class while her father flies coach or if this is just a little joke that Lachende is playing to amuse himself.

"The whole terrorist thing," says Prior.

"Don't even get her started," says Lachende.

"I prefer Fringe fighter," says Molly. "What the hell you care? You're going to clear your name by blaming mom for everything and then head back to Antigua. Isn't that your plan?"

"Speak of the devil," says Lachende. "Give this a look-and-listen."

From their point of view, they are flying above the Sky-Screen. Lachende broadcasts the latest news report inside his balloon skin for their viewing pleasure.

"Now, with the fugitive Jeremiah Prior under the watch of armed guards, we take you to a historic interview with his Mod ex-wife who, of course, is fully cooperating with the Mod Police in their investigation."

Sky-Screen plays grainy footage of an interview with Felice. She's still pretty, in a two-dimensional way. Her dirty-blond short hair and face have been artfully composed. She smirks as she looks right at the camera with the most earnest and sincere expression.

"Well, I always suspected my ex-husband of betraying his country but I never thought his mania would reach such levels of atrocity. I mean, overthrowing the government? Who does he think he is? I have given everything for this country. And my deepest act of charity was marrying that Fringe idiot. As Dr. Anton Ferri's Chief Scientist, I just want to protect his good work and the status quo and all who live peacefully on this planet."

"Lachende, what was that you were telling me about not throwing up inside here?" says Prior.

"Isn't this fascinating?" says Lachende. "NanoGov is running with my fake story about you being caught." He chuckles and the air inside the bubble sways with his rhythmic laughter.

Lachende descends gently onto the rooftop of Penny's apartment building. Lachende does a perimeter check and makes sure the coast is clear. After he confirms no Mod Police are present, he lets loose his passengers and returns to three-dimensional form. Prior opens the rooftop door and they take the stairs down to Penny's apartment.

Penny answers the door, surprised to see them.

"Sorry to barge in on you like this," says Prior. "But our options on hideouts are kind of limited at the moment."

Prior senses she's glad to see him but ambivalent about Molly and Lachende.

"Of course," says Penny. "Come in."

Her place is spare. It gives Prior the impression she hardly spends anytime here. It has the usual cardboard box furniture and some old tarps for bedding on the floor.

"I'd offer you some water but I just ran out," she says.

"Thanks anyway," says Prior. "Anyone come asking for me today?"

"Miss Simmons came by the office yesterday, asking about the status of her brother. That's it." She turns to Molly. "Molly, I don't know if you..."

"Yeah, I remember you," says Molly coldly.

"And you remember me, Miss Penelope," says Lachende, all charm.

"Of course. Little Lachende. How are you?" says Penny. She's tentative, unsure of what's happening.

"Engaged," says Lachende, putting his arm around Molly. "Keeping the business in the family."

"Alright, let's break it up," says Prior. "Lachende, show Molly and Penny the video you got from NanoGov."

"What happened to your copy?" says Lachende.

"Disappeared."

"What is this?" says Penny, backing up to the door.

"Your husband's case," says Lachende. "It's got a surprise ending."

"I'll leave you to it," says Penny. "I need to go out for some water anyway."

"I think you'll want to stick around and watch," says Prior.

"No thanks," says Penny and shuts the door behind her so quickly that Prior doesn't have time to respond.

"The touchy widow," says Lachende. He shines a light on Penny's ceiling and the video footage of Penny knocking out Prior and shooting her husband while Felice runs off plays in a loop.

"Jesus," says Molly.

"My guess is they want to draw me out," says Prior. "Why else would they want to make me feel comfortable to go out in public now?"

"Or to draw mom out," says Molly. "She's gone into hiding. NanoGov needs her more than ever since Ferri went missing."

"So, Lachende, tell me about these two-percent, new-evolution Mod-things," says Prior.

Molly looks at Prior directly for the first time since he's been back. "Dad, I'm sorry," she says. She jerks forward but draws back just as quickly, not quite able to bring herself in for a hug. Prior appreciates the gesture.

"I'm not really supposed to talk about it," says Lachende.

"Spill it, kid. That's what's been devouring Fringe, right?"

Lachende, faltering back to the old social dynamics that are imbedded in his personality, reverts to being the office kid and answers his old boss' question.

"The next wave of technology, after the Nano-Revolution, came too quickly. But it's here. It was rushed to market and, like cell phones and old flying cars, it has problems that NanoGov wants kept secret."

"What the hell are you talking about?" says Prior.

"The idea of becoming Mod was to be unique. You understand? That was the allure. But then everybody became one. Some Mod got bored of being like everyone else. Can you imagine? They can have anything they want but they wanted more. So some gave in to this new technology offered by NanoGov. I remember them asking me when I converted. Trying to upsell. Very exclusive. And Mod that agreed gave up even more mass in exchange for more nanos."

Molly shakes her head in defeat.

"You mean..." says Prior.

"These Mod have become one-dimensional, you understand? They're the new ruling class. We are the new second-class citizens..."

"And that makes us third-class. Great. What do these things call themselves?"

"Points," says Molly

"Points. Shit," says Prior. "And what's the problem with these one-dimensional Points besides their unique diet?"

"No idea. Very hush-hush."

Chapter 23

"Hey," says the bouncer, looking like a ton of spoiled beef. "We don't serve threeds here." The early derogatory term for three-dimensional Fringe is dispensed with menace.

Prior steps forward so he's standing to the side of the bouncer. The bouncer is practically invisible, shimmering in the cool, night breeze.

Prior is laying low, hoping no one recognizes him. Now that NanoGov broadcast that he's been caught, Mod are less suspicious. Prior still has a job to do. And he figures Addison, tucked away in his wallet, might be the key to the whole thing.

He needs to duck into this fancy Mod bar where Mod occasionally go slumming with some privileged Fringe. Some, like this Mod meathead, even fantasize about having a blue-collar job and decide to play make-believe once a week. Prior hopes the bouncer's not asking for ID.

"It's alright, he's with me," says Miss Simmons, sticking her beautiful face out from the entrance.

The Mod bouncer opens the three-dimensional velvet rope and waves them in.

"You're very convincing," says Prior to the bouncer as he brushes past him. "For a second there, I thought I was in real trouble."

"Move along, meat bag."

Miss Simmons is waiting just inside the door. "Right on time, Mr. Prior," she says, leading him to a quiet table in the corner. Her scent is so sweet you could pour it on pancakes.

The place is a classy joint with actual tables and real chairs. Red velvet curtains and drapes encapsulate the room while a small band plays the same retro-punkflapper music that seems to be all the rage. Some people, mostly Mod, are smoking. Some are drinking alcohol. It's like something out of an old digital stream.

"Nice vibe," says Prior.

"We'll be safe here," says Miss Simmons, sitting down, her dress exposing more leg than Prior needs to see right now. "Cigarette?"

"No thanks." The truth is that Prior is dying for a smoke. He hasn't had one since Antigua. But he doesn't trust this broad and certainly won't accept something from her that he would put in his body. For all he knows, her plan is to have her nicotine nanos invade and occupy him so he'd be her slave. He can think of worse things.

"Well, then. What have you found?" she says.

The room lighting changes and Miss Simmons changes with it. Now she smells like lilacs, her aroma-nanos working overtime. Her dress changes shape to accommodate the shift in lighting. It's cut just right.

Prior gets a grip, reminding himself who he's dealing with. He's spent the afternoon researching her, discovering everything about her.

"Let's start with your real name," he says.

"What do you mean?"

"Quit it. You're not Miss Simmons. It's no good."

She puts out her cigarette, her silence calling his bluff.

"Fine. Shall I refresh your memory?" says Prior. He shouldn't have been fooled so easily. But her looks overwhelmed him. She's been wearing a nano-disguise on her face. Very expensive. And all to hide her true identity and the fact that she's Mod. "Modela Nova. Ring any bells?"

"Lower your voice," says Modela. Her face is no longer sweet. It looks real. Prior likes it this way better.

"I don't get it," says Prior. "People would be ecstatic to see the world's first Mod. Hell, they're all named after you."

She starts to cry. But that's not the part that unnerves him. With each heaving sob and tear rolling down her cheek, she grows flatter and flatter until she's dissolved into a sheer wisp of a person.

Prior never thought he'd be meeting Modela Nova in the flesh, so to speak. She hasn't changed too much. Still beautiful. Back in the day, every boy wanted her. So did every man.

Years earlier, at the thirty-fifth annual Virtual Streaming Awards, she created a sensation when she turned up on the red carpet. In the middle of her interview, she threw off her fur coat and revealed herself to be the world's first Mod. It was the ultimate act of celebrity. She couldn't have been any thinner. She was translucent, luminescent. She captured all the attention. It was the only thing the entire world talked about for months afterwards. At the end of the award show, she strolled onto the stage for a fifteen-minute ovation. She left the stage and paraded back out with Anton Ferri on her arm. He announced himself to be her creator and the world officially changed forever.

Immediately afterwards, everyone wanted to be Mod. It spread like the popularity of microwave ovens or smart phones many generations earlier. Only it was quicker and less regulated. People's greed got the better of them. They saw Modhood as the cure to all the world's ills.

The rich and powerful were resentful of Modela Nova for leading such an obvious cultural change. They kicked themselves for not thinking of it first. Ferri became the premier ambassador to the future. The world's leaders and privileged class followed suit, financing scientists to make them all Mod. The world's scientists were stumped, not ready to embrace or replicate this untamed technology. Ultimately, everyone went begging to Ferri. Then, they formed NanoGov. And once NanoGov had Ferri's secrets, he was discarded like an overripe banana.

"It's difficult being the first," says Modela. "You don't know what it's like."

"No, I guess I don't. Maybe you, Jackie Robinson, George Washington, and Jesus can start a club."

"My brother," says Modela. "Have you found him?"

"That's where you lose me. You don't have a brother. Records say you're an only child. So who the hell is this Addison?"

"Mr. Prior, you have to believe me…"

"I don't have to believe anything. You set me up. You sent me on a death errand to chase down a Mod. I'm in big trouble, lady. So, you start spilling or people are going to see your face in the news again. Only this time, it'll be one of those crazy celebrity deaths." Prior is taking a risk threatening a Mod but he figures he knows how to play her.

"Alright. I'm sorry," she says, not used to being spoken to this way. "But understand Addison is my brother. My real brother. He was kept out of the press and my history for his protection. You have to believe me. And you must promise not to tell anyone."

"I'm listening."

"The public thinks I was the first Mod. But that's not entirely accurate. Dr. Ferri experimented on Addison first. He was the prototype. And it drove Addison a little mad."

"I know the feeling."

"Addison developed...special abilities. He's no danger to you, me, or anyone but I'm afraid he could hurt himself."

"Trust me, he's a danger to you and me and everyone."

"So you've found him?" she says.

The Mod clientele keep looking towards Modela, shaking their flat heads disapprovingly. They can't recognize her in this lighting but don't like her hosting a Fringe. Prior figures he'll be asked to leave soon.

"Yeah, I found him."

"I just want to protect my little brother, Mr. Prior. You have to believe me. Everything else I told you was true. You had to find him before they did."

"The Points?"

Modela looks legitimately shocked. "You know?"

"I have a rough outline. More fun with evolution. I mean, as long as we're all going to hell anyway."

"It's terrifying."

"One-dimensional beings threatening your cushy two-dimensional existence? Sorry if it's hard for me to cough up empathy," says Prior.

"Where's my brother now? I must see him."

Prior gets up. It's time to head for the exit before he attracts any more attention. "Stop by my office tomorrow and I'll take you to your brother. It's too public here."

She stands up and faces Prior directly. He gets a great look at her. The kind of look men might sell their souls for.

"Why don't you come back to my place?" she says. "I feel naked and exposed now that you know all my secrets."

"Tempting," says Prior, eyeing the door, needing to get the hell out of Dodge before he does something stupid. "Very tempting. But no."

"How about your place then?" she says, not letting it go.

"Sorry, Modela. I have a daughter who's coming over to visit. Meet me at my office tomorrow."

The streets are deserted and the hush allows Prior's mind to be distracted. Prior thinks about how much he misses women. He's never been lucky in the women department. The women in Antigua were spoken for and their role in everyday life was sacred. The local men were jealous of their women.

Before he knows it, he's back at his office. It's late and Penny is gone which means his office is now his apartment. Prior lights some candles.

Right now, he's wondering where Molly is. He hadn't lied to Modela Nova. Molly is really meeting him at his office in a rare display of interest in their relationship. He is hoping the chill is finally coming off that crust. Instead of Molly, Prior finds a note slid under his door. Molly must have sent it over with a messenger kid.

"Dad, I was followed to your place. I got as far as two blocks away, turned, and ran. I'll see you tomorrow when it's safe. Molly."

Prior blows out the candles and sneaks back outside. He sneaks slowly around the block of his building, hugging the walls, making as little noise as possible. He thinks of the woman who got devoured on his first night back.

He makes his way to the nicer part of town, following a hunch. He's hides in an alleyway and peers across a concrete park towards a large, ornate building. It's a Mod Clinic where Fringe go to be converted. He waits for an hour before he sees her.

Molly treks towards the Mod Clinic building, waves her hand, and is allowed entrance. Prior hopes she's not actually converting tonight. As he moves out of the alleyway to get a better look, Prior catches something in the corner of his eye. A shadow. It quickly disappears into the night but there's no doubt what Prior just saw.

Prior makes a beeline straight to the shadow in the adjacent alleyway.

"Alright, let's go. I'm wise to you," says Prior, putting up the brave snake oil.

There is silence followed by the shifting of feet on the alleyway gravel, as if this guy is making up his mind.

"I said let's go, chum," says Prior.

Footsteps from the alleyway race towards Prior. At first, Prior only makes out the shadow's outline. Someone in a long overcoat. Prior knows it isn't Addison this time. He's still safely tucked away in Prior's jacket pocket in his office.

The shadow stops just short of Prior. "Good evening, Prior." It's a deep male voice. Unafraid.

The shadow takes a few steps further out into the street. Prior catches sight of his face by moonlight. He recognizes the face from the photo in Penny's office.

"Beauregard Sanders," says Penny's husband. There is a casual tone about him, as if he's used to stalking people.

"You stay the hell away from my kid, Sanders," says Prior, taking a step forward, his hands balling into fists.

"And you stay from my wife," says Sanders.

"Penelope? She works for me."

"Sure."

"That's why you and your NanoGov buddies took away my detective license. I ought to re-work your face."

"You've been warned," says Sanders.

"Look, pal…"

Before Prior can finish, Sanders strikes Prior square on the jaw, sending him down to the ground. Prior never sees it coming. He rubs his jaw, It aches but isn't broken.

The Sky-Screen shines a light on them. Prior is temporarily blinded. Nursing his jaw, he dives back into the safety of the alleyway. When he turns back, Sanders is gone.

Chapter 24

As untrustworthy as Belden is, Prior needs his help. Prior has to be careful not to be seen approaching Belden's house. He's taking a chance but he's running out of time. Soon, the Mod Police will outsmart him and throw him into whatever medieval dungeon they've concocted for their amusement.

Prior moves slowly through the city, avoiding detection. His jaw is still throbbing. By early evening, it feels better as he knocks on Belden's door.

"Well, well," says Belden from inside his house. "Shall I release the hounds?"

"Alright, Professor. I come in peace."

Prior stretches out his hands so the nano-scan can be completed easily.

"Ta-da," says Belden, opening the door and facing Prior. He's wearing a silk Japanese kimono, his hair in a topknot. With his enormous, protruding belly, he looks like a demented Buddha. "Welcome, my friend. All Fringe are welcome to my humble abode."

Belden turns ninety degrees to allow Prior to pass and he slips from Prior's view.

"Son of a bitch, Belden," says Prior, rushing by without glancing at him. "A Mod?"

Belden's drawing room has been re-decorated in the style of Imperial China. Lots of red lacquer and gold embellishments. Prior grabs a seat on a wooden throne.

Belden enters regally and poses at the doorway. "Is that all you have to say?"

"I can tell you I'm not surprised."

"Oh, Jere, you simply must give in to all your temptations and convert. Best decision I ever made."

"Used to be you were happy with Chinese takeout. This seems a bit extreme."

Belden descends into his drawing room and swoons dramatically onto a beaded settee.

"And to what do I owe the pleasure? I must admit I was miffed after your treatment of me earlier," says Belden. "But those were my long-ago sordid Fringe days."

"What do you know about Addison?"

"I see," says Belden. "Still working the beat."

"Goddamn Mod," says Prior.

"Perhaps I can explain it this way."

"It's getting late."

Belden sighs, a little exasperated, not used to being spoken to in a snide manner. He gathers himself, then proceeds. "A man drinks water from a paper cup. The total mass of the man, the paper cup, and the water remains the same. The mass is just transferred."

"I've already been to your nano-lectures," says Prior.

"Now," says Belden, ignoring Prior's remark. "The paper cup represents Man, squashed flat after the water has been consumed. The water represents nanos, ever fluid. And the man represents the possessions that the nanos afford him. Understand?"

"Too well." Prior doesn't have the time, or quite frankly, the intellectual depth, to get into a nano-philosophic discussion at this point in the evening. "Here's my working analogy, Professor. In Roman times, the upper-class elite set themselves up for plumbing. Pipes for fresh water, laundry, as well as pewter jugs, plates, and goblets. High living. The lowly peasants had none of these things. They were still wiping their asses in the river. But here's what history teaches us: the upper-class elite died in droves from lead poisoning in the water pipes and pewter jugs. The commoners just kept on living their lives. Low tech always beats high tech."

"I've heard that fable," says Belden. "Unimpressive. Yet, how can you compare macro-level pewter with the nanoscale, where the mind-bending principles of quantum physics apply? Where the characteristics of materials change? Carbon becomes a hundred times stronger than steel, aluminum turns highly explosive, and gold melts at room temperature."

"Uh-huh," says Prior. "And what's your point?"

"Point?" says Belden. He laughs in a way that is almost sinister and yet sincere. "Everything that has come before is prelude to the next evolution. I know because I have witnessed Anton Ferri create it. And Addison Simmons holds the key."

"The key?" says Prior.

"You know, it's a real shame about you and Felice, what with her working so closely with Ferri all those years. She was the most brilliant nano-scientist I ever encountered. Now, she could help us all solve this problem."

"What problem? What does Addison know?"

"Just find him, Detective Prior. Velocemente."

"You know, if this guy is as popular as you say he is, Mod and NanoGov are going to throw everything they have looking for him."

"Yet he has proven remarkably elusive," says Belden.

"I'm on the lam, in case you've forgotten."

"And that's why you've come to me," says Belden, floating up in delight. He produces a real-looking syringe from his paper-thin kimono pocket. A strange, viscous liquid floats inside the ampoule.

"What the hell is that?" says Prior.

"The help you so desperately need to do your job."

"What is it?"

"You have trust issues, don't you? We'll have to work on that."

Prior shakes his head. Things are moving too fast. He isn't use to this. In Antigua, things happened so much slower.

"You're going to have to trust me, Prior," says Belden. "I gave you the plasma gun for protection. Now I need you to find Addison. This elixir will help you evade Mod detection during your investigation. My own personal cocktail. Wonderful invention."

Prior is standing at a threshold again and decides to ring the doorbell. He's running out of choices. He rolls up his sleeve and looks the other way, like a child.

As the needle injects Prior's arm, Belden whispers, "The active ingredient is the Georges Seurat sketch, broken down into nanos, that everyone is in such a tizzy about."

Chapter 25

Prior stops by Molly's place, curious to hear more about her and Lachende. If she's serious about him, it means trouble. It means she's going down a dangerous road that ends with her selling her soul to NanoGov and becoming Mod. He's not sure if it's all a front to infiltrate NanoGov and take it down or if she really wants to lead a flat existence with Lachende.

Prior knocks a couple of times on her door. No answer. Her neighbor with the earrings isn't home either. He squats in the hallway to wait for Molly, a tangle of thoughts wrapping around his head. Who else knows about Addison and the Points? Grainger doesn't seem concerned. Do the Mod police really suspect Prior of any of this? Certainly, they have no trouble finding him when they want. And what is Penny's angle in all this?

An hour later, Prior hears someone climbing up the stairwell.

"What are you doing here?" says Molly. She's alone.

"You know, it's not safe walking around this late by yourself," he says, relieved she's still Fringe.

"Don't start, Dad. I'm going to bed. You can use the bathroom or whatever but then it's good-bye."

"Why don't you…"

"Because I can't trust you," says Molly, louder than she probably intends. "For all I know, NanoGov or Mom are in your head, controlling you."

"Well, as long as you're safe," he says, putting his coat back on, never getting past the threshold.

She closes the door on his face and latches it loudly for good measure.

Against his better judgment, Prior decides to hang around Molly's apartment building, partly to be near her, and partly to make sure no one else is stalking her. After a while, he sees a leaf float into her window. A few minutes later, it's not a leaf but a bubble that floats out the same window. He figures Lachende picked up Molly for a late date. He runs along the street, following the bubble like a little kid chasing his lost kite. The bubble glides along the slight breeze and lands in the nearby park.

The park is deserted and barely lit. Prior, a little out of breath, hides behind an elm tree. He watches Molly emerge from the bubble and Lachende turn himself into his three-dimensional Fringe disguise.

Prior is so focused on trying to listen to their conversation that he doesn't hear the Fringe approaching him. The Fringe, a barefoot Fringe woman dressed in more rags than the usual Fringe, sidles up to Prior with her hand out. Prior waves her off, indicating he's busy. The Fringe, desperate to get anything that she can trade for food, deftly digs her hand into Prior's back pocket and takes his wallet.

By the time Prior realizes his wallet has been picked, the Fringe has taken off. Her flapping rags tear off as she runs away. Prior, dressed more appropriately for speed, gives chase and tackles her. As Prior and the Fringe roll on the ground, Prior's wallet flies out of her hand and lands hard on a rock. The Fringe holds Prior down, her long fingernails digging into Prior's neck. The wallet opens up and releases its contents, including a suddenly-loose paper clip. The unclipped Addison Simmons rapidly unfolds himself. Prior manages to throw the Fringe off him and crawls towards his wallet a few feet away. Addison stretches to his full height, hisses at them violently, and flies off into the evening sky. The Fringe groans and disappears into the night, off to easier prey.

Terrific. Prior just lost the only evidence to help his case.

Molly and Lachende run over to Prior.

"You okay?" says Lachende, helping Prior up.

"Addison," says Prior. "He got away."

"Nice going," says Molly. "What the hell are you doing here? Following us?" She marches away and Lachende and Prior consider each other before following her further into the park.

The three amble in silence for a few minutes.

"So, I don't understand something. How exactly are the two of you involved with the FU movement?" says Prior.

"How could we not be?" says Molly.

"So it's for real, this freedom fighting and plotting against NanoGov?" says Prior.

Molly takes a seat on a bench. Lachende sits next to her and puts his arm around her. Prior remains standing nearby, trying to gauge their sincerity. He dabs at his neck where the Fringe scratched him.

"Prior," says Lachende, "we're not stupid. We know it's impossible to take down NanoGov. But we have to try. Even as a Mod, I get that."

"Otherwise, we're no better than Mod who have given up on humanity and just navel-gaze their existence," says Molly.

"How are you planning on burning down the house, exactly?" says Prior.

Molly and Lachende look at each other like each one is hoping the other can answer that simple question. Finally, Molly says, "We're more in the fact-finding phase of the plan."

"No chinks in the armor?" says Prior.

"None," says Lachende. "We know we can transmit a signal that would reach all Mod but nothing can hurt them. The best we can hope is to make them feel ashamed of their behavior."

"Not very promising," says Prior.

They stare into the silence of the trees.

"How's your neck?" says Molly.

"I got bigger problems," says Prior, thinking about Addison on the loose.

"I mean, you could probably..." she says.

"He would love to help," says Lachende to Molly.

"Molly, I'm happy you found someone," says Prior, indicating Lachende. "But I'm in enough trouble as it is. I can't get involved in the wholesale takedown of the planet's government."

"So glad you came back," says Molly, getting up. She runs away. After a moment, Lachende goes after her, leaving Prior alone in the park.

Prior sprints to his office, the stabbing wind feeling good on his face, reminding him he is still in this world. The office is empty, Penny having gone home hours ago. He writes a note, then lays out on his desk for some sack time.

The next morning, Prior flags down a Fringe girl runner in front of his building. He sends the kid over to Modela's address with the note.

He needs to find out why everyone is after Addison. And he needs the money from the case.

Later that morning, Penny reports for duty, looking better than she has a right to.

"Hi, Prior. Where the hell you been sleeping?"

"Listen, Pen, about your husband…"

"It wasn't Beauregard. You have to believe me."

"Come on, he pulled my license so we'd be forced to close up shop and you'd have to go back home to him." He pauses as a hurt look crosses her face. "Well, I don't know what you've got going on in that head of yours but…"

"I just wanted to be with you. Like the old days," she says, damming up the waterworks.

"The old days are over. There was nothing ever there to begin with. Now, you're married," says Prior.

Penny sighs and sits down, resigned. "Speaking of spouses, you got a note from your ex," she says, all business again. "Arrived yesterday."

"Call a kid," he says. Prior opens the note.

"J, I must see you right away. I can't tell you where I am. We have to arrange to get together. It's urgent. My life has been hell since I stopped working for Ferri. Everything's changed. Please send a response to the old Grand Central Station Terminal, Locker 5412. F."

Something doesn't smell right. Felice is Mod. They have no troubles.

A messenger Fringe boy steps into the office. Prior grabs a piece of paper.

"F, are you having me followed? I can't help you if I don't trust you. And stay away from Molly. She's scared out of her mind that someone is following her too. What does this have to do with Ferri's disappearance? J." Then, he adds, "Hope you're well."

He hands the note to the kid and gives him some water.

Thoughts of Felice swell up inside Prior's head. Good times mixed with bad. He used to think all this was behind him but when you get kicked in the gut long enough, you start to miss the feeling.

Back when Prior was obsessing about finding the guy his wife was having an affair with, nothing was right at home. It was worse, later, when it turned out to be Feynman. In his pursuit of the truth, he lost his grip on the situation right in front of him. He lost Felice. He wasn't there for her. He shouldn't have started the affair with Penny. Maybe his sense of justice was more powerful than his commitment to her or maybe he was just pissed off at her having an affair. Either way, he couldn't solve the case and it made him feel impotent all around.

Right around this time, Felice's boss, Ferri, started talking to her about the advantages of turning Mod. Prior is sure that Ferri played to her vulnerability. Ferri also played on her vanity. The thing that kills Prior is that it didn't take that much convincing. Was it such an easy choice to leave Prior?

"Penelope," Prior says.

"Yeah, chief?"

"I need you to be straight with me. We're continuing this practice without a license. It'll work if you and I maintain a professional relationship."

"I'm with you, Prior."

"You go home to your husband at reasonable times. You convince him we're serving a public good."

"That's not going to work with him. He thinks that you and I…"

"Then you tell him I'm still in love with my wife," says Prior.

Penny remains stoic but something inside of her breaks. Prior still doesn't trust her. He's not sure if she knows that he knows she killed Feynman.

"Penny, the last thing we need is for NanoGov to come sniffing around here."

"Gotcha, chief."

"Why did you come find me in Antigua? I was happy there."

"No, you weren't," she says and goes back to her part of the office.

Later, Prior is sitting at his desk trying to figure out where Addison could be holed up. Penny's gone home early to be with her husband per Prior's orders. Prior can't afford any misunderstanding with her.

A Fringe messenger girl opens the office door and drops off a note.

"Detective Prior, thank you for staying on with my case. The last known whereabouts of my brother were at the Mod Clinic in the Wall Street section. I'll stop by tomorrow so we can talk some more. Good luck, Miss Simmons."

She's still pretending to be someone else so the publicity about her brother stays low. Prior tips the girl and waits for her to leave before he burns the note.

There's a horrible scream outside. It's followed by a slurping, gurgling noise that sounds terribly familiar. Prior bolts toward the broken window.

In the street below, Prior sees Addison floating in the air holding Sanders's arms a few feet off the ground. Sanders dangles helplessly, screaming. Sanders' arms tremble as his life force pulses into Addison's waiting hands. Sanders is slowly shriveling up, desiccating as Addison literally sucks the life out of him. In less than a minute, the screams and gurgling die down. As does Sanders. When Addison has his fill, Sanders is completely gone.

Addison flicks his two-dimensional head toward Prior, hisses, and flies away like a rocket.

Chapter 26

Prior knows better than to just show up to the funeral as himself, especially with NanoGov after him. He stops by Gluestick's stable. In the back of the stable, hidden under the floorboards and covered with hay, is his old work trunk. Skippy left it undisturbed. There are still a few items in the trunk that function. He never thought he'd be using them again. Somehow, naively, he thought if he returned to the mainland, things would be different.

Searching through the trunk brings back memories of past cases. Some of the tools are old technology and he's sure that nanos have advanced way past this. That could be helpful. In his experience, old technology always beat new technology. A lot of the stuff used to belong to Feynman. And here he is using it to sneak into his widow's next husband's funeral.

He dons a mid-eighteenth-century tunic, vest, coat, stockings, pants, and hat. Before he leaves, he gives Skippy some last-minute instructions.

Mod are fanatical about displaying their wealth. They feel they're timeless and superior to their own era. They do not like being tied down to the present and often ravage the past of its fashions. Immortality tends to make you lose a bit of perspective.

Sanders' funeral has a pretty good turnout. The service and actual burial take place on top of a hill in a remote part of the cemetery park. Penny, dressed all in black, plays the part of the grieving widow beautifully. Prior doesn't have the heart to watch this scene for the second time. Her first husband's funeral was tough enough. It seems everyone Prior touches or gets involved with ends up hurt or dead. He should have stayed in Antigua.

But it's too late for that now. People want him out of the way and the only clue he has to the whole ball of string is the Mod who killed the guy that's getting buried. He's hoping Addison turns up at the funeral.

Prior progresses further towards the funeral service, confident as any Mod pretending to be a Fringe, and evades detection. He feels embarrassed, like a bit of a dandy, so he knows the trick is working. He watches Penny carefully through the crowd. She's greeting mourners and accepting everyone's sympathies as they file by. To any observer, she is the twice-grieving widow.

Prior doesn't buy it. There is still something suspect about recent events that somehow tie back to her. Would Ferri have disappeared if Prior had stayed in Antigua? Would Addison have killed Sanders? Would Molly be safe?

The coffin is lowered into the ground. Everyone sits down in high-backed chairs, a reverential tone in the air. Prior hangs back, looking for Addison or any familiar face that might help him. No sign of him. Might he be in disguise as well? Doubtful. They never take advantage of this skill. Mod are so satisfied and in love with themselves, they never think to alter their appearance except to make themselves younger, thinner, or more fashionable.

Prior tries picturing what a younger or thinner Addison might look like. The Mod priest begins the sermon. These Mod priests don't actually practice religion any longer. They just play the part to amuse themselves. The communion wafers are thicker than the Mod priest by a million-fold.

"We gather here to mourn the loss of one of our own," says the Mod priest, having taken on the persona of an old, wise man.

Prior lets out a chuckle.

"The miracle of the nanos in our world and the Holy Promise of Immortality somehow eluded our brother, Beauregard Sanders. But let not this anomaly dissuade us from our Faith in Nanos. The Nanos were the Second Coming spoken of in the Old World. The Nanos removed any notion of Apocalypse and replaced it with Eternal Life on Earth. We embrace Nanos. They have revealed to us the Sacred Secret of Life. The Nanos have made us our own Creators. Thanks be to Nanos for they bring us closer to the God in each of us."

"Thanks be to Nanos," says the congregation in unison.

"Thanks be to ourselves," says the priest.

"Thanks be to ourselves," says the congregation.

Prior doesn't know how much more of this he can take. The damn priests stole the church's real estate and riches in their mad rush to become Mod.

Prior takes a stroll around the cemetery, hoping to run into Addison. No such luck. There's no one he sees that can help. Turning past a tract of land that used to be filled with tombstones, he bumps into Penny.

"Prior, nice look."

He momentarily forgets his ridiculous disguise. "Yeah, how about that? Still fits," he says. "Shouldn't you be back there with all the mourners?"

"It's the priest's words. They made me think of you. How you had so many opportunities to turn Mod but didn't. How you stayed Fringe."

"You think it's for you?" he says.

"Prior, you don't know what it's like."

"Pen, we've been all through this. It was never for you. You know that. And tell me, what's with the Mod send-off for Hubby Number Two? He didn't turn, did he?"

"He was Mod," she says, crying.

"Mod don't eat Mod."

Her sobs grow with every inhalation.

"Penny, I'm being straight with you. It's time you be straight with yourself."

She turns and shuffles away, head down.

"What are you doing?" says Prior.

"What do you mean?"

"I mean why did you set me up? Why did you bring me here from Antigua with your husband's money? Was it so Sanders would get jealous?"

"Prior..."

"I think you arranged for Modela Nova as a client. I think you knew Addison would be out to protect her and would end up killing your husband. Did you do all this so you and I could end up together with his money?"

Prior finds it difficult to make out her face behind the veil. She never drops her gaze while he lists off his accusations. They hang there, thick like smoke.

"Prior, listen to yourself. Just listen to yourself," says Penny, finally. "You're not worth all that. You're not worth any of that."

She sprints away.

He chases after her. As he makes his way down the hill, he catches sight of Modela Nova. She must have turned up looking for her brother as well. She's in her Miss Simmons disguise, wearing a large, pointy black hat that would make every other woman who wore it look like a witch. On her, it looks ravishing. If only the mourners knew who she really was. There was a time when you couldn't spit without hitting a picture of Modela Nova around the world.

Penny grimaces at Prior.

Modela looks over her shoulder and pouts. Prior figures she knows she's being followed. Prior and Penny make their way down the hill towards Modela.

"Pen, she's a client. Her brother is the guy I've been hired to find. He's also the guy who killed your husband. Aren't you remotely interested?"

"Celebrity trash," she says. "I'm sorry she ever contacted us. I figured she had money and would make a good first case for you. You know, easy. Lots of exposure."

"Did you know she was Modela Nova when she first came in?"

"Be careful," says Penny.

"Why?" says Prior. "Does she have nano-cooties?"

"Sort of. Beauregard told me about the experiments that Ferri conducted on her brother. He also did things to Modela."

"What things?"

"She attempted another upgrade. Tried to become a Point. I hear she's dying. Her nanos aren't self-repairing."

"That's impossible."

"So don't get too close to her."

"And you'll be there to catch me when she breaks my heart, huh? Well, my condolences to the bereaved widow."

Prior continues down the hill. He turns around to Penny, who's already heading the other way, and thinks, "One of these days, you'll have to regale me with how you ended up marrying a Mod."

By the time he reaches the bottom to join the other mourners, Modela is gone. He scans the crowd, carefully weaving through them. There is a commotion behind Prior. He spins around.

A flock of sheep are running down the hill, past the mourners. Their bleating adds some much-needed entertainment to the proceedings. They trample all the flowers and shrubs and come within inches of people, having learned over time not to fear them

The Mod mourners merely turn ninety degrees, rendering themselves essentially invisible, and let the sheep pass by without incident.

"Well, well. Former Detective Prior."

It's Grainger and his torpedoes. The disguise isn't fooling them. They weren't here before as part of the service. Prior immediately suspects Penny called them after she saw him here. He really needs a new secretary.

"Grainger. Come to pay your respects? After all, you're a NanoGov man now."

"Nice get-up," says one of the torpedoes and proceeds to laugh.

Prior turns casually and sees they have him surrounded. He needs to buy some time while he reaches into the folds of his costume for some defensive measures.

"Now, why the hell would you be here disguised as Mod, Prior?" says Grainger. He flicks his hand slightly and Prior can tell he's giving commands to his team. Grainger is doing his own stalling for time until his team is in the right formation to move in. "Don't you know that's illegal?"

"I aspire to be like you guys, I guess."

"Bullshit," says Grainger. "We're Fringe, just like you."

"Follow the money, Grainger. Who's paying you? Mod? NanoGov? It's all the same pile."

"You knew this guy?" says Grainger, gesturing towards Sander's burial spot.

"My secretary's husband. Nice guy. Shame, really."

"Well, ain't that cozy?" says Grainger. "That leaves you and her both single. Now you're able to play in the big sandbox filled with his money."

"Shouldn't you and your monkeys be chasing public nuisances like the sheep that ran by?"

"Only public nuisance I see here is you," says Grainger.

The mourners disperse and the field gets eerily quiet. It just leaves Prior alone with these goons.

"You come across this Addison?" says Grainger.

"Not yet."

"And what about Dr. Anton Ferri? Any contact with him?"

"Yeah, a famous guy like Ferri has a lot to discuss with me," says Prior.

Grainger's face is blank and impossible to read. Prior isn't quite sure what he knows. The wind picks up and Prior hears a distant flutter in the sky. It's a familiar sound that grows closer. In a few seconds, it sounds as if a flock of birds is descending on them. The little red light on Grainger's wristwatch is flashing.

Grainger's torpedoes immediately back off and position themselves behind Grainger, like scared children. Grainger, for his part, takes a few steps away from

Prior as well. They all focus submissively on the ground, not wanting to make eye contact with the gathering objects.

The flat, bat-like objects flap to the ground where they unfold and grow in dimension. They stretch and pull themselves like two-dimensional taffy until they're human scale. There are four of them, wearing their traditional black robes; the same types of robes worn by twelfth-century European monks.

The Mod Police. Children playing at cops and robbers like they've joined a fantasy camp.

"We'll take it from here," says the lead Mod Police Officer in a raspy voice.

"I understand," says Grainger, in a quiet, almost reverent voice, never taking his eyes off the ground. "Please be advised that this perp has information…"

"Are you presuming to speak to me?" says the lead Mod Police Officer.

"No, sir."

"He thinks we're all partners," says one of the other Mod Police Officers.

The Mod Police emit a wheezing noise, like steam escaping. It's the closest they can approximate to human laughter.

The Mod Police behold Prior with their empty, lifeless eyes.

"Jeremiah Prior, you are hereby charged with…"

Prior pulls a plastic water gun out of his jacket and aims it at the Mod Police. During this whole conversation, he's been filling the gun with Antoine's Antiguan red fish jerk sauce within his robes. Now is as good a time as any to see if it really works.

The Mod Police are ten feet in front of Prior with Grainger and his torpedoes a few feet behind them. Prior figures he can knock out the Mod Police and bolt before Grainger and his gang pry their heads loose from the Mod Police's asses and start chasing him.

"How dare you…" says the lead Mod Police Officer.

Prior pumps the trigger and sprays them with the fish sauce. It coats the Mod Police and even splashes onto Grainger and his goons before they have time to react. The spray noise sounds like Mod Police laughter.

Nothing happens.

"Shit, Antoine," says Prior.

Prior bolts past the edge of the cemetery and into the city. Grainger and his torpedoes pursue him on foot, trailing him by about fifty feet. The Mod Police shake themselves off like dogs after a swim and fly off into the sky. They circle thirty feet over the ground, hunting for Prior.

Prior jumps into the nearest warehouse and pulls out one of Antoine's pica-tams. At least he knows this works. He pulls it over his entire body until it looks like a big sack. He hops into a corner of the warehouse and remains still.

The Mod Police and Fringe cops use their nano-scanners to search for a signature pattern that matches Prior's nano-signature on file. Because the pica-tam is made from pica-fibers, the nanos never even get close to him. They're like an ocean cruiser trying to sail through a keyhole.

After an hour, Prior figures he's evaded the cops. He takes back any ill-will towards Antoine, looks up at the sky, and thanks him for the elastic pica-tam. It also gives him an idea.

Chapter 27

Prior goes to his office, makes a few inquiries delivered by Fringe messengers, and gets an appointment with the Letter-Writer. He throws the plasma gun into his back pocket. It makes him feel better about his chances of survival. Now that the Mod Police have made an overt attempt to arrest him, he doesn't feel bad carrying it around.

Prior heads to the park and hears an oncoming stampede. The dappled sun makes the park look even more like a jungle. The Mod playing Ben-Hur roars by on his chariot driven by a pack of Fringe. The chariot slows down to make a right-angle turn and avoid a row of trees, practically rolling on just its two right wheels. Prior leaps to the back of the chariot and holds on, ducking low to avoid detection. The Mod stands up high, donning a leather helmet with side straps that make him look like he's on his way to a Brunhild audition. He's too entranced with his majesty to look back. Prior should be safe for the mile he's hitching a ride.

At the other end of the park, Prior hops off, glad to leave the chariot race. His mouth is full of dirt and his ears are still ringing with the screams of the whipped Fringe as they pull their Mod-Master through his deranged fantasy. Prior stabilizes himself as best he can and heads to the Letter-Writer's tent.

As usual, the line to the tent is long. But Prior has set up a reservation. He's gotten word to the Letter-Writer that he's onto something big that might bring down Mod. The Letter-Writer has taken the bait and obliged Prior. Prior gives everybody in line a nod as he lifts the tent flap and enters.

"Quickly," says the Letter-Writer. He's sitting on his box, surrounded by a citadel of paper stacks.

"People looking for me?" says Prior.

"Better I give you a list of who's not looking for you. Let us get to what you need. It would not be good for business if they killed me too."

"That's very thoughtful of you," says Prior.

"The thing," says the Letter-Writer, his eyebrows indicating impatience.

Prior hands him the mahogany pipe he lifted from Belden's robe a few days earlier.

"And the specifics?" says the Letter-Writer.

"Modela Nova's address."

"Well, well," says the Letter-Writer. "Trouble doesn't need to look for you. You're walking right into it." The Letter-Writer completes his task with a flick of his quill like a conductor waving his baton. He hands Prior a slip of paper. "You were never here."

Prior grabs the paper. "Never am," he says.

As he heads in Modela's direction, he formulates a plan in case she isn't willing to cooperate. Between the pica-tam and the plasma gun, he's on solid ground. It won't be the first time a beautiful woman has set up Prior or left him holding the bag. He just has to find out how much she knows and how deep she's involved.

Modela lives in a nice section of the city, even by Mod standards. But then, when you're the object of worship and the first of a new species, people tend to throw a few shekels your way.

Prior slides the pica-tam over his body. It feels oddly familiar and comfortable.

Prior saunters through the front door of her building. The security nanos remain at-ease as he enters without detection. They probably notice the air particles moving in a different direction or the ambient temperature of the room rise a hundredth of a degree. If they do detect these disturbances, they do nothing about it. He pictures a nano asleep in a chair, a half-eaten doughnut in one hand, drool emanating from its mouth down to its lap. But that's crazy. Nanos aren't alive. They are things. Ferri figured out a way to convert organic mass to nano-scale robots, programmed to do their Mod-Master's bidding.

Prior climbs up to the eleventh floor and proceeds down the quiet hallway. Modela's neighbors seem to be away for the evening. It is also possible that, despite the dozen or so doors in the hallway, there are only two apartments, one on each side of the hallway. It isn't unheard of for a Mod to consume the interior walls and take over the neighboring space. It isn't that much different from what Addison did to Sanders.

Modela's door is carved iron and has some type of electronic surveillance camera attached to the top of it. He checks the door. Of course it is unlocked. He enters Modela's home and closes the door behind him, undetected.

Once inside, he stands still for a few minutes, listening for any activity. He's hoping that Modela is home by herself. He can never be too careful. The place is completely silent.

He sniffs around slowly at first, hugging the walls like a moving poster. When he's sure the apartment is empty, he takes off the pica-tam.

The apartment is decorated sparely with minimal furniture. It is all sleek, chrome, and white. She must be going through a weird, late-twentieth century phase. Mod usually decorate with more pretension and gaudier displays of wealth and power.

There is a tapping and a rush of wind from the bedroom. Prior ducks down to the floor, reaching for his pica-tam. The noise doesn't repeat.

He creeps to the bedroom. The window is open, the room sucking in big gulps of wind. There is glass on the floor and it appears that the window was broken earlier. The tapping is the window curtain blowing and fluttering in the wind. A chair next to the window has been knocked over and smashed.

There's been a struggle. Maybe it's supposed to look like this. Maybe somebody did come in and kidnap her. All he knows is that he needs her and she isn't here.

He peers out the window. The city is quiet tonight. Peering down eleven stories, he says a little prayer that Modela, or what's left of her, is not down there. The sidewalk is clean. He knows that, under normal circumstance, if Modela were thrown out a window, she'd simply float away. But after what he saw Addison do, even Mod aren't safe.

Prior decides to search her place thoroughly since it appears he has the luxury of time. Naturally, her walls are filled with pictures of herself, a shrine to her former and everlasting glory. There are framed pictures of Modela with various dignitaries from around the world, most of whom have already turned Mod in the photos. In a darker part of the hallway, there are a few shots of Modela when she was younger. These were taken when she was an actual Fringe model and actress.

She was absolutely gorgeous. Why somebody would try and fix what wasn't broken eludes Prior. There's a lot about people he doesn't understand.

Prior heads back into the bedroom and continues his search for something. Anything. A clue that might help him see this case in a new light.

In the living room, her desk is in neat order but contains nothing extraordinary. A half-hour into his search, he finds what he's been looking for in her kitchen. Next to an old-fashioned microwave oven, there's a hand-written note. It's an appointment for a consultation at the Mod Clinic. Attached to the note is an ID and a Mod Clinic access badge. Everything except the note is a fake.

Why is Modela trying to sneak into the Mod Clinic? That's where Fringe are turned to Mod. Modela is already a Mod. And certainly, she is famous enough that she can saunter in as an honored guest, not as an intruder. Prior's head heats up, like the good old days. Back when he was in the zone and everything clicked.

Addison. The access badge is for Addison.

Prior checks the note. The appointment is for tomorrow morning at eleven.

Prior leaves Modela's apartment and quietly heads downstairs, slipping on his pica-tam. He figures there is nothing more he can do today on the case. He'll check on Molly again, then pay another visit to Brewster.

As he walks across the lobby towards the front door of Modela's building, Prior notices that the air is dustier than when he came in. What is more puzzling is that the dust particles aren't behaving according to the laws of Brownian motion. They seem to cluster together into what appears to be factions, like a century-old high school cafeteria.

The dust cliques are following Prior.

Even though he is undetectable covered by his pica-tam, the dust cliques are swirling around him, trying to sniff him out, like they've discovered a black hole.

Points.

Somehow, they have discovered Prior. But they aren't sure yet. That's why they haven't attacked, devoured. The silence is the eeriest part. Being one-dimensional and infinitely small, they make no sound, even when thousands of them are gathered together into mini galaxies orbiting Prior's head.

Prior stands still, unsure if he should make a run for it. Probably not. Points are surely faster than a Fringe on foot. He isn't even sure if the Points are here searching for him, Modela or Addison. Or are they after the stolen Seurat sketch coursing through Prior's veins?

He slowly turns back around and advances toward the elevators. There is no sense in worrying about raising suspicions with the building tenants anymore since a giant Point cloud, moving like a weather front, is following him. The elevator doors open and Prior steps in, along with several thousand tiny, one-dimensional people. The generic music playing through the speakers has a heavy bass line. The Points throb in midair with each bass note.

Prior gets off at the eleventh floor and re-enters Modela's apartment. The Points, flying more erratically as they become excited, continue to follow him, resembling soda water carbonation. The Points act as if they have stumbled onto whatever they were seeking.

The giant dust cloud grandly sweeps into the room and disperses in every direction. Immediately, the Points start consuming the mass in the room. Prior watches as the entire contents of the living room melt in front of him. It is all done with great soundless precision.

Prior grabs a golden goblet sitting on a windowsill and runs into the kitchen, not caring if they realize he is a Fringe in hiding. Modela's microwave oven is an old model, probably collected during the mid-1980's craze. Prior makes sure the microwave oven is plugged in and works. He waits until there is hardly anything left in the room.

Prior cranks up the microwave oven to its highest setting. He flings open the door and sets the golden goblet into the tray inside. The Points, moving as one again, each hungry for golden leftovers, fly into the microwave, coalescing like steam. Prior slams the door. Finally, there is noise in the room.

Not only is the microwave's fan whirring at an ungodly decibel pitch, there is a muffled screaming from within the microwave, like old-fashioned popcorn, as each greedy Point explodes into a mini starburst. A huge fireworks display is contained within a small box and Prior is the only one who gets to watch.

Old technology always beats out new technology. Prior understands something that is so old, it has been forgotten. In their arrogance, the new Gods of the land assume that anything old is not worth knowing. But nature has a steadfast rule.

Everything burns.

Chapter 28

When Prior gets back to his office the next day, the widow Penelope is waiting for him.

"Jesus, Penny, shouldn't you be mourning somewhere?"

He can't bring himself to mention that he isn't glad to see her. He needs to get some research done. And there is nobody better at research than the woman standing before him dressed in black.

"I need to get back to work," she says.

She sits in the corner of his office, organizing files. Her hands shake slightly which is the only indication that she's been through a traumatic experience. Either she has deep reserves of strength he isn't aware of or she's hiding something.

"Maybe this isn't the best time to lose yourself in the details of my case," says Prior.

"I need to work," she says.

He sits down next to her and offers a cigarette he stole from one of Grainger's torpedoes. He even stole the lighter. It's been a while since Prior has had a smoke. It's nice. The smoke in the air brings back a lot of memories. Mostly, they're good.

Penny inhales deeply and seems to relax. Mod enjoy smoking so cigarettes are now designed with nanos to repel the bad effects of smoking. Those nanos race through their lungs, vanquishing all the nicotine and whatever the hell else they put in cigarettes.

"Nice funeral," says Prior, not knowing what is appropriate in this situation.

"He was an asshole."

"Eh…"

"But a rich asshole."

"Ah."

"The best kind," she says, trying to blow smoke rings to accentuate her position. The smoke just ends up being an expanding stream like the exhalations of a dragon breathing fire.

"So, what are you going to do now?" says Prior.

"I just want to help. I've got all his money. But I don't want to be alone right now."

"Fair enough."

"I've decided to focus on someone else's misery for a while."

"Meaning me?"

"Meaning Modela Nova. And her missing brother. I could do with watching Mod be miserable for a while."

Prior puts out his cigarette.

"Tell me what you need," she says as she continues to straighten his files.

"My old chemist pal, Brewster. I need to know…"

"Got it," she says, handing him a folder.

"Penny, how did you…"

"Prior, you'll never learn. You need me a whole lot more than I need you."

By the time Prior makes it to the street where Brewster lives, it's still early. Prior needs to be at the Mod Clinic by eleven. If his hunch is right, he'll nab Addison at the Mod Clinic and get him to explain everything.

A sole light flickers from the house at the end of the street. The light emanates from Brewster's former greenhouse in the backyard.

Prior hopes that Brewster has solved the problem of his two-headedness. In the good old days, Brewster was commonly acknowledged as a chemistry genius. Especially his work in plastics. One of the first things that Mod did was appropriate all plastics in the world. Plastics were prevalent and a cheap source of mass for their Mod to convert into whatever the Mod desired. Mod soon found out that they were only interested in thermoset plastic; the kind that didn't melt. Bakelite was really popular for a while. Prior made a pile authenticating Bakelite products for Mod so they could consume them like fast food. The melting kind, thermoplastic, was too dangerous for Mod to play with. Brewster's work was in thermoplastics. Prior figures Belden stole Brewster's thermoplastic collection as collateral for his Mod conversion.

Unwittingly, Brewster helped define the nano-chemistry that led the way to Ferri creating Mod. Prior is sure that Brewster's research was exploited to create Points as well. It makes sense that Brewster lives in a greenhouse so he can continue living off the grid, working his experiments, trying to make the Fringe world a better place. Prior is hoping that Brewster is deep into something important. Maybe he discovered a way to escape this circling-the-drain existence.

The front of Brewster's house is dark. The stone feels cold. Prior sneaks around to the back towards the warm, translucent glow from the fogged glass of the greenhouse. Prior hopes the good half of Brewster's head-duo is home tonight. And that the other half has been vanquished.

As Prior taps on the greenhouse door, a chilling thought occurs to him. The only way Brewster can truly exist in this type of environment is if he is under the protection of NanoGov. Prior shakes off the feeling. Brewster would be the last person to sell out to them. His life is devoted to undoing what Ferri brought upon the world.

Perhaps Brewster is telling NanoGov he is doing research on their behalf in exchange for an assurance of safety. But, locked behind these doors, hidden by glass that somehow keeps out the NanoGov and Mod security nanos, Brewster takes their money and equipment and applies it to experiments that will ultimately lead to their downfall. Now, that sounds like the Brewster he knows. Or some optimistic glimmer hiding deep inside Prior.

Prior taps on the greenhouse door with more confidence.

A silhouette gathers on the other side of the door.

"Yes?" says the voice. It is muffled by the thick glass.

"Brewster?"

A security camera, above the door, previously hidden by clinging ivy, pokes out and gives Prior a good once-over. Satisfied, the camera recedes back into its foliage.

The door sweeps open. Prior braces himself.

"My stars, Jeremiah Prior," says a one-headed Brewster, grandly twirling his cape. "As I live and flourish. I thought you were dead."

Brewster is Mod.

Prior doesn't know what to say. He needs time to absorb this.

"Don't stand there like the Avon lady," says Brewster. "Enter."

Brewster places the film of his hand on Prior's shoulder and leads him inside. Counter to Prior's expectations, the greenhouse is not filled with plants. Nor is it filled with science experiments, lab benches, test tubes, or any signs of radical societal upheaval. It is just another hyper-luxurious Mod palace replete with tapestries, furnishings, art, and treasures scavenged from the world and its less-fortunate occupants.

Brewster seems to favor the Egyptian motif more so than others. That explains why he is dressed like King Tut.

"Don't look so astonished," says Brewster, leading Prior to the main part of the room, which is much bigger than it appears from the outside. Brewster offers Prior a small stool, then sits languidly on a velvet throne that his nanos create.

"You of all people."

"Oh please, Prior. Don't start in with that. You are many things but naïve isn't one of them. Now, to what do I owe this great pleasure?" says Brewster.

"Official business, actually."

Brewster stands up from his throne, takes a step down, and turns slightly to his left. Suddenly, Prior can't see him anymore.

"Look, Brewster, I don't have time for this." Prior stands and takes a step to his right until he can see Brewster again.

There is a large ultraviolet light near the greenhouse window behind Brewster that shines artificial amber rays of sun translucently through his head.

"Then what do you need of me?"

"When I have time, you'll have to explain to me just what the hell you were thinking," says Prior. "But for now, please step here." From his right pocket, Prior pulls out something he knows will capture Brewster's attention. "There are bigger things at play here, Brewster. I may have shambled onto something deep. I need your help." Prior nonchalantly waves the eighteenth-century brass needle Belden used on him.

"Whatever do you mean?" says Brewster, entranced. "And where did you get that nasty needle? Here. Let's have us a look-see."

Brewster grabs the needle and holds it the way a monk would grasp a holy relic. Brewster studies the carvings on the sides of the needle, hoping to unlock some ancient riddle. Maybe there's another authorship in it for him. After material possessions, the most important thing to Mod is recognition of a new discovery.

"It's gorgeous," says Brewster. His eyes remain focused, their reverential gaze on the needle.

"Remember Professor Belden," says Prior. "He stuck me with this needle. Said it was for my own good."

"The man sounds enchanting as ever."

The scenery rushing by the back window blurs like a faded water color.

"And he injected something in me. He says it's the stolen Seurat sketch. Maybe because he didn't want to be caught with it when NanoGov came snooping around. Maybe he wanted to throw them off his tail. But I have a bad feeling I know what he did."

"You're not implying that…"

"I am," says Prior.

"Here, gimme," says Brewster, having heard the only bit of news that could divert him from the enchanting brass artifact in his pasty hand. He gazes at Prior the way a bandage salesman might look upon a hemophiliac. Brewster devolves quickly from the educated chemist into a Thing That Wants, grabbing Prior's wrist, rolling up his sleeve. Prior pulls his arm away and slaps Brewster hard on the face. It feels like putting your hand through plastic wrap. Before Brewster can react, Prior snatches the needle away from him.

"Well, well, aren't we touchy."

"Maybe it's just Seurat's black crayon lines and blobs," says Prior, hoping to hook Brewster further. Prior reaches into his backpack and pulls out a portable turntable. It is standard issue for his line of work. Prior winds it up and places it in front of Brewster. "You're not going to like this."

Brewster backs up a few steps. "So completely unnecessary," says Brewster.

"I know," says Prior. "But I have to be sure."

"Now, you know I don't have to subject myself to anything of this sort without a NanoGov warrant," says Brewster.

"Humor me."

"Very well. But you'll have to return the favor someday."

This is the only tool available for Prior to determine if Brewster has any NanoGov nanos floating within him. Prior needs to know that Brewster is clean, that he just has his own nanos to command. Somewhere, Prior hopes, deep inside Brewster, is that hippie that still wants to take down the government.

Brewster steps on the turntable. Prior cranks it to 45 rpm and nods to Brewster. Brewster summons his nanos and begins spinning in place, slowly at first, then at full speed, his axis remaining at the center of the turntable. There is nowhere to hide.

"Are you having fun yet?" says Brewster, his voice attacking Prior's ears in waves. "We Mod have given up so much for a real life yet we're still subjected to these humilities."

"I don't know what world you've been living in but it doesn't take a chemistry genius to recognize when your head is so far up your ass," says Prior.

"Charming, Jere."

"The Vermeer stolen last week?" says Prior, searching Brewster's spinning facial expressions for any clues.

"Officer and a Laughing Girl," says Brewster. "Of course. What Mod hasn't heard? Horrible. What have we become?"

Brewster steps off the turntable. Waves of him ripple through his flat body. He steadies himself and lies down on a Louis XIV chaise lounge that appears instantly.

"Looks like you're clean," says Prior.

"Detective Prior, surely you're not implying that I would know the whereabouts of this Vermeer?"

Brewster places his hand on his lap and an Egyptian silver bowl filled with peeled grapes appears. He pops a peeled grape into his slit of a mouth. The grape-lump stretches his skin tightly as it works its way down his upper torso. Gradually, the grape-lump dissipates as it reaches his abdomen. Mod still creep Prior out, old friends or not.

"You still dealing in black-market body chemistry?" says Prior, tentatively.

"In the good old days, a body's chemistry was worth about $1.83," says Brewster, warming to his subject. "Now, with phosphorous prices being what they are and the ban on Fringe potassium…"

"I think my blood futures might be worth more than that," says Prior.

Brewster eyes Prior closely with his monoscopic expression. "That's what they all say. But when you die, you're mostly water. And in case any of this is news to your voluminous brain, water is still free. Even for Fringe."

Prior makes a decision. He has no choice. He has to trust this guy, hoping there's some humanity left.

Brewster stands up and drifts over like a sail. "My poor boy, no wonder you're looking pale. Are you suggesting…?"

Brewster puts his tracing-paper hand on Prior's shoulder again.

"That's why I'm here," says Prior.

Brewster produces a small piece of paper indistinguishable from his left hand. From his right hand, his nanos attack the brass needle. The needle is dissolved in one second, incorporated into the mass of his nanos. The brass needle reassembles in Brewster's hand as if he conjured it. He approaches Prior, who takes a step back.

"There are bigger things at play here, Prior. You're in deeper than you know. Now, I played with your toy. You play with mine."

Prior reluctantly offers his finger. Brewster pricks it with the needle and hands Prior the piece of paper.

Prior applies his finger to the paper, swirling and smearing a few drops of his blood. Vermeer's "Officer and a Laughing Girl" coalesces instantly in postage-stamp size.

"Amazing," says Brewster, flat tears sliding down the plane of his cheek. "No one's ever owned the real painting. Why, do you realize that the last true masterpiece available for public consumption courses through your veins?"

"Yeah, it occurred to me."

Brewster peers at Prior with a penetrating gaze. Brewster used to look at Prior that way back in the old days when he needed Prior's help.

"And knowing this, and seeing me like this, you still chose to disclose your secret to me?" Brewster seems genuinely touched. Emotions don't sit well on Mod. They're out of place.

"Because I have to believe you're still inside there, Brewster. Hidden in one of those square inches."

"True enough."

"The thing is, Brewster, I don't know why I was injected. Or where the stolen Seurat is."

"Well, I suspect Belden took the Vermeer. Couldn't he have simply panicked and injected you with the goods?"

"Maybe Belden planned on smuggling the painting by killing me and transporting my body."

Brewster floats around his room, thinking. "Prior, let me tell you something about the great Anton Ferri. After I turned, I found out that Ferri was involved in some shady deals with these Points. The word in the sky is that Ferri was trying to restore his reputation and legacy. He was on the verge of a major discovery in the next step of evolution when he disappeared."

"Sounds like high-level NanoGov to me," says Prior.

"Or the Fringe Underground Movement. I never would have turned if I had known about the Points."

"You didn't answer my question, Brewster. Now that you've seen it, what's my blood chemistry worth these days on the open market?"

"My estimate would be five-and-a-half billion. But I can do better than that," says Brewster. "Come here." He takes Prior's hand and holds it open. A silver skeleton key appears in Prior's hand, then melts into his skin.

"What's the key for?" says Prior.

"To open the lock, obviously."

"What lock?"

"For the vault I just placed the Vermeer in," says Brewster. "Mod can't get to it. The Vermeer nanos in your blood are now encapsulated by thermoplastics. Perfectly harmless until someone tries to steal it."

"Thanks," says Prior.

"One more thing," says Brewster. "You'll need to think of a password. Something no one can guess. It will help secure the key."

"Got it," says Prior.

Brewster disappears behind a thirteenth-century tapestry, reappearing a few minutes later. He hands Prior a small plastic device. It looks like one of those old disposable cigarette lighters.

"More items for your goodie bag," says Brewster.

"What is it?"

"The result of some experiments. But only use it if you have to. And for God's sake, point it away from you when you push this button."

Prior demonstrates how he'll use it. Brewster nods approvingly as Prior pockets it.

"And if I go kaboom when someone tries to steal the Vermeer?"

"I'm sure you'll be fine. You take care of that key. That's the real trick," says Brewster.

"I wish Mod believed in Fringe consent," says Prior, rubbing his hand.

Chapter 29

He finds that his whole perspective has changed with the knowledge of the Vermeer painting coursing through his veins.

Officer and Laughing Girl.

The irony of the painting doesn't escape him. The only thing more off-putting might have been if Vermeer decided to call the damn thing Unlicensed Authentician and His Freedom-Fighter Daughter, Wherein the Latter is Supremely Pissed-Off at the Former.

Prior decides to take a stroll. Back on the street, he flags down a Fringe messenger boy, writes a note and sends the kid off to Felice's place. He sends another note to Lachende. He knows that Fringe messenger boys aren't allowed to communicate directly with Mod but these kids have a way of getting their messages sent. Mod never can trace these messages since the kids pass them in a hasty manner, like worker bees, and Mod just don't have the attention span or focus to see it through. These kids will do anything for a tip. That's how they feed and clothe themselves.

He clings to the shadows of a building's doorway, avoiding as much detection as possible. A while later, the messenger boy runs back with a response from Felice and Lachende.

"J, Molly is not with me. Listen, I really need to see you. It's urgent. F."

"Daddy-O, I'll be at the radio station. Your sonny-boy-in-law, Lachende."

Prior tips the kid and throws away the notes. The kid darts away, onto his next mission. Prior thinks about Felice's note. No dice. He isn't biting. The further he stays away from Felice, the less trouble he'll be in.

Prior heads to the city's only radio station, covered by his pica-tam. There, he crouches in the shadows and waits for Lachende. He can't shake the unsettling thought of being strapped to a slab while the Vermeer in his blood is auctioned off to the highest bidder.

The radio station building is on the perimeter of the city and has the traditional tower for broadcasting. Mod have allowed these metal towers to stand, uneaten by their nanos, for the singular retro-pleasure they provide. The tower stands in the skyline as a quaint reminder that the world was so vastly different not that long ago.

Prior takes off the pica-tam so Lachende can find him. He reaches into his pocket, hoping to find another cigarette. His finger still stings from Brewster's needle. He checks the time. He needs to interrupt Addison's eleven o'clock appointment.

Old habits are not an affordable commodity in this world. Prior shouldn't have had a cigarette the night before. First, he treated himself to something luxuriously forbidden. The next thing he knows, he'll be nano-flat and selling his soul for a tobacco plantation run by Fringe and his nano-slaves. It's no way to live.

"Hey, Poppa."

Prior spins around on his knee, still crouching. Molly stands casually, holding hands with Lachende in broad daylight.

"Are you nuts?" says Prior, shooting straight up. He grabs their hands and disentangles them.

"What's the prob?" says Lachende, wearing a 1970's velour track suit.

Lachende's face reveals his intense focus. He is willing his nanos to make him resemble a Fringe. Even still, Mod don't hold hands, much less socialize, with Fringe in broad daylight.

"The problem, Lachende, is that certain people might be after Molly. She might be in danger. She should be in a safe house."

"Don't talk about me like I'm not here," says Molly.

"No one's come around looking for you?" says Prior.

"Well…" says Lachende.

"Lachende!" says Molly. Her tone expresses their familiarity, which makes Prior more uncomfortable.

"Well what?" says Prior.

Molly pouts her lips like she used to. It has a momentary soothing affect on Prior, ratcheting down his anger, surprise, and insecurity. It makes him feel safe, like his daughter is a little girl again, like the world hasn't completely changed.

"This morning, before Lachende came to pick me up, Detective Grainger showed up. He said he was looking for you," says Molly. "He had some bad news."

"What?" says Prior.

"Dr. Brewster is dead. Killed in his lab," says Molly, stoically. Her life is so filled with death that one more doesn't seem to move her to tears.

Prior's not a religious man but says a little prayer for poor Brewster.

"What happened to your finger?" says Molly.

Prior doesn't respond, still thinking about Brewster. He held out hope that Brewster was his strongest ally. He needed an old friend to trust.

"Looks like someone drew a blood sample," says Lachende.

"I just saw him. Brewster," says Prior. "Devoured by those things, I bet."

Lachende looks disappointed. It's close to a human reaction. "I'm so sorry, Prior. I know he was your friend." He places a flap on Prior's shoulder but Prior pulls away.

"Cut it out, Lachende," says Prior. "Is that all you have to say?"

"You think Lachende had something to do with it?" says Molly. "Brewster was his mentor."

"Come now, this is curious," says Lachende. Before Prior can react, Lachende's finger extends into a wand, ever telescoping into a thinner strand until it reaches Prior's injured fingertip. With no hesitation, Lachende's fishing-line thread enters Prior's finger for a second. It then retracts and snaps back to its normal shape and scale.

Lachende's eyes grow twice their normal size as he takes a step toward Prior. "Well, well, what have we been hiding?" says Lachende, pushing Prior away from the street.

"Back off," says Prior.

Molly takes a step back. She looks genuinely surprised.

"How long have you had that?" says Lachende. "Not long or I would have detected it sooner. It has a sweet smell." Every step he takes towards Prior is countered with a step backwards from Prior.

"What?" says Molly, interrupting the dance.

"Vermeer's 'Officer and Laughing Girl.' Guess whose blood holds the world's greatest free-agent treasure?" says Lachende to Molly.

"Dad?"

Prior holds up his hands to stop them from advancing. "Belden, the idiot Professor. He injected the painting into me a few days ago."

"You could have sold it for a fortune. Gone back to Antigua," says Lachende. "I would have, if I were you."

"I know," says Prior. "And someone killed Brewster for it."

"Why didn't you escape?" says Molly.

Prior takes a deep breath. "Why do you think? I wanted to be with you." It's harder to say that he imagined.

It's difficult to read her expression. She's either touched or annoyed.

"Alright, hold that thought," says Lachende, putting himself between Prior and Molly. "Time to go to work."

Lachende deflates in front of them, his mass escaping while his nanos rocket away, swirling and orbiting around the Lachende galaxy. Lachende quickly turns back into his Mod self. A microphone and headset instantly appear on his head and his clothes change from the 1970's velour track suit to a giant walking electronic display that is wrapped tightly around his body. Small, colorful, blinking lights skate across Lachende's two-dimensional frame in front and back of him like a sandwich board. The lights spell out, "...WNAN RADIO...THE GOLDEN OLDIES RADIO HOUR...LACHENDE IN THE MORNING...WNAN RADIO..."

"Great," says Prior. "Limitless technology and I'm walking around with a human billboard."

"Quiet, I'm on the air," says Lachende and adjusts his head set and microphone.

"You know about this?" says Prior to Molly.

"It's how we met." She's less defensive when she says this, like a small door has opened.

"Dandy," says Prior.

"Hey, it's Lachende in the morning on your radio station, WNAN. The only nano-radio station sanctioned by NanoGov. All nano, all the time. How are we doing out there today, people? A big shout-out and good morning to all my Mod listeners! And a happy how-da-ya-do to all my Fringe friends out there. If you're listening to this, you have access to a radio, electricity, or are connected to a Mod who does. Either way, this all bodes well for you!"

"Is there a job you don't have?" says Prior to Lachende.

Lachende motions for Prior to be quiet, pointing to the microphone, as they parade down the street. Lachende keeps talking into his headset, his billboard body announcing radio contests and commercial breaks. Several Fringe and Mod see him on the street and point, surprised and pleased with their brush with fame. Prior hides behind Lachende, hoping not to be noticed. He tries to draw Molly in with him but she proudly marches beside Lachende.

"Is this for real," Prior says to Molly. "I mean, who is he talking to?"

"Oh my Mod, Dad, sometimes I can't believe how out of it you are."

"Thanks."

"Lachende gets to do this once a week. His radio show is broadcast up there," she says and points to the sky. "Lachende's radio show bounces off the Sky-Screen where it transmits directly into Fringe radios and, via nanos, into the brain of every Mod."

"So he was serious about Fringe listening to this on radios?"

"Golden Oldies," she says.

"This is just a city thing, right?"

"City thing? Look at the Sky-Screen. It's NanoGov. Since when do they think small? This is worldwide."

Prior feels odd following Lachende and Molly down a public street in daylight while Lachende broadcasts his morning show to the planet. Lachende is so comfortable in his new skin, so assured in his place in this crazy world. Prior wonders if Antoine can hear this in Antigua. He hopes there still is an Antigua.

"That was 'I'm Your Steamship of Love,' part of the 2020's retro-punkflapper music craze. Now, you're in for a very special treat, listeners," says Lachende. "Today, we're going to be exploring the old neighborhood they used to call Greenwich Village. As always, I'll be your tour guide.

"Greenwich Village may have just been a small section of New York City but it was one rich in history. Did you know that the ancient Mayan, conquerors of Europe, settled here in 1657? They were the original founders. Since then, this quaint neighborhood has given birth to thousands of people who went on to lead marvelously prosperous lives as Mod."

"Mayans?" says Prior, still following them down the street, nowhere near Greenwich Village.

Molly whips around, embarrassed. "Yes, Dad, Mayans."

"But the Mayans weren't from Europe. They didn't settle here."

"Who cares?" she says. "Don't you get it? People aren't interested in details. They just want to be assured that they stand on the shoulders of magnificent people from the past."

"In fact," continues Lachende as they stroll down another street, "the name 'Greenwich Village' has an interesting origin. It's a rather cute misunderstanding from these ancient people. You see, the settlers to these strange lands used to eat all their food wrapped in various edible leaves. Decades later, the British came to this country and discovered this unique eating practice. The British called what the Mayans ate a 'green sandwich.' After the British invaded the city and decimated the Mayan culture, taking over all that was now rightfully theirs, they decided to call the Mayan village 'Green Sandwich Village.' Years of changes to the language caused the name to shorten to what it is now historically remembered as."

Lachende beams, seeking Prior's approval.

Prior remembers Lachende as a little boy, so eager to help out on a case. Feynman would usually send him out to spy on someone. Lachende was always great at disappearing into the background. He'd pretend, without much difficulty, that he was a homeless street urchin, disguising himself with mud on his face and rags for clothing.

He was so cheerful and optimistic. Mostly, he just wanted a home. And he was so damn adaptable. Prior told him he needed to be careful. In the world they lived in, possessing an eagerness to be liked and wanting to constantly please was a bad thing. Predatory people conspired on a daily basis to take advantage of that exact instinct. These predators ended up forming NanoGov.

They stroll around for the full hour during Lachende's broadcast, aimlessly turning down mostly abandoned streets but occasionally coming into contact with some disheveled Fringe who pathetically wave hello. Mod drift overhead, blinking their lights back to Lachende in recognition of the radio show they're listening to.

The entire time, the Sky-Screen covers everyone like a blanket, monitoring and projecting Lachende's radio show.

By the end of the show, Prior's demeanor has changed. He feels less paranoid under that blanket. No one has come up to them. No nano-search, scan, or interrogation of any kind is performed. Prior chuckles, realizing the irony that the situation is now reversed. He is now in the protective cocoon of Lachende's presence.

They reach the Mod Clinic as Lachende signs off. The electronic billboard body dims and Lachende is back to his 1970's velour track suit. He's added a pink, fur pimp hat for added measure.

"Hell of a show," says Prior.

"Did you like it? Don't think I didn't notice the eye-rolling," says Lachende.

"Lachende, you of all people should know that as an Authentician..."

"Well, as promised, here we are," says Lachende.

Prior takes a look at the Mod Clinic's façade. It's just another large, square warehouse, bland and without charm. Its only distinguishing feature is its lack of dilapidation. The dull bricks and glass look newly installed.

"I have special privileges that allow me to bring in one guest each month. It's all heavily monitored by NanoGov but I'll just tell them that you're a very strong candidate for Mod conversion. I brought some fake identification nano stuff as well," says Lachende. He produces a small pill.

"What about Molly?" says Prior.

"I'm going in with you, Dad," she says as if it is the most natural and obvious response.

"They won't let you in there. No way," says Prior.

"Oh, Molly's been inside several times to visit me. It's all taken care of," says Lachende, turning to the front door.

"What?"

"Been studying these Clinics," says Molly. "Looking for chinks in the armor."

"They think you're a terrorist. Unless that was just for me," says Prior. "Either way, I don't want you in there shopping for ideas."

"Oh, please," she says.

"You might as well tell him," says Lachende.

"No way," says Molly.

"Oh, come on," says Lachende. "He could have run off with the Vermeer but he stayed for you. You owe him that much."

"Don't talk about me like I'm not here," says Prior.

"Not happening," says Molly.

"Fine. Come on, then," says Lachende, sticking his hand into the doorway crack. He's searched for rogue nanos. The door opens and Prior and Molly are searched as well.

"You know, Molly," says Prior, "this isn't like getting your ears pierced."

"Tell me about it," she says and crosses the threshold.

Chapter 30

There are thousands of Mod Clinics throughout the world, two in this city alone, each operated by NanoGov, each in direct communication with one another using Sky-Screen and instant nano-communication. Collectively, NanoGov has performed millions of Mod conversions worldwide. These Mod Clinics are the nerve center of this new world. The womb.

These facts alone make Prior nervous as he sets foot inside. He's never been inside a Mod Clinic. This is the one place in the entire universe where he shouldn't be walking into. And he's waltzing in with the one person who he swore to protect.

But Prior's apprehension pales in comparison to the rigid fear he experiences once inside the Mod Clinic. He holds his breath and reaches out for Molly. There are no clearly delineated walls, floor, or ceiling inside. Rather, everything seems to be underwater. The three of them stand in a rushing stream with white water caps, awaiting audience with the Great Oz. The rushing current does not take them anywhere. It speeds by, ignorant of their presence.

Prior feels heavy, sluggish. His limbs require great effort to move, being dragged down by the tremendous weight of the water. The smell of wet, electric air is tangible but he's not getting wet. There are waterfalls overhead, fish swimming alongside, and the crash of waves and swirl of eddies in the distance. No borders or boundaries are visible, the perfect architecture of the Mod Clinic emphasizing the limitless nature of Mod. Prior closes his ears and eyes, imagining he's someone else discovering Atlantis.

A faint, metallic voice says, "Fringe gestation detected. Admission granted. Proceed with caution."

There is a tugging at his hand. He re-orients himself, opens his eyes, tries to get his bearings.

"Dad."

"Huh?"

"Dad. Come on. You can't freak out here."

Molly holds his hand as they proceed down the raging river. Prior faintly hears his footsteps but the feeling of seasickness is difficult to stave off. Every muscle is strained as he advances. It is a concentrated effort just to stay erect. Molly and Lachende hold hands and prance along.

"Come on, Prior, just stand still now," says Lachende. "The nanos need to check you out. You'll be fine."

Lachende and Molly are solid rocks being battered by the angry seas. What was that old saying? Something about how the sea is a maker of widows.

"Dad?"

Prior looks back. He is five feet inside the front door. It feels as if he's traveled for miles. Exhausted. How could a Fringe volunteer for this type of treatment?

Prior stands still as a swarm of nanos, resembling a school of eels, swirl around him in long ribbons. They wrap around him tighter and tighter, as if trying to force him to spill the truth. A boa constrictor could study the nanos' methods and take notes. With sudden and equal dispassion, they loosen their grip and shoot away. Prior slumps to the ground at the bottom of the sea.

"Well, you're alive," says Lachende. "That's always the hardest part. We're aces."

"What's happening?" says Prior, taking short breaths, not knowing if his next one will be available on the sailing tide.

"What do you mean?" says Lachende.

"Wait a minute," says Molly to Lachende. "Dad, do you think you're underwater?"

"Aren't we?" says Prior, gasping.

"Shit, Lachende, you forgot to give him the Moses pill," says Molly.

Lachende whips out his hand and feeds Prior a small pill before he can react.

"Oops," says Lachende.

The effect is instantaneous. A giant drain becomes unplugged and the ocean in Prior's mind parts into two sections. Prior's disorientation also dissipates. He stands up on his landlubber's legs. Everything dries up.

Prior faces an extravagant lobby to an enormous building. It is in the Greek style, punctuated with columns along its perimeter and luxurious silken drapes along its walls. The lobby's showpiece is a thirty-foot statue of Ferri. A small water fountain operates in front of the statue. The spraying, leaping water practically bows to the great inventor. In the distance, several sets of white double-doors open and close as men in lab coats dash around with Fringe and Mod patients.

"Oops?" says Prior.

"Sorry," says Lachende. "I forgot this was your first visit here. They use the drowning thing as a security measure. Scared the hell out of me the first time."

"Anything else I should know? Will I be hallucinating that I'm being eaten by lions in the Coliseum while Roman citizens cheer me on?"

"I don't...lions? Hmm. No...I don't think so," says Lachende, advancing towards the double-doors.

"I heard something while I was underwater," says Prior.

"People hear all kinds of things in that stress," says Molly, pulling Prior along.

"Lachende, you almost drowned me."

"Now, you be nice to him," says Molly to Prior in a conspiratorial tone. "He could get into big trouble bringing you here," says Molly.

"What about you?"

"I'm in love with the schmuck," says Molly.

"That's not what I...what?"

"But don't tell him. It'll just go to his flat head."

She squeezes his hand and they go through the double-doors. It leads to a long hallway, doors officiously dotting each side. At least the scale of this hallway is more in line with Fringe proportion.

"Excuse us," says a Fringe man as he makes his way by. He wears a trench coat draped over his shoulders. As he proceeds, Prior realizes that the coat is a Mod draped over the man. Every Fringe is required to have a Mod sponsor in order to convert.

"Ooh, I want to see this," says Molly, catching up with Lachende.

Grabbing Lachende's hand, she pulls him and Prior towards the Fringe with the Mod overcoat.

"Oh, please. It's not that big a deal," says Lachende.

"Maybe not for you," says Molly.

The Fringe and his Mod sponsor disappear behind a set of doors.

"Molly," says Prior, "we don't want to attract attention. I have to find Addison."

"Exactly," she says. "We should act like tourists. Don't you think it would be suspicious to be in this place and not gawk?"

"She's got a point," says Lachende.

"Fine."

They head through the set of double doors where the Fringe with the Mod overcoat entered. It leads to another empty hallway. Next to the doors is a small metal panel with a thin slot.

"Hmmm, let's see here," says Lachende.

He slips his paper hand into the slot like a toaster and looks curiously around for a moment. He pulls out his hand.

"Mod conversion scheduled in three minutes in Theater Three. Up the hallway and to the left," says Lachende.

"You are amazing," says Molly.

"If we hurry," says Lachende, "we can catch the sneak previews."

They make a left at the end of the hallway. The door immediately to the right is labeled "Theater One." Prior peeks into the door's small window, keeping his eyes peeled for Addison. Theater One is filled with dozens of Fringe men and women, each strapped to a bed and connected with hundreds of little wires to their heads.

"My co-workers. Mod Dreamers," says Lachende. "A whole bank of them. One of the cushier jobs available to a Fringe."

"Looks enchanting," says Prior.

"Hey, it's important. How would you like to live forever and be bored out of your flat mind? Mod are many things but creative isn't one of them. These guys fire out Mod Luxury Catalogs to every Mod on the planet."

"Sounds like bullshit work to me," says Prior.

"You try lying down for eight hours, day after day, coming up with luxury items and hobbies and vacations for Mod. Believe me, after the third day, it becomes quite taxing."

"Do they know you're Mod?" says Prior.

"They let me slum."

"Come on," says Molly, "we're going to miss it."

They enter Theater Three through a set of heavy doors. It is a square room set up with a single row of chairs on each of the perimeter walls. In the center of the room, a large horizontal plastic tube glows dimly. The Fringe enters through another door and approaches the tube. He is completely naked, in his thirties, and extremely rotund. He lays down in the tube in serene tranquility, his arms folded over his chest. There is something overtly corpse-like about him. Prior has already had his fill of funerals this week.

The room is filled with observers. Prior, Molly, and Lachende quietly take seats in the corner. Molly sits between Prior and Lachende.

"When you…did you?" says Molly.

"Naked? Oh sure, you have to," says Lachende. "You don't want foreign textiles contaminating your new nanos."

The lights dim around the room's perimeter so the center of attention is the Fringe in the tube. His Mod sponsor floats down and drapes himself over the tube. Prior can only make out the Fringe's head and feet.

"A bit freaky," says Prior in a whisper.

"A little respect," says Lachende. "This is a sacred religious act."

The overhead duct exhales a puff of smoke. The smoke wafts down toward the tubed Fringe. As it descends, it reconfigures itself into a double-helix shape, taking on a steel-blue hue. It spirals down, looking like a miniature tornado in slow motion. The smoke tornado alights onto the top of the tube, eliciting a slight electric pop sound. The smoke banks sharply, and proceeds towards the Fringe's face. The tube glows brightly now, throbbing, endowed with new energy and expectation. The smoke enters the tube and completely fills it.

The Mod drifts away towards the ceiling, prompted by a silent cue from some unseen conductor. Prior squints, unable to see the Fringe through the smoke-filled tube except for the slightest silhouette of his head.

Suddenly, the tube trembles and rattles and the Fringe lets out a horrifying scream. There is a terrible sucking and ripping sound like a giant vacuum cleaner breaking down. In an instant and with a tremendous shudder, the smoke penetrates the Fringe from all directions as if he is a sponge. It leaves him exposed, naked, and in tremendous agony. He lets out another agonized shriek.

"Oh Mod," says Molly. "What are they doing to him?" She grasps Lachende's hand, realizing that her lover experienced the same agony.

"Easy," says Lachende. "It's beautiful."

"He's in terrible pain," says Prior.

"Sweet ecstasy," says Lachende.

Molly remains transfixed on the sight of the Fringe writhing and screaming as the nanos rocket through the very core of his being.

"Lachende, how did you…" says Molly.

"Believe me, it doesn't hurt at all. It's the most intense feeling you'll have but I assure you, it's the good kind of intense."

"Take a good look, Molly," says Prior, trying to divert her thoughts away from where he knows they're going. "You want to volunteer for that type of torture?"

There is a hiss from the tube and the Fringe melts away. Steam rises from him in the tube to replace the smoke. The steam escapes through the pores of the tube, covering the outside of it and the room until the theater itself resembles a sauna. The hum of ventilation fans emanates from the floor. When the steam is finally cleared away, the tube is gone. In its place is a flat sheet of Mylar that lies lifeless on the floor, shimmering and reflecting the lights from above.

The Mod sponsor descends once again from the rafters and lands gently on the Mylar sheet. After a moment, the Mod sponsor stands, becomes human scale, and sits down on a reserved chair.

The Mylar sheet trembles. It floats on the warm air currents. Suddenly, it explodes into a shifting sequence of random shapes, like a slot machine window. Prior knows things are not coming up cherries.

The new Mod screams but the sound is one of elation. The shape-changing slows down and the new Mod assumes the same human form it had when it entered, only about five years younger and about a hundred pounds lighter. And now, he exists only in two planes.

Everyone in the theater applauds. Molly and Lachende have tears in their eyes. Prior suddenly feels ill. People around him praise the event as if they have witnessed a birth. Prior knows what he just witnessed was the death of another human.

"When I was underwater," says Prior to Molly, "I heard the security-nanos say that you were pregnant. That's why they've left you alone."

"Nonsense," says Molly.

"Because now you're sacred to them. Especially if you're looking to convert." Prior stands up, raising his voice. "My God, it's like they'll get two-for-one with you."

"Sit down," says Molly. "You don't know what you're talking about."

"I'd do what she says," says Lachende.

In the corner of his eye, Prior sees someone familiar stand up and exit the theater. It looked like Penny.

"Stay right here," says Prior.

"Where are you going?" says Lachende.

"I'll be right back."

Prior goes out into the hallway but there is no sign of Penny. She must have ducked into Theater Two next door. Prior peeks into the window on the door. The room is dark. He takes a deep breath and goes in.

The door closes behind him. Theater Two is pitch black. Prior reaches out, keeping one hand along the wall so he won't lose his bearings. The air in the room feels musty. Fresh air hasn't visited this place in a long time.

Even though it is completely silent in the theater, Prior can sense the presence of someone. Or something. He isn't alone in here. And whatever it is that's in here, it's comfortable with this dank darkness. Which is more of a declaration than Prior can lay claim to.

There is a low growl somewhere in the room not that far from Prior. Prior's hand gropes the wall. He flicks on the switch and the florescent lights flicker on like a miniature explosion.

The growl grows louder, this time accompanied by the figure of Addison in the middle of the room. Addison is bent down over a half-digested Fringe body, blood ringing his mouth like war paint. The remainder of the Fringe body lies slumped over Addison's knee, a knot of muscle, half-torn limbs, and bones.

Addison's growl is not directed at Prior. There is an audible gasp in the room and Prior realizes that the theater is filled with Points, each hovering above a chair, each intensely inspecting Addison's behavior and handiwork.

Chapter 31

"Addison!" says Prior.

Addison bolts up, dumping the body's remains on the floor. He shrinks into a bubble, shooting across the other end of the room and out the ventilation system.

The Points float casually from their chairs to the remains of the body, hovering, as if unsure of the proper social protocol in these matters.

While the Points are momentarily distracted with the remains of Addison's lab experiment, Prior takes off after him. The door he busts open leads to another long hallway. He knows that Addison is probably making his escape through the duct work. Prior grabs one of the fire extinguishers hanging on the wall, aims it at the vent over him, pulls the pin and squeezes the trigger.

He runs to the next vent and lets loose with the extinguisher again. The white foam sprays up into the ductwork. If Addison is there, the foam is not making things easier for him.

Prior hears a bang around the corner and sprints down the hallway. He's sure it's Addison. He takes out the plasma gun Belden gave him. This seems as good a time as any to field-test it.

He turns the corner and spots something that makes him put on the brakes. His momentum sends him flying into the wall. He bounces off and lands on the floor, the plasma gun sliding several feet in front of him.

"Detective Prior."

It's Grainger and his men. They are armed and have the drop on him. They are also holding Addison, trapped inside some kind of translucent bag that resembles a giant jellyfish.

"Grainger," says Prior, getting up, rubbing his shoulder.

"Easy now," says Grainger and points his gun closer to Prior's face. One of the torpedoes puts his boot on the plasma gun.

"What the hell is that?" says Prior, indicating Addison's jellyfish bag.

"You don't get to ask the questions," says Grainger.

"Right, wouldn't want to get your bosses angry with you."

"Speaking of..." says Grainger.

Prior turns to see a swarm of Points flying down the hallway. They descend on Addison, or rather, the bag he is wrapped in. Inside, Addison looks terrified. He might be screaming but Prior can't hear anything through the bag.

"What the hell is going on?" says Prior.

"Don't you know?" says Grainger. "You got front row seats to the freak show. Your old pal, Addison, here, snuck in to get some files about Ferri's research. And he couldn't help himself to a snack. Points love to watch. For a finale, they were going to consume our doggy-bag-buddy here. We've been trailing him all along. Which brings me to you, pal. You are in deep, deep shit."

The next thing Prior experiences is a blanket over his head. The blanket slips over his body. It feels a little like his pica-tam but he doesn't want to show off that technology to anyone. He initially thinks Grainger's torpedoes are fitting him for a body bag. But then he hears Lachende.

"Just be quiet," says Lachende.

Prior hears Grainger and his men but their sound is muffled. He squints through the blanket and sees they are chasing him. He sits back and gets oriented.

"So now you just pop me into your bubble?" says Prior.

"He's helping you escape," says Molly.

Prior leans forward and realizes he's riding in the backseat of Lachende's bubble again. Molly has her back to him. The bubble rises and exits the building. Prior looks down and sees Grainger and his men pointing at him.

"Where are we going?" says Prior.

"Your office," says Lachende. "And you're welcome."

They glide quietly over the city and arrive to Prior's office through the open window in a few minutes. Lachende brings himself in for a landing in the middle of the office. He shrinks down to human proportion. They all stand there, breathing heavy. Prior tries to re-orient himself.

"You mind telling me..." says Prior.

The door opens and Penny bursts in, latching the door closed behind her. She's breathing heavy. She looks at the three of them and nods. "We got company," she says.

Before Prior can respond, Grainger and his men burst through the door. Grainger still holds Addison in the cocoon bag. The bag squirms as Addison attempts to escape.

"You ain't getting away that easily," says Grainger. His torpedoes take a few steps and encircle Prior, Penny, Lachende and Molly. One of the torpedoes points the plasma gun at them.

"How the hell did you know we'd be at the Mod Clinic?" says Prior, looking for a way out.

"How do you think?" says Grainger. "Your sweet client. She thought you were applying the screws to her brother." He holds up the bag with Addison.

Lachende and Molly hold each other. Prior figures Lachende can protect her again. "You're so stupid," says Prior.

"Yeah, why?" says Grainger.

A swarm of Points enter the room in a long line, zigzagging like a sky snake.

"Oh shit," says Grainger. His men quickly fall behind him again.

"You think they'd give up the day's entertainment?" says Prior.

"Prior," says Penny, grabbing a World War II hand grenade from her desk. She races past Grainger's men, holding it the air, her other hand on the pin. Grainger and his men back up a few steps.

"Penny!" says Prior.

She seems nervous, slowing down as she gets closer to Prior. Grainger's men don't advance on her.

"I'm not going to let them get you," says Penny. She turns around to Grainger and his men. "Now back off. We're getting out of here."

"This is very touching," says Grainger. "But I got a job to do. And we all know that's a dummy."

Prior slowly reaches for the grenade Penny is holding. "I appreciate the gesture, Penny."

The Points remain still, hovering in the air, like they're watching a soap opera.

"I just wanted to help," says Penny, defeated. She looks around the room, embarrassed. "Come with me?" she says to Prior.

"Go on, sit down," says Grainger to Penny.

"Sorry, I..." says Penny. She charges the torpedo with the plasma gun, sending him to the ground. Prior grabs hold of the plasma gun.

"No! Get him," yells Grainger.

It's too late. Penny rushes to the corner of the room as Prior pulls the trigger on Grainger and his men.

The plasma gun clicks, making a hollow, pointless noise.

Somewhere, in the back of his mind, Prior conjures up an image of Belden, chuckling in his bemused way.

"It's a goddamn toy," says Grainger. "Grab him."

The Points seem to lose interest in Addison since they can't get at him through the bag. They start hovering around Prior, rubber-necking the new freak show.

Prior makes a silent prayer. It's time to test his faith in his other friend. He reaches into his pocket and grabs the lighter gizmo that Brewster gave him. He flicks the button.

An intense yellow light shoots out of the lighter and turns into a star-shape burst that fills the office. Grainger and his men shield their eyes and hit the ground.

The Points don't hit the ground because they are too busy exploding. Each Point goes spectacularly super-nova in mid-air until there is nothing left of them. The tiny explosions give off a high-pitched squeal and bright spark. Then, just as quickly, the yellow starburst fades. Prior looks up and thanks Brewster.

Prior runs over to Molly. He takes her hand and starts leading her out of the office.

"Wait," she says. She grabs Lachende's hand and pulls him like a kite.

"Prior," says Grainger, aiming his gun at him.

Prior points the lighter at Grainger and his men.

"This thing just took out a thousand Points. You think it can't take you guys out with a little flick of my finger?"

Grainger, unaccustomed to being outflanked, stares, blinking in a dumbfounded way. His men look to him for some kind of guidance.

Penny goes to her desk, looking nervous.

"Alright, put down your guns," says Grainger to his men.

"But chief…"

"Goddammit, put 'em down!"

"That's the first smart thing you've done today, Grainger," says Prior.

"Dammit, Prior, how long you think you're gonna last out there? With the full force of NanoGov on your ass?" says Grainger. "You got your own client setting you up."

"We both got bigger problems than that," says Prior. "Take a look in the bag."

Grainger looks down and sees that Addison is missing.

"Let's go," says Molly.

Immediately, Lachende turns himself into a bubble and envelops Molly. Before Prior can say anything, the Lachende-bubble flies through the exit and into the waiting sky.

Grainger swings his arm and knocks the lighter away from Prior. "It's over, Prior," says Grainger. His torpedoes pick up their guns and line up behind him.

Prior takes quick stock of his choices.

"Don't," says Penny, still sitting at her desk.

Prior makes a dash for the door. Grainger's torpedoes train their guns on him and shoot an energy bolt. The steel-blue beam emanates like a mist conjured from thin air.

Penny bolts from her chair. "No!"

"Penny, don't!"

"Prior!" she screams.

Prior ducks as Penny takes the full force of the energy bolt. Prior rolls on the ground and watches Penny get vaporized. Her mass is instantly turned into nanos. Some of her nanos enter Prior's mouth. He breathes her in and can smell her perfume. Her mass seems to vibrate in his body, each molecule saying, "I love you, Jeremiah Prior."

Grainger and his torpedoes approach Prior. "Jesus, Prior, sorry," says Grainger. They tie his hands together and help him up. "But you're under arrest."

Chapter 32

Prior has been languishing in the nano-prison for three hours, courtesy of Grainger who has thrown him in here with almost childish glee. In typically humiliating logic, Mod have forced Fringe to build the nano-prisons to encase and contain Fringe who commit crimes against them. Prior had been personally responsible in the past for filling up his share of the nano-prisons with Fringe felons on behalf of his Mod and upper-crust Fringe clientele. He doesn't find the irony remotely amusing.

The nano-prisons are based on the old-fashioned concept of prisons with the exception that there are no bars or cells. Prisoners wear a specially made nano-prison suit that resembles a gelatinous, embryonic sack, similar to the one that Grainger used on Addison before he escaped. Prior slithers around the prison yard as the sack jiggles while remaining tightly wrapped around him. From the view of the nano-monitors outside, the prison yard is filled with giant, upright slugs slouching and shuffling around. From Prior's view in the slug suit, the prison yard is a hazy blue fog with clearly drawn boundaries. The suits prevent escape since they don't allow progress further than the prison yard.

The beauty of the design is that no guards are needed. That's fortunate and deliberate since Mod aren't remotely interested in such a filthy job and no Fringe would accept the responsibilities and ramifications of the work.

As Prior paces in the yard, the thought of never seeing Grainger again makes him momentarily happy. Then it occurs to him. Grainger and his men had him in their grasps. They had every opportunity to take a sample of his blood. They could have verified if he really had the Seurat that Belden wants everyone to think he has. Hell, they could have given him a transfusion and grabbed the whole thing and auctioned it off. They could have just sold Prior to a Point and had it devour him. And there wouldn't have been anything he could do about it. Prior still isn't sure where the stolen Seurat is but he's glad that Grainger hasn't discovered he's got the Vermeer. Prior deduces that Grainger isn't working for Mod or Points or anyone else who is in search of the Seurat. Maybe Prior misjudged Grainger. Maybe he's just a guy doing his job.

Prior's thoughts keep getting interrupted by the late-breaking news in his head that he's in nano-prison. Escape seems impossible. Prior thinks about his backpack which Grainger threw in a corner of the prison office without inspecting it. Then he recalls poor Penny and he crumbles inside the suit.

Prior figures he'll make for an excellent patsy for all the people Addison killed. They'll pin the gruesome and extremely public slurping of Fringe and Mod on Prior somehow. He still can't figure out who is behind all this and what they have to gain.

Mostly, though, Prior's thoughts keep circling back to Molly and whether she would really convert to Mod to be with Lachende, especially in her condition. The thought of being a grandfather doesn't fill his heart with warmth in this world. He wonders whether Lachende really is trustworthy.

Prior sees the sun setting and knows he's run out of luck. He isn't looking forward to spending the rest of his time on this bankrupt and despoiled earth like a slice of banana in a Jell-O mold.

The wind changes, blowing hard at him. Leaves fall off the trees that surround the yard, sticking to Prior's slug sack exterior. Dust and pollen drift towards him in small waves. They obscure his vision further. He stays still, hoping that the leaves and dust will blow away once the wind dries out his gelatinous suit.

Over the sound of the wind and leaves slapping against him, Prior hears a slight hum. The portion of the nano-prison suit in front of his face begins to shimmer. Something is drilling its way through his suit, making a pinhole-sized tunnel. There is the smallest popping noise. Something breaks in through the interior surface of the suit.

A typed letter appears in front of Prior's face inside the suit. The letter slowly pans from left to right, then shifts again to the left and slowly scrolls upwards like a sheet of paper inside an antique typewriter. Prior imagines that none of this is evident from the outside of his leaf-covered suit. He figures he might finally have gone bat-shit crazy. The feeling is not unwelcome.

"Dear Jere, please excuse this crude communication but it was the only way to reach you under these dire circumstances. I've previously tried getting your attention but now that you're a captive listener, I suppose you have no choice but to comply with my wishes. I need your help. But in order for you to be of service to me, I have to bend some rules and extract you from your current confinement.

"I am told by our mutual friend that you are in possession of a certain piece of artwork considered to be a rare masterpiece. It is this artwork that interests me. Within its ridged paper and crude, charcoal crayon lines may lie clues that can help us both.

"Therefore, I need you to come to me. I am placing directions to my whereabouts in the nanos of your shirt fabric. At the appropriate time, your shirt sleeves will point the way to me. For now, I have embedded a computer virus in this transmission which will disable your nano suit. Walk slowly and you won't arouse suspicion.

"See you this evening, Felice."

The letter fades away.

Prior debates momentarily whether to believe the truth of the situation or instead that his own delusions have permanently detached from reality.

Felice said that the art in his blood was charcoal crayon on ridged paper. But the Vermeer is oil on canvas. Seurat was famous for his charcoal crayon on ridged paper drawings. Felice doesn't know about the Vermeer. What does she want? Why does she think there are clues in the Seurat sketch?

Prior's nano-prison suit vibrates. The leaves and pollen slide off as the suit melts away at his feet. Who else but a Mod genius like his ex-wife could slip him a file in prison that will allow him to bust out? Prior can move easily now. He makes his way towards the nano-prison yard office, the suit a chum trail. He retrieves his backpack. By the time he reaches the prison gate, the suit is completely gone, dissolved into the dusty ground. He looks down and is surprised to discover he is wearing his old Fringe cop uniform. Just another Fringe cop checking up on a prisoner. Prior strolls out of the place with no questions or obstructions. His ex-wife has come through for him. Now, he just has to find out why.

As soon as Prior leaves prison, he makes a straight line for the stables. He figures he has a few hours before the nanos and Grainger discover he's not one of the walking dead in the nano- prison slug suits.

Skippy is grooming the horses outside when he sees Prior approaching. Skippy presses a button under his wooden bench and waves him into the fenced stables.

"Lachende's inside," says Skippy, a welcoming smile on his face. "He's been worried."

"Thanks, kid. And Molly?"

Skippy shakes his head. "Heard you were in the pokey."

"Now, you see, that's how rumors get started," says Prior. "Do me a favor and get Gluestick ready for me, will you? I'm riding out in five minutes."

"Sure thing."

"And Skippy?"

"Yeah, chief?"

"Thanks."

Prior enters the stable and sees a horse blanket thrown over one of the gates. "Lachende."

The horse blanket sits up. "Prior, I was hoping you'd come by."

Prior looks around, making sure this isn't a trap. "How'd you know I broke out?"

"After I brought Molly back to her place, I kept an eye on you. Felt guilty about how things ended."

Prior thinks about Penny and how he's still carrying parts of her around. "Molly alright?"

"Always."

Prior takes a step closer. "Lachende, I need to see the real you."

"What?" says Lachende, changing to his two-dimensional person shape.

"You saw the Vermeer. I was hoping you could hook into the main banking system and tell me what I could get for my blood futures now."

"Your what?"

"My blood futures."

"Whoa," says Lachende. "What are you thinking of doing?"

Prior considers giving Lachende the Vermeer thermoplastics vault key that Brewster gave him but decides now is not the time.

"Just do this for me. Please. I'm going to check on Gluestick. Before he died, Brewster told me my blood is worth five-and-a-half billion on the black market. I need a promissory note for my body chemistry. I want to see how much money I could get now for what my blood will be worth when I die. My blood futures."

"You must really trust me," says Lachende. "The Futures Exchange doesn't exist any longer. Any other Mod would just kill you now and take the painting."

"Except it's locked away. But I do trust you." He takes out a small scrap of paper and pricks his finger. The few drops of blood land on the scrap and form the Vermeer painting.

"Here," says Prior, handing the scrap to Lachende. "This should be enough to convince Mod to give you the money. Leo the Fence. Remember him? He can tell you which Mod would be interested."

"He's a Mod now."

"Leo the Fence?" says Prior.

"This is crazy," says Lachende.

"The money is going to Molly."

"Assuming your Mod buyer doesn't just take all your blood and the Vermeer with it," says Lachende.

"Like I said, it's locked away. Make sure you tell them that. They get the key later."

Lachende nods.

Prior heads out of the stable. When he looks back, Lachende is already gone.

Prior mounts Gluestick and rides out into the city. Gluestick is in great shape. The breeze across Prior's face feels great. It helps him clear his head.

Prior reaches into his backpack. He pulls the pica-tam over his head and stretches it over his entire body. Now, he is a giant woven burrito riding through the city. It's not unlike being in nano-prison yet the complete opposite. To an outsider, Gluestick is galloping free on his own.

When he arrives into the center of the city, Prior's right sleeve moves on its own, causing his elbow to jut out and rub against the pica-tam. He pulls Gluestick's reins and they turn right. Then, after about a mile, his left pant leg brings his left knee in and Gluestick slows down, turning slightly to the left.

With his clothing spasmodically directing his horse, Prior makes his way north, past the city. He enters a more mountainous region that becomes more rural with each passing mile.

He keeps wondering why Felice would need to take such security precautions. Who is she running from? Once she turned Mod, she had everything she wanted. There is really nothing to fear except Points.

Prior and Gluestick ride to the end of a gravel path about three miles away from the main road. It brings them to a large stone house in the middle of the woods. Still wearing the pica-tam over his whole body, Prior dismounts Gluestick. He escorts Gluestick to a barn behind the house where there is fresh water and hay waiting for him. He ties off the horse who seems content for the break.

Prior's clothes lead him to the back door of the house. It is unlocked so he steps inside. It's a simple, ranch house. He takes off the pica-tam and breathes in the fragrant air, keenly aware that at least seven different security systems and twenty-five cameras are allowing him this entry, watching and assessing his every move.

There is a faint chemical smell in the air.

"Felice?" says Prior.

This isn't like her. Prior envisioned a much more opulent and fashionable home for a Mod.

The back hallway leads into an enormous antique apothecary. It is filled with floor-to-ceiling wooden cubbies and replete with long soapstone benches and bars in the middle of the room, packed with test tubes, burners, open bottles of chemicals and piles of various powders.

Prior enters her full-scale nineteenth-century apothecary somewhat apprehensively.

A small speck wafts in the air. The speck floats down in a lazy, half-circle arc towards Prior, landing in his ear. It's a Point.

"Hello, Jeremiah Prior."

That voice. It can't be.

"Jere." The voice is muffled but familiar. "Jeremiah."

Prior feels disoriented and sits on an Elizabethan-era couch. He feels a flutter in his ear which causes him to shake his head. Felice, or what's left of her, comes flying out of his ear and hovers before him.

"Jesus," says Prior. "Not you too."

"Surprised?" she says.

She doesn't really speak in a conventional sense since she doesn't have a mouth. Instead, she focuses the nanos to cause vibrations inside Prior's ear.

"I could have killed you, you know," she says. "Every ex-wife's fantasy."

Prior looks around at her meticulously appointed apothecary.

"I'd say you've had enough fantasy," says Prior. "Sounds like you need a re-boot, Felice. Join the human race again."

"Here," she says.

A cup of hot tea floats over to Prior from the lab bench. He examines it closely.

"Oh, come now, Jere, it's just tea."

He decides he's in no position to argue with her. He takes a sip of the tea and it makes him feel better instantly.

"So why did you invite me over? Molly?" says Prior.

Felice shifts a little bit, as if the thought of her Fringe daughter disturbs her.

"Not directly. How is she?"

"Fine," says Prior. He's having a hard time talking to the air. It makes his conversations with Mod seem normal. "I understand now why she moved out."

Felice floats around the room before landing on his nose. He blows her off, annoyed with her presumed intimacy. She flies away on the currents caused by the tea's steam.

"You always were an asshole," she says.

"Yeah, but I was your asshole."

She hovers again in front of him. "I need your help. I'm in trouble," she says. She dims the volume of her nanos to affect a desperate tone.

"Trouble," says Prior. He puts down the tea and stands up. "How exactly does a Point get in trouble? You're above the law. You're immortal. You're the top of the food chain."

"That's exactly the problem," she says.

Her voice sounds hurt but he can't tell if she is manipulating the air particles for effect.

"How so?"

"NanoGov lied to me. They lied to all Mod who converted to Points. They never told us about the Flaw."

"The Flaw?"

"Points. We have a major design flaw within us. The whole Point concept was rushed to market. Not nearly enough testing and research."

Prior recalls that Lachende told him the same story. "What's this Flaw?"

"You've seen it," she says.

"Humor me."

"Think of it as having a half-life," says Felice. "Points have a sort of accelerated life span. When our nanos start to dissipate, we need to consume more mass to keep us stable. We're not sustainable. You understand now what this means?"

"My God," says Prior. "That's why you're devouring Fringe. It's not for their sheer mass. It's to keep you alive." He lets out a chuckle.

"What the hell is so funny?" says Felice.

"Irony is a bitch, that's all. Hundreds of years of folk tales and urban legends destroyed within a lifetime by your superior technology and yet you've still managed to turn yourselves into vampires."

"Not me," she says. "I haven't devoured any Mod or Fringe. That's why I need your help. Before I do end up taking someone else's mass."

"Jesus," says Prior.

"It's too horrible," she says. There's a heaving rush in the air and it sounds like she's crying.

"Felice, how did this happen?" says Prior. "You were the smartest person I knew. How did you get yourself into this?"

"You can help me," she says. "You know where the Flaw began. The Point anomaly. The prototype. He holds the cure."

"Addison," says Prior.

"Addison."

So that's why everyone is interested in Addison. Points want to cure their Flaw and keep on ruling the world.

"I hate to disappoint you, baby," says Prior, "but I don't have Addison. He slipped through my fingers a few times. Wily bastard."

"But you can find him again, can't you?"

"So you can dissect him?"

Prior thinks of Modela. Maybe she's the only one who's truly looking out for the well-being of her lunatic brother.

"We need him, Jere. Don't you see?"

Prior throws out the bait, seeing if she'll bite. "I don't know. What about Ferri? Can't he help?"

"Ferri's dead. You know that. Don't play games with me. Not now."

"Felice…"

"Ferri didn't have the stomach for all this. At his age, he was all about his legacy. Would you want it written on your tombstone that you invented a race of people that needed to devour its own kind to survive?"

"First of all, we are not the same kind. Not by a long goddamn shot. And if you ask me, Ferri was a sap."

"He was the lucky one," she says. "Without him, I'm stuck with the burden of trying to cure us and fix his mess before I self-destruct."

"Well, I can't pull Addison out of a hat. Despite what you think, I don't know where he is and I'm just not that clever these days. Plus, as you're keenly aware, I'm an escaped convict."

"The Seurat. I know it's in your blood. It might hold the answers."

"Code buried in the charcoal lines?" says Prior. "No one would ruin a rare piece of art so they could pass a note."

"What about the Movement?" she says. "There are rumors that Fringe have found a way to get at our Flaw. The gold…"

"Now what made you ask that?" says Prior.

"No, it's just that…"

"Did you have anything to do with the Point attack at the FU meeting the other day? Because, if you did, Felice, so help me…"

"Can't you see I'm grasping at straws here?" Her voice is a wind-flutter.

"I need time," says Prior.

She ignores him.

"Don't you care about our daughter?" says Prior.

Felice begins spinning in place on her sub-atomic axis, slowly at first, then ever more quickly. After a moment, she floats back to his ear. Prior hates her silences but the two of them have a history together. He loved her once. When she was a Fringe. Before she let her figure go.

She drifts back into his ear. "Alright, Jere," she says. He suddenly finds himself missing her smile. "But since you don't know where Addison is," she says, "I need you to find the Seurat. Get it and, in exchange, I'll get NanoGov off your back."

"Fine," he says. "I'll need access."

Prior takes out Penny's leaf-letter. Felice lands on it delicately, momentarily. The leaf-letter glows as if its charged with new energy. Prior pockets his new passport.

"Thanks. But my chances are better at finding Addison than the Seurat."

"Too bad you can't ask your secretary to help," says Felice.

Prior wondered how long it would take to circle back to this. "You worry more for our daughter," says Prior. He's had enough. He gets up and heads for the door.

"Thank you, Jere," says Felice.

Prior slips the pica-tam on and leaves. When he's several miles away, he dismounts Gluestick, doubles over and vomits, shedding the nanos that led him to Felice's. This overwhelming blanket of desolation takes over and he shivers on the side of the road.

He and Felice. They met when she was still three-dimensional. Their future laid before them like the finest picnic spread. How did it come to this? How could she have changed so much? She's an asteroid orbiting around his constant planet, rocketing through his sky, propelled by unseen forces; her next move unable to be determined by probability theory.

Prior misses his wife. His vomit is just the symptom. He gets back on Gluestick, breathes in a cold, harsh dose of air. Making sure no one saw him, he straightens his clothes and continues on.

He's gotten Penny and Brewster killed. The Fringe mindset is one of a defeated race. He should have stayed and fought for Molly years ago. For the Fringe. He helped get his partner killed and should have stuck around to accept the consequences.

After he drops off Gluestick at the stables, he knows what he has to do.

He heads to the Holland Tunnel.

Chapter 33

The wet muck and foul smell of the Holland Tunnel welcome him back. He retrieves the newly charged leaf-letter and dons his pica-tam. Instantly, he's transported to the palm tree-lined shores of Antigua. This side of the island is quiet. Not a bird in the sky. He surveys the landscape but there is no one on the beach. He can see his hut about a half-mile away. It appears intact. Prior spots the Sky-Screen amidst the clouds on the other side of the island.

Maybe Mod moved on to other islands and left his home alone. He takes off his shoes and shirt and dives into the ocean, the warm sea foam and waves cradling him. After a moment, he treks back to his hut. The ocean breeze feels good on his skin. He doesn't miss the oppressive stench and decaying buildings that surrounded him in the city. With each step towards his hut, he settles further into the island life. He's only been back for twenty minutes but it feels like days.

Prior is astonished, happily, to discover that his hut remains largely untouched. Some precious items have been stolen but his bed, blankets, and chair remain, greeting him as he crosses the threshold. He sweeps the leaves and insects from his bed and lays down. When he wakes up, it is the next day.

After a breakfast of coconuts, Prior heads northeast towards his shop, curious if it's still there. The island is quiet, devoid of any signs of life. He uses his hands to cut a new path since he lacks any tools. The path used to be well worn but nature has quickly taken over in his absence.

It takes Prior several hours to make it to the bay on the north shore. He clears some bushes from his view and rests his eyes on the spot where his shop should be. In its place is a three-story shopping mall, completely encased in glass windows, that runs for at least a mile along the shore. Inside the mall, Prior can make out thousands of Mod going about their daily shopping of furs, dinosaurs, medieval dungeon chains, knick knacks, what-have-you. Their Fringe servants trail respectfully behind.

No matter. He hadn't planned on opening his shop anyway. Good thing, actually. The past belongs in the past, along with all its trophies and memorabilia. Prior figures these Fringe are just marking time until they can turn Mod as well. It's the same everywhere.

He sets off to find Antoine. Antoine would have saved most of the villagers. He's probably hidden everyone underground which is why Prior hasn't seen anyone outside the mall yet. He doesn't recall exactly where Antoine's pica-factory is. After a few hours, Prior reaches the apex of Barnes Hill near the center of the island. He can see a good portion of the entire island from here. Most of the trees have been removed by Mod and replaced with tacky displays of wealth including yachts the size of cruise ships, a mansion in the shape of an old-time space shuttle, and a giant golden toilet. Prior wonders if these things change weekly based on the whims of their Mod-Owners.

There is a low hum coming from the south. Prior cranes his neck but can't make out anything. Overhead, the palm trees provide shade from the sun's glare. Prior can't make out what the Sky-Screen is broadcasting but the hum is coming from the ground. Prior goes down the hill to investigate.

He wraps himself in his pica-tam in case there are any Mod or nanos around. The last thing he needs is for Sky-Screen to catch wind of his island arrival. The hum appears to be coming from behind an enormous sandcastle. Since there is no shore and the sandcastle is two hundred feet high, Prior is on the alert for Mod. He treads lightly. Although he is invisible to Mod, he could still step on a twig or snap a branch which would give away his position to a security-nano.

Prior enters the sandcastle and descends a flight of sand stairs. At the bottom of the stairs is a sand dungeon complete with steel bars. Hundreds of Fringe lay on the ground behind bars. Some are crying. They look like they haven't eaten in weeks.

One of the Fringe catches Prior's eye. It's Tindonna, still wearing her green scarf around her head. She sits in a corner, shaking her head.

Something moves behind Prior, the sand shifting with the weight of Fringe feet. Prior sees a Fringe run down a hallway. He takes off after the Fringe who runs out the other side of the sandcastle. Prior gives chase, gaining. He can make out that it's a small girl. He catches up to her as she heads towards Barnes Hill. He looks around but no Mod or nanos approach.

Prior scoops her up. She's startled since she can't see him in his pica-suit. She doesn't scream and Prior figures her survival instincts tell her not to. To a passing animal, the little girl appears to be floating through the air. Prior stops at the foot of a tree and puts her down on the ground. Before she can get up and run off, he stretches his pica-tam and envelops her in it. Now, the two of them are invisible and camping inside this magic tent.

"Shh," says Prior. The girl looks scared. She can't be more than ten years old. "You're okay."

"I know you," says the girl. "The man who left."

Prior recognizes her. She's gotten a little taller but still looks like her mother.

"Mr. Prior," says Prior, sitting down. "Your mother is Tindonna."

"I'm Tamesha," says the girl. She remains standing, eager to leave.

"Where are you going?"

"To get food for my people," says Tamesha. There is no trace of hate or despair in her voice. Only survival. Like escaping between the dungeon bars and stealing food is the most common thing.

"I can't help your people," says Prior.

"But I can," she says. She pushes against the pica-tam, testing its plasticity.

"Antoine. Where is Antoine?" says Prior.

"Dead. Betrayed by Philippe. They're all dead. My mother in the dungeon. And the others. They are all that's left. Unless you want to work as a slave. Better a prisoner, I think."

"I'm so sorry," says Prior. He gives her a hug and realizes it's the first bit of human contact he's had in so long.

"Soon. Soon it will change. Mod find and destroy the pica factory. But every day, I dig a little more. One day, there will be a tunnel and my people will be free. Then, Mod will see what is what."

"How is your mother?" says Prior.

"I have to go. Guards will be back and I cannot be missing. Leave me so I can find food."

"Wait," says Prior, peeling the pica-tam off from around them. "Antoine would want you to have his pica-tam. It's all I have left from him except for his jerk sauce. But you need it more than I do."

Tamesha takes it, excited, knowing a weapon when she sees one. "That jerk sauce nasty. Little sparkly things floating inside. Nasty." She turns and runs off, leaving him alone.

He closes his eyes and hears his own breathing. This little girl has the courage to go on, to survive. One day, she thinks she will thrive. It reminds him of Molly; a radical who wants to take down the system. Molly would never turn Mod.

Prior falls to the ground and cries, his stomach heaving. He thinks of Penny throwing herself in front of him, dying for him. Molly and Lachende risking everything. Poor Antoine. Even Skippy sacrificing so much to survive.

Prior gets up and heads back to his side of the island. Prior stands on the shore of Antigua, the ocean lapping at his feet. Behind him, untold destruction of Fringe as Mod mold this sandbox to their whims. The sky is blemished by clouds, a complete lack of birds, and Sky-Screen. This is no way to live.

He grabs a few supplies from his hut and leaves for the last time. He can't stay on this island. He has work to do.

Chapter 34

Prior takes Penny's leaf-letter out of his pocket. It still sparkles with Felice's nano-juice. From his backpack, Prior retrieves his last bottle of Antoine's jerk sauce. The gold flecks dance in the red, viscous liquid, obscured by the dirty orange glass vial. He unscrews the jerk sauce top, rolls up the leaf-letter, and sticks it into the bottle. He screws the top back on and gives the damn thing a good shake. He takes the top off again and brings the vial to his mouth.

"To you, Antoine," says Prior, and drinks the whole thing in one gulp. It's not in his mouth long enough to register any taste or discomfort. It feels warm going down his gullet. When it hits his stomach, he can feel his innards tingling. Prior feels light-headed. He starts to fall, thinking the soft sand is a good cushion for a lay down. But instead of falling down, his body rises, hovering above the sand and sea by a few inches. The tingling feeling now radiates through his entire body.

He looks up, the Sky-Screen getting larger, approaching him instantly until all he can see is the detailed optics. No, the Sky-Screen hasn't come to him. He's been transported on a light beam to the Sky-Screen. He's in it now, a light particle bouncing around the entire scope of the screen. The light shines through him. He looks down hundreds of feet below onto Earth. He is one with the propaganda and feels dirty that he's contributing to NanoGov's disinformation. But the thought is fleeting. Perhaps two seconds. He feels a tugging at his chest as a white light blinds him. He shuts his eyes, his weightlessness causing him to fold into himself. He is hurled across a great void at speeds he's not meant to experience.

The feeling is brief. Maybe three seconds. Suddenly, he hears retro-punkflapper music playing. A wispy voice announces the next song.

Prior realizes that he's inside Lachende's Golden Oldies broadcast. Inside Lachende himself. Back in New York City. The colorful lights blink as they advertise the broadcast. Prior is part of the light and part of the broadcast.

Lachende shakes his frame like a wet dog, perhaps sensing an uninvited host.

Prior flies off Lachende's frame. He's flung into the Sky-Screen's orbit again but instead of being absorbed into the giant eye in the sky, he circles around the Sky-Screen and ricochets back towards the city. He's a bolt of energy, a light particle, nano-sized. He descends from the sky in a straight line. A building approaches, getting bigger. He sails through the smallest crack between the closed window and the sill. He lands, skipping several times on the wood floor. By the time he has made his way across the room, he is full grown again, three-dimensional, and bumps hard against the wall. It knocks the air out of him.

Prior remains lying face down on the floor, disoriented. After a moment, he looks up. He's in Penny's apartment. The leaf-letter, dull and spent, rests near his hand, having escaped the confines of the jerk sauce. The vial's gone, its contents having acted as a reactor core to the leaf-letter.

He figures the leaf-letter was programmed to ultimately return to its origin once it exhausted its purpose. Prior knows how the leaf-letter feels.

"I need a drink," he says, getting up slowly, checking to make sure nothing is broken.

Prior investigates the apartment. He sees the little red purse on the floor; the one Sanders gave Penny. He pockets it for Molly.

He can't shake the feeling that Penny sacrificed herself for nothing. What had Prior ever brought her but misery?

Something catches the light on top of one of the stacked boxes. Prior reaches up to the top stacked box. Atop the box is Feynman's old detective badge. It's metal and still bears his name and detective number. Prior isn't sure how Penny managed to save this all these years. Surely Mod would have scavenged the metal for its own selfish purposes. Prior pockets the badge. He knows its secrets.

Prior leaves through the door like a proper Fringe. When he hits the street, he realizes he doesn't have the protection of the pica-tam. But he knows that Mod's arrogant mindset would never contemplate Prior escaping from prison or returning again from Antigua. He's safe if he can accomplish what he must quickly.

Prior hoofs it to Brewster's. The place remains ransacked. Some items have gone missing since Prior's last visit. Probably Fringe desperately in search of supplies. At least they've managed to remove Brewster's poor body. There's no more of this world that Prior can take. His friend will do him one last service. Prior digs out an old-fashioned Smith-Corona typewriter from the rubble, protected in Brewster's thermoplastic sack, and places it in his backpack. It's the typewriter he gave to Brewster as a present after one of their cases. They were so happy that night, celebrating the resolution of a mystery. He wishes Brewster was here with him again. The weight of the typewriter feels good. Solid.

Keeping to the alleys and shadows, Prior hikes to the park and waits in line with everyone else. A few hours go by. Prior doesn't mind. It lets him think through his plan. When he gets to the front of the line, the Letter-Writer looks up and smiles, recognizing him.

"Jeremiah Prior. Your forwarding address keeps changing."

"I have something for you," says Prior, taking out the typewriter. "You've done me a few favors. Ribbon is still good." He places the typewriter on the cardboard desk and takes off the security sack. The desk sags under the weight.

The Letter-Writer stares in disbelief at this beautiful object. Tears well up in his eyes. Prior isn't sure if it's because of the typewriter or the gesture. The Letter-Writer reaches out with an aged hand and touches the side of the typewriter. He's full-on crying. He hugs the typewriter as if it's a lost child who's finally found their way home.

"I have no words..." says the Letter-Writer.

"You better have words," says Prior. "These people depend on you."

"If you ever need anything..."

"I do have one small favor to ask," says Prior. "Tell my daughter, Molly, that I'm alright and to meet me at her usual drinking hole. If she isn't home when the note's delivered, give it to her neighbor across the hall." Prior thinks about the neighbor girl with earrings. She's kept her gold earrings hidden with veiling technology that Molly stole from Felice. But now Prior's thinking Felice stole that technology from Feynman.

The Letter-Writer nods, never taking his eyes, or hug, away from the typewriter.

Prior smiles and leaves the park. A few blocks from his office, he stops by the convenience store with the red spiders. He needs all the gold he can get his hands on.

221

"What you want?" says the old woman who sits behind the cardboard box countertop. Conditions haven't improved for her.

"Remember me? We traded a lye cake for Antiguan jerk sauce?"

"Antique what?" says the old woman, fighting with gravity to stand.

"Juju. I gave you a bottle of juju."

Prior tries to help the woman stand but she shrugs him off.

"Get away," she yells as Prior moves to the customer side of the boxes. "I remember you. Juju to kill spiders. No good. Spiders still here. Maybe I kill you." She draws her hand from behind the counter brandishing a baseball bat. "I kill you for permanent."

Prior backs away. He knows she doesn't pose much of a threat but he doesn't need Fringe cops or Mod Police attention right now.

"Wait," says Prior. "Did you use it all or do you still have some juju left?"

"Why, you want to watch it not work on red spiders? You special kind of freak?" She draws closer to him, waving the bat in the air, warming up.

"Here," says Prior. He pulls out several bars of Antiguan soap that he took from his hut. "This is more valuable than gold. Real soap. Think of what you can sell it for." He offers it to her as he lowers his head.

The old lady stops advancing and lowers her bat. "You give to me? Why? So I no kill you?"

"To make a trade," says Prior. "You can have the soap if you give me back the bottle of jerk sauce."

"You crazy," says the old lady. She trudges from behind the counter, still holding the bat, and produces the vial of jerk sauce. It is more than half full, the gold flecks dancing in the light. "Give me soap."

Prior hands her the soap and she drops the bat. It makes a loud satisfying clang on the floor. She hands Prior the jerk sauce, stares him in the eye and says, "If this soap no good…"

"Yeah, I know," says Prior, already leaving the store. "You kill me for permanent."

Prior walks right past his office. Too many memories for him inside there. He thinks about Penny and how all she wanted was to be with him. How he ruined her life. Ruined all their lives. Feynman, Felice, Molly. Everyone he touched. He knows where his actions have led. And knows what he has to do.

He finally arrives at the graveyard. The one he was too scared to enter his first night back. He searches the streets for the bum he gave a bottle of the jerk sauce to. He supposes the chances of finding the bum are slim. Prior wends his way past the small mounds of dirt. The graves seem delicate, vulnerable without their headstones. There are hundreds of small dirt mounds set on the open land in a scattershot fashion. No identifying markers let him know which one is Feynman's.

The wind howls, warning him to get out. He doesn't obey. He caused this unnecessary death. He recognizes that now. There is nothing he can do about it. Prior would like to forgive himself but it wouldn't help the world at all. All he can do is try and make things right.

He reaches into his backpack and pulls out Feynman's old badge. He presses the badge hard against his hand. The badge begins to vibrate slowly, then picks up pace. Feynman always was a wizard at veiling technology. That was a handy skill to have as an Authentician.

The badge leads Prior to Feynman's grave. Prior knows that the badge's encrypted nanos aren't leading Prior to Feynman's body exactly. Nanos wouldn't care about four-year-old dead flesh. But if Feynman got buried with his stolen gold bars and hid them using his veiling tech, his badge is acting as the key to the safe.

As Prior approaches Feynman's resting place, the badge escapes Prior's hands and floats over the grave. The ground begins to shake, causing Prior to take a step back. There's a grinding sound emanating from the grave. Something metallic pushing against something wooden. The ground opens up and heaves, creating a mini volcano. Six gold bars erupt from the volcano, float over the grave, then orbit in a circle. As they complete their first rotation, they vaporize, the gold mass turned into nanos. The nanos move as one and flow directly into Feynman's badge. The badge glows momentarily before resuming its dull luster. The badge flies back into Prior's hand. It feels a bit heavier.

Golden Oldies indeed.

Prior glances down at the grave. He puts away the badge and gets down on his knees. He fills the hole in the ground as best he can, burying his partner again.

"Sorry pal," says Prior. "About Penny. About everything."

Chapter 35

Prior enters the dirty watering hole brimming with Fringe. He searches for Molly but all he sees is the water-monger serving his swill to desperate groups of Fringe huddled over a small fire. It's dark and the only light comes from the small campfires that dot the place. The water-monger nods at Prior, making him feel like a regular. Prior takes a seat in the corner, hoping Molly got the message.

Through the smoke, a figure approaches Prior's table. Prior squints but can't make out who it is.

"Detective Prior," says Grainger. "You're like...what did they used to call 'em?"

"A bad penny," says Torpedo No. 1. Torpedo No. 2 isn't far behind. Grainger and the two torpedoes grab chairs and sit at Prior's table. They appear different, determined. They mean business this time.

"Evening, Grainger," says Prior, trying to buy himself some time, hoping that Molly doesn't get mixed up in this.

"We heard you flew away like a little birdie back to Antigua," says Grainger. "When I heard that, I thought, nah, that doesn't sound like Prior. Going back to his island would be a smart thing to do. Instead, here you are. Thanks for proving me right."

"He's here alright," says Torpedo No. 1 into his wrist. Prior is pretty sure the remark was not intended for Grainger. He starts to piece together what's going on.

The torpedoes straighten up, looking less buffoonish. They've cut a deal with someone else. Grainger isn't wise to their intentions or he would never have brought them along. Prior scans the room. No sign of Molly.

"What'd I do now?" says Prior.

"Impersonating Mod, for one," says Lachende, taking a seat next to Grainger. Lachende is pretending to be Strutsky and by the looks of Grainger and the two torpedoes, they still don't know they're sitting next to a Mod.

"Strutsky, is it?" says Prior.

"You're not giving us the slip this time," says Grainger. "Let's go."

Grainger gets up and motions his torpedoes. They each grab Prior by an arm before he can react. He gazes at Lachende who is having fun playing the part of the tough guy. Lachende trails behind them as they escort Prior out of the bar.

"How'd you find me?" says Prior.

"Wasn't hard," says Grainger. "We got a tip from some broad in your daughter's building. Next time, choose better friends."

Molly's neighbor with the earrings. She sold him out.

They take him out back into the same damn alley. He doesn't want it to end this way. The two torpedoes escort him to the end of the alley, their tight grip on his arms unyielding. Grainger and Lachende are a few steps behind.

"You got him?" says Torpedo No. 2.

Torpedo No. 1 nods and Torpedo No.2 lets go of Prior.

"Say, what the hell are you doing?" says Grainger to the torpedoes.

"Ready," says Torpedo No. 2 into his wrist.

A spotlight hits them from above. Sky-Screen. Grainger and Prior gape up while the torpedoes remain still. Lachende takes a step back.

A small swarm of Points descends in a double-helix formation from the sky. They're heading straight for Prior. Lachende jumps back and hides behind some boxes.

Grainger charges Prior, yelling, "Watch out!"

Prior calculates the physics and knows he can take out one of the torpedoes. He grabs Torpedo No. 1 with his free hand and swings him hard into the brick wall. Torpedo No. 1's face takes the brunt of the impact, losing a few teeth in the process. Prior slams Torpedo No. 1's face back into the wall. Torpedo No. 1 drops to the ground, unconscious, maybe dead, before Torpedo No. 2 grabs Prior from behind.

Torpedo No. 2 pulls Prior away from the wall as Grainger approaches. Prior uses Torpedo No. 2 as leverage and kicks his two legs out, knocking Grainger back.

"Get the hell out of here, Grainger," says Prior.

Torpedo No. 2 keeps a tight grip on Prior as the Points arrive into the alleyway. They hover momentarily. Torpedo No. 2 holds Prior out like a lamb to slaughter.

Prior turns to the mist of Points. "You hungry? Bon appetit."

Prior throws himself and Torpedo No. 2 into the Points. The Points surround Torpedo No. 2 whose mass is easily double that of Prior.

"What are you doing?" says Torpedo No. 2. He lets out a scream as the Points begin devouring him, starting with his head. Torpedo No. 2's muscles, frozen in a death grip, continue to keep a tight hold of Prior's right arm.

Prior manages to slip out of the grip but not before the Points take a hold of his right hand. Prior screams in agony as he watches his right hand dissipate into the Point fog. He falls back to the ground, scrambling up. With his left arm, he pushes Torpedo No. 1, still on the ground, towards the Points for further feasting. He tucks his right arm under his left armpit. There's no bleeding, just a stump where his right hand used to be.

Prior runs down the alleyway, hoping Points will be satisfied with eating the two torpedoes. Someone grabs his shoulder and spins him around.

"What the hell is going on?" says Grainger.

"Let's get the hell out of here and I'll tell you," says Prior. "Where's your rookie?"

"Strutsky!" says Grainger.

Lachende peers out from some boxes and follows them out of the alleyway.

They run a few blocks, glancing over their shoulders. The Points don't give chase. When they get to the edge of the park, Grainger points a gun at Prior. Prior spots it and halts.

"OK, what was that?"

"Your goons. They were spies. Probably NanoGov. Or Points. Who knows? But they definitely weren't working for you. Or any other Fringe," says Prior.

Grainger considers Prior, then puts away his gun. "Thanks for getting me out of there."

"Same," says Prior.

Lachende sighs, amused.

"Your hand," says Grainger, pointing to Prior.

"Something about the Points' nanos," says Lachende. "They make it so it doesn't bleed. Like a miracle."

Prior stares down at his stump where his right hand used to reside. No pain. The wound is completely repaired.

"Hardly a miracle," says Prior. "More like a horror show."

"What's your problem, rookie?" says Grainger.

"Grainger, you really have no idea what's happening," says Prior.

Lachende stretches, shedding his Strutsky disguise. "Gentlemen, this has been fun. But I will not be a main course simply because I enjoy playing cops and robbers."

"He's a goddamn Mod," says Grainger.

Lachende starts to float away.

"In my coat," says Prior, his right arm still tucked under his left armpit.

Grainger reaches into Prior's coat pocket and pulls out the Framer that Prior took from Brewster's lab. Lachende is only ten feet away. Grainger hits the button and flings the Framer. It makes a beeline towards Lachende and easily traps him in its frame. Grainger converges on the Framer, picking it up. Lachende is stretched inside like a canvas. Grainger draws his gun on Prior.

"Now what?" says Prior.

"I need to figure out what's going on," says Grainger. "Figure you two can answer my questions."

"Where to?" says Prior.

"FU meeting. You two bozos are gonna get me in."

"Interesting move, Grainger," says Prior.

They walk a few blocks, Prior in front, Grainger behind him with a gun in one hand and the framed Lachende in the other. Brewster must have fiddled with the Framer because ordinarily, Lachende would have figured out a way out. Somehow, his nanos can't come to his rescue.

Prior doesn't mind. If a tussle with Grainger is the worst that happens to him for the rest of the evening, he's getting off easy.

"Slow down," says Grainger.

"How do you know where we're going?" says Prior, not turning around.

"Got a tip about an underground meeting in this building," says Grainger, indicating an abandoned brownstone apartment building down the block. The street's deserted but Prior keeps an eye on the sky in case Points want dessert.

"Ever think it might be a trap?" says Prior. "I mean, your goons and the alleyway…"

"Not from this source," says Grainger, walking alongside Prior. He's still got the gun pointed at him. "I heard about it from your daughter."

Prior halts.

The Framer vibrates so Grainger puts away the gun, holding the Framer steady with two hands, like he's holding a steering wheel that's out of control. Lachende still can't escape.

"Little help here?" says Grainger.

Prior sees this as his moment to bolt but he's done running. He grabs the Framer with his one hand until it stops struggling.

"How long have you known he's a Mod?" says Grainger.

"Remember the kid used to help me and Feynman out?"

"Lachende? Little Lachende?"

Prior nods.

"Well, I'll be damned," says Grainger.

"How could Molly…"

"She's the terrorist Mod Police have been going after," says Grainger.

"So you were keeping an eye on me in case she showed up?" says Prior, trying to act surprised.

"We don't have hard evidence so I needed to catch her in the act."

"You're figuring tonight might be the night. Get me and my daughter."

"Something like that."

They arrive at the building and climb up the stoop. The wooden door is latched shut. Prior knocks on the door. There's an echoing knock from inside. Prior slides his FU key through the mail slot in the door. Grainger slides the Framer through. After a few seconds, Prior's key and the Framer are slid back to them. The heavy door opens, the wood creaking from its weight.

An old Fringe, dressed in rags, lets them in. He closes the door behind them and leads them down a flight of stairs to the basement. There's a room at the bottom of the stairs. Probably where they held tenant meetings when this place was in full operation. There are twenty Fringe scattered around the room, most of them sitting on the dusty floor. There is no stage or grandeur to this room. It's just a bare room with no windows, greasy walls, concrete floor, lit by a few candles.

An old Fringe woman, standing against a wall, shuffles in front and shushes everyone, indicating the meeting is starting. The Fringe take their seats. Grainger and Prior stand in the back. From the shadows, Molly emerges, holding a candle. She places it on a chair in front of her so the glow illuminates her face.

"This is an FU meeting, huh," whispers Grainger, scanning the crowd. "Pretty much what I expected."

"Hey, Grainger," whispers Prior. "How about you give me back my Framer. And Lachende."

"Why should I…"

Grainger peers down and sees Prior holding Grainger's gun on him. Prior pickpocketed it when Grainger was distracted. Grainger slowly hands over the Framer.

"What are you doing?" says Grainger.

"Shhh," says Prior.

Molly starts her speech. It's the usual self-defeating talk that Fringe are used to.

Prior peeks into the Framer. "Lachende, I'm letting you out but don't start a commotion. I don't know what Brewster did to this Framer but I can put you back in here again. And next time, I'll feed you to Points."

Prior pushes the Framer button and part of Lachende pours out of the frame like melted ice cream, puddles on the floor, and spreads. Then the part of him not in the Framer takes on a more solid form and quickly coalesces into the top half of Strutsky. The bottom half narrows down into a flat canvas still jailed in the Framer.

"This is unpleasant," says Lachende.

Prior is about to respond but his attention is taken by Molly's speech. He keeps a tight grip on the Framer like it's Lachende's leash. Grainger and Lachende turn their head towards her as well.

"You've all heard about the stolen Seurat sketch?" says Molly. "It wasn't stolen from a Mod's underground vault. It was my mother's. And I took it. It holds the key we need."

"What the hell is she talking about?" says Prior, leaning closer to Lachende. Grainger leans in as well.

"She's really serious this time," says Lachende. He turns to Prior. "Felice, sorry, the ex-Mrs. Prior, has been searching for that Seurat sketch. She's been trying to draw Molly out anyway she can. Including using you."

"What's so special about the Seurat sketch?" says Grainger.

Molly screams and they all turn their heads. The old Fringe woman host has unfurled to reveal herself to be Mod. The Mod turns into a sack and completely envelops Molly, despite Molly's struggling. The Fringe get up and scream. Chaos erupts. Prior and Grainger fight their way through the crowd to get at the Molly-cocoon. Prior grips the Framer and drags Lachende behind him. The Mod floats up to the ceiling. A face forms on the bottom of the sack.

"Ladies and gentlemen. Always a pleasure."

It's Belden. He smiles. The sack disappears through the ceiling, leaving behind the echoes of Molly's screams.

Chapter 36

Prior and Grainger escape the brownstone building. They stand at the stoop, catching their breath, as Lachende extracts himself fully from the Framer.

"Sorry about that," says Prior. Lachende hands him back the Framer. "Got to hand it to Brewster though."

"Molly," says Lachende.

"I know," says Prior. "I have a plan."

"You ain't going nowhere," says Grainger.

Prior sighs. "Dammit, Grainger, don't you get it?" Grainger just stares at Prior. "Show him," says Prior to Lachende.

Lachende's face turns into a screen that projects the actual video footage of Richard Feynman being murdered by Penny.

Grainger stares at it. "Play it again." Lachende obliges. After a moment, Grainger says, "This for real?"

Lachende and Prior nod.

Grainger paces half a block and returns. "Well, flatten my ass."

"It's alright," says Prior.

"What's your plan, boss," says Lachende.

"We need Addison. He's the key to this whole thing. He can help us find Molly and take down NanoGov."

"Holy shit, Prior," says Grainger.

"Problem?"

Grainger contemplates his ex-rookie and Prior. "No, no problem. I could do with a little revolution myself."

"Alright, you two go and see what you can find at Mod Police Headquarters," says Prior. "I'm going to Modela Nova's place. Addison's sister might know where he's hiding."

Grainger and Lachende turn to go. After Grainger is a block away, Lachende turns back to Prior.

"Okay, I did this as quietly as possible and just as a hypothetical. I found a Mod who's interested," says Lachende. "He said he could get you four billion today for your blood."

"Thanks, Lachende. Do it."

"I hope this crazy idea of yours remains a hypothetical. Despite outward appearances, Molly would be crushed if anything happened to you. You should have seen her before when…"

"You're a good kid."

Lachende goes silent. It's an odd sight. Finally, Lachende nods his head and catches up with Grainger.

Prior makes his way to Modela's apartment. If anyone knows where Addison is, Modela will. If anyone can get the information out of him, she can. Prior hasn't heard from her in a while. Maybe she's been keeping away from Prior ever since she set him up.

As soon as he knocks on her door, he hears that horrible, familiar sound. Then he catches Modela screams. Prior sets his shoulder to work and busts down her door.

Modela Nova is splayed on the floor in the middle of her living room. Addison stands ominously over her, in the process of devouring her mass.

Addison doesn't notice Prior entering the room. He is too focused on relishing his feast. His eyes are rolled back in his head like a Great White shark during a frenzied attack. Modela's screams seem to make Addison more determined.

Prior leaves quietly and closes the door. He stands outside in the hallway, the adrenalin pounding away at the inside of his skull. He reaches into his backpack and pulls out Brewster's Framer. It's time to test its limits. Instantly, Modela's screaming ceases.

He kicks open the door and throws the Framer at Addison.

Addison roars, his arms flailing and legs kicking, trying to get the Framer off him. In a matter of seconds, it envelopes him.

"Goddamn you, Addison," Prior says, grabbing the Framer tight so he won't escape. Modela is gone, completely devoured.

Addison quits squirming and holds still. There is a muffled puff of air from the Framer like a food container getting burped. Addison appears secure, stretched thin.

"My daughter's been kidnapped," says Prior to Addison in the Framer. "You may not care but you're going to help me."

There's a muffled sound coming from the Framer. Cautiously, Prior puts the Framer up to his ear, like listening for the ocean in a seashell.

"Modela! I'm sorry," says Addison in a faint voice. "I loved my sister. You have to believe that. I wanted to make sure she wasn't getting into more trouble with Ferri."

"Yeah, my heart bleeds for you," says Prior.

There is a rapping on the window. Prior peers out as a small fog rolls up to the window and permeates the room.

"What is this?" says Addison.

"Funny, I was going to ask you the same thing. You had nothing to do with Molly's kidnapping?"

"Of course not."

The fog coalesces along a wall. The wallpaper develops small scratches. The scratches turn into letters as the wallpaper is peeled back by the fog.

"J," reads the wallpaper. "I have Molly. It's not the Seurat I'm after but Addison. I know you have him. There will be an exchange in one hour because I demand one. And I want Addison alive. I await your reply. F."

The fog repairs the wallpaper as if it had never been damaged, then it swirls around Prior's feet, hovering. She isn't kidding when she said she awaits his reply. The fog moves up to his knees.

"You're going to help me Addison." says Prior. "You owe me that much. For my daughter. For your poor sister."

The fog swirls around Prior's face. He knows the fog isn't Felice. These are her nano-messengers. He tilts his head down and talks right into it, delivering the message he knows will be promptly delivered to Felice in seconds, wherever she actually is.

"Alright Felice, you've taken this child custody thing a little far, haven't you? Addison doesn't know anything. And if you think I've found out some great underlying secret and discovered that the world's going to hell, you're about four years too late.

"I don't know what the hell is going on in that flapjack brain of yours but you better not let anything happen to our daughter. You bring her to my office in an hour. You bring her personally or no exchange. And you tell the fat professor if he wants to see his Vermeer, he better not touch a hair on Molly's head."

The fog registers the change in Prior's breathing and knows the message is over. It dissipates into the air and flies out the window.

Prior breathes a sigh of relief.

"What did you mean by her meeting you at your office in an hour? You will not hand me over to her," says Addison.

"Look who's in a position to give orders."

Chapter 37

Prior's office has been ransacked. The suspects are innumerable. He places the Framer, with Addison still captive, on his desk.

Penny kept a tidy file system. He hadn't realized how much she did for him. And how much she meant to him. He continually ruined her life and she kept coming back for more. It's a lot more than he can say about the other women in his life. Prior tries to focus but his memories of Penny keep creeping in. He thinks of Molly and it brings him back to reality. And poor Modela. She'd still be floating around if she hadn't chosen him to help her.

Prior is taking a chance but figures he's running out of options.

"OK, Addison, I'm trusting you." He clicks the Framer button. The Framer shakes violently and drops on the floor, empty. There's a shift in the corner of Prior's office. It causes him to spin around.

Addison stands in the corner, shaking. Suddenly, he unfolds and there are two of him. The Addison on the left changes shape and assumes the form of Modela. The couple resemble a set of happy sister-and-brother cut-out dolls. Prior's breath stops as he realizes Addison could devour him on the spot.

"Mr. Prior," says Addison. His voice is tinny and devoid of emotion. "I'm sorry about my previous behavior. It's...it's the hunger." His mouth quivers and a pink ribbon tongue snaps at his lips. "Pretending my sister is here makes it easier." The fake Modela stands still like a flat mannequin. He grips her hand tightly.

"Well, Addison, I sure hope you can hold off a little while longer."

"I want to help. To atone," says Addison. His voice seems sincere but it could be his nanos' ravenous desire talking. "My darling Modela."

"I'll get you your lunch," says Prior. "And I'll do what I can to help you. Just follow the plan."

At exactly one hour after Prior gave Felice her fog-message, there's a knock on the door. Prior lets out a nervous chuckle at the formality and predictability of the timing as he opens the door.

Felice, in Mod form, stands in the hallway, looking younger than Prior remembers. Her hair is shorter. Behind her, stands Belden, his flat, wide arms surrounding Molly like a coiled anaconda.

"You okay?" Prior says to Molly.

"What happened to your hand?" says Molly.

Prior considers his right arm which ends in a stump at his wrist. "So now I can only count to five. I'm fine," says Prior.

The three of them step cautiously into Prior's office.

"Prior," says Belden, still holding onto Molly. "You don't look surprised."

"Don't I?"

"To see me in cahoots with your wife, to use the parlance of days gone by."

"Ex-wife," says Prior.

"Hello, Jere," says Felice. "I see you've got…company."

Modela Nova, sitting in a chair by Prior's desk, legs crossed, smiles weakly but doesn't say anything.

Felice regards the room, searching for hidden dangers. Prior hasn't seen Felice in a long time. As a Point, he could feel her presence and hear her but now he's viewing a moving poster of her. It disgusts him but he can't stop staring. He reminds himself he has to move quickly.

"Felice," says Prior as coldly as he can muster. "Grab a seat. All of you."

Felice nods at Belden, who lets go of Molly. She runs over to Prior who gives her a quick hug. He pulls up a chair next to Modela. Modela and Molly contemplate one another with a silent nod. Felice and Belden move to the other side of the office and sit down.

"Well, you've managed to get the sister here," says Felice, with an annoyed glance at Modela, "but I don't see the brother. Is Addison expected soon?"

"Because if he's not," says Belden, "I can assure you we are more than perfectly prepared to take Little Miss Terrorist back with us."

Prior paces the room and stops in front of Belden.

"What is it with you people, huh?" says Prior. "I know you have no respect for Fringe but when does it end?"

"I honestly have no idea what he is saying," says Belden to Felice. "It comes out all 'blah, blah, blah.'"

"Who the hell gave you the right to threaten my daughter?" says Prior.

"I did," says Felice.

"Of course," says Prior. "So you can work on your cure for being too goddamn greedy."

"It's for the common good," says Belden. "Altruism, my dear boy, is a concept too primitive for your weak mind."

"And how do you figure into all this, Professor Pancake?" says Prior.

"Well, I hardly believe insults..."

"Yeah, well, get used to it, Belden," says Prior. "When you turn traitor, you stop getting invited to all the really swell soirees."

"Professor Belden was given the money for his conversion by me in exchange for his help in securing Addison," says Felice. "I was his sponsor."

"I see. And you didn't care that his plan involved kidnapping our daughter."

"Actually," says Felice, "that was my idea."

Prior turns to Molly who sports her stoic face. She isn't reacting to any of this. She knows something but her poker face isn't telling Prior what it is. Modela tries to sit still and not appear frightened but her paper foot slaps the rug nervously.

A smile crosses the map of Belden's face. "And how is my little investment doing?" says Belden. "Still coursing through your veins?"

"Is that why you're here?"

"You'll kindly return it to me," says Belden.

"Tell me again what's stopping me from grabbing Molly and kicking your sorry ass out of here?"

Belden is momentarily taken aback, not used to being spoken to in this manner. Then, his smile returns. "Because, Prior, I know something you don't. And this particular something gives me a bit of leverage in this little game we seem to be playing."

"Games bore me," says Prior.

"You'll like this one," says Belden, turning to Felice. "Shall I tell him? Or would you like to?"

"You," says Felice. She examines the floor. It's unusual behavior for her. Up until now, she's been focusing on Prior's eyes, trying to gauge if he has any surprises planned.

"Like Felice said, she and NanoGov gave me the money to convert in exchange for helping them find Addison. However, I also provided Felice with some insider information to help her find her cure. Very important insider information."

"Such as?" says Prior.

"They took the Seurat," whispers Molly.

Prior goes over to Molly and holds her face. She won't look him in the eye.

"In exchange for…" says Prior.

"During Molly's brief, recent stay with me, while I was extracting the Georges Seurat sketch, I had an opportunity to…how shall I put this delicately…augment her biology."

"What?"

"Molly bears my child," says Belden.

Prior turns to Molly. "Is this true?"

Molly continues to look down, ignoring all of them.

"Felice?" says Prior, hatred in his eyes.

"If you could understand the hunger," says Felice in a flat tone.

"You bastard," says Prior to Belden. "You featureless bastard." He rushes over to Belden and blows in his face. The momentary air shift blows Belden back over the chair and against the closet door. "Now!"

Modela flies across the room, changing back to Addison, screaming with a ravished vampire hunger. In mid-air, Addison turns himself back into a Point and swirls like a tornado around Belden, enveloping him.

Belden emits a temporary but high-pitched scream. Then, almost too quickly for Prior's taste, it's over. In a matter of two seconds, Belden's mass is completely gone. There is nothing left of him.

Felice sits in shock.

Molly closes her eyes from the horror.

Addison turns himself back into a Mod and politely sits down. Although he is sated, he eyes Felice hungrily, assessing his dessert.

"Now," says Prior, breaking the silence, "Felice, honey, sweetheart, I think it's time we had a friendly chat."

"I have the Seurat. I just need Addison," she says.

Addison erupts in a scream. It isn't the hunger screech that he let out before. It's a shriek of utter agony. For the first time, Prior sees genuine horror and fear in Addison's eyes. A cloud has materialized over his head and it quickly draws him upwards, nano by nano, sucking him up into its vortex. Addison shrinks, trying to get away, but he is caught in its pull. Prior feels a rush of air created by the vacuum. The air pressure drops and rises erratically as a screaming Addison is devoured. When he is completely sucked up into the cloud, his screams cease.

"Addison!" says Prior, running to the spot where he had been sitting. There is a sonic blast that knocks everyone across the room.

"Well, now, I've been looking forward to that for a very long time," says a familiar voice from the cloud.

When Prior gazes up, the cloud turns into Anton Ferri.

Chapter 38

"Hello, Jeremiah," says Ferri in Mod form. He takes a step forward and Prior and Molly reflexively step back. Ferri waves his hand. The one chair in the room that hasn't been upturned slides over to Ferri. He sits languidly in repose, completely confident. His bald head shines from a light emanating from within. His strong features are exaggerated in his current form.

Molly remains silent, trying to assess what's happening.

Felice approaches Ferri, nods to him, and submissively positions herself behind him.

"I apologize for the dramatic entrance," says Ferri. "But you have to admit, it was effective."

"What have you done?" says Prior.

"Oh, please, Jeremiah, you're a detective," says Ferri. "A good one, I thought. But then again, you're so personally invested in this case, I imagine it's difficult to remain clear-headed and objective. For a Fringe, anyway."

"Then suppose you explain it so a Fringe could understand," says Prior, trying to buy time.

"I should think it's perfectly obvious," says Ferri.

Felice looks down, afraid to catch Prior's eyes. She avoids Molly's gaze as well. "Anton," says Felice.

"The Seurat," says Molly.

"This was all about you finding Molly," says Prior to Ferri and Felice. All the tumblers are finally clicking into place.

"Look, it's trying to think. Most amusing," says Ferri.

"Molly stole the Seurat sketch when she left you," says Prior to Felice. "There was something embedded in the sketch you needed. Something you didn't want anyone else to find."

"I thought I could trust my own daughter," says Felice.

"Don't even..." says Molly.

"But Molly was hiding out," says Prior to Felice. He's paces in front of her, working it out. "And you couldn't afford to have her picked up by NanoGov. You had to find her on your own. So you used me to lead you right to her," says Prior.

"Precisely," says Ferri.

"I don't understand," says Molly.

"Easy," says Prior, "Ferri here fakes his death. You think he did it because he got tired of the Moderazzi? No. It's so he could lie low and keep NanoGov from snooping around. Then your mom is free to keep looking for you with no one being suspicious." He turns back to Ferri. "Ferri here knew that there were only two people I could safely trust. So he killed Brewster. That forced me to make contact with Felice. I led you right to Molly."

There is silence as this explosive news permeates the air and penetrates Molly's reality.

"Excellent summation," says Ferri.

"And Addison?" says Prior.

"A pawn," says Ferri. "A troublesome pawn."

"Belden," says Prior.

"Oh Prior. Poor sentimental Prior. Belden?" says Ferri. "A fool. Brewster? Everyone else? Road bumps."

"Right, Anton," says Prior. "Life is cheap. But now the important question. Why? Why go through all this? Is your legacy that important?"

"Prior," says Ferri, "for all your days, you will never truly understand me. My motives are far above your pay grade."

"You created this Point mess," says Prior. Then he turns to Felice. "Both of you. Now Points have to devour Mod and Fringes to stay alive. But I think you figured out how to solve the Point Flaw. And the solution is in the Seurat sketch."

Ferri chuckles and applauds, amused. "I like you, Prior," says Ferri. "I've met every fancy Mod and NanoGov executive you can imagine and I'd like to think I know a little something about people. And you I like."

"Swell."

"But how is it possible for you to be so right and so wrong?" says Ferri.

"We were never looking for a cure to the Flaw," says Felice.

The statement cuts through the room.

"The Point problem can't be reversed," says Felice. She remains calm. There is something condescending in her tone, as if she's explaining this to children. "They told me that turning Point was glorious. Now, I'm as cursed as the others. At least as a Mod, I knew I was immortal, though my powers of consumption were limited."

"You're crazy," says Prior.

"Let the woman finish," says Ferri. He's indulging her.

Prior holds tight to Molly.

"Your science was flawed," says Felice to Ferri. "The Point conversion was rushed to market." She turns to Prior. "We had to find a solution before we ran out of Mod and Fringe to consume."

"And me?" says Molly.

"I couldn't bear to consume my own child," says Felice, cold, bloodless. "Not if I could talk you into turning Point with me. Then we would scour the planet, feeding together."

"And if she says no?" says Prior.

Felice shrugs. "If she turns against me like all the rest, I'll be forced to take her mass as well."

This is not the Felice that Prior married. She doesn't want a cure for the Points. She just wants to fix herself. And she wants to take Molly with her. At any price.

"Are we quite done here?" says Ferri.

"Not yet," says Prior. He begins pacing. Ferri and Felice witness with curiosity. "You said it yourself. The two of you aren't looking for a cure to the Point Flaw. You just need a constant food source to keep feeding."

Ferri smiles broadly. "That's wonderful," he says. "You know, I didn't think you'd work it out."

"Let's leave, Anton," says Felice.

"Not when I can gloat," says Ferri. "You're right, Jeremiah. My solution was an elegant one. And Felice helped me design the machine. A nano-machine that produces Fringe as a food source for Points. The design is secured in the Seurat. We're utilizing nanos in a radical new way, combining the nano's ability to self-repair with the ability to self-perpetuate on a massive scale. That's how I solved the Point Flaw."

When Prior makes sense of the machine's design, he shudders at its implications. This must also be Ferri's plan for finally overthrowing NanoGov and taking over as its leader. Fringe and Mod will be completely expendable, obsolete. Prior rights himself and breathes deeply. No way is the world going down like this on his watch.

Ferri implodes to a Point and hovers in the air for a moment, an intense light the only marker of his presence. He's literally a miniature star. Then he begins to vibrate slightly. Suddenly, he inflates himself to three-dimensions and is again the kindly, old grandfather everyone wants.

"Don't you see?" says Ferri, calmly. "I have plans to correct a horrible wrong. Points need my help. Addison was a guinea pig. An experiment that should never have left the test tube."

"You arrogant bastard," says Prior.

"I think this draws our little summit to a close, don't you?" says Ferri. "We've all gotten what we came for."

"The girl," says Felice to Ferri.

He flashes a wicked smile. "Patience," says Ferri.

Prior holds Molly tightly.

There's a sonic blast that knocks Prior down to the ground near Molly. It feels just like the one they experienced minutes earlier.

When the dust clears, Felice and Ferri are gone.

Chapter 39

Prior checks the windows to make sure there are no signs of Ferri, Felice, or an invading army of Points or Mod. Prior and Molly sneak out into the street, watching overhead and keeping to the shadows. He puts his arm around her. She lets him.

His mind is turning recent events over and over and what he knows he has to do. He searches for alternatives but none come to mind.

After they've wandered a few blocks, Prior decides to ask Molly what is an obvious but still delicate subject.

"So, Molly…"

"You're going to ask me how I could accept the terms to be impregnated by Belden."

"Terms? I thought…"

"Everything is transactional with these bastards," she says. "Belden and mom offered me a ton of money if Belden could inject me with his DNA," she says. "Of course, I knew that sex was totally out of the question with that fat fuck, Mod or not. Sorry."

"No, go ahead."

"Anyway, I accepted it because I need the money. No surprise there. They already paid me. The money is for the baby."

"But…"

"The money is so I don't have to turn Mod," she says.

Prior grabs her close to him and kisses her forehead. "That's the nicest thing you ever said," says Prior. "Here." He gives her Penny's little red purse.

"What's this?" she says, holding it up to the light.

"A totem. For your protection."

"Thanks," says Molly, pocketing the purse. They continue strolling. "Besides, the joke's on them. I was already pregnant. Belden thought it was his kid after he injected me with his DNA. Lachende got there first by a long shot. It felt good scamming them."

"Your mother…"

"Yeah," says Molly, putting her arm around him. "Suddenly, I'm starting to suspect she may not have my best interests at heart."

They walk the next few blocks in silence.

"Where are we going, by the way?" she says.

"Your apartment."

"What?"

"You have to admit," says Prior. "It's the last place anyone would be looking for you."

"Why can't I come along?"

"Too dangerous. I'll stop in soon."

"I can handle myself," says Molly.

This is difficult for Prior but he tries not to show it. It may be the last time he ever sees her. At least this time, it's for the right reason. "I know. But you need to take care of that baby."

They continue walking towards her apartment building. No one seems to be following them.

"I'll get a hold of Lachende to watch over you," says Prior. "I just need him to help me with something first."

Molly smiles. "Thanks, Dad. But I don't need anyone to watch over me. I'm not going home."

"Where are you going?"

"You have to stop treating me like a child," she says. "I'm off to an FU meeting."

"Why? You saw what happened last time."

She sighs. "Because we have to maintain the illusion that we have some control or can actually do anything. Do you know what it's like to have years of this helpless, restless energy? And what's my ridiculous contribution going to be? Nothing."

Prior considers her but she avoids his gaze. "Can you ask the FU to meet me at McCloskey's Bar tonight?"

She nods her head.

"Please be careful," he says. He goes to hug her but she withdraws.

"You too," she says and ducks down an alley, disappearing into the night.

Prior takes a deep breath and sighs. Within two hours, there are fifteen FU members at McCloskey's Bar. Molly isn't among them. Their eagerness makes Prior feel less lonely. Still, they are badly outnumbered and have no technology.

"How can I help?" says Grainger, arriving with Lachende.

"Thanks for coming," says Prior, and fills them all in on current events.

The FU members appear more disheartened than ever.

"Gather round," says Prior. He dumps the contents of his backpack on the floor. It's the Fringe Underground Movement key, the gold flecks from Antoine's jerk sauce, and Feynman's badge teeming with the gold bar nanos. "I've got a plan."

Prior goes over it. They listen, nodding, agreeing; some reluctantly.

Before they leave, Grainger catches up to Prior. "Glad you're on our team," says Grainger.

"Glad there is a team," says Prior.

When they get outside, Lachende envelopes Prior in a balloon and they float towards the Mod Clinic. Prior sits inside, contemplating if his plan will work. He needs to do something for this world. No one else will. The reason he went to Antigua makes sense now. He didn't develop the same defeatist mindset as the Fringe. The world demands a different point of view. This whole crazy world has to be re-booted.

It seems like Prior is the only one who has even thought about trying. He has the support of Grainger, the FU Movement, and Lachende but they need to be led, not take a leadership stake. It's as if that part of their brain has deteriorated. Grainger has never questioned authority before because he has been conditioned not to. Everything seemed so futile. They are all in some kind of drugged stupor, chemically lobotomized by NanoGov. Prior doesn't put it past NanoGov to alter the citizenry like that. Consider what they've done so far in the name of progress with a willing populace.

Lachende accompanies Prior to the Mod Clinic. Lachende escorts Prior inside. Prior pretends to be a Fringe ready for conversion. For Lachende's part, he is eagerly playing the role of Prior's benefactor and mentor, observing how their stations in life have been reversed. Lachende gets Prior processed through without any fuss. NanoGov is always eager for new recruits.

Lachende leads him down a hallway. They enter a small, sterile room furnished simply with a modest bed. Prior lies down and Lachende straps him in.

"Good luck," says Lachende.

Prior nods weakly, hoping he's made the right choice for the hundredth time.

"You sure you know what you're doing?" says Lachende.

"Of course not. Now you remember to get the hell out of here after the blanket part."

"You owe me one," says Lachende.

"Funny, I was going to say the same thing."

Lachende smiles a crooked smile and floats above Prior.

A soft woman's voice wafts in Prior's room through a small speaker.

"Welcome," she says. "Now just relax."

It is the nicest voice that Prior has heard in a long time. It almost makes him relax. Lachende drifts onto Prior like a blanket. There is a rush of air. Prior can feel the nanos flying through the walls into the room. They hover over him like a microscopic flock of birds before descending through Lachende and into him. It doesn't feel like anything at first but then Prior's molecules start shape-shifting and everything is immediately different.

The part that is difficult about going Mod is the disorientation as Prior's mass evacuates him. It is an excruciating pain he's heard about but never experienced. Laying on the bed, Prior feels every molecule in his body ricocheting, juggling, shimmering as they shift and warp into their new form. It's not unlike the feeling when Felice left him. Lachende is there, holding Prior together.

Prior screams as the woman continues to relentlessly insist in that pleasant voice that he relax. Prior feels like he is being pulled in every direction at once. Once the salt-water taffy sensation is over, the burning sensation begins. Every pore of his skin intensely burns. Then, just as quickly as the pain begins, it subsides. The whole conversion takes four seconds. It feels like an hour. Lachende ascends and leaves the room.

At first, Prior doesn't feel any different. Then, the bed straps come loose and there's an emptiness, a lightness. He floats. Prior has only felt like this when he was hammered on Wadadli rum. Then, he realizes that it isn't a metaphorical floating, it's the real thing. He concentrates and raises his arms in front of him.

His hands and arms are flowing ribbons of skin. He focuses on his smoke body and realizes he's naked. And two-dimensional.

"Now concentrate on sitting up," says the female voice.

Prior finally drifts back down to the bed where he obediently sits. It takes all of his focus not to float back up. He is alive to every air current and micro-change in temperature in the room. Every fiber on the bedspread is nuanced and detailed to his discerning eye.

"Dress yourself. Remember, it's anything you want. Your nanos will always provide for you," she says.

Prior is really starting to take a shine to this woman. He makes a mental note to find out who she is when he gets out of here.

Prior gives some serious thought to the notion of how he should be dressed. He finds it hard to think about his attire and remaining seated at the same time. When he tries to do two things at once, everything becomes foggy.

There is a tingling sensation all around him that tickles. It feels electric. It's his nanos. They have converted from his former mass into free-floating servants of his will, permanently connected to his every whim. A trillion, trillion butlers, valets, and handmaidens waiting to fulfill every one of his desires. They hover, waiting to be beckoned. Waiting to be put into service.

It feels like an infinity of arms protruding from his body, each easily commanded. He sees and smells everything perfectly. He stretches out into infinity. There is nothing he can't possess.

Prior concentrates and grows back his right hand.

He thinks, "A full Rastafarian robe and tam." Before he has finished thinking about Antoine, a portion of his nanos have assembled around him. He is wearing the wardrobe he just requested. The vast remainder of his nanos await further instruction. They swarm around him like he is the sun to their galaxy, flying through him, worshipping him, encircling him. Infinite hugs from an endless nursery of babies.

The sensation is overwhelming. Prior loses sight of the outside world beyond his own reach. There is a social bubble around him that exists solely to satiate his desires and pleasures. Everything else is irrelevant. Prior has everything he can possibly ever need to sustain his perfect flat life. That lightness is all around him. He even thinks about forgiving Felice. This freedom is intoxicating and he understands the allure. Perhaps he could join Felice and try to find an actual cure for the Point Flaw.

Then he thinks about Molly. And he feels heaviness again. He knows what he has to do.

His nanos push him in one direction as his Fringe guilt pulls him in another. The guilt wins. Big surprise.

After an hour, Prior is able to concentrate on several things at once. He floats out of the room, a bit groggy and disoriented, and turns the corner.

He suddenly remembers and checks for the Vermeer. It is still within him, locked safely in Brewster's thermoplastic vault; still part of his nano-sphere.

He floats down the hallway, then banks sharply into a ventilation duct, just the way Lachende explained it. Prior couldn't have Lachende as an accomplice. Lachende can't be implicated in any of this in case it goes sideways. Molly's kid needs a dad. Prior has to do this alone. The security nanos don't notice him since they are trained for Fringe infiltration. Mod would never be a security risk since they have everything they could ever want. Why would they infiltrate?

He ends up in a small empty room. He steps up to the concrete wall and touches it with both hands. It feels cold and smooth. His nanos await instruction.

He thinks, "Retrieve secret NanoGov files related to Points."

A stream of data rushes through him directly into his brain. He pulls his hands away from the wall. Dazed, he steps back, aware of dark secrets he should not be privy to. Instantly, Prior's insulated world gets vastly larger.

He learns how Mod are converting to Points. The Pandora's Box of data buzzing about his brain also confirms what Felice and Ferri told him: Mod are able to turn to Points but the conversion process makes the Points' nanos unstable. All the Points are projected to implode after a few years; some after a few months. The Points' only recourse is to continually steal and consume the mass of Mod and Fringes in order to survive. It is the biggest crisis NanoGov has ever encountered.

The world is suddenly much darker and alien. And flatter.

Chapter 40

Prior floats over to Molly's apartment. The ease with which he can traverse the city astounds him. He has limitless access afforded to him. He slips through her building and arrives in her spare apartment.

"Molly?" he says.

Prior momentarily concentrates and the apartment is completely furnished with comfy couches and chairs.

"What is this?" says Molly, walking into the foyer. She sees Prior and steps back.

"Molly, it's OK."

"Oh my Mod," she says, looking for an exit. "How could you?"

"I did this for you. I have a plan."

"Yeah?" says Molly. "Like what, join mom?"

"We're taking down the Points."

She considers him. "Are you alone?" she says.

Prior takes a step closer and she doesn't move. She surveys her surroundings like she's expecting others to jump into the room and capture her.

"You're insane," she finally says. "What were you thinking?"

"I had to do this. It's the only way to get in."

"Where?"

"Ferri's lab."

She scrutinizes him and bursts out laughing. "Lachende told me but I didn't believe it. My own dad. The guy who kept lecturing me about turning Mod."

"I thought…"

"You look ridiculous," she says.

He tries to hug her but she's all business.

"I'm coming with you," she says.

"No way," he says.

"I know my way around the lab better than you," she says.

"There's no way…"

"Remember mom and her 'Take Your Daughter to Work Day?'" she says. "I guarantee I'll have you in and out of there so you can convert back right away."

Prior evaluates her offer. There's no time. "Shit. OK. But you're going to stay out of trouble. I don't need you going all terrorist-mode on me."

"Sure you do," she says and smile. "Now bubble me up."

Prior sighs, then wraps her like a cocoon. They float to Ferri's laboratory outside the city.

"I figured out what's going on at Ferri's lab. It's where Mod are converted to Points. Ferri's lab is a goddamn Points factory," says Prior. "And even though Ferri faked being dead, his lab continued honoring appointments with Mod who wanted to go in for the latest fashion. Ferri carried on turning Mod to Points knowing they were inherently flawed."

Molly shifts her weight which causes him to navigate higher and to the other side of the building. "Ferri's lab is heavily guarded with security nanos," she says. "This way."

She guides Prior to a manhole outside the lab. "This waste pipe leads into the boiler room in the basement," she says. "No one but Fringe would even know what a waste pipe is and no Fringe would think of using it for these purposes. The arrogance of Mod. No insult intended, your flatness."

Prior envelops Molly tighter and they enter the manhole. They float through the pipe and into the basement, unscathed and unsullied. Molly exits Prior's bubble and he flattens himself out, following her.

As expected, the boiler room is dimly lit and humid. They make their way past the hissing equipment to the double doors and stairwell. The clang of footsteps on metal echoes with an odd sound. It is strange to see this much metal in one place. Prior walks behind Molly up to the first floor. They have no weapons in their possession.

Now that Ferri and Felice have the Seurat, Prior has a hunch that they'll return to the lab to extract Felice's nano-machine so they can keep working on his

Point project making Fringes. Prior and Molly sneak into the lobby of the building. It's an enormous atrium, at least a hundred feet high. The glass walls glisten and sparkle behind the humid, heavy mist that pervades the air. The lobby is outfitted with a rainforest motif. Giant, broad-leafed trees sprout up and create an umbrella for the entire room.

"No Mod," says Molly.

"That's not what worries me," says Prior.

"What then?"

"No security nanos," says Prior.

"I don't like this," says Molly. "We should head back. Get some weapons."

"Listen," says Prior, louder than expected. "It's not about weapons. It's about mindset. People have forgotten how to fight for anything important. They just accept what they're told. Yeah, you blow some stuff up but it's not enough. You have to think bigger. People got lazy. But here's the thing. The assholes in charge got lazy too. They're not expecting this. Trust me."

"It's a little bit about weapons," says Molly.

Suddenly, they hear screaming outside. They drop to the ground and Prior covers Molly with his body like a blanket. The screams continue. Three passing Fringe are getting devoured outside the building.

Molly shakes Prior off her and runs to the exit. "The hell with this," she says. "We've got to go save them."

"Stay down!" says Prior.

A Fringe man runs to the glass entry door and bangs it, desperate to be let inside. A small shower of raindrops descends on him. The raindrops bank sharply and enter his ears. Points zip into his brain and bounce around as his head rattles like a maraca. Before he hits the ground, Points have converted his mass; there's nothing left of him. He simply disappears mid-collapse. The Points fly back into the building lobby and camouflage into the rainforest.

"My God. Now what?" says Molly, panicking.

Before Prior can answer, they hear thunder. The room shakes and a furious rainstorm descends into the room in big, sloppy drops. They are under a major Point attack.

"Head that way," Prior says to Molly, pointing to the labs. "Do you have the little red purse I gave you?"

She takes the purse out of her bag. "I'll distract them and circle back this way," says Molly.

"You shouldn't have come," says Prior.

Molly runs off towards the labs. Most of the Points chase Molly.

Prior opens the entry door. A stiff wind blows into the building and knocks the Points off-course. Prior understands that they are prone to the same laws of physics and Brownian motion, like dust particles, when it comes to reacting to outside forces. Prior has to buy Molly some more time.

He decides to test another theory. He spreads out like a giant tarp and rubs himself on the carpeted floor. The Points react to the static electricity and avoid him. They fly towards the labs to chase Molly who is easier quarry. One thing about Points: they are even lazier than Mod.

Just as the Points are heading through the lab doors, Molly comes bolting out. A squadron of Mod flies after her. She dives to the ground as Mod fly over her. The Mod collide with the Points, letting out a horrific screeching noise. The Points, incensed that their air space and quarry hunt is being interrupted by lesser creatures, attack the Mod.

Prior realizes that the old-fashioned notion of rock-paper-scissor would easily explain the social and evolutionary paradigm that is their world.

Molly reaches Prior, who has drawn himself up to human dimensions.

Prior watches as Points and Mod battle in the sky, completely forgetting the lowly Fringe below. Mod are no match for the ravenous Points who completely consume them in seconds. The Mod numbers are quickly depleted. Molly looks up in fear and awe.

"Notice that?" says Prior.

"What?" says Molly.

"Points. They're pulsating with some type of vibrating energy."

"Yeah?"

"They're all in sync with one another. Come on." Prior is betting that Points operate on the same frequency. That's how they communicate with each other.

Prior and Molly run to the shelter of the lobby corner, behind an enormous tree. Its root system is large enough to give them cover.

"Hand me the radio transmitter," says Prior.

Molly hands Prior the small transmitter that Prior stole from the Mod Dreamer room at the Mod Clinic. He sets the radio transmitter to the frequency that Points use.

"You know what you're doing?" says Molly.

"Do we have better options here?" says Prior.

The remaining Mod continue to emit their high-pitched screaming in the atrium sky. The tree leaves occasionally burst into flames from the energy the Points give off consuming Mod.

Prior holds out his hand and a bottle of Antoine's jerk sauce with the gold nanos appears in his palm. He injects it into the transmitter. The transmitter fires up with energy. Prior turns a dial to the right frequency and waits until all the Mod are devoured. Then he hits the transmit button. The gold nanos are transmitted directly into the Points via the transmitter.

"What the hell is it doing?" says Molly.

"Gold nanos melt at room temperature," says Prior. "And Points, already unstable, aren't going to like that very much."

The Points begin to explode. The effect is dazzling. Within minutes, Prior and Molly are treated to a great second fireworks display under the canopy of the indoor rainforest. Just as quickly, it is over. There's no smoke, only some ash that dissipates in the silence.

Prior knows their job here hasn't even started.

"The nano-machines. They have to go," says Molly.

"I know," says Prior. "Take care of it. I have to check something out. Meet back here in ten minutes?"

Molly nods, then heads down the hallway.

Prior floats up to the top floor and sees what he was hoping to find. A giant transmitter. Prior closes his eyes and concentrates. His nanos rush out of him, eager to do his bidding. Seconds later, Lachende floats into the transmitter room.

Lachende is in the middle of his Golden Oldies broadcast, just like Prior had scheduled. Lachende doesn't appear surprised to see Prior.

"And we'll be right back after these words from our friends at NanoGov," says Lachende. He turns to Prior. "Well, look at you."

"What? Did I lose some weight?" says Prior.

"Pretty nice, huh?"

"I don't want to get used to it," says Prior.

"Oh, but you will."

Prior quietly explains the plan to Lachende. Lachende studies Prior as if he is crazy. Maybe Prior is.

"I need your notes," says Prior.

"Molly agreed to this?" says Lachende, transferring to Prior the notes that he and Molly assembled from their Mod Clinic stakeouts.

"She's all in."

"How are you going to do this?" says Lachende.

"Think fat fish, not flat fish."

There is a huge explosion in the building's basement. The building shakes but remains otherwise stable. The security-nanos go into overdrive and act as structural engineers, trying to repair the damage.

"I'll go down and check on Molly," says Lachende.

A second later, he brings her up to the top floor. She is fine; happy even.

"Well, that was fun," says Molly.

"You blew up all of them?" says Prior.

"No more nano-machines. Pity," she says, smiling.

"How can you not love her," says Lachende, giving her a hug.

"Let's finish this," says Prior.

"They were just sitting there. Unguarded. It seemed so easy," says Molly.

"Just needed the will," says Prior.

Lachende continues with his broadcast, coaxing listeners to stay tuned with the promise of a special guest. Prior hopes that the distraction will last long enough before Points know what hit them.

Prior floats into the transmittal room and takes a deep breath. He turns the dials to the correct frequency. With his nanos, he turns the remaining gold from his stash into dust and deposits it into the transmittal equipment.

Prior sends some of his nanos to whisper into Lachende's ear. "Now remember," says Prior, "what's going to render the whole venture successful is if you broadcast at the same frequency that the Points communicate in."

Prior considers Felice one last time. One last chance to try and save her.

No. She's made her choices. Now, a Fringe will finally make a choice. His plan is so simple. It's not that the Fringe were incapable of coming up with the same plan. It's that they couldn't conceive of it. Years of brutal defeatist news dulling their ability to reason critically, making them doubt they had any power whatsoever. Prior hasn't been conditioned. He has the will.

Molly screams, shaking, holding her head tight. "She's here!"

"Felice!" says Prior.

"Get out of my lab!" says Felice.

"Make her stop!" screams Molly.

"Get away from her!" says Prior.

"No Jere!" Felice's voice crashes into Prior's ears in waves. "She's mine."

Prior flicks the switch. Instantly, the gold dust is depleted as it turns into liquid, then into gold nanos. The gold nanos swarm around the transmitter, then shoot out into the atmosphere at each and every Point.

"No!" screams Felice. "Don't…"

Molly drops to the floor, breathing heavy. Prior rushes to her. "I'm OK," she says. "Mom's gone."

Prior can hear explosions in Ferri's lab followed by screaming. He floats outside and spots Lachende, who sports a pair of headphones on his flat head.

"Working?" says Prior.

"Listen for yourself," says Lachende, sounding stunned.

Prior puts on the headphones and listens to the global response. Throughout the world, the gold nanos are being transmitted to Points who readily absorb them. When one Point tunes into the broadcast, the adjacent Point tunes in and so on. Within seconds, the gold nanos melt, causing each Point to explode like a giant connect-the-dots game.

Prior thinks of Felice and suddenly feels sorry for her.

Molly gets up slowly. She's dizzy, holding her head. Something about her seems off. Prior's nanos scan her and quickly discover she has a stowaway.

"Molly, the red purse," says Prior. "Open it!"

Molly opens the purse. Prior's nanos cause a rush of wind under the purse. Felice the Point flies out of the purse.

"Damn you all," say Felice, revenge in her eyes.

"Goodbye, Felice," says Prior.

"No! What are you…" screams Felice in waves that reach Molly and Prior. In another second, she explodes in front of them.

"Oh my God," says Molly.

"Sorry," says Prior. He floats to her. "NanoGov developed this crude fabric to capture Points," says Prior, examining the purse. "Sanders gave it to Penny to protect her in case Ferri ever showed up."

"Sorry, dad," says Molly.

Lachende floats into the room. "They were so vulnerable," says Lachende.

"All of them?" says Prior.

"All of them. Every Point in the world," says Lachende. "Right after the commercial break from the Golden Oldies radio show. Kaboom. As a race, they are officially extinct."

"My mom," says Molly.

"I'm sorry, Molly," says Prior. "They became vulnerable once we started thinking of them as vulnerable. They had all the Fringe doubting themselves, thinking we were nothing."

"Still, I can't believe it worked," says Lachende. "What a show."

"Then you're really going to enjoy the encore," says Prior.

Chapter 41

Prior is saddling up Gluestick. The skies are clear but there's a nervous energy in the air.

"We're heading out," says Molly. Lachende is with her. They're off to find the remains of the Fringe Underground Movement.

"Will your friends join us after what happened this morning?" says Prior to Molly.

"More than ever," she says.

"Good," says Prior. "Tell them to meet us at the Mod Clinic in one hour."

"Us?"

"Lachende, I want you to come right back here after you drop Molly off," says Prior.

"What's going?" says Molly.

Prior smiles and puts his arm around Lachende the way Antoine used to put his arm around Prior. "Oh, you know, father and son-in-law stuff."

"Oh God," says Molly. "I may nano-puke."

"You take care of yourself," says Prior.

As soon as Molly and Lachende are off, Prior sends Skippy to go find Grainger. He needs Grainger for his plan.

Prior floats over to Belden's house and enters. He rummages through Belden's cabinets and discovers what he's searching for: the case of glass vials Belden stole from Brewster.

Lachende returns to the stables a few minutes after Prior.

"Molly alright?"

"Of course. A few FU members will meet us at the Mod Clinic," says Lachende. "What's this about?"

"You know how you told me Brewster developed a cheat code or workaround for you to convert back to Fringe?"

"I've used his prototype. Why, having second thoughts?" says Lachende.

"Not for me," says Prior, staring Lachende right in the eye.

"No way," says Lachende. "Molly needs all the protection…"

"It's because of Molly, kid," says Prior. "You have to convert back to Fringe. Permanently."

"Why?"

"Haven't you thought this through? You're going to be my grandkid's father. You need to be with Molly. Fully with Molly. And you can't be a husband or dad as a Mod."

"Yeah, but…"

"It's time to choose sides, kid," says Prior.

Lachende takes a deep breath. "I do love her, you know."

"I know."

"Shit," says Lachende. "Alright, in for a penny…sorry." He summons his nanos. A wine glass materializes, filled with purple liquid. "And I was just getting used to being a DJ." He drinks the liquid. He lets out a small scream and falls to the floor. He envelops himself in a cocoon. The cocoon expands into an egg. It lies still for a few minutes, then shimmers. The egg cracks open as Lachende bursts through. He sits up, sweating. He's three-dimensional. And a bit older looking. "This better be worth it."

"Mazel Tov. Now you're a man," says Prior.

A half-hour later, they arrive at the Mod Clinic, this time, Lachende inside the Prior balloon. Mod are fleeing the Mod Clinic in droves, clearly nervous about the news that Points have exploded. The sky looks like it's throwing a giant ticker-tape parade. As the cloud of fluttering paper whips by, Prior catches sight of Grainger and seven Fringe cops heading his way.

"The cavalry," says Prior. He sets down near Grainger.

"You make those fireworks this morning?" says Grainger, reaching the Mod Clinic.

Prior shrugs.

"Nice," says Grainger. Then he gets a good ogle at Prior. "Whoa, what am I looking at here?"

"How's it feel working with the right side of the law, Grainger?" says Prior.

"You a Mod," says Grainger. "Jesus. You always did like taking down your own."

"Don't ever change, big guy," says Prior.

"It's not over yet," says Lachende, his full three-dimensional Fringe mass creating shadows on the ground.

Grainger takes a step back. "What the hell is happening here? Mod are Fringe, Fringe are Mod."

"Science," says Lachende.

"Why aren't you running scared?" says Grainger to Lachende.

"Mr. Jeremiah Prior here is my future father-in-law, that's why," says Lachende. "We're family."

"Okay," says Grainger, too focused on the immediate issues of global meltdown to process this new information.

"Molly?" says Prior.

"Should be here soon," says Lachende. He's observing his hands, feeling the weight of his arms. He's like a toddler who just learned to walk.

"NanoGov is going to be pissed. Hell to pay," says Grainger. His men nod in agreement.

"Look, all of you. Don't you want to live in a world with just flesh-and-blood humans?" says Prior. Everyone leans in to listen. "Just honest-to-goodness three-dimensional people with a decent chance at living a long, happy life? Where your day is filled with things like courage and dignity again?"

There is a silence that falls over everyone as they suddenly realize this fantasy is actually within their grasp.

"Of course," says Grainger in a quiet manner.

Molly arrives with four FU members to the Mod Clinic. She runs over to Lachende. "You did it," she says, touching his face.

"Yeah, your dad..."

"I love it," she says and hugs him.

"I hate to break this up but my men are getting antsy," says Grainger.

"Alright. I'll sneak all of you in," says Prior.

"Can't do it," says Lachende.

"What?"

"Security has the place on lockdown, even to Mod," says Lachende. "Nanos scrambled the code to get in."

"Great," says Grainger. "Now what?"

"Maybe we come back with a better plan and more weapons?" says Lachende.

"Oh my God," says Molly. "Mindset, Lachende. It's not about weapons." She runs up to the Mod Clinic front entrance, takes out a small disc from her backpack, and places it at the door. She calmly saunters back to the group. "You might want to tread on my heels," she says. She runs one block away and they quickly follow her.

"Now what?" says Grainger, as they hide behind a line of trees.

"This," says Molly and pushes a small button on a remote switch.

There is a fiery explosion and the front door to the Mod Clinic goes flying past them in a cloud of smoke and sparks.

"Door's open now," says Molly, calmly sauntering towards the Mod Clinic.

"Jesus," says Lachende.

"Old technology always beats new technology," says Molly, smiling at Prior.

They quickly enter the Mod Clinic.

"What are we looking for?" says Grainger.

"Mod Dreamers," says Prior.

"This way," says Lachende.

They find the bank of Mod Dreamers asleep in their glass chambers, completely plugged in and unaware of the shift in the world's population and power structure. There are twenty Mod Dreamers in all, each transmitting to the world's Mod.

"I heard about these things but I never thought they were real," says Grainger.

"Their information flow is one way," says Lachende. "Mod don't talk to Mod Dreamers. It's too beneath them. These guys here are completely in a vacuum."

"We used to call them Mushrooms," says Molly. "That was easy when we never had to look at them."

The Mod Dreamers are pasty-white and frail Fringe. Their muscles have atrophied in the service of their Mod Masters.

"The Mod Dreamers don't have a clue what's just happened," says Lachende.

"Good," says Prior. "That's the plan." Prior sticks out his hands with his palms facing upwards, like he's a convict from a hundred years ago, turning himself in.

Dozens of tiny glass vials grow out of Prior's palms, like sprouting hairs. They're the little glass vials filled with Brewster's thermoplastic nanos he picked up at Belden's house.

"Interesting magic trick," says Grainger. "You gonna make a rabbit pop out of your hat next?"

"Here," says Prior, handing out the vials to Grainger's men and the FU members. "Each of you take these vials and feed them into the Mod Dreamer chambers."

"What's in them?" says Grainger, holding the vial to the light, the prism dancing across his rough face.

"Nanos."

"Great," says Grainger. "Just what we need. More nanos."

"This better work, pal," says Prior, more to himself.

"Wait," says Molly to Prior. She reaches into her backpack and pulls out a pica-tam the colors of the Jamaican flag.

"Your friend, Antoine, sent it to me a few weeks ago," she says. "Pretty good friend."

"Molly," says Prior.

"How do you think I've been eluding NanoGov? Just get in."

"Good old Antoine."

Prior coils into a spiral, then snaps into a small ball that bounces into the pica-tam. Molly places the pica-tam on her head.

"This could be a new look for me," says Molly.

Outside the Mod Clinic, the blare of the Mod Police alarm is sounding.

Grainger, his men, and the FU members enter the Mod Dreamer chambers and each carefully opens a vial. The nanos race out of the vials, visible through the smoke in each chamber, and enter the Mod Dreamers. The Mod Dreamers inhale sharply and open their eyes, stunned momentarily by the nano-injection. Then, just as abruptly, they return to their dream-state. The Mod Dreamers become hyperactive as the nanos are dispersed through them to all the planet's nanos. Every Mod is eager for more ways to use nanos, more mass. The thermoplastic nanos combine with every nano in the world.

The Mod Police reach the Mod Clinic. They see the infiltrators and are momentarily taken aback at their audacity.

Prior has a front row seat, safe within the pica-tam on Molly's head. He smiles. Brewster figured out a way to create thermoplastic nanos. The kind that melt given the right conditions. The kind of nanos that melt when receiving a specific radio frequency.

"Now," projects Prior through his nanos to Lachende.

Lachende projects the radio frequency to the world through Sky-Screen.

The thermoplastic nanos reveal their true nature, creating a global meltdown. They are a wolf in sheep's clothing. Brewster's thermoplastic nanos are a computer program with instructions for every nano.

The Mod Police start popping and expanding like prehistoric bags of microwave popcorn. They writhe in agony, then suddenly explode.

The monitors tell Prior that there is a popcorn-a-thon all over the world. Mod are bursting like confetti, their nanos sizzling into nothing.

Prior breathes a sigh of relief and wishes his old pal Brewster was here to experience this. Effectively, Prior has just reversed immortality.

"My God, it worked," says Grainger.

"Prior," says Lachende to Molly's pica-tam. "This is why you wanted me to convert to Fringe. Pretty clever to get your futures money now. You knew you were killing all the Mod."

After a few minutes, the explosions cease around the world. The Sky-Screen explodes into itself like a black hole, allowing the sun to shine down in its entirety for the first time in a very long time. The planet's background hum goes silent. Soon, the silence is taken over by Fringe cheers.

Molly takes off her pica-tam and Prior unfurls himself.

"No more NanoGov," says Prior. He still can't believe it.

Lachende catches his breath, then stands up.

"Just tell me we're done today," says Lachende to Prior.

"Oh, not quite yet," says a familiar voice.

Prior spins around and gets slapped in the face with the sight of Anton Ferri.

Chapter 42

Ferri has assumed full Fringe form. Prior is surprised that Ferri is a Fringe. He figured that Ferri would somehow be immune to the thermoplastic nanos or any other crazy scheme that Prior cooked up. Prior's fear of Ferri is palpable and clouding his judgment. He understands how the rest of the world's Fringe felt about NanoGov and Mod now.

"I see our roles have been reversed, Jeremiah," says Ferri. "Now you have the evolutionary upper hand."

Ferri advances towards Molly. She takes a step back, tension in her eyes.

"Ferri, if you hurt her…" shouts Prior.

"Jeremiah," says Ferri, oozing alpha confidence, continuing his march towards Molly. "If I wanted to hurt your daughter, I'd…"

Prior lunges for Ferri in mid-speech, hoping that the rude timing might throw Ferri off. Prior commands his nanos to attack. He unfurls himself to envelop Ferri, knowing this is the simplest of Mod tasks. Ferri sidesteps Prior gracefully, sending Prior flying past him. As Prior falls to the floor, Ferri grabs the last nano-vial out of Prior's hand.

Prior hits the ground with a thud, landing on his back. His nanos offer no response. Ferri kicks Prior hard in the face, forcing him onto his stomach. Prior tries to get back up but Ferri delivers another kick to Prior's mid-section, leaving him sprawled painfully on all fours. Ferri leans down and, before Prior has a chance to catch his breath, injects Prior with the thermoplastic nanos.

Grainger, his men, and the FU members are frozen with fear in the corner.

"No one move," says Ferri, winded. He grabs Molly, plucking her from Lachende's weak grasp. Prior sits in the middle of the room like wounded prey.

"What did..." says Prior.

"You're a walking, ticking bomb now," says Ferri. "Children shouldn't play with grownup things. You know what effect the thermoplastic nanos will have on you. The damage they'll do. You're set to go off very soon now."

Molly appears terrified. Ferri tightens his grasp on her.

"I want to personally thank you both," says Ferri to Molly and Prior. "For getting rid of that chatty Felice. Taking too much credit. Typical."

"You're such an asshat," says Prior.

Ferri smiles, ignoring the slight. "I can replicate her technology now that I possess her notes from the Seurat."

Lachende comes barreling towards Ferri, fists ready to pummel the old man. He dives towards Ferri who merely ducks and lets Lachende continue his experiment with gravity unfettered. Lachende crashes into the wall and slumps on the floor, shaken.

Ferri looms menacingly over Molly. Everyone in the room is afraid to move. They're in a new world but still fearing the old one. Ferri closes his eyes and begins to tremble. A dust cloud puffs out and away from him. The dust cloud begins to swirl around him like a tornado.

Prior stands up, keeping his distance, waiting to make his move.

The dust cloud. Ferri still has control of his nanos. Somehow, even as a Fringe, he is commanding nanos. It's impossible but leave it to the father of nanotechnology.

The nano-cloud begins to swirl around Molly, enveloping her in its cyclone. She screams.

"Leave her alone!" says Prior. He takes a step forward. As he does, the nano-cloud dissipates. Ferri takes a step back, confused.

"Well, well. New data," says Ferri, almost under his breath. He's trying to process something. His eyes blink, lost in his computations. "Lachende, what is your nano-data doing inside this girl...unless..."

Lachende stands up and faces Ferri.

"Of course," says Ferri. "She's pregnant with your child." Ferri turns to Prior. "The trouble with these pesky kids today. Always getting into hijinks."

"Get away from her," says Lachende.

"Now, gentlemen," says Ferri. "Haven't you tired of these heroics yet? My nanos will have a field day extracting all kinds of information. Who knows what secrets Felice revealed to her?" Ferri turns towards Molly. "It will be excruciatingly painful."

"Ferri," says Prior, holding a vial in his hand.

"What have you got there?"

"Normally, you'd send your nanos to investigate but you're not that powerful anymore, are you?" says Prior.

"Don't push me, Mod," says Ferri. Then, impatiently, "What is that?"

"Some of Addison's nanos. Highly unstable. Wouldn't play well with you. Especially since Molly knows how to shed Lachende's nanos so they'd mix with Addison's. Now, back off."

"You're bluffing. Badly," says Ferri.

Ferri's right. But Prior can't let it end like this.

"Am I," says Prior. He glances at Molly and Lachende. "You guys ready?"

"Oh yeah," says Lachende.

Molly nods, unsure of what to do.

Ferri chuckles but there's a trace of fear in his voice. The nano-cloud swirls around him again like a witch's cauldron.

"Now!" says Prior. Prior opens the vial in his hand and distracts Ferri. Molly slips away from Ferri and runs towards Lachende. Prior releases his nanos to attack Ferri.

Ferri's nano-cloud expands and covers most of the room, the thick paste of it making it hard to breathe. Everything vibrates as Ferri directs his nanos to attack Prior's nanos. The nanos clash in the air, an infinitely small traffic jam with aggressive rush hour drivers. It's getting harder to see or breathe in the gloom of it. There are small explosions as the air current shifts violently. Finally, the nanos part, quietly. Ferri's nanos seep back into Ferri.

Prior, Molly, and Lachende clear their eyes, trying to get their bearings. Grainger, his men, and the FU members are on the floor, covering their heads.

Ferri, unchanged, stands against the wall, a defiant gleam in his eye. "Very dramatic," says Ferri. "Perhaps next time..."

There's a cracking explosion followed by a wet, smacking sound. Ferri's head shatters, his brains and blood splattered on the wall behind him. His decapitated body slumps to the floor, lifeless.

Skippy stands there, holding the rifle. The smoke wafting from the business end of the barrel is natural, completely different from the inhuman smoke of the nanos.

"Molly, are you okay?" says Skippy, still poised with the rifle.

"Skippy..." says Prior.

"I heard Molly was in trouble. Is it okay that I came?"

"Old technology," says Lachende, reaching for Molly. "Old technology."

"You can give me the rifle now," says Prior to Skippy.

Skippy smiles, still shaky. He hands the rifle to Prior.

"Jesus," says Grainger. He and his men are dusting themselves off. The FU members approach Ferri's dead body cautiously. One of them is brave enough to touch it with his foot.

Molly lets go of Lachende's hand and rushes over to Skippy.

"Skippy, I don't know what to say. Thank you."

"You would have done the same."

"I would have. Absolutely," says Molly, brushing Skippy's hair away from his eyes.

"Yeah, I know. Maybe you can name the kid Skippy?"

"Let's not get crazy," says Prior.

One of the FU members spits on Ferri's lifeless body. When it doesn't react, they all spit on him. Satisfied, they leave. Hopefully, they have enough members left around the world to re-build.

"Molly?"

"Yeah Dad?" says Molly, turning towards Prior.

"I love you. You know that, right?"

"I'm starting to get the idea."

"You guys get out of here," says Prior.

"Here," she says, handing Prior the pica-tam. "It's an antique now. You should have it."

"Great work, boss," says Lachende. "Now you get back to being a Fringe so we can celebrate."

"Absolutely," says Prior, maybe louder than he intended. "Molly?"

"Yeah?"

"What are you gonna do now? To get rid of that restless energy?" says Prior.

"What do you think?" she says, putting her arm around Lachende. "Someone has to watch over these monkeys."

"The FU movement. Restoration phase," says Lachende.

"Men just know how to destroy," says Molly. "I'll round up the women and we'll build."

"That's good," says Prior.

"I mean, someone has to lead these idiots," she says. "It's gonna take some time to reorient them to what women can do."

"And I'm just the idiot to follow," says Lachende.

"Dad," says Molly, "Ferri didn't hurt you with those thermoplastics, did he?"

"Never. Brewster built in a safeguard. Now get out of here. I'll meet up with you later."

Prior hugs the three of them. Molly turns and leaves with Lachende and Skippy. Prior watches them leave and sighs.

There goes his heritage, his mark. He's glad he came back. His Antigua life was a shelter, not a family. As great as Antoine was, he was a friend, not a brother. He found Molly and connected. She's with Lachende and seems blissfully happy. Skippy will be alright too. Prior feels it in his core.

Grainger talks to his men, shaking their hands. They head out but Prior waves Grainger over. Grainger tells his cops to go on without him.

"You OK?" says Grainger.

"I suppose. You?"

"I don't understand," says Grainger. "Why did you stay Mod? You could have converted back the way Lachende did, no?"

Prior brings his form into human dimension. "I needed that edge to protect Molly."

It's just the two of them left in the Transmitter Room. Two cops finishing up a case.

"This is good," says Grainger. "I'm getting reports there's no more NanoGov. I mean when they all blow up, how could there be? And Fringe all over the world are taking over. Not a bad day's work."

"Not a bad day's work," says Prior. He rubs the pica-tam, working out a problem.

"Come here, I want to show you something," says Grainger.

They head downstairs where Grainger's men are destroying the Fringe-Mod conversion machines. They've saved one for Prior. Two of Grainger's men have dragged Ferri's headless body into a giant incinerator.

"Beautiful, isn't it?" says Prior.

"Never thought I'd enjoy my work so much," says Grainger. "Want to give me a hand?" He hands Prior a metal screwdriver.

"Where did this come from?" says Prior.

"Freakiest thing," says Grainger. "These metals tools just appeared. Must have been the nanos. Went back to their former selves or something."

Prior inspects the screwdriver. It's real. "This is really good news," says Prior.

"Tell me about it. Now I just gotta learn how to use metal tools again," says Grainger.

"Grainger, can I ask you a favor?"

"Name it, you're the hero of the hour."

"Help me with this Mod-converter."

"The last one," says Grainger. "After turning back to Fringe, you thinking about starting a museum or something? Because I can't wait to get rid of these damn things."

"Nothing like that. It's just..."

"You believe what Ferri told you?" says Grainger "About the thermoplastics?"

"It's true. I don't have very long."

Grainger's face gets wrinkled with concern, the blood draining away. "Oh geez, Jere, I'm so sorry." Grainger sounds sincere and heartfelt for the first time that Prior can recall. "What can I do?"

"Help me get into this thing."

"You can't convert to Fringe now. With the thermoplastics, you'll explode."

"I know. But I have a plan."

"You always have a plan," says Grainger.

Prior climbs into the Mod-converter.

"What the hell is that?" says Grainger, pointing at the pica-tam.

"I had a friend in Antigua. A good friend. You would have liked him. He made it."

"A hat?"

"I think I can use the pica nanos in the tam to bind the thermoplastics in my bloodstream. Maybe disable them," says Prior.

"Wait a minute," says Grainger. "You do that and chances are good you'll stay Mod. But like a really weak, inanimate Mod."

"Just strap me in," says Prior.

Grainger closes the door, not wanting anyone to see this. He adjusts the straps on the Mod-converter bed. He starts to close the lid.

"Not yet," says Prior. "Here." He produces the Vermeer thermoplastics vault key hat Brewster gave him and hands it to Grainger.

"It's vital you get this to Molly. The password for the key is Wadadli."

"Wadadli?" says Grainger.

"When I'm done here, you deliver me and the key to Molly. Clear?"

"You're wishing you stayed on your island, aren't you?" says Grainger, nodding.

"And miss this?"

"You're a good man, Prior."

"Don't get all mushy on me, Grainger."

Grainger and Prior smile at each other, knowing this is where it ends. Grainger closes the lid and fires up the Mod-Converter.

Prior stretches his pica-tam. He concentrates and absorbs the picas, thinking about how Addison ate Modela. He directs the pica nanos to stabilize the Mod nanos within so they can't be replicated. He concentrates and the pica-tam fibers swarm and bind the thermoplastic nanos in Prior's body, disabling them. Prior doesn't want to explode. He wants to keep alive the memory of Penny, whose nanos he has within him, Antoine, whose picas are part of him, and Brewster, who's inert thermoplastic nanos flow through his bloodstream. He begins to vibrate and buzz as his whole world goes dark. The last thing he hears is his own racking scream.

Chapter 43

Prior has been framed. He stares out at the room like he does every day. Sometimes, he gets visitors. Sometimes, it's just him. He likes the ones who talk to him. The ones who ask questions and are curious. The ones who just stare make him uncomfortable. Occasionally, someone will stop by and provide him an update on current events. Mostly, it's the same story but Prior never tires of listening to it. NanoGov has been vanquished globally and people (they call themselves people now) are back to self-rule.

He hears the clicking of heels on the hardwood floor followed by the rubber thumping of boots. He knows that Molly and Lachende are walking down the hallway towards him. Perhaps they'll stop by for a visit today. That would be nice.

Felice always did have wonderful taste in houses and decorations, even though they leaned towards the extravagant side. Prior is happy that Molly and Lachende moved into Felice's old house. They even built a stable for Gluestick and have Skippy staying in the guesthouse. They're renovating the main house, bringing it up to modern standards. Some things remain old and appreciated though. Prior likes that. He believes it's his contribution to Molly's upbringing.

The flump-flump-flump of running bare feet drown out Molly and Lachende's footsteps. It's their son, little Brewster. He's adorable. Prior can always count on a visit from him. Prior doesn't even mind the occasional poking by Brewster with his sticky strawberry jelly hands.

"Brewster," says Lachende. "Have you said hello to your grandfather today?"

"No," says Brewster. Brewster's favorite new word is no.

"But he loves you," says Molly.

Molly picks up Brewster and stands in front of Prior. Lachende puts his arm around her and the three of them smile at the giant Vermeer painting that is Prior.

He remained Mod rather than die. He's glad of it. He expanded his altered nanos to become a living painting. An authentic Vermeer.

It makes up for his years of neglect and absence. And he was able to provide for his family with the money from his blood futures so they could start a new life.

Life as a framed Vermeer canvas isn't so bad. He's become his own family heirloom. He gets to see his family. Prior smiles.

It makes his life less pointless.

ABOUT THE AUTHOR

Dan Kopcow's fiction short story collection, *"Worst. Date. Ever."*, was published by Regal House Publishing in March 2020 and was named one of 2020's top 100 novels by the Community of Literary Magazines and Presses (CLMP). The anthology, "Thank You, Death Robot," which included his short story, *"The Cobbler Cherry,"* won an Independent Publishing Award for best science-fiction and fantasy and was voted a *Chicago Tribune* Top Ten Fiction book. His rom-com novel, *Head Voice*, will be published in late 2022.

Dankopcow.com

ACKNOWLEDGEMENTS

Thanks to my wife, Angie, for the constant love and support. You're the best Fringe I know.

There are many FU Movement members in my local chapter but two that constantly inspire me to continue writing are my son, Chris, and my friend, Paul.

Prior Futures was first born as a short story at the Ambler Writers Group and I am thankful for the encouragement from my fellow writers to expand it into a full novel.

And finally, a profound thanks to the late American physicist and Nobel Prize laureate Richard Feynman, the father of modern nanotechnology, for his brilliant and insightful writing and speeches on theoretical physics which served as a great resource and inspiration and for whom this ungrateful author chose to honor, rather perversely, by bestowing his name on an unrelated fictional character whose ass is unceremoniously kissed goodbye before the curtain even rises.

NOTE FROM THE AUTHOR

Word-of-mouth is crucial for any author to succeed. If you enjoyed *Prior Futures,* please leave a review online—anywhere you are able. Even if it's just a sentence or two. It would make all the difference and would be very much appreciated.

Thanks!
Dan Kopcow

We hope you enjoyed reading this title from:

Subscribe to our mailing list – *The Rosevine* – and receive **FREE** books, daily deals, and stay current with news about upcoming releases and our hottest authors.
Scan the QR code below to sign up.

Already a subscriber? Please accept a sincere thank you for being a fan of Black Rose Writing authors.

View other Black Rose Writing titles at
and use promo code
PRINT to receive a **20% discount** when purchasing.

www.ingramcontent.com/pod-product-compliance
Lightning Source LLC
Chambersburg PA
CBHW010729100726
47899CB00009B/2988